Return to the Bosque

Other novels by Ken Miller:

Evening of Pale Sunshine

Weep Without Tears

Return to the Bosque

A Novel

Ken Miller

iUniverse, Inc.
New York Lincoln Shanghai

Return to the Bosque

Copyright © 2007 by Ken Miller

All rights reserved. No part of this book may be used or reproduced by any means, graphic, electronic, or mechanical, including photocopying, recording, taping or by any information storage retrieval system without the written permission of the publisher except in the case of brief quotations embodied in critical articles and reviews.

iUniverse books may be ordered through booksellers or by contacting:

iUniverse
2021 Pine Lake Road, Suite 100
Lincoln, NE 68512
www.iuniverse.com
1-800-Authors (1-800-288-4677)

Because of the dynamic nature of the Internet, any Web addresses or links contained in this book may have changed since publication and may no longer be valid.

This is a work of fiction. All of the characters, names, incidents, organizations, and dialogue in this novel are either the products of the author's imagination or are used fictitiously.

ISBN: 978-0-595-44687-2 (pbk)
ISBN: 978-0-595-68955-2 (cloth)
ISBN: 978-0-595-89010-1 (ebk)

Printed in the United States of America

This book is dedicated to my sixteen siblings: from Eileen, the eldest, to Clifford, the youngest.

PROLOGUE
Central Texas, 1856

A tremor ran through Sarah Parker as she looked up at the bareback rider, a tremor of excitement not fear. The stranger was clad only in a loincloth and outlined against the copper and gray of the late afternoon sky. For the first time in her fifteen years, she sensed a stirring in her blood, a stirring that surged upward from her loins, through her torso, and flushed her face. She felt the coming of her womanhood, and it disturbed and excited her.

Self consciously, Sarah glanced over her shoulder at the log house set among the mesquite trees to see if her father had noticed the solitary observer on the embankment across the Bosque River. Although he was a Baptist minister, she knew he would reach for the rifle leaning against the door if he saw him. The nearest neighbor lived several miles away, and there had been rumors of resurgence in the raids by the Comanche. But he seemed unaware of her concern as he chopped kindling and stacked it on the porch.

Turning back, Sarah gasped in wonder as the slender, bronzed man on the ridge stared down at her and raised his long lance in salute, a ribbon fluttering from the shaft. Without thinking, she lifted her hand and returned his silent communication. For a long moment, she gazed at him with her arm upheld and her emotions in turmoil. Then the rider turned his horse and rode into the bright orange orb of the setting sun, his presence lingering in her thoughts.

The next morning, while the narrow valley still held on to the darkness and before her father awakened, Sarah waded across the river and climbed up to the place where she had seen the rider. The memory of her aunt, Cynthia Ann Parker, who had been kidnapped as a child, returned to haunt her, but she continued her quest undaunted. The hoof prints of an unshod horse still disturbed the grass, now damp with dew. And lying there, as if awaiting her arrival, was the ribbon from the Indian's lance, a long vibrant, blue strip of cloth. Kneeling, she picked it up and pressed it against her lips.

Often, after that day, Sarah would glance toward the ridge hoping to catch sight of the young man who had looked down upon her from afar. He never returned and, in time, she quit watching for him. She cherished the ribbon, which she folded and placed in her Bible. When her memory faded with the passage of time, she would take out the shimmering piece of cloth and think about the mysterious stranger.

Chapter 1

▼

Central Texas, 1876

"Riders coming, Mama. And they ain't riding slow."

"Ain't, Maggie?" Sarah Parker Whitman questioned the tall, slender girl who entered the door carrying a bucket of milk.

Perhaps Jim has finally come home after being gone for over two months, Sarah thought. A smile lit up her face and brightened the dim room illuminated by a fireplace at the rear and several flickering candles on the long wooden table, which was set for dinner.

"Aren't," Maggie said with a shake of her long, thick red hair and a flash of her emerald green eyes, both genetic traits passed on to her through her mother's Irish heritage. "Please don't call me Maggie. That's a girl's name. I am sixteen years old now, soon to be seventeen. My name is Margaret."

"Okay," Sarah said, "I'll call you Margaret if you'll quit using *ain't* for *are not*."

"Oh, Mama," the girl retorted with a smile on her lips, unable to resist her mother's infectious joshing. "Don't you ever stop being a school teacher?"

As Sarah took the bucket of milk from Margaret and set it on the sink counter below the string of dried Mexican chilies, *ristros*, hung in the window, snuffling noises issued from a massive dog sleeping by the fireplace. Sarah watched bemusedly as the mottled black, orange, and gray mongrel gave voice to his dreams, and then settled back into rhythmic snoring. Her father had named the animal, part Gray Wolf and part German Shepherd, Beelzebub after the biblical fallen angel who was next to Satan in power. "Looks like he got his colors from running through the fire and brimstone of hell," he often said before his disappearance ten years before.

Sarah took her four-year-old son Jody's thumb out of his mouth and tousled his curls, soft as lamb's wool and shiny as spun gold, as she walked with him to the open door. His blanket, grasped in his other hand, dragged on the floor. She looked through the dim evening light as three riders leading a packhorse thundered up to the yard and came to a quick stop, showering dust into the air. The wind, a gentle zephyr from the south early in the day that jostled the trees and the feathery tops of the corn stalks, now whistled in from the northwest along the Bosque River bringing with it a promise of falling leaves, lengthening nights, and cold weather.

"Daddy?" Jody said peering out into the gathering darkness.

Jim wasn't one of the riders, Sarah realized, the disappointed sinking in her stomach giving way to fear. The strangers dismounted and, brushing dust from their clothes with their misshapen hats, stomped up the stairs to the porch. She stepped backward, dragging Jody with her. The first to approach was a small man dressed in dark trousers, a weathered plaid shirt, and a black jacket that ended just above the gun he wore low on his right hip. His face was thin and pockmarked and stringy black hair fell over his forehead. His shifty dark eyes darted back and forth, never settling on anything for longer than a moment. He reminded her of a rattlesnake searching for a prey to lash out at.

Sarah looked over his shoulder at his two companions standing on the porch. One of them was a slender young man with dark swarthy skin, black eyes and long, dirty pigtails. His shoulders were covered with a Mexican serape. As the third visitor moved into the light streaming out through the doorway, she could see that he was short and stooped with age, his pale eyes rheumy and wet with tears of weariness. Filth lay on him like a shroud, covering his worn clothes, his long unkempt gray hair, and his scruffy, tobacco stained beard. A terrible stench exuded from him in waves and extended from the porch in to where Sarah stood inside the door. She wanted to step back into the room with its soothing aroma of bread, warm from the oven, and the tangy smell of beef stew bubbling on the stove top, but she didn't want to allow the strangers to enter. She remained at the door with tentacles of fear clutching at her.

"Evenin' Ma'am," the man in the doorway said in a quiet voice, barely above a whisper.

"Mama," Jody murmured around the thumb he had jammed back into his mouth, "Daddy? Is Daddy here?"

"No, Jody," Sarah answered. "Your father isn't with them."

Looking directly at the man standing in front of her, she said, "Good evening, Gentlemen. You are not welcome here. Please be on your way. I am Mrs. Sarah Whitman. My husband, Jim, is due any minute. He went to the neighbors to deliver some horses."

Sarah could see the man's gaze dart over her body, dwelling for a moment on the swell of her breasts. Then he scanned the room, his searching eyes taking in Margaret, the door to the single bedroom set to one side, the sleeping loft on the other side, a large rocking chair, and the dog snoring in front of the fireplace. Sarah tensed as his scrutiny paused momentarily on the old Sharps buffalo gun mounted above the books stacked on the mantel. Suddenly, she realized that the man was staring at the table set with three plates and three sets of eating utensils. The fear she had felt earlier returned even stronger, this time enveloping her in a tight grip.

"Husband, huh!" The man's scar caught the light from the candles and shimmered against the sunburned skin of his face. His eyes slid past Sarah as he continued, "I count three of you. If your husband's about to get here, why didn't you set a place for him?"

"Come on, Pete," the old man wheezed. "Breed and I are hungry enough to eat the south end of a north bound skunk. That there food sure smells good."

"I told you, old man, no names," Pete snarled.

Turning to Sarah, he smiled, his thin lips pulled back from his dirty, broken teeth. "Looks like it would only be hospitable if you'd let us partake of that supper you fixed. I expect there's some hay and oats in your barn. Our horses need taken care of."

Over his shoulder, he snapped, "Breed, take the horses to the barn. Unsaddle and feed them. And bring them saddlebags in here."

"Sir," Sarah said. "You are not welcome here. Please—"

"Shut up, woman," Pete snarled as he pushed past her and went to the sink. Grabbing the pump handle, he forced it vigorously up and down.

The old man shuffled through the door bringing his smelly aura in with him. Spying the rocking chair, he let out a sigh and said, "Lordy, Lordy. Will you look at that? Just the place to rest my weary bones fit and proper." He plopped down in the chair and withdrew a thin bottle from his filthy jacket pocket. Taking a noisy gulp, he began rocking vigorously.

"This damn thing's emptier than a whore's hope chest," Pete snarled as he flailed at the pump handle.

"You might get some water if you'd stop cursing and prime it," Margaret said tartly.

Pete ignored Margaret as he sloshed some water from a pitcher into the pump. With a few more strokes, the water began flowing into the sink, and he washed his hands and face. After drying on a dishcloth, he turned to Sarah, who still stood by the door.

"Listen, woman," he said. "You have a nice family here: daughter and baby boy. You don't want them to get hurt do you?"

Sarah started to respond when Breed stomped through the door and threw several saddlebags on the floor. They hit with a loud clunk as if they were heavily laden with metal.

"Lots of horses in the corral behind the barn, Pete," Breed said. "Some pretty good mounts." A wide grin, highlighted by his shiny white teeth, spread over his swarthy face as he stared at Margaret.

Sarah followed his lascivious look and stepped in front of him. Margaret's breasts had begun to swell during the past year, and she was suddenly aware that her daughter's nipples showed through the thin material of her dress. Margaret had always been her little girl, the flower of her life, she thought. Now, she's a young woman, her beauty as bright as a candle in the winter darkness. Although it was warm from the fireplace and the cook stove, Sarah felt a chill creep over her as she sensed the touch of a ghost from the unknown future.

"Well!" Pete said. "Looks like we done hit the jackpot. Watch these folks while I go to the outhouse."

"Most people wash their hands after they go to the toilet," Margaret remarked.

"Nobody asked for your advice," Pete snapped. Turning in the direction of Sarah, he added as he stomped to the door, "What about that food, woman? Been a long time since we ate hot grub."

Keeping herself between Breed and Margaret, Sarah took a loaf of bread from the sink counter and carried it to the table. "Please be seated," she said to him.

Breed hesitated, and then he pulled a chair out from the table and sat down. Snoring noises rode the waves of odor emanating from the old man in the rocking chair. His bottle had fallen from his hand, and a small puddle of liquid stained the floor.

When Pete returned, Sarah confronted him at the door, "You're welcome to share what we have, mister. Then I expect you and your friends to be on your way."

"Well, we'll just see about that, won't we," Pete retorted as he pushed by her and plopped down in a chair.

Margaret placed the steaming stew pot in the center of the table. "We eat family style here, mister," she said quietly, looking directly at Pete, who as usual, avoided her eyes. "Please wash your hands again before you touch our food."

Pete uncoiled from his chair and slammed his left fist onto the table while drawing his pistol with his right hand. Spittle bubbled from his mouth as he roared, "Shut your mouth, or I'll shut it for you."

Sarah, standing beside Margaret, was reminded again of the uncoiling of a rattlesnake. But she realized that Pete was even more deadly than a poisonous snake. He possessed a malevolent evil that put her, Margaret, and Jody in terrible danger. Moving quickly, she put her arm around her daughter's shoulder and pulled her back from the table.

"She didn't mean anything," Sarah said to Pete as she leaned over the table in front of Margaret and ladled a portion of stew into his plate.

Pete sat down, mumbling, "I don't take kindly to sass from nobody."

Breed pulled a long, thin knife from inside his *serape*, cut off a thick slice of bread, and stuck the knife into the table top where it quivered in the candlelight. He licked his lips as he stared at Margaret.

The commotion at the table had awakened the old man. Sitting up, he sniffed the air and belched, adding the fetid odor of his alcohol breath to the miasma extending around him. "Grub, by gawd," he spat out. He tried to rise from the rocker, but the effort was too much for him and he fell back. "Grub, by gawd," he murmured again.

Turning to Margaret, Sarah said, "Feed Jody while I fix that man something to eat."

Sarah stood as far away from the old man as she could as she handed him a filled plate. His hands shook as he took it and set it on his lap. When he reached for the spoon, the plate tipped precariously. Holding her breath, Sarah held it until he could steady himself.

"Thankee, Ma'am," he said as he looked up at her through his red, teary eyes. "Much obliged. This here is worth more than all that gold in them saddlebags. Yes sir—"

Pete darted from his chair and slapped the man across his face sending the plate of food spinning to the floor. "Damn!" he shouted. "First you tell them our names, then about the gold. What the hell's the matter with you?"

Pete pulled his pistol and pointed it at the pathetic creature, who was holding his face in his hands and sobbing loudly. "I should of done you in a long time ago," Pete said. "You ain't nothin' but a loud mouthed drunk."

Sarah stepped in front of Pete, "Sir, I wouldn't shoot that gun if I were you. The neighbors will hear it and come running."

"Neighbors? What neighbors? We didn't pass any houses."

Sarah tried to remember the direction Pete and his companions had come from. "The Sigmund Ranch is just down the river a short way."

"That's right, mister," Margaret said. "Sometimes, when the wind is right, we can even hear them talk."

Pete's eyes darted from Sarah to Margaret, "Don't know if I believe you."

The old man had stopped his sobbing, and he was trying to pick up his plate from the floor. Sarah took it from him and, after cleaning it at the sink, refilled it, and replaced it in his lap. She watched Pete carefully as he returned to the table and helped himself to more of the stew, his eyes searching around the room, stopping several times on the closed bedroom door.

When he finished eating, the old man began drinking again. Within a few minutes, he fell back into the rocking chair and began to snore loudly, his lips fluttering with spittle.

"Reckon it's about time to get some sleep," Pete said as he gazed toward the bedroom door. "We got to hit the trail early."

"There's plenty of room in the barn for you and your men to sleep," Sarah said from the sink.

As she looked at Pete, with his shiftless eyes, and then at Breed, who was lusting after Margaret, she realized that they were going to kill her and her family. She also sensed that she and Margaret would be raped. Looking at her gentle, virginal daughter, the thought overwhelmed her. Thanks to the old man, they knew Pete's and Breed's name and about the gold—gold that was no doubt stolen. She had to do something and do it quickly. Wiping breadcrumbs from the cutting knife, she turned away and slid it into the pocket of her apron.

"Barn?" Pete remarked. "Might be a tad cold in the barn. Expect we'll sleep right here." He glanced at the bedroom again, a hungry grin slashed across his face. "Reckon your husband been held up. Ain't you thinking?"

"He'll be here soon," Sarah replied. Then glancing at Margaret, she added, "We need some more wood for the fire, Margaret. There's a stack on the porch."

Without waiting for a response, she walked to the fireplace, took Jody by his hand, and started toward the bedroom.

"Where the hell you going?" Pete snapped as he started to rise from the table.

"To put Jody to bed," she answered. "And to get a blanket for the old man."

"Okay. Just don't be dallying. And leave the door open so I can see you're not up to any tricks."

Sarah laid Jody in his small bed and wrapped him in a blanket. He murmured for a moment, and then closed his eyes. Standing up, she peered through the bedroom door. She saw Margaret go to the fireplace with an armful of wood followed by Breed, who had risen from the table. Pete was also looking at Margaret and not at the bedroom door.

Sarah glanced up at her husband's double-barrel shotgun, which he kept loaded and stored on a wall shelf that was high enough to keep it out of Jody's curious hands. Although she had fired the gun several times at Jim's insistence, it frightened her because of the loud sound of its discharge and the destruction it wrought. She wondered if she had the strength and the will to use it. A sudden shiver came over her, and she stood motionless in indecision. She believed that life was God's gift, and it was a grave sin to kill another person. She thought about the Lord's Commandment, "Thou shalt not kill, sayeth the Lord."

A vision of her father came to her, his calm presence providing her strength. Sarah took a deep breath, plucked the shotgun down, and swung it up to her shoulder as she stepped out of the room. Pete turned toward her and, gasping in astonishment, reached for his pistol.

"Don't move!" Sarah shouted as she cocked the two hammers and leveled the barrels at him. "Just don't move!"

Pete froze with his gun still holstered. Breed, with one hand on Margaret's arm, turned and looked at his knife, which was still stuck in the tabletop.

"Damn me," Pete said, his eyes no longer shifting back and forth, but locked on the shotgun. "Should have checked the damn bedroom out. Thought that buffalo rifle was all you had."

"Too late, Pete," Sarah said. "Unbuckle your holster and let it fall on the floor. Now!"

As Pete was unfastening his belt, Sarah rested one finger on each of the two shotgun triggers. Suddenly, unconsciously, one of them twitched. The gun roared as a stream of flame shot out of the barrel carrying with it a load of large pellets. The projectiles spread out as they rushed through the air and struck Pete a murderous blow, sending him tumbling backwards with blood spurting from multiple hits in his face, throat, and chest. The deafening roar of the shot and the acrid smell of the gunpowder filled the air.

"Oh Lord," Sarah cried. Jim had warned her about the gun's hair trigger, she thought. She hadn't meant to fire it.

She turned to Breed, who had thrown Margaret to the floor and was pulling his knife out of the table. She swung the gun toward him, but then realized that she couldn't shoot because Margaret and Jody were in the line of fire. As she watched in horror, Breed drew his arm back to throw the knife at her. But, before he could release it, a mottled mass of snarling animal launched through the air as Beelzebub, awakened from sleep by the sound of the shotgun blast, leaped up. The dog hit Breed's shoulder and knocked him across the room where he stumbled over Pete's body. Rolling over, Breed scrambled to his feet, again drawing back his knife into a throwing position.

The second barrel of the gun exploded as if it had a mind of its own. The deadly shot tore across the room and slammed into Breed's torso. It ripped flesh and meat from his bones and scattered his blood across the room and onto the wall behind him.

"Oh Lord," Sarah moaned again when the sound of the firings quit echoing in her ears. An excruciating pain, caused by the shotgun's recoil, numbed her shoulder. She could hear Jody wailing in the bedroom behind her and the astonished shout of the old man as he fumbled his way up through his whiskey-induced stupor.

"Mama!" Margaret screamed in horror as she looked at the bodies strewn on the floor. "What are we going to do now?"

Shaken by the deafening blast and the pain in her shoulder, Sarah looked at the two motionless bodies on the floor. It took her several moments to collect her thoughts. Then she went to Breed and knelt beside him. He was lying on his back and his eyes were staring lifelessly at the ceiling. A quick look at Pete told her that he was also dead.

"Bring me some blankets from the bedroom," she asked Margaret. Turning to the old man, she said firmly, "You! Don't move. Just don't move."

Chapter 2

"I'm telling you, I didn't mean to shoot him," Sarah said as she covered Pete's body with a blanket.

"Didn't mean to!" Margaret exclaimed. "Mama, he was going to kill us. And that ... monster," she pointed toward Breed's body under another blanket against the wall. "He ... he was going to—" Tears streamed down her cheeks as she held Jody in her arms. Beelzebub had settled back down on the fireplace hearth and was resting from his exertions.

Sarah looked up at her daughter and said quietly, "I know what he was going to do. I'm just saying that I didn't mean for the gun to go off. I was going to tie them up and send you to fetch Lars Sigmund."

Sarah rose and walked over to the old man rocking in his chair and staring wildly up at her. "I don't know who you are, or why you came here tonight," she said. "I suspect you've been up to no good. Now we'll have to have to bury your partners. But first, you are going to tell me the whole story."

"I ... I—" he stammered. He held his hands up in front of his face, "Are you going to shoot me too?"

"No, there's been enough killing. I want to know why you stopped here. Who are you?"

"Jackson Pollard, that's my name. Well, you see ... we ... we—" The old man looked at the saddlebags lying near the door, and then back to Sarah, "We held up the train station in Fort Smith. Yes, we did. Gold ... it had government gold and silver."

"Government gold and silver?"

"Yes. It was for the Indian agents to buy land from the Comanches and Kiowas. That it was."

"Mama," Margaret interrupted. "It's starting to smell bad in here. What are we going to do?"

"Just a minute," Sarah said. Turning back to the old man, she asked quietly, "How much gold and silver did you get?"

"Don't know, exactly. We ... we only got part of it. They caught all of the others—"

"The others? Who were the others?"

"Well, there was eight of us when we started. The guards at the station killed two and the posse got the rest. Even killed Mansfield. He was the leader, you know."

"Mama," Margaret said as Jody began to sob around his thumb stuck in his mouth. "What are we going to do about these bodies? We can't go for the sheriff until morning."

"Take Jody in the bedroom and put him to sleep," Sarah said as she stood up and backed away from the stench surrounding Pollard. "Then we'll take care of them."

Turning back to the old man, Sarah said, "Don't move from that chair, Mr. Pollard. I don't know what we're going to do with you."

"Oh, you needn't worry about me. I'll be quiet as a church mouse."

Sarah knelt at the saddlebags on the floor by the door. After she opened them and checked the contents, she went into the bedroom. Margaret sat in a chair next to Jody, who was turned on his side in his bed, still sucking his thumb. Sarah raised her finger to her lips at Margaret's questioning look, "Shh—" Reaching under the bed; she removed a large cloth valise. "Come out when he's asleep," she said quietly.

Sarah stood in the doorway and looked down as Margaret put her hand tenderly on Jody's shoulder and began to sing *Brahm's Lullaby*:

> Lullaby and good night, with roses bedight.
> With lilies o'er spread is baby's wee bed.
> Lay thee down now and rest, may thy slumber be blessed.
> Lay thee down now and rest, may thy slumber be blessed.
> Lullaby and good night, thy mother's delight.
> Bright angels beside my darling abide.
> They will guard thee at rest; thou shalt wake on my breast.
> They will guard thee at rest; thou shalt wake on my breast.

The old man was snoring when Sarah reentered the main room. She removed some of the gold and silver coins from the saddlebags and placed them in her valise. When it was nearly too heavy for her to carry, she divided what was left into two of the saddlebags. While she was separating the small gold bars, she noticed something stamped into the surface. Holding one of them close, she read the inscription and shook her head in wonder. Then she carried her bag to the fireplace and set it beside the sleeping Beelzebub.

Kneeling, she ran her hands over the dog's thick fur, warm from the heat of the open fire. He bristled at her first touch, and then settled back into a rhythmic, shallow snore.

"Thank you, old fellow," she said endearingly. "I didn't know you still had it in you. You can rest now. If you hadn't jumped in—"

Sarah shuddered as she recalled the horrible scene with the noise of the shotgun and the sudden death it dealt the two strangers. She knew the images would haunt the rest of her life.

"What are we to do now?" she asked the slumbering mass of fur.

As she looked down at Beelzebub, nearing the twilight of his life, her thoughts went back to the day when her father had brought him home. He was a scurrilous and gangly puppy, barely able to run without slamming into things around him. Margaret was only four years old at the time, and she was frightened of the smelly, multi-colored bag of bones with a deep, mournful wail inherited from his Gray Wolf father.

Preacher Parker—as he was known to family, friends, and strangers alike—had delivered a baby during one of his circuit rides through the sparsely populated country to the west. Like most of the hardscrabble families struggling to build a farm between the annual spring raids of the Comanches, the droughts of the summer, and the cruel winds and snows of the winters, they had no cash or negotiable paper. Instead of payment, they asked him to take one of the five puppies bouncing off each other and the walls in the dirt-floored cabin that served as a home for the humans, the dogs, a few pet chickens, and an occasional armadillo that wandered into the menagerie. The fact that this particular puppy was twice as large as his siblings and had a nasty disposition, both traits inherited from his father, made the selection easy for them.

Against his better judgment, Preacher Parker took the mongrel home with him. He thought the dog might protect his daughter and granddaughter when he was away on the Lord's business. After Sarah's first husband, Dennis Hopkins, had been shot when he was caught dealing cards from the bottom of a deck in a

Waco saloon, he had moved in with her and Margaret at the ranch that he had given her as a wedding present.

The once recalcitrant animal soon became Margaret's protector and companion. Anyone or anything that came near her suffered his wrath. As the years passed the legend of the massive part dog and part wolf with a nasty disposition grew until everyone in the area became aware of it and avoided the Parker Ranch on the Bosque River. Even the Comanche Indians, warned by one of their medicine men to stay away from the huge dog with a red-haired child companion, bypassed the homestead during their spring raids out of the Staked Plains, *Llano Estacado*, to the northwest.

Sarah looked up from the fireplace hearth as Margaret came out of the bedroom. "Wake Mr. Pollard," she said. "He'll help us dig the graves."

"Ugh! He stinks. What are we going to do then?"

"I don't know. Let's take it one step at a time. First, we need to get these two buried and clean up this mess."

While the old man was digging a hole near the barn, Sarah and Margaret wrapped the bodies in blankets and drug them out of the house.

"Mama," Margaret said after they put the bodies on the ground near the growing pit. "Grandpa said telling a lie is a sin. Did we commit a sin by telling them our neighbors could hear a gun shot? You know they're almost five miles away."

"Don't worry," Sarah said with a smile. "I think the Lord will understand and forgive us for telling a lie when we were threatened." But, she wondered with a heavy heart, will He forgive her for breaking one of His commandments, "Thou shalt not kill."

"Why are we digging the grave here by the barn?" Margaret asked as Sarah climbed down in the hole and took the shovel from Pollard, who was wheezing loudly.

"I don't want them in our family cemetery. We can drive the cattle over the grave so no one will know where they are."

"Aren't we going to tell the sheriff about them and—" Margaret looked at Pollard who was sitting on the edge of the water trough still gasping for breath.

Sarah ignored the question as she climbed out of the shallow grave. With Margaret and Pollard to help, she rolled the two shrouded bodies into the hole and covered them with the excavated dirt.

"Mr. Pollard," Sarah said. "Put the saddles on your horses ... all of them. Bring them and the pack horse to the house."

"Yes, Ma'am," the old man wheezed. "What you gonna do to me?"

"We'll discuss that when you finish."

Sarah waited until Pollard entered the barn, and then she drew Margaret near and said, "Go into the house and start cleaning up. When I finish here, I'll help you. We need to get some sleep; we have an early morning start."

"Why? Where are we going to?"

"Where I should have gone long ago … to find Jim. And," she added with a smile, "don't end a sentence with a preposition."

"Oh, Mama," Margaret pouted.

"Go on now," Sarah said. "I'll run the cattle by here a few times."

When Sarah entered the house, Margaret was mopping the floor where Pete had been shot. Beelzebub still slept by the fireplace. Every now and then, he would raise his hackles and snuffle as his nocturnal dreams moved him to action. Jody was also asleep when she went into the bedroom and packed an old leather suitcase with several changes of clothes for the two of them. Going to the shelf that held her books, she took down her Bible. As she placed it in the bag, it opened and a blue ribbon fell out. She picked it up and, with a smile accompanied by memories of the past, folded it and put it back into the bound book. Closing the suitcase, she set it on the floor by the bed.

She helped Margaret clean the blood from the floor and the wall. Hearing the sound of neighing horses from outside, she picked up one of the saddlebags and stepped out onto the front porch with Margaret following. Pollard, sitting astride his horse, held the reins of the other two saddles horses and the packhorse. He started to dismount.

"Hold on, Mr. Pollard," Sarah said as she stepped down into the yard and looked up at him. "I don't want you to set foot in my house again."

"No, Ma'am," the old man said. "What … what am I to do now?"

"Let's talk about that for a minute," Sarah responded. "You know the law is looking for you. If they don't hang you, at your age you'll never see the outside of a prison again. Is that what you want?"

Pollard started to talk, but the effort was too much for him, and he began to cry. "No … no," he snuffled when he regained his composure.

"What were you doing with those two scalawags?" Sarah asked in a quiet voice.

"Needed the money. My luck done run out and—"

"Needed the money! For what, to buy whiskey?" When the old man didn't respond, Sarah continued, "Do you have family, Mr. Pollard?"

"Yes. Well … just a daughter and couple of grand younguns."

"Where do they live?"

"Down near Houston. Had a farm till her husband died in the war. Now, I'm not sure where they are. Reckon they're still somewhere near there."

Sarah went to the packhorse and loaded it with the saddlebag she had been carrying. Then she forced herself to enter Pollard's aura of aroma as she searched though his bags until she found a bottle of whiskey. Uncorking it, she poured the contents out on the ground.

"Mr. Pollard," Sarah said as she stepped backward, "I'm going to make a deal with you. Are you agreeable to that?"

"Yes, I am."

"We're not going to turn you over to the law," Sarah said. "In return, you leave here right now. Take all those horses with you. Wait till about midday, then turn the two saddle horses loose. The sheriff may have a description of them. If you do get caught, don't say anything about being on this ranch."

"Where ... where can I go?" The old man began to cry again.

"Houston," Margaret said from the porch.

Pollard looked up through his tears, "Huh?"

"Houston," Sarah echoed what Margaret had said. "You have family there. It's about time you lived up to your responsibility to them. I'm sure your daughter needs help. I put some of the gold and silver on the packhorse. If you spend it quietly and wisely, you can take care of your family and yourself for a long time."

The old man's eyes cleared, and he stammered, "Th ... thank you. I appreciate what you're doing. I really do."

"Appreciation isn't enough," Sarah said. Turning to Margaret, she asked, "Please get my Bible out of the valise inside the door."

When Margaret returned, Sarah took the Bible from her and approached the old man again. "I want your sworn word, on the Lord's book, that you'll go to Houston and help your family. Also, you won't touch the bottle again. Do I have your word?"

"Yes ... yes you do," he said as he placed his hand on the Bible Sarah held up to him. "I swear on God's book."

When he gathered up the reins from the other horses and turned to leave, Sarah stopped him. "One more thing, Mr. Pollard. Wait a moment, please."

Sarah went into the house and returned with a towel and a bar of soap. Handing them to him, she said, "When you come to water, wash yourself and your clothes. You don't want your family to see you like this."

Sarah felt Margaret's hand squeeze her shoulder as they watched the old man ride away from the house into the moonlit night. "Thank you," she said to her daughter. "You are very understanding and forgiving."

"No, Mama, you are. I will pray he'll return to his family."

"I will also," Sarah said.

"What are we going to do now?"

"We're going to get some sleep and put today away," Sarah said as she took Margaret's arm. "Tomorrow can take care of itself."

In the early hours of the morning, when the fireplace logs had burned down to a dull glow and before the roosters began to crow, Sarah roused Margaret in the sleeping loft. "I'm going to hitch Contrary and Precious to the wagon," she said in a whisper. "Throw some wood on the fire. Fix breakfast and feed Jody and Beelzebub. Then pack a bag with clothes and toilet articles for at least a week."

Sarah left before Margaret, stirring and rubbing sleep from her eyes, could respond. Picking up the saddlebag she had left near the door, she went by the barn and grabbed a shovel before going to the small family cemetery on a rise up the river from the house. Dawn was beginning to lighten the eastern sky and force the darkness into low-lying recesses. She could just make out two headstones outlined against the pale grass, damp with dew. The pleasant chirping of birds in the mesquite, post oak, and cottonwood trees blended with the musical rippling of the river to put life into the dawning of the new day.

Although it was still too dark to read, she knew well the carved inscription on the large marker on the left:

> Alice B. Parker
> Born 16 May 1825, Died 25 June 1847
> Beloved Wife and Mother
> Resting in The Arms of the Lord

Sarah was only five when her mother died from pneumonia, but she remembered the beautiful and gentle woman. For many years, she couldn't separate the dreams of the long, dark nights from the fantasies of her daytime imaginings. In both, her mother comforted her when she hurt and rejoiced with her when she climbed another step toward womanhood.

Tears welled up in her eyes and ran down her cheeks as she knelt in the grass and spoke aloud, "Mother, I must leave you now. We can't stay here any longer. I fear each day for Margaret and Jody. I have to find Jim. I'm just not strong enough to stay without his protection. I will return when I can."

The inscription on the headstone to the right of her mother's was incomplete:

Robert C. Parker,
Born 16 June 1821

Sarah took a deep breath and began speaking, "I don't know where you are, Father. I do know you were with me last night. It was your strength that pulled the triggers of that gun, not mine. Thank you for saving us from those evil men."

For a long moment, Sarah knelt in prayer. A gentle, lowing murmur wafted in on the cool wind blowing from the pasture as the cattle began their daily grazing. It mingled with the trill of the river as it rushed onward to the southeast. The sounds of the morning soothed her tormented mind as she remembered her father, gone now for so many years. She imagined that he died at the hands of the Comanches in the open country to the west, later to be ravished by wild animals. The vision of him lying in some god forsaken and desolate place with his bones bleaching in the hot summer sun and drifting before the strong winter winds haunted her. She wanted him here, resting in the ground beside his wife.

Before he left on his final visit to the scattered families hungering for the word of the Lord, Sarah remembered him railing against the Catholic Church again, which was his favorite subject after the Bible. He had come into the Texas territory with his father and several uncles long before the Civil War, when it was still part of Mexico. If they had been Catholic, or had agreed to convert, the Mexican government would have given them land grants in the Gulf of Mexico lowlands or along the Rio Grande drainage basin. But the "Hardshell" Baptist families refused to relinquish their faith. They believed in backbreaking labor, strict morals, and fire and brimstone preaching. So they were forced to settle in the Comancheria area on the Edwards Plateau and on the fringes of the *Llano Estacado* where they were interlopers on the Comanche hunting grounds and subject to their terrible wrath.

"Dang burn Papists," her father had said to her, which was the closest he ever came to cursing. "They have a so-called Pope who lives in a foreign country and tells his flock they can't pray to the Lord, they have to go through their priest minions. Confess their sins to them, after paying a tithe to the church coffers. Balderdash, I show folks how to get down on their knees and pray directly to the man upstairs. In English, not that bedeviling Latin. And, if they don't have any money or items of trade, I'll take their good will and friendship in payment and call it square."

Sarah, with Margaret's hand in hers, had watched her father ride away that fateful day. An early winter covering of snow, swirled by the wind, chilled the morning. Normally, her father never looked back after he left the house. His eyes were always on the road ahead and his mind preoccupied with the sermons he would preach in the days to come. For some reason, that day he turned before fording the river and looked back at the house. Lifting his hat, his long black hair, which was streaked with white, streamed out in the wind. He waved in solemn farewell before galloping on.

"Father," Sarah said, returning from her daydream, "I am going to find Jim. I pray he is still alive. I fear staying here alone. Those people last night … others like them could come again. Or the Indians. They still raid this area. I don't know why they haven't found our ranch."

Sarah looked at the saddlebag beside her, "I hope you don't mind me using your grave to hide the rest of this money. I know stealing is not God's will. I promise you I'll put it to good use."

"Besides," she continued with a slight smile, "I expect it came from hard working people being taxed. I know you think the only tax we should pay is to the Lord."

Rising, Sarah buried the bag. She was careful to return the sod so the evidence of digging wouldn't be apparent. When she stood up, the gusty north wind fluttered her dress and blew her long red hair around her face. Far off, down the river bottom, the lonely cry of a loon floated on the morning air. The mournful sound rose above the water, the cemetery, and the trees until it dissipated in the vastness of the sky.

"Good-bye," Sarah said quietly to her mother.

Turning, she walked slowly to the house trying to orient her thoughts toward the things she needed to do before leaving the ranch.

Chapter 3

▼

"Mama, are we going to Fort Worth to look for Jim?" Margaret asked as Sarah clucked the horses across the river and turned the wagon along the road heading to the southeast.

Margaret held Jody on her lap with a blanket wrapped around him to ward off the early morning chill. After Beelzebub had awakened from the dreams that bedeviled him by the fireplace and ate some ground meat and bread sopped in milk, he was invigorated. Running ahead of them, he swung his ponderous head back every now and then to make sure they were keeping up with him.

"Yes," Sarah answered. "That's where he went to sell the horses. And where he was last seen."

The wagon jerked and bounced as the right front wheel struck a large rock that had rolled onto the narrow roadway. Sarah grabbed for her wide-brimmed hat with one hand while holding tight to the reins with the other. Dust motes rising from the dry dirt in the ruts caused her to sneeze.

"Whee, Mama," Jody screamed in joy as he bounced on Margaret's lap. "Go faster."

"Are we going to take this wagon all the way?" Margaret asked as she brushed dirt from the bodice of her dress. "We'll shake to pieces."

"No," Sarah answered. "We'll leave it at the livery stable in Waco and take the stage. It leaves early in the morning. We'll stay in a hotel tonight."

She didn't add that she thought it would be dangerous for two women and a boy to be traveling so far alone.

"Do we have enough money?" Margaret asked. "I thought we were—" looking back at the valise lying on the wagon floor, she became quiet.

Sarah glanced at Margaret and said, "We haven't had a chance to talk about the money those three brought into the house last night. You heard the old man say they stole it from the federal government."

"Yes. It was to buy land from the Indians."

"More than likely, it would line the pockets of the Indian Agent and his cohorts," Sarah said. "I don't think the Comanches and Kiowas would see much of it."

"Are we going to give it back?" Margaret asked as Jody began to whine.

Sarah pulled the wagon to a stop and stepped to the ground, taking Jody in her arms. She unbuttoned the front of his pants and turned away while he urinated into the brush at the side of the road. Beelzebub ran in from his position at the point and came to a sliding stop, raising a cloud of dust. He stood still, panting rapidly, while Jody finished his toilet.

After Sarah buttoned Jody's trousers and handed him up to Margaret, Beelzebub looked at the wagon and whimpered, his long tongue dripping saliva as he begged for a ride. Sarah had to let down the tailgate and help him into the bed. "I can remember when you could run twenty miles and jump over a horse," she said as she rumpled the dog's ears and blew into his face.

Standing alongside the wagon, Sarah looked up at her daughter's pretty face, smudged from the dust and open with childlike trust and naivety. "I don't know yet what we'll do about the money," she said quietly. "You know, we gave part of it to Mr. Pollard. I pray he will make good use of it."

Pausing for a moment, she added, "The gold bars were minted by the Confederate States. Somehow they got into the U.S. treasury. Probably during the war."

Strange, Sarah thought, her father would chuckle if he knew the gold had been taken from the rebellious states. He was a staunch supporter of the Union, even though Texas had aligned with the Confederacy during the recent conflict. The statewide southern sympathy had cost him a large number of his congregation, and he had been forced to close his church on the bank of the Bosque River in Old Clifton. Unable to give up his Lord's calling, he had taken up circuit riding in the territory to the west and northwest. Other men of the cloth feared to venture there because the protective government military had been pulled into the terrible eastern conflict that tore the nation apart in the cause of states rights versus anti-slavery.

Putting her hand on Margaret's leg, Sarah continued, "If anything should happen to me, the other saddlebag is buried in your grandfather's grave. He'll keep it safe for you."

"Happen to you—" Margaret gasped. "Mama, ain't anything going to happen to you, is there?"

"Don't worry. I don't intend on anything happening. I just wanted you to know in case of an emergency. And, there you go using that word *ain't* again. We're going to have to enroll you in a finishing school so you can learn proper English. I certainly haven't done a good job of teaching you." Climbing back into the wagon, Sarah snapped the reins and started it rolling before Margaret could respond.

"Mama," Jody said plaintively as he crawled into the back with his blanket to lie on Beelzebub, rising and falling with the dog's deep breathing. "I'm hungry. So is Beebub." Since struggling with his first attempts at pronouncing the dog's full name, he had shortened it to a form easier for him to say.

"Me too," Margaret added. "And I have to go to the toilet. I don't want to go out in the bushes. Yech!"

"We're almost to the Sigmund's place," Sarah replied. "Hilda will be pleased to fix us something to eat. Besides, we need to ask Lars if he'll watch our ranch while we're away. The horses can fend for themselves for a while, but the cows will need milking and the chickens and hogs need to be fed and the eggs gathered."

"How long will we be gone?" Margaret asked.

"I don't know," Sarah said. "Maybe several weeks." As she thought about her response, an empty feeling grew in the pit of her stomach. She wondered if she would ever again see the ranch in the valley by the river where she had lived most of her life, and where Margaret and Jody had spent all of their years.

She thought about the river, low enough to ford except during periods of heavy rain and spring runoff. She had learned to swim in the clear, cool flowing water and Margaret after her. She had caught her first fish there, a large catfish that frightened her when she pulled it ashore, but elated her when her father filleted it and served it for supper. It was on the banks of the stream among the willows and switchgrass that she found her first injured creature, a small silver, pink, and black scissor-tail flycatcher that had fallen from a nest high in the cottonwood tree above. With her father's moral support, she had nursed it back to health, climbed the tree, and returned it to its noisy siblings.

She had watched impatiently for signs of spring along the river swollen with upstream rain, looking for the budding of wild flowers and the first of the ungainly sandhill cranes, the highflying Canadian Geese, and the Mallard Ducks to return from their southern sojourn and bring with them a promise of life reawakening after the long dormant winter.

In the summer, when the fields dried and cracked from lack of rain, among the grasses and bushes set back from the flowing river she had experienced the wonder of fireflies. "Nature's tiny night angels," her father had called them as she romped after the intriguing insects trying to catch their magic in her hands.

In the fall, the magnificent Monarch Butterflies fluttering south on their annual journey to the mountains of Mexico made the trees come alive with motion and color. Although they rested for only a brief time, Sarah had looked at them with joy in her heart as they swarmed in abandonment, and she mourned their passage with tears in her eyes as they soared gracefully into the sky to continue on to a place she could only wonder about.

The Bosque with its magnificent splendor and its wondrous gifts would beckon to her to return. Because of the river, she had become aware of the joy and the mystery of nature. She had observed the cycle of birth, life, and death. And through the river, she had come to the realization that water was very important to life and growth in a land of sparse rainfall.

The ranch house, so full of love, warmth, and memories, would also call to her. Her father had built it with only one room when he settled onto the property with his new bride, Sarah's mother. But when she was old enough to observe her parent's nocturnal activities, he had expanded it to add a sleeping loft for Sarah and a separate bedroom with a door for privacy for himself and his wife. The house had been built solid enough to withstand the extremes of nature: the bitter cold and strong winds of winter, the heavy rains of spring, and the fierce blasts of the summer sun. It was a home for a family, not just a place to live.

But now she had two children who depended on her. They were going into an unknown future with little knowledge of where to search for Jim—if he was still alive—and with stolen money that might land her in prison if the federal authorities found out about it.

After they left the rutted path leading from the Sigmund Ranch and turned east toward Waco, Sarah snapped the reins over the backs of the horses to increase their pace. She had tried to leave Beelzebub with the Sigmund's dogs to no avail. Revitalized after eating, he had crawled under the wire fence and caught up with the wagon before it was out of sight of the house. He loped alongside as the road veered away from the river and its cover of trees and willows and started up a long incline sided with green ferns and rocks turned a bright orange by their symbiotic covering of lichen. The cool temperature of the fall morning gave way to a warm afternoon sun that looked down patronizingly over their shoulder. The sharp aroma of alkali and sagebrush permeated the air.

"We stayed longer at the Sigmund's than we should have," Sarah said as she removed her woolen jacket and stowed it behind her seat. She looked back at Jody sleeping peacefully with his blanket wrapped around the arm that held the thumb in his mouth. The blanket, white at one time and covered with the outline of tiny animals, was now soiled beyond recovery. She recalled when he would cry mournfully every time she would take it from him to wash. Finally, she started cleaning it late at night when he was asleep, because he would not part with it without a fight. His golden curls caught the sun's rays and held them suspended as if their vibrant color was a gift from Heaven. What a beautiful child, she thought. With his tiny, pug nose, chubby cheeks, and large, angelic eyes he was the darling of everyone who met him. Nothing, she vowed silently, nothing must ever happen to him.

Margaret held her bonnet against the wind and said, "Hilda and Lars sure are nice people, aren't they? Too bad they don't have some boys."

"Boys!" Sarah laughed. "Wouldn't one be enough?"

"Oh, Mama," Margaret blushed, a red tint highlighting her face, which was tanned to a golden glow by the long summer.

Sarah looked at her daughter, the smile on her lips fading as she thought about Margaret. She was getting to be a young lady. A beautiful, young lady living on an isolated ranch miles from the nearest neighbor and even further from any young man who might be a prospective suitor. She didn't even have the advantage of attending school with other children since it was over a half-day ride away. As a result, Sarah, who had been a schoolteacher when she met Jim, taught her at home. She thought something good might come out of the journey ahead. Perhaps Margaret would meet a fine young man; someone like Jim.

After they crested a steep hill formed by granite outliers, the land flattened out into a plateau that ran several miles before dropping away in the distance. The spears on the prairie grass sighed and waved in the wind in concert to an unheard symphony orchestra. Alongside the trail, nature's palette had cast splashes of gray sage, yellow goldenrod, and red Indian Paintbrush to provide a pleasant contrast to the layer of dust scattered over the roadway by the churning wheels of passing travelers and the stomping hoofs of lowing cattle. Overhead, high cumulous clouds with fluffy white tops and gray bottoms piled one on top of the other forming outlines of grotesque creatures and cuddly animals.

The flat plain they had been riding on began a gentle descent back to the sandy river bottom where the water flowed among spreading broad-leaved post oaks and elm trees enjoying the last warm days before shedding their leaves to the cold, biting north winds of winter.

"We'll stop for a rest at the river and water the horses," Sarah said as she wiped dust from her eyes.

"Mama!" Margaret cried. "Look!"

Sarah turned to see a large group of riders approach the river from the far side at a gallop. Even at this distance, she could see that they were heavily armed. They had pistols strapped to their legs and rifles carried over the pommels of their saddles, as if they were ready for combat. She pulled the wagon to the side of the trail and stopped it short of the crossing area. Beelzebub, unaware of the horsemen, plowed into a shallow area and began wallowing in the water.

"It's okay, Margaret," Sarah said. "We'll let them pass on. I'll do any talking that's needed." Even as she said it, she knew Margaret would speak her mind if she had the notion. It was one of the traits Sarah admired in her.

Two lead riders, slowing for the river fording, looked up at the wagon and its occupants. At a shout from one of them, the main body stopped on the far bank. Then they holstered their rifles and splashed through the belly deep water toward the wagon.

"That's the McLennan County Sheriff, Wilson," Sarah remarked as she recognized the first rider mounted on a brown stallion. He was a big man with florid cheeks, a bulbous nose, a tobacco stained handlebar mustache, and long straggly hair. "I don't know the other one."

As the sheriff and his companion came to a stop in front of the wagon, Sarah could tell that they had been riding long and hard. The horses, sweat streaked and wheezing for breath, turned their heads and stared at the river in anticipation of a drink. Both men also looked tired and thirsty.

"Just a minute, damn you," the sheriff said as he pulled his reins to stop his horse from fleeing to the stream. Perspiration stained the armpits of his long-sleeved plaid shirt and dark leather vest. Across the river, the other riders had dismounted and were scooping up water in cupped hands alongside their drinking horses. Beelzebub had ceased his romping and came up the bank to plop down along side the wagon near Margaret. Closing his eyes, he was oblivious to the activity around him.

Sarah heard Margaret gasp as she looked at the second rider. She could see why her daughter was so affected; he was the most handsome man she had ever seen in her life. Tall and thin, his face glowed from the touch of the sun. He sat his white horse with the easy assurance of a born horseman, the long fingers of his hands gentling his mount with slight movements. Black hair peeked out from under his light brown, wide-brimmed hat and emphasized his piercing blue eyes. When he looked at her, Sarah felt that all her thoughts were suddenly revealed as if he had reached into her very soul. Clad in dark, creased trousers, a white shirt, and a vest that matched his hat, he appeared to be cool and unruffled by the arduous journey. A holstered revolver sat low on his left thigh.

Shaken by the man's masculinity, Sarah turned to Wilson, "Good afternoon, Sheriff. What brings you so far from Waco?"

"Harrumph!" Wilson said as he spat a long stream of tobacco juice onto the ground. "Good day to you, Mrs. Whitman. We're chasing some folks—"

"Sheriff, don't you think you should introduce me to these fine ladies," the blue-eyed stranger said with a smile that revealed even, white teeth. His voice, a soft tenor, was friendly, warm, and invited conversation.

Wilson glanced at his companion with respect as he said, "Mrs. Whitman. This here is Jack Kilpatrick. He's a—"

Kilpatrick interrupted the sheriff with a laugh, "Just the name is all that is needed." He enunciated his words in the manner of a highly educated person. "Good afternoon ladies. I am pleased to make your acquaintance."

"Have you had any word on my husband, Sheriff?" Sarah asked, tearing her eyes from Kilpatrick and looking at Wilson.

"No, Ma'am. Nothing from Fort Worth or any other law offices."

"Her husband?" Kilpatrick asked.

"Jim Whitman … he disappeared several months ago," Sheriff Wilson answered. "He was last seen in Fort Worth where he sold some horses to the U.S. Army. No one's seen hide nor hair sign of him since."

"You have my sympathy, Mrs. Whitman," Kilpatrick said. "I'll do what I can to help locate him. Marshal Jim Courtright in Fort Worth is a good friend of mine."

Jody, awakening from his nap, climbed up into the seat between Sarah and Margaret rubbing his eyes. He crawled into Margaret's lap and stuck his thumb in his mouth as he stared wide-eyed at the two mounted men.

"And who might this fine young man be?" Kilpatrick asked.

"Jody," Sarah responded. "He's my son."

"Kilpatrick," Wilson said in a plaintive voice. "We're losing time. Going to be dark soon. We need to find out what these folks know and get on about our business."

"Why, certainly, Sheriff," Kilpatrick said softly as he nodded his hat brim at Sarah. "You may have surmised that we are chasing someone, Mrs. Whitman. Actually three men."

"What are they wanted for?" Sarah asked.

"Let us just say they are robbers and murderers, Mrs. Whitman," Kilpatrick responded with another one of his dazzling smiles. "I understand you live on the Bosque River west of here. The scoundrels appear to be heading that way. Have you seen any strangers pass by lately?"

Suddenly aware of the valise lying on the wagon bed behind her, Sarah avoided Kilpatrick's eyes as she responded. "No. No, we haven't. We're going into Waco for groceries."

"And you, Miss Whitman?" the overwhelming smile returned as Kilpatrick impaled Margaret with his penetrating gaze.

Margaret squirmed on the seat, as she answered, "No sir. As Mama said, we haven't seen anyone ... just Lars and Hilda Sigmund."

"The Sigmund Ranch is about ten miles ahead," Wilson said in response to Kilpatrick's questioning look. He spat another long trail of tobacco on the ground near Beelzebub. Some of it splattered onto his snout.

The dog roused himself from his sleep and looked up at the rider looming over him, a glint of fire in his eyes. Rising to his feet with his hackles extended, he issued a low, deep growl.

Sheriff Wilson's horse whinnied and reared backward at the sight of the angry beast confronting him. Wilson drew his pistol as he brought his steed under control and pointed it at Beelzebub. "Damned dog. What the hell!"

"Don't you dare shoot him, Sheriff," Margaret shouted. "Beelzebub. Quiet now. Quiet!"

At the sound of Margaret's voice, the dog retreated to the shadow of the wagon. But he still glared up at the sheriff with hatred in his eyes and a rumble in his throat.

Kilpatrick's voice filled the air like a soothing balm, "Sheriff, instead of shooting that big animal with a strange biblical name, you should swear him in. He'd make three or four of your posse."

"He didn't take kindly to you spitting at him, Sheriff," Sarah said. "It's a nasty habit I don't condone either."

"Time for us to water our horses and head up river, don't you think?" Kilpatrick said quietly but firmly after Wilson holstered his pistol.

"Good day to you Mrs. and Miss Whitman," Kilpatrick added as he touched his hat brim. "Have a pleasant visit in Waco."

Sarah clucked at Contrary and Precious and started into the river with Beelzebub splashing along behind. As they passed Kilpatrick, she noticed that he was staring at her in an open and forthright way as if he had a question in his mind. But it went unspoken and Sarah turned to look at the foaming water rushing by the horses as they stepped into its depths. She was afraid to look back, afraid that Kilpatrick was still looking at her and fearful that he would see the flush rising on her cheeks. When they reached the far bank, the posse riders were mounted and awaiting the wagon's passage so they could ford across. They gawked at Sarah and Margaret with wide, appraising eyes.

After they topped the rise leading away from the river, Margaret interrupted the silence, "Wow, Mama. Have you ever seen anyone so handsome?"

"Whom are you speaking about?" Sarah asked as she kept her eyes on the road ahead.

"Oh, you know! Jack Kilpatrick. Didn't you see the way he looked at you?"

"Looked at me," Sarah responded quietly. "I don't know what you're talking about."

"He couldn't take his eyes off you," Margaret said with a laugh. "You are a beautiful woman, even if you are my mother."

"I wouldn't know about that. I'm married. I don't see those things the way you unattached women do."

As she was making light of Margaret's comments, Sarah felt the flush return to her cheeks, and a strong, sensual feeling, missing for months, overwhelmed her. While Jim was a pleasant man to look at, his features were large and small pox scars dotted his cheeks, inviting sympathy more than admiration. What he lacked in physical and social grace, he made up with brute strength and a quiet demeanor. By contrast, Jack Kilpatrick was devastatingly handsome. He moved with the ease of a trained athlete or an actor on a stage and, seemingly without any conscious effort, he knew just what to say to diffuse the tension caused by Sheriff Wilson. She thought that Kilpatrick could look into her mind and search around. He would be a formidable adversary.

"What an idiot that sheriff is," Margaret said. "I thought he was going to shoot Beelzebub."

"Yes," Sarah agreed. "He's about as smart as that stump in our yard. There are stories going round that he embezzled funds from the county and beat up some prisoners. He's coming up for re-election next month. I don't think he has a chance."

She looked over her shoulder at the late afternoon sun, which was nearing the tops of the trees skirting the horizon. Stopping the wagon, she said, "It will be dark before we get into Waco. We better put Beelzebub in with us. He and Jody can nap together."

"Do you think they will find anything at the ranch, Mama?" Margaret asked quietly, a frown of concern on her face.

"I don't know. I hope not. It'll be hard to find the grave under all those hoof prints. If Mr. Pollard is wise, he'll get rid of those two saddle horses and not stop until he reaches Houston."

Sarah looked at her daughter, touching her arm. "Let's not worry about it now," she continued. "Today has had enough worries."

"Can we put them in Grandpa's bag of worries and woes?" Margaret asked with a laugh. "Like we used to do?"

"Yes. Father left me his worry bag when he went away, you know. He said I'd have a use for it some day."

"Really! Where is it?"

"I can't show you. Worries and woes are invisible, so the bag has to be invisible. I packed it in my suitcase."

"How do you know it's packed if you can't see it?" Margaret asked.

Sarah smiled to herself as she went to the rear of the wagon and helped Beelzebub up into the bed. Closing the tailgate, she told herself that it was time to put her own frets and concerns into her father's worry and woe bag. She was tired, and they still had a long way to go before they reached Waco.

Chapter 4

The sounds of morning rushed into the small hotel room on the main street of Waco, just off the confluence of the Brazos and Bosque Rivers, with a crash and a bang. Sarah awoke suddenly, not sure where she was for a moment. The cacophony of noise from outside pulled her into reality. She heard the clang of a blacksmith's hammer on an anvil, the neighing of horses, the barking of dogs, the creak of heavy wagons, the crowing of a wayward cock, the burble of voices passing by, and the far-off crack of a gun shot. The gray light of dawn struggled to penetrate the dirty lace curtains over the small second floor window as she lay on a blanket on the floor next to Beelzebub.

She had always enjoyed her visits to Waco over the years. Her father started his ministry as an assistant pastor at a local Baptist Church, and he took pride in acquainting her with the area's history each time they came to town. She knew that the old settlement, known as the "City of Waco" after the displaced local Indian tribe, was on a spur of the Chisholm Trail, which was used by cattlemen to drive herds to markets further north. It was an important debarkation point for thousands of prospective settlers headed west and north and the primary shipping point for a large area of North Texas and Eastern New Mexico. The town's many saloons and gaming houses attracted cowhands, drifters, and other nefarious characters who earned the city the nickname of "Six Shooter Junction." When she was a teenager, her father had even taken her to the red light district called the "Reservation." He snorted and fumed as he told her that prostitution was legally recognized, licensed, and regulated by the city. "Dagburned Sodom and Gomorrah," he ranted. He didn't blame the sporting women, or "soiled doves" as he called them. They wouldn't take up the world's oldest profession, he often preached, if men with greed and evil in their hearts didn't snatch them up and cast them into the houses of ill repute. He also blamed the human weakness that drove men of all classes to spill their seed outside the bonds of the matrimony sanctified by the Lord.

Unfortunately, Sarah thought, there was no time for shopping or sightseeing this time. She took off her nightgown and put on a white long-sleeved cotton shirt with frilled cuffs and a high collar and a dark woolen floor length skirt over a thin slip. Although she needed to use the guest outhouse behind the hotel, she delayed leaving the room until she awakened Margaret and Jody who were sleeping on the narrow bed.

"Jody," she said, taking his hand. "Come with me to the toilet."

Turning to Margaret, she added, "Get everything packed. Don't leave the room until we return."

"Mama," Margaret moaned as she rubbed her eyes, "It's early. I'm still tired from last night."

"I'm sorry. But the stage leaves at seven. If we miss it, we'll have to stay another day."

Buying the stagecoach tickets at the Wells Fargo office for herself, Margaret and Jody was no problem. But when Sarah asked the agent if Beelzebub, who was asleep on the porch, could also ride, she met firm opposition.

"Dogs don't ride, Ma'am," the little bespectacled man at the counter said in a petulant voice.

"I'm willing to pay ... half fare of course," Sarah said. She knew that Beelzebub would never be able to keep up with the stage all the way to Fort Worth, and he wouldn't stay behind even if she could find someone foolhardy enough to keep him.

"Well, I don't know," the clerk said. Then thinking about the increased money the company would make, he added, "We'll have to talk to the driver. If he's willing, I guess we can take the mutt. He is a small dog, ain't he?"

"Isn't he?" Margaret corrected the man after a glance at her mother. Jody was holding onto her skirt with one hand while the other held a licorice stick.

Sarah ignored the clerk's question as she counted out the additional fare on the counter. "Who is the driver?" she asked.

"Why, Old Smelly, of course," the clerk answered. "Every body in these parts knows he has the route north out of Waco. Since they built the bridge, anyway. He don't like running water, won't ford any rivers. The story is he was caught in a spring flash flood and washed down the Brazos River. But the water couldn't penetrate the dirt covering his clothes, and he floated like a cork. He might have made it all the way to the Gulf of Mexico had not a cowboy, searching for lost cattle, spotted him bobbing up and down in the current. He threw a loop over him and pulled him to the bank. Since then, Old Smelly won't cross any water higher than the axle of his coach unless there's a bridge."

"Oh Lord," Margaret said as they walked out onto the porch where Beelzebub lay snoring. "Sounds like we have to put up with another stinky old man who hates water."

The Concord Coach stage pulled up to the station in a cloud of dust, a creak of leather, the neighing of horses, and the crack of a whip. Sarah stepped off the porch to confront the driver as he climbed down from the top seat.

Old Smelly's razor thin face was sunburned and heavily lined. He looked old before his time from years of drinking, smoking, and working outdoors under the brutal Texas sun and the nearly constant wind. His skin resembled the gnarled bark of an ancient post oak tree. His insipid, pale gray eyes were almost hidden beneath his heavy, dust-laden eyebrows. Long woolen underwear showed at the open collar of his shirt; a shirt that was missing several buttons and stained with sweat, dirt, and tobacco dribbling. A pair of black suspenders held up his ragged and patched black pants. The remnants of a Confederate States of America infantryman cap perched on his straggly gray hair. It looked like it had been left too long in the rain and the sun, and then stomped by a few stout hogs in a wet sty.

Sarah had met many men who never bathed, avoiding water with the best of the West's great unwashed knights: a large group that included farmers, cattlemen, plains Indians, and puritanical preachers from the Northeast whose European ancestors believed that washing removed a layer of protective oils from the skin, which resulted in various and sundry ailments, most of them fatal. She never accepted that absurd notion, insisting on frequent baths for herself and her family. Sarah appraised the driver from a distance, reluctant to approach him.

"Howdy, Ma'am," Old Smelly said as he removed his shoddy cap and dusted it off on his hip. "How can I help you?"

"I have tickets for me and my family to ride to Fort Worth," she said. Motioning to their baggage on the steps, she added, "We have that and our family pet."

"Pet?" Old Smelly snorted. "An animal?"

"Most pets are animals," Sarah said with a condescending smile. "We paid half fare for him."

"Paid for an animal?" Old Smelly barked incredulously as he spat a long, brown stream of tobacco juice into the dust near Sarah. "I'll be horn-gawd-damn-swoggled," he added.

"Yes," Sarah snapped. "We paid his fare. And I will thank you kindly to spit away from me, far away. It is a most deplorable habit, sir. Also, your speech is atrocious. In the future, do not take the Lord's name in vain near me or my family."

A red flush rose up Old Smelly's neck as he took offense at Sarah's tongue lashing. "You are rude," he said in a wounded voice.

"Yes," Sarah replied. "Perhaps I am. It is a temporary failing of mine, which can be corrected. However, Sir, you are ugly, foulmouthed, and you stink. Those, I fear, are permanent conditions."

Old Smelly started to spit again. Then thinking better of it, he stopped and, in his consternation, swallowed his chew. Hacking and coughing, he brushed by Sarah and went into the stage office, slamming the door behind him.

Loud voices issued from the room for several minutes before Old Smelly and the clerk emerged. Going to the pile of luggage on the steps, they placed them in the rear boot of the coach.

Then the clerk turned to Sarah. "Your pet?" he asked.

Sarah turned and pointed at the huge mass sleeping on the porch. Beelzebub took that moment to give voice to one of his dreams, perhaps one where he was fighting for his life alongside his wolf father against a passel of large bears. Whatever it was, with his eyes still closed, he lifted his huge snout and roared. The sound blasted off the porch and resounded up and down the street. Horses reared at their reins and neighed in fear. For several blocks, people stopped what they were doing and stared in the direction of the monstrous dog. But Beelzebub had settled back into a snuffling snore.

Old Smelly and the clerk were unsettled by the blast of noise rushing over them. "Oh, dear me!" the clerk said. "I thought it was a family pet, Mrs. Whitman."

"He is," Sarah said. "He's been with us for many years. He won't stay behind, so we are taking him to Fort Worth with us."

"I ain't taking nary animal that size on my stage," Old Smelly said when he regained his senses. "He's as big as my horses."

"I paid good cash money for his fare," Sarah said to the clerk. "What would the owner say if I told him you refused to take him?"

"Give her money back," Old Smelly croaked around a mouth full of spittle. He looked around for a place to unload it away from Sarah. "I have to pick up two more passengers at the hotel. There ain't room for him inside."

"Then he can ride on top with you," Sarah said.

Fear showed around the whites of Old Smelly's eyes as he stared at the multi-colored monster with a voice like a blast of dynamite. "On top! No! Ain't no way." He sputtered and nearly swallowed his tobacco again.

Addressing the clerk, Sarah said, "Ask the owner if he wants me to return the fare. If you don't, I will personally tell him you are turning down hard cash."

The clerk turned to Old Smelly for support, but he was on his way across the road to spit. Sarah turned away as the clerk looked imploringly at her. Then he walked up the boardwalk and disappeared into the hotel restaurant. After several minutes, he returned in a slow trot.

Meeting Old Smelly in the middle of the street, the clerk told him, "Mr. Erath said we got to take the animal. He don't want to give up the money. And … that's not all. There won't be no shotgun rider on this route no more. Mr. Erath said we got to cut down our expenses."

Old Smelly started to curse but, when Sarah glared at him, he stopped and pointed at the top of the stage. "How do we get that … that animal up there?"

"I'll help you," the clerk said uncertainly.

The two men approached the porch with trepidation. Sarah smiled as they stared at Beelzebub in fear. She glanced at Margaret, who was also smiling, and said, "If I may suggest, gentlemen, don't startle him. He has a terrible temper when he comes out of his dreams."

Old Smelly and the clerk backed quickly down the steps as Sarah turned to Margaret and said, "Wake him up. We need to get him loaded."

Margaret snapped her fingers and Beelzebub awakened instantly. He followed her to the stagecoach and stood docilely where she positioned him. As the two men approached him warily his throat started to rumble, but he calmed down when Margaret put her hand on him and said, "Quiet. They're going to load you so we can leave."

"Be a good doggie, Beebub," Jody said around the thumb that had snuck back into his mouth.

Old Smelly and the clerk put their arms around the now docile animal and tried to lift him up. But it was futile; he slipped through their grasp and plopped back down on the ground. Sweating and straining, they finally got hold of Beelzebub's hindquarters and front shoulders and were able to lift him halfway to the driver's seat. Then the clerk's strength gave out, and he dropped his end. Old Smelly couldn't bear the entire weight of the dog, and he collapsed under him. He hit the ground with Beelzebub thrashing around on his chest.

His curses rose with the cloud of dust caused by the impact, "I'll be horn-gawddamn-swoggled."

"Sir!" Sarah's voice lashed out. "I will not abide your language. You will *never* ... I repeat, *never*, use those words in my presence again."

Old Smelly, chastened again, struggled to his feet and stared at Beelzebub who was standing calmly, his tongue wagging and spittle dropping onto the dusty street. The clerk, brushing dirt from his jacket, backed away wild-eyed, holding his hands out in front of him in surrender.

"I have a suggestion, if you will listen," Margaret said. Old Smelly and the clerk looked at her as if she were the bearer of salvation. "Why don't you move the luggage to the top? Then back the stage up to the sidewalk. We can put him in the boot. It's a lot lower."

With the help of Sarah and Margaret, they were able to get Beelzebub into the rear baggage compartment, where he promptly fell asleep. Sarah put a container of water in with him and, at Jody's insistence, added some beef jerky for him to chew on when he awoke.

As the stage pulled out of Waco and bumped over the bridge across the Brazos River, the two passengers Old Smelly had picked up at the hotel introduced themselves. "Mr. Barton, John, Barton," the thin, gray faced, elderly man, dressed in a gray suit with a stiff white shirt collar and a narrow-brimmed gray hat, said as he nodded at Sarah. "My wife, Abigail," he added with a glance at the woman beside him.

Abigail, pleasantly plump and with a florid red face that generated heat like a pot belly stove, was also dressed in gray: dress, gloves, and matching bonnet. Setting in the seat beside her was a large hatbox bordered with frilly pink ribbons. "We are going to Dallas for our daughter's wedding," she squealed in a high-pitched voice that reminded Sarah of the screech of chalk on a school blackboard. "We'll change to the train in Fort Worth."

"Pleased to meet you," Sarah responded. "I am Sarah Whitman. This is my daughter, Margaret and my son, Jody. We're going to Fort Worth."

"Mama, look," Margaret exclaimed pointing at a sign on the cabin wall behind the Barton's. With a smile on her face she read it aloud:

> Wells Fargo Stage Line Notice to Passengers
> 1. Abstinence from liquor is required, but if you must drink, share the bottle. To do otherwise makes you appear selfish and unneighborly.
> 2. If ladies are present, gentlemen are urged to forego smoking cigars and pipes. The odor of same is repugnant to the gentle sex. Chewing tobacco is permitted but spit with the wind, not against it.
> 3. Gentlemen must refrain from the use of rough language in the presence of ladies and children.

4. Firearms may be kept on your person only for use in emergencies. Do not fire them for pleasure or shoot at wild animals as the sound riles the horses.
5. Gents guilty of unchivalrous behavior toward the lady passengers will be put off the stage. It's a long walk back.

Mr. Barton laughed when Margaret finished. "Well, Ladies," he said, "I will certainly watch my language and behavior. I don't chew, but if I did, I'd certainly spit with the wind."

"Thank you, Mr. Barton," Sarah said, with a smile. "It's nice to know we are in the presence of a gentleman."

Mrs. Barton opened her large handbag and took out her knitting supplies as her husband pulled his wide-brimmed hat down over his eyes and leaned back in the seat. Margaret put a small pillow behind her head and closed her eyes. Jody, also tired from the short night, lay his head on Sarah's lap and fell asleep.

Cushioned by large leather supports under the cabin, the stage rose and fell rhythmically and the miles fell behind them. Sarah looked at her son and daughter with love and concern. She thought about the quest they were undertaking. If she had to do it over, she would have left them with the Sigmund's. Lars and Hilda had tried to talk her into it when they were there, but she gave in to the pleas from Margaret and Jody to go with her. The terrible realization that she would not find Jim caused her to shiver, even though the morning sun, streaming through the window onto her, was warm and comforting.

The stop at the stage relay station in Hillsboro for lunch and a change of horses was a welcome respite from the tiring ride. After visiting the filthy outhouse crawling with spiders and other crawling and flying insects and washing in the horse trough, they were fed a meal by the stationmaster. He introduced himself to Sarah as Ned Bunning. A short, stooped man garrulous by nature, he was cleaner than most men in his line of work and very respectful to the women passengers. Taking an immediate liking to Jody, he let him wear his wide-brimmed hat with an eagle feather stuck in the brim. He served venison stew with loaves of baked bread and warm buttermilk. He salted the meal with constant references to his heroism under fire from bandits, Indians, and other reprehensible characters. Old Smelly filled his plate and took it outside to eat with Beelzebub and his horses. His absence freshened the air in the small cabin considerably.

Mr. and Mrs. Barton ate quietly. The stale air and the heat from the stove brought out beads of sweat on Mrs. Barton's brow. Waving a small fan in front of her face, she sighed between bites.

Sarah was surprised that the food was so palatable. "This is an excellent meal, Mr. Bunning. You have my compliments," she said, interrupting his story about wrestling an alligator in Louisiana as a younger man.

"Thank you, Ma'am," Bunning said as he turned back to a wide-eyed Jody and continued his wild tale of intestinal fortitude. "I held that gator's mouth closed with one hand while I pulled out my trusty Bowie Knife with the other. Bam … bam. I stabbed him in the eye—"

"Really, Mr. Bunning," Margaret interrupted. "You shouldn't be telling Jody stories like that. He'll start believing they are true."

"Were you there?" Bunning inquired with a sly grin and a wink at Jody.

"No, I was not there."

Bunning laughed and asked, "Then how do you know they're not true?"

"Oh, hogwash," Margaret said.

At that moment, Old Smelly stuck his head in the door and said, "Time to head em' up and move em' out. Got a schedule to keep."

When they climbed into the stage, Margaret turned to Bunning and said, "It wouldn't hurt to clean out that horrible outhouse. That is, if you have nothing else to do with your time except make up stories."

As the afternoon miles ground under the stagecoach wheels, the sun climbed higher in the sky, now painted with slashes of white cirrus clouds to the east and growing piles of cumulous puffs to the west. Grass covered rolling plains, devoid of trees, stretched out as far as Sarah could see. Circling high above, a black speck grew larger as it descended until it formed into a large eagle hawk. It plummeted out of sight beyond a rise as it swooped down on an unsuspecting field mouse or other ground animal.

Then a sudden blast of air formed a dust devil that whirled toward them. "Look, Jody," Sarah said as she held him up to the window to see the rising dirt storm as it raced alongside them.

"Ooh, a whirly bird," Jody screamed. "Mama, is it going to hit us?"

At that moment, the nature's force, which had formed the twisting phenomenon, decided to stop its play, and the dust devil faded into oblivion. Disappointed, Jody stood up in the seat between his mother and sister. Turning to the rear, he peered through a small crack between the boards making up the back wall of the cabin.

"Mama!" Jody cried. "Beebub is gone."

"Gone!" Sarah exclaimed as she turned around. "How do you know?"

"I can see. Beebub's not there."

Sarah looked through the narrow opening. She could see into the boot at the rear and make out the water bowl but, other than that, it was empty.

"Oh Lord," she said as she put her head out the door window and looked back in the direction they had come. Dust from the wheels rose in suffocating clouds and covered her face. Sneezing and coughing, she returned to her seat.

"What's the matter, Mama?" Margaret asked as she opened her eyes.

"Beelzebub's gone."

"Gone!" Margaret's voice was taut with fear. "He can't run all the way to Fort Worth. We have to stop for him. Please!"

Sarah leaned out the window and shouted, "Stop! Stop the stage!"

Receiving no response, she hollered again, "Old Smelly. Stop this stage. Right now!"

When Sarah returned to her seat covered with dust, Mr. and Mrs. Barton stared at her in astonishment. "Why do we need to stop?" Mrs. Barton squeaked. "We'll be late for Missy's wedding."

"Our dog was riding in the baggage boot," Margaret said. "He must have jumped out. We have to find him and put him back in." Turning to Sarah, she asked, "How are we going to get Old Smelly's attention? He must be hard of hearing."

Wiping dust from her face with a white handkerchief, Sarah looked at Mr. Barton. "Are you carrying a gun?" she asked.

"Well ... yes, Mrs. Whitman," he stammered. "Why do you want to know?"

"May I borrow it, please?"

"Borrow it! Why?"

"I'm going to fire it out the window and get the driver's attention. We do have to stop."

"I can't do that," Mr. Barton said. "No. Can't do that."

The stagecoach was jostling and bouncing as it sped onward. Sarah thought that Beelzebub might be able to keep up with it for a few miles unless he injured himself when he jumped out. They had to stop as soon as possible and look for him.

"Mr. Barton," Sarah said. "Please let me use your pistol. I will pay for the bullet."

Glancing at his wife, who was casting him stern looks, Mr. Barton responded, "No. It would be dangerous. Lord knows what you might hit. The rules posted right there says we are not to fire guns. It might spook the horses."

Sarah reached across Mrs. Barton's lap and snatched up her hatbox. Before the woman could stop her, she held it out the window. "Mr. Barton, I want your pistol. Now! Or do you want me to drop this wedding hat."

"Oh, gracious me," Mrs. Barton cried. "I could never replace it. Why are you being so mean?"

"I'm sorry," Sarah said. "I apologize for my rude behavior. Tell your husband to hand me his gun, and I'll return your hat to you."

"John," the woman shrilled. "Give that nasty woman your gun. I must have my hat."

Mr. Barton reached inside his jacket pocket and removed a small, pearl handled revolver. Taking the pistol in her hand, Sarah aimed it out the window and fired. The report, quieter than Sarah had imagined due to the small caliber, echoed inside the coach. But the stage pounded on, not reducing in speed. Mrs. Barton cowered back into the far corner of her seat and covered her mouth with her handkerchief. Once again, Sarah fired out the window. As before, the sound reverberated over the passengers, but the wagon continued with undiminished speed.

"He really is hard of hearing," Margaret said as she took her hands away from her ears.

"Mama, can I shoot the gun?" Jody asked excitedly

"No!" Sarah responded.

Standing, she opened the door and leaned out. Holding the pistol high in the air, she prepared to fire it once more. At that moment the wheels hit a hole in the road and tossed the stage violently upward. As Sarah grabbed at the doorframe, the gun fired. The bullet leaped forward and upward. Striking the metal support on the edge of the driver's seat near Old Smelly's elbow, it ricocheted and narrowly missed him causing catastrophic results.

"I'll be horn-gawddamn-swoggled," Old Smelly swore, loud enough for Sarah to hear over the sounds of the stage. "Bandits!" With that, he snapped his whip over the rumps of his lead horses and put them into a dead run.

Sarah was thrown backward by the acceleration of the coach, and she would have fallen out the window if Margaret had not grabbed her skirt and pulled her into the cabin. She fell onto Mr. Barton's lap with her breasts across his arm.

"Really, John," Mrs. Barton snapped, her face growing redder by the second.

Gathering herself, Sarah straightened her clothes and moved to the seat next to Margaret. The coach was bucking and rolling with the increased speed, and it was difficult to talk over the noise of the wheels, the rush of the wind, the crack of Old Smelly's whip, and the bellow of his cursing.

"Mama, what are going to do now?" Margaret shouted as she held Jody in her arms and bounced up and down.

"Whee!" Jody cried. "Go faster. Go faster."

Sarah looked around the careening coach. What was she going to do, she wondered? The stage won't stop for many miles. If Beelzebub is injured, they might not find him even if they turn back. The thought of losing him cast a pall of depression over her. She knew how much he meant to Margaret and Jody.

Drawing a deep breath, she said, "Okay, Margaret. I'm going to climb to the top and tell Old Smelly to stop."

Turning to Mr. Barton, she asked, "Will you help me."

"Help you," Mr. Barton cried with his eyes wide. "How?"

"Give me a boost until I can reach the top rails and pull myself up."

"John Barton, you will do no such thing," Mrs. Barton interjected with a toss of her head. "If you touch that woman again, why I'll—"

Sarah, ignoring the outburst, stood up and opened the door against the wind. Looking up, she could see the metal rail just out of her reach. "Boost me a little, Mr. Barton. I can't quite reach the top."

Sarah thought that Mr. Barton, conscious of his wife's objections, was about to refuse when she noticed him staring at her legs as she reached up.

"Grab hold, Mr. Barton," Sarah shouted over the crescendo of noise enveloping them.

Ignoring his wife, who was gawking at him in astonishment, Mr. Barton grasped Sarah's ankle and held her while she took the weight off her lower foot and lurched upward.

"Why I never—" blustered Mrs. Barton as she covered her eyes against the sight before her.

Sarah was able to reach the metal railing at the top of the stage and, with the assist of a toehold in a small window beside the door, pull herself up and roll onto the area where the baggage was held down with criss-crossing ropes. The effort exhausted her, and she lay on her stomach gathering her breath. At that moment, the hurtling wheels struck a deep hole, and the coach bounced violently. She bounced with it and was only able to avoid being thrown over the side by grabbing the baggage ropes.

When the wagon settled down a bit, Sarah rose to her hands and knees and clambered forward to where Old Smelly sat on the driver's seat. He had lost his cap during the mad dash from the imaginary bandits, and his hair was stringing behind him in the wind like a dirty mop.

"Stop!" Sarah shouted in his ear. "Stop the stage."

Old Smelly reacted like he had been shot. His eyes widened, and he jumped as far away from Sarah as the seat would allow. "I'll be horn-gawddamn-swoggled," he shouted as he swallowed part of his tobacco chew and began coughing and spitting.

Sarah decided to allow Old Smelly this one verbal transgression, since she had frightened him half out of his wits. Then he spit out into the wind stream and particles of the effluence splattered back onto her face.

"I'll thank you to not spit on me," Sarah snapped as she held onto the seat with one hand while she wiped the spittle off with the other. "I do not intend to tell you again."

"What're you doin' up here?" Old Smelly asked, ashen faced from fright and from swallowing most of his chew. He turned his attention to the horses, still galloping swiftly down the rutted dirt road.

"If you'll quit spitting on me, I'll tell you."

"Don't have time to talk. Bandits," Old Smelly said as he picked up his whip and cracked it in the air over his steeds.

"There are no bandits," Sarah shouted. "That's why I came up here. I fired that shot from below to get your attention."

"No bandits?" Old Smelly shouted. He didn't appear to want to accept the possibility that he and his stage were not in mortal danger.

Exasperated and at the end of her patience, Sarah leaned forward and shouted in his ear, "I fired that shot to stop you. Our dog jumped out of the boot, and we need to find him. Stop this stage. Now!"

Slowly, Old Smelly seemed to comprehend what Sarah was telling him. Pulling back on the reins, he slowed the horses to a trot and then to a walk. Blowing from the exertion of the extended run, they slobbered their appreciation into the air.

As the stage slowed and the noise of its travel diminished, Sarah spoke in a lower voice, "I'll tell you one more time. Our dog either fell or jumped out of the boot. There is no way he can keep up on his own. We have to find him and put him back on board."

"We can't stop for no dog," Old Smelly said plaintively. "Got a schedule to keep. We're carrying the U.S. mail, you know."

"I appreciate your sense of loyalty. However, we paid a fare for our dog. I expect you to honor that obligation also."

Old Smelly looked down at his sweaty horses while he considered Sarah's argument. Finally, he turned to her and said, "I'm sorry. But I cain't stop and look for no dog. When we get to Fort Worth, we'll refund your money." He clicked his tongue and snapped his reins to increase the pace of the stage.

Sarah took a deep breath and looked skyward for advice. Then, reaching into the pocket of her skirt, she withdrew Mr. Barton's pistol. Leaning forward over the driver's seat, she held it where Old Smelly could see it in his peripheral vision.

"Lordy," he gargled. "What're you going to do with that? You ain't going to shoot me over a dog, are you?"

"No. I hold your life precious," Sarah responded. Aiming the gun at the rear end of the left horse in the first row ahead she continued, "I will shoot that horse if you don't stop."

"My horse?" Old Smelly groaned in anguish. "My gawd. You cain't shoot my horse."

"Yes, I can. And I will, if you don't stop immediately."

The horses slowed to a walk, and then came to a shuddering stop as Old Smelly reared back on the reins. When the dust settled, Sarah stood up and looked back along the road. The sun was bright in the sky above the low clouds to the west, and the horizon to the south shimmered in the afternoon heat. Small mesquite trees, parched shrubs, and sagebrush stretched as far across the flat, dusty plain as she could see.

Old Smelly climbed to his feet. After spitting off the far side of the coach away from Sarah, he shaded his eyes and scrutinized the trail behind. "Nary sight of hide nor hair," he said, staring at the pistol as Sarah returned it to her pocket.

"Mama," Margaret shouted as she stepped down from the stage. "Are you okay?"

Sarah climbed down from the driver's seat and faced her daughter, "Yes. I'm fine. We couldn't see Beelzebub from the top."

"We'll just have to go back," Margaret said.

Old Smelly plopped to the ground beside Sarah, who moved away from his ripe scent. "We cain't go back," he said. "No, Ma'am. We got a schedule to keep." He looked warily at Sarah, expecting her to draw the pistol from her pocket again.

Mrs. Barton chose that moment to stick her head out the window and whine, "Driver, we'll miss the evening train connection into Dallas if we dilly dally here. Let us be off."

Margaret turned to Sarah, "We can't leave him behind. He's too old to take care of himself." Looking back along the road, she added with tears in her eyes, "He'll die out there."

"How much time can we delay and still make that Dallas train?" Sarah asked Old Smelly. "We must have made up some time when you were running the horses."

Taking his watch out of his shirt pocket, Old Smelly looked at it before responding, "Not much more than half an hour. Cain't be later than that."

"Okay," Sarah said. "I'll give you a ten-dollar gold piece if you'll give us that half hour. We can go back along the road for fifteen minutes before turning around."

"Well, darn," Old Smelly said, the glint of greed in his eyes as he looked at the shiny coin Sarah removed from her pocket. "I don't know. Guess we can do that. But that's all the delay I'll allow."

When fifteen minutes of backtracking revealed no sign of Beelzebub, the stage came to a halt again. Sarah, Margaret, and Jody climbed to the top baggage area. They examined the plains behind them for any sign of Beelzebub while Old Smelly held his watch in his hand and waited impatiently.

"Beebub ... Beebub," Jody cried out in his tiny voice. "Beebub, where are you?"

"Driver," Mr. Barton's voice floated up from the coach cabin. "If we are late in Fort Worth, I intend to report you to the authorities."

That was enough to galvanize Old Smelly into action. Snapping the face cover of his watch closed, he spat off the far side of the driver's seat and said, "That's it. We got to go now."

"Oh, hold your horses," Margaret snapped. "A few minutes more won't make any difference."

"Calm down," Sarah said as she put her arm around her daughter's shoulder. "It looks like we're going to have to leave him."

"We can't do that, Mama. Please!"

"Time to go," Old Smelly barked with impatience.

Taking Margaret's hand, Sarah helped her climb to the ground. Jody clambered down like a monkey and starting playing in the dirt along the side of the rutted roadway.

Picking Jody up and dusting him off, Sarah lifted him into the coach. "Come on, Margaret," she said. "I know how you feel. But there isn't anything we can do now."

"No, you don't know how I feel, Mama. Beelzebub is a part of me. I can't leave him behind. He's used to us feeding him, and he's too old to fight the wild animals out there."

Sarah drew Margaret close and hugged her. Tears formed in her eyes as she shared her daughter's pain. "I know. But the stage has to go on."

"Let it," Margaret said as she pulled away from her mother's embrace. "I'll stay here and wait for him. You and Jody can come back for us."

Sarah looked at the vast expanse surrounding them. Since leaving Hillsboro several hours earlier, they had not passed a single inhabited building. The only sign of life was a few dusty cowboys driving a small herd of cattle north alongside the road. The thought of Margaret alone and helpless in this wilderness frightened her. Jim had once offered to teach Margaret to shoot his rifle and pistol, but she had refused. Her gentle nature would not abide violence. Adopting sick and injured animals and birds and nursing them back to health had been more important to her than playing with dolls when she was a child. And Sarah knew how much Margaret adored Beelzebub.

Sarah took her daughter's hand and said, "Let's go on to Fort Worth. I can't leave you here. It's too dangerous. We'll rent a wagon and find someone to help us look for him tomorrow."

Margaret wiped tears from her eyes with the sleeve of her dress. Then, with one last hopeful look down the road, she allowed her mother to lead her into the stage. When Jody climbed into her lap sucking noisily on his thumb, she stopped crying and held him tightly.

Chapter 5

As they neared Fort Worth, Sarah could see an increase in the number of cattle alongside the road. By the time they reached the first buildings on the outskirts of the city, the hoofed beasts spread as far as she could see across the rolling plains on both sides of the stagecoach. Gangs of shouting, rope swinging, and cursing cowboys formed the milling masses into rough groups to keep the herds from intermingling.

Sarah recalled that her aunt, Cynthia Ann Parker, had lived near Fort Worth after her involuntary rescue from the Indians. But she hadn't remained there long. Her family had taken her to East Texas where she had died grieving for her Indian family.

The noise, dust, and stench surrounding them pulled Margaret out of her melancholy. "Mama," she said. "I've never seen so many cows. What are they doing here?"

Mr. Barton, after glancing at his wife who was knitting furiously, cleared his throat and said, "They're waiting to be loaded onto the trains headed east. The Texas and Pacific Railroad stopped construction just outside of Fort Worth due to lack of funds three years ago. The town folk then took it upon themselves to complete the rail line, and the first train came in July of this year. With the arrival of the railroad, Fort Worth is now a major point for the shipment of livestock, cotton, corn, wheat, and what's left of the buffalo hide industry. The long cattle drives north to Kansas are about over."

"How do you know all this?" Margaret asked.

"I'm a banker in Waco," he responded proudly. "The State National Bank here in Fort Worth is one of our branches. I expect it will soon be one of the biggest banks in Texas."

"Look, Mama," Jody shouted as he stuck his head out of the window. A hatless rider pulled up along side the coach, handed him several pieces of folded papers, and then he raced away toward a nearby group of drovers huddled around a campfire at the rear of a chuck wagon.

"Let me see that," Sarah said as she took the first sheet and read it aloud, "This notice good for five pounds of potatoes (batatas) at Bateman & Bros. Wholesale Grocers and Commission Merchants, West Second Street and Throckmorton."

She started the second paper, "The Stag Saloon. Corner of Sixth and Main Street. Bring this for free beer, cheap good whiskey, and the sweetest gals—" She let her voice trail off.

"What else does it say?" Margaret asked.

"Never mind. It is not a place we will frequent."

Darkness was starting to fall when they pulled into the outskirts of Fort Worth. Gas lamps and oil lanterns cast flickering lights out into the roadway. As the stage approached a two-story house set behind a picket fence beside the road with a chimney on each side and a wide porch in front, Sarah could see a white-bearded old man sitting in a chair. Two boys, slightly older than Jody, sat swinging their legs off the edge of the porch. One of them, when he saw Jody hanging out of the window, threw a stick at him. It struck the side of the coach near the rear and ricocheted back against the fence to the accompaniment of the boys' laughter.

Jody ducked back into his sister's arms with fright in his eyes. "Why did they do that, Maggie?" he cried.

"City boys," Margaret answered as she took him in her arms and comforted him. "They haven't been taught manners. They ain't got—" Glancing at her mother, she finished, "They don't have better sense."

They turned off the road winding along the bluff of the river and clattered south from the courthouse along Main Street. A wide boulevard, it was fronted on both sides with wooden buildings, mostly two-story structures that looked like they had been thrown up overnight, and a few more substantial brick structures. The discordant noise and the hustle and bustle of the busy frontier town overwhelmed Sarah. The sounds of horses whinnying, the pounding of construction, dogs yapping, people shouting, gunshots, honky tonk pianos, and a far off train whistle caused a crescendo that increased in volume to an unbearable level the further they progressed into the city. There was an incessant stream of buggies, carriages, hacks, freight wagons, and horseback riders on the street. Jostling pedestrians hurried aimlessly like streams of ants up and down the sidewalks, across the traffic-clogged streets, and in and out of the establishments.

Sarah thought Fort Worth was quite a change from the quiet and solitude of the country ranch on the river where they lived. She had no idea where they would start to look for Jim in such a mass of humanity.

Jody, unable to contain his enthusiasm, was leaning out of the coach window jabbering and pointing wildly. Sarah had to hold him tightly to keep him from falling out.

A raised board sidewalk ran along each side of the rutted, dirt roadway. Sarah quickly read the signs on the business buildings as they passed by: King Brothers Blacksmith Shop, D. W. Helm Grocer, H. Dugan Wagon Yard, Ye Olde Ice Cream Parlor, Archibald Leonard's Flour Mill and Calhoun Livery Stable. And on one street corner resided an impressive two-story brick establishment: Washer Bros. Clothiers & Furnishers. It was topped by an ornate crown holding up a world globe. Scattered among the reputable businesses were the watering holes, dance halls, and bordellos frequented by visiting cowboys, buffalo hunters, entrepreneurs, peddlers, freighters, Reconstruction Government employees, soldiers—white and black—and locals. They included: Farmers Saloon, Stag saloon, The Headlight Bar, The White Elephant Saloon, and Tivoli Saloon.

"Look, Mama!" Margaret exclaimed. She pointed past Sarah and Jody and read a large banner strung above the first floor of a massive brick building, "'Theatre Comgue, Madame Centz' Female Minstrels performing the Paris sensation, the Cancan.' What's a Cancan?"

Sarah smiled and collected her thoughts before answering, "It's a dance."

"I've never been dancing," Margaret said wistfully. A gleam came into her eyes as she asked, "Can we go?"

"I don't think it would be wise. We'll talk about it later."

Leaning across Jody's legs, Sarah caught Mr. Barton's attention. "We need to find a hotel. Can you recommend one?"

"Why, yes I can," Mr. Barton replied loudly over the noise hammering the stage as he avoided Sarah's eyes. "When we come here on bank business, we stay at the Mansion Hotel. It's quiet and very clean. They have a most palatable dining room. It's on Fourth Street between Main Street and Commerce."

As they continued on, the raucous sounds diminished, and the whistle of a train and the whoosh of its panting engine grew louder. When the stage stopped in front of the well-lit railroad depot, an overpowering stench pervaded the night air. Huge, shapeless piles of dark, hairy hides encroached onto the loading area.

"Yuck," Margaret said wrinkling her nose. "What is that horrible smell?"

Mrs. Barton covered her face with a lace handkerchief while her husband responded, "Buffalo hides waiting shipment."

"Buffalo hides?" Sarah queried. "I thought most of the buffalo were gone."

"Yes," Mr. Barton said. "They are a dwindling species. But there's still a demand for them in the East and in Europe. It's a cash business. Our bank buys many of the hides and consigns them to a company in New York."

Jody was staring at the huge metal monster, which was gasping and wheezing, with steam blasting out of its churning engine and black clouds billowing from its large smoke stack. "Mama," he squealed happily, "I never saw a train before."

Sarah noticed the sadness in Margaret's eyes. She put her arm around her shoulder and said, "I know you're thinking about Beelzebub all alone out there in the dark. We'll go back for him tomorrow."

"Promise?"

"Yes," Sarah responded as she pulled Jody away from the window. "Let's get settled in the hotel and have supper. We'll find a wagon to rent in the morning."

The Mansion Hotel was an imposing four-story brick structure. As Sarah signed in at the desk, she could see a large dining room set off to the rear. She put the valise, heavy with its valuable contents, under one of the two beds in the second floor room they were assigned. As Margaret watched her, she pulled the bed spread down to the floor to hide it.

While they were eating from the well-stocked buffet table, Margaret picked at her food and kept her head down. "Mama," she said. "I saw a livery stable two blocks down the street. It looked like it was still open."

Sarah wiped Jody's face with a napkin after he dived into a slice of apple pie. Looking at Margaret she said, "Okay. We'll walk down there as soon as Jody finishes. It will help settle the food so we can rest easier tonight."

The owner of the McGregor Livery Stable and Wagon Yard was a grizzled, lean man sporting curly, crimson locks streaked with gray. He smoked a crooked stem pipe and wore a long sleeved, white shirt open over his red chest hair. His tartan skirt and calf length stockings gave him the natural air of a highlander viewing his flock of sheep in a meadow above a shining loch.

"Mac McGregor is me name," he said, a heavy burr thundering through his mutton-chop mustache as he met Sarah, Margaret, and Jody at the gated yard entrance. Flickering gas lamps lit the area, casting garish shadows into the street.

"Sir," Sarah said. "We have need of a wagon or buggy early in the morning."

"And someone to escort us, too," Margaret added. "We need to find our dog. He jumped out of the stage north of Hillsboro."

"Dawg, ye say," McGregor said with a noisy pull on his pipe.

"Yes," Sarah answered. "He's been a member of the family for twelve years. He's too old to survive out there on the plains alone."

"Aye," he said as he tousled Jody's curly locks. "Ye have a fine wee laddie and a bonnie lass, but as me old grandmither used to say 'many a mickle makes a muckle.'" He took a long suck on his pipe and snorted the smoke out through his wide, florid nose before continuing, "Ye shouldna ha' trouble finding the creature. I'll send me muck hand wi' ye come morning. He's a fair hand wi' a rifle and ha' a keen sense a direction."

As they were crossing the street from the stable, a group of riders raced up the road toward them, firing pistols into the air and whooping loudly. Sarah grabbed Jody's arm and pulled him back to the safety of the porch of a mercantile store, where Margaret joined them.

"Wahoo," shouted one of the dusty horsemen as he spotted Sarah and Margaret and swerved toward them. "Will you look at that? I just love the ladies."

When Sarah glared at him, he doffed his hat, dug the trowels of his spurs into the sides of his horse, and raced forward to catch up with his rowdy companions.

Suddenly, even the noise of the galloping riders was drowned out as the roar of a shotgun split the night air. It was followed almost immediately by another blast. The rampaging cowboys came to a milling halt facing a lone man, who was standing in center of the street illuminated by the light cast from the windows and doorway of a large saloon.

"Look, Mama," Margaret said in wonder. "Who is that?"

"I don't know," Sarah responded.

She held Jody in her arms and stood transfixed by the unusual sight of the single shotgun wielder facing down so many riders. A tall man with shoulder length hair, he wore two pistols with the butts forward, and he seemed fearless as he calmly reloaded his firearm. A bright glint of light reflected from a star pinned on the vest of his dark suit. He appeared bigger than life as he looked up at the angry faces staring down at him.

Several of the cowboys started forward to ride him down, but they stopped as a heavyset man at the head of the group raised his hand. "Hold on a minute, boys," the leader said, his words slicing through the sudden silence. "Good evening, Marshal Courtright. To what do we owe this honor?"

"New city ordinance, Mr. Sanders," the marshal said in a strong mellifluous voice, which carried with it a ring of authority. "The town folks are tired of dodging bullets from your boys out for a little fun. Only law enforcement officers and soldiers can carry guns inside the city limits."

"Well, the town folks sure don't mind taking our hard earned dollars," shouted a short, misshapen dwarf of a man with a hat twice the size of his head and mounted on a giant horse slick with sweat. "I say to hell with you and your two-bit town. No one's relieving me of my guns."

"Mr. Sanders," the marshal said as he spit a stream of tobacco juice on the road raising a tiny cloud of dust. "I can understand how your cow hands feel. It's a long dusty trail walking with them beeves. Been there, done that. But Fort Worth is growing into a respectable city. Stray bullets have a way of hitting the innocent more often than the guilty. You're welcome to leave your weapons at my office and pick them up when you've sampled all our fair metropolis has to offer."

The outspoken dwarf stepped his horse forward and, drawing his pistol, fired it in the air. "That's what I think of your goddamn ordinance," he taunted the peace officer with a laugh.

So quickly did the marshal move that Sarah, from her vantage point on the porch, only saw the tiny hulk of the man as he pitched sideways out of his saddle and slammed into the ground with a bang and a squeal. "Goddamn," he cried as he rolled over and recoiled from the twin barrels of sudden death staring down at him.

"Mr. Sanders," Marshal Courtright said in a calm, unruffled manner as he pressed his shotgun into the dwarf's chest. "This man will pay a ten dollar fine for violating the ordinance and another ten for public cursing. I'll personally lock up his guns. The rest of you know where my office is."

Sanders removed his dusty ten-gallon hat and wiped his neck bandana over his balding head before responding, "Okay, Marshal. Last time I brought a herd here, I lost two hands. After I paid them, for Christ's sake. Killed each other they did. Reckon they'd still be alive if you'd taken their firearms." He paused a moment, and then asked, "Is there really a law against cursing? Afraid we're all guilty of that."

"I just made that up to cover the situation," Marshal Courtright said with a tight-lipped smile. "The other alternative was to shoot this SOB. I didn't want to do that."

"Glad you didn't," Sanders said. "Shorty's a hell of a hand on the trail."

He took a roll of bills from his jacket pocket, peeled off several, and handed them to the marshal. Looking around at his men, he said loudly, "Follow me, gents. There's lots of whiskey and women waiting for us. Couple of you pick up Shorty and put him back on his horse. Let's check our guns and get on with the rat killing."

The riders respectfully split formation and rode on either side of Marshal Courtright as they continued quietly up the street, two of them holding Shorty up in his saddle. Sarah watched the cowboys until they disappeared up a side street in the distance. Then she noticed that the marshal was staring at her. When she met his eyes, he removed his hat and waved it in acknowledgement before re-entering the saloon through a group of watchers who had spilled out onto the porch to observe the spectacle.

Sarah suddenly recalled that Jack Kilpatrick had said that he knew this Marshal Courtright. Perhaps his office would be the place to start looking for her husband after they found Beelzebub.

"Wow, Mama," Jody gasped. "That was a bang-bang."

"Yes, it was a bang-bang," Sarah agreed. "I don't think it was good for—"

She stopped speaking at the sight of a tall, big bosomed woman in a bright purple full-length dress following the saloon crowd back inside. Carrying herself regally, her shoulders were thrust back and her head held high.

"Mama, do you know that woman?" Margaret asked incredulously. "Isn't she a soiled dove—as Grandpa would say?"

"I don't know what she is but, yes, I think I do know her. When I was teaching at the two-room schoolhouse in Meridian, the other teacher was named Rose Travis."

"That was before I was born, wasn't it? When you met my father?"

Sarah turned to her daughter and said quietly, "Yes. That is when I met your father."

Over the years, as Margaret grew older, the questions she asked about her father had become more penetrating. Sarah deflected her insistent queries by telling her that he had died of an unexpected illness. In fact, he had died a cheating gambler's death from a bullet racing across the table over a stack of bills, silver coins, several empty whiskey glasses, and a pile of marked cards.

Sarah was only seventeen years old when she met Dennis Hopkins, the dashing and handsome son of the founding family of the town of Meridian. Thanks to the solid foundation her father had given her in reading, ciphering, history, and the classics, the nearby community had called on her to educate their children in the fundamentals of learning in the new schoolhouse. There, she had met the man who was to seduce her in a few short weeks, only to disappear after leaving the seed in her womb that was to enter the world as Margaret, gentle and beautiful Maggie.

Her father understood the situation at once. After jerking Hopkins out of the bed of a prostitute in Waco and pistol-whipping him, he brought him forcibly to his church where he joined him and Sarah in the bonds of matrimony and, in the process, avoided the unpleasant likelihood of having a bastard grandchild.

Over the next four years, before he met his untimely but warranted demise, Hopkins re-entered Sarah's life on rare occasions and only long enough to ask her for money or beg her to satisfy his sexual needs with someone outside the sordid world of prostitution. To both requests, she responded negatively, never wavering in her rejection of him or his way of life, refusing even his pathetic professions of love.

After Dennis' death and her subsequent marriage to Jim, her father assisted in Margaret's adoption and assumption of the Whitman family name. When Margaret was old enough to comprehend, Sarah had told her that Jim had adopted her. It didn't seem to matter to the child who worshipped and loved him. Jim returned her feelings and became a gentle, loving, and hard working head of the household. Sarah knew that one day Margaret would find out the truth about her real father. She prayed that Margaret would forgive her for the falsehood she had told her.

Sarah remembered the other schoolteacher, Rose Travis, as an intelligent, strong, and assertive person who seemed to know a lot about life. She had been raised in Austin and had traveled to New York City and Boston before marrying a rancher who brought her to the frontier village of Meridian. She was adamant about not having children, and she needed something to occupy her time, so she volunteered to teach school with Sarah.

After Sarah left the school, she and Rose corresponded on occasion. She was always thrilled to receive notes from Rose from the exciting places she visited and lived in after leaving her husband behind the reins of a mule: New Orleans, St. Louis, Denver, and San Francisco. The letters had stopped nearly five years before, and Sarah had lost track of her. If the woman on the saloon porch was indeed Rose, she certainly had changed.

"It's getting late," Sarah said. "If that is Rose, she might help us find Jim. I'll just say hello to her, and we'll go back to the hotel. We do have to leave early to find Beelzebub."

"Beebub gone," Jody said. "I miss Beebub."

"So do I," Sarah said, starting down the sidewalk. "We'll find him tomorrow."

As they neared the saloon, the raucous noise of the nightlife inside the brightly lit room bombarded them. The tinny tunes of a piano floated above the buzz of voices, mostly male. Occasionally, the high-pitched squeal of a woman cut through the other sounds, shrilling in the night air like the cry of a female hawk.

A huge sign stretching across the posts of the second-story deck proclaimed in large block letters:

>THE RED BULL SALOON
>CAN'T FIND IT HERE
>WON'T FIND IT ANYWHERE

When they reached a narrow alley that ran between a single story building and the taller two-story saloon, Sarah stopped and turned to Margaret. "Stay here with Jody," she said. "I'll just say a quick hello to Rose and arrange to meet her later."

"Oh, Mama, can't we see what's happening inside?" Margaret asked wide-eyed.

"No!" Sarah said firmly. "Wait right here. I won't be but a minute."

As Sarah entered the saloon through two large swinging doors, most of the crowd, filling the large room and spilling up a flight of stairs near the bar, began singing boisterously:

>When Johnny comes marching home again,
>Hurrah, hurrah.
>We'll all feel gay,
>When Johnny comes marching home again,
>Hurrah, hurrah.

Sarah stopped at the doorway as she noticed that a number of the patrons were standing tight-lipped and staring at those who were singing with a look of hatred. The two groups began separating, those still singing gravitated toward the piano at the front of the room, and those who were not milled to the rear, next to the bar and the stairs. She tried to locate the woman she had seen outside, but couldn't find her in the swirling crowd.

"Oh Lord," she said as she sensed the animosity between the two groups grow into a dark, evil thing threatening to break loose in a destructive force. As she backed out through the swinging doors, she thought that if Marshal Courtright was still in the saloon, he was about to earn his pay.

Hurrying down the sidewalk, she just reached Margaret and Jody when the sound of a pistol shot barked, and the music and singing fell off to a strange silence. Then the loud, commanding voice of Marshal Courtright filled the void, "There'll be no more singing tonight, gentlemen. The Civil War is over. It will not be fought again in this saloon. I have a good poker hand here, and I thank you to let me play it. Jinks, play a tune that will remind us of our dear mothers, please."

The soft tinkle of piano keys and the murmur of voices slowly increasing in volume followed Sarah as she herded Margaret and Jody out of the alley and shooed them down the sidewalk.

Then she heard a husky female voice calling her, "Sarah ... Sarah!"

Turning, she saw the tall, imposing figure of a woman standing at the top landing of the stairs leading from the alley to the second floor of the saloon. The light from the open door spilled out and illuminated her huge bosom and her long purple dress, blossoming full from a multitude of petty coats.

"Sarah, honey, it's me, Rose."

Sarah looked up and raised her hand in recognition. "So, it is you," she said loud enough to be heard over the storm of noise from the saloon as the patrons returned to their former state of vociferous mischief making.

"Wait here," Sarah said to Margaret as she started up the stairs. "Watch Jody. I'll go up and talk to Rose for a moment."

Sarah noticed that Jody had spotted a pile of dirt alongside the wall of the building across from the saloon. The primeval motivation that had bedeviled little boys for thousands of generations drew him unerringly toward the mound. Plopping himself down, he dived into the dirt with his hands and began making a wagon trail. She could see Margaret standing in the shadow of the stairs watching Jody play as she climbed the stairs.

"Why, honey, I'm so happy to see you," Rose said as she embraced Sarah.

Taller by nearly six inches and given additional height by her long-heeled pumps, Rose's breasts smothered Sarah and caused her to gasp for air. She remembered that Rose had been amply endowed, but the extra weight she had gained, and the tight corset she wore, pushed her massive mammary glands upward and outward. The deep cleft between the two enveloped Sarah's face.

Stepping back, Sarah said, "Hello, Rose. I'm happy to see you also. I enjoyed your letters from all those places you went to. I didn't know you were here in Fort Worth."

Rose laughed with a deep rolling movement. Her magnificent chest bounced up and down and threatened to burst loose from its constraint. "I've got a bird's nest on the ground here. I own half of this fine establishment. And—"

Hesitating, Rose looked down at Sarah appraisingly. "As I remember, your daddy was a preacher wasn't he?"

"Yes, he passed away about ten years ago. Actually he disappeared somewhere west of our ranch."

"Sorry to hear that," Rose said. "A righteous man he was. I don't think he'd approve of my line of work. Hope you can turn the other cheek, so to speak."

Sarah smiled as she looked past Rose at the many doors that opened onto the hallway behind her. A young black woman, dressed in a pale blue dress, was entering one of them with a hiccupping, whiskered old man. Looking up at Rose's heavily rouged face and her orange hair piled upon her head and shining like a beehive in the sunlight, she said, "I don't make judgments about people. I leave that up to the Lord. It's good to see you. And," she added, "I need help."

"Help? Why you come to the right woman. Ain't nothing goes on in this town that I don't know about."

"Rose, I'm surprised at you," Sarah said with a smile. "You were a schoolteacher, and now you're talking like a field hand?"

"I have to talk like my clientele, honey," Rose said with another rumbling laugh. "I don't want them to think I'm getting uppity. Most of them have to sign their names with an X. Now, come in off the porch, and tell me what you need help with. This room in the corner is my office and bedroom."

Before Sarah could respond, a dark-haired young woman with a red birthmark across her nose and right cheek opened the door and said, "Beg pardon, Rose. We have a problem downstairs. Better come quick. Liddell needs you."

With an exasperated sigh, Rose looked at Sarah and said, "That's my partner. Guess I better see what's got his tail in a ringer. You wait here, honey. I'll be right back."

Sarah leaned on the railing and looked down into the alley. She saw a tall, thin young man turn the corner of the saloon and saunter down toward the alley. Not seeing Margaret standing under the stairs or Jody playing in the dirt pile, he walked into the shadows and began relieving himself.

Just as he was about to finish watering the sparse weeds on the ground, Jody's tiny voice piped up through the darkness of the alley, "Maggie, he's going pee-pee."

"Good Lord, Almighty!" the man said in surprise. "Who is that? Where are you?"

Margaret stepped out from under the porch into the light cast from one of the saloon windows. With a stern look on her face and her hands on her hips, she remarked to the stranger, "I'll thank you to not use that language in front of me and my little brother."

Sarah smiled to herself as Margaret's words sliced through the night like a knife.

The young man, now completely flustered, glanced down to see if he had buttoned his trousers.

"Are you quite finished, mister, whoever you are?" Margaret bore in. "They make outhouses for that, you know."

The man stepped forward into the window light. Gangly, black-haired, and brown-eyed, he was freshly shaved above his prominent Adam's apple. A silver badge sparkled on the vest of his tan suit. His black cowboy hat was pushed back over his long forehead, which opened up his look of consternation. Sarah thought he was pleasing to look at in a juvenile sort of way. He'd probably be a handsome man, when he filled out his thin face. A few good meals would do him a world of good. He had one of the most pleasant voices Sarah had ever heard. It was a soft, mellifluous tenor that filled the alley with sound and easily reached her on the second floor balcony.

"Must I ask you again?" Margaret demanded. "Do you have a name?"

"Yes. I do ... that is, I have a name."

"Well, what is it?" Margaret's exasperation was reaching the boiling point.

"Pee ... pee," Jody laughed as he looked up at the stranger from his dirt hill.

"Shall we call you Mister Pee Pee?" Margaret said.

"No, no ... my name is Daniel, Daniel Worthington."

"Thank you, Daniel," Margaret said as she stepped out onto the brightly lit sidewalk. "My name is Margaret Whitman, and the little boy who gave you your nickname is my brother Jody. Come out here. I don't like to talk to strangers in dark alleys."

When Worthington joined her on the walkway, Margaret asked, "What is that badge for?"

"Why, Ma'am, I'm a peace officer."

"You may call me Margaret, Daniel. I don't think Ma'am is appropriate for someone my age. What's a peace officer?"

"Yes, Ma'am ... I mean Margaret. I work for Marshal Courtright. He said we are hired to keep the peace, so he calls us peace officers."

Sarah was about to call down to Margaret when she heard a low rumbling noise come from down the alley. She saw the movement of objects in the near darkness, like the darting of a school of fish under the surface of a pond at night. As she watched in horror, a large mass separated from the main group and stayed behind. The rest of the nocturnal ghosts closed in on Jody who was driving his imaginary toy over the mound of dirt. The first specter materialized in the dim window light shining onto the surface of the alley. It was a large, male dog with matted black fur and skin torn from many fights. His jaws were drooling saliva as he leaped forward and then backward, as if testing Jody's ability to fend him off. His companions stood in a snarling mass behind him, their long tongues flapping from side to side, and their red eyes staring hungrily at the boy.

Sarah tried to scream but no sound would come. She started down the stairs, her legs moving in slow motion, as if she were wading in quicksand.

Jody finally looked up and saw the menacing animals for the first time. Frozen with fear, he was unable to move.

Daniel turned as the leader of the pack of dogs snarled and stepped forward. The others, emboldened by their leader's example, surged after him. When Daniel finally realized what was happening, he started to draw his pistol.

At that moment, the large object, which had held back from the attack, moved swiftly. It was a mottled creature with gigantic fangs and, borne on the wings of a primeval howl, it hurtled up the alley and intersected the pack of dogs. Before the first one could reach Jody, the huge interloper tore into them, his initial charge scattering furry, yelping bodies in all directions. Then, turning, he leaped on the nearest dog and seized its throat in his massive jaws. With a roar, he flung the bleeding body up against the saloon wall, and then he whirled to search out another victim. The remainder of the pack leaped on the terrible avenger who had struck so suddenly out of the night. Snarling and howling, the alley became a deadly battleground of gnashing teeth and deadly roars.

Then, another of their companions fell to the terrible wrath of the ferocious animal, and the wraiths of the night still able to run fled howling down the alley. By this time, Sarah could see that Daniel had his pistol in his hand. Several times, he aimed and prepared to fire into the fighting dogs, but each time he held his fire not knowing what he would hit. Finally only one target remained standing: the great black, gray, and orange beast that had fought the others to a standstill. Raising the gun, Daniel started to pull the trigger.

"No ... No," Sarah screamed as she leaped at Daniel and struck his hand upward.

The pistol barked and spat out a flame, the bullet whistling harmlessly into the dark sky.

"That's Beelzebub," Margaret sobbed as she knelt and took Jody in her arms. "He saved Jody."

The sound of the saloon piano died as patrons rushed outside to see what was happening. In a short time, Sarah, Margaret, Jody, and Daniel were surrounded by a crowd of people gesturing and jabbering. Rose towered among them.

"Oh, Mama," Margaret said tearfully. "A pack of dogs were heading for Jody when Beelzebub attacked them. I ... I think he may have been running with them until they took after Jody. Then ... then he—"

"It's okay, I saw it all," Sarah said quietly as Beelzebub suddenly plopped down in the dirt and put his head on the ground. She could see raw, open tears oozing blood from his face and shoulder.

"Officer Worthington," an authoritative voice rang out. "What transpired out here? Why did you use your firearm?"

"Marshal," Daniel responded as he stood stiffly at attention. "Some wild dogs were attackin' this boy." Pointing at Beelzebub lying near Sarah and Margaret, he continued, "I thought that ... that creature was one of them, and I was goin' to shoot him."

"He's our family pet," Sarah said. "We thought he was lost, and now he's saved my son's life."

"Marshal," Rose interrupted, "This is a friend of mine, Sarah Whitman and her family. You said you were going to rid the streets of those wild animals. What are we paying you good money for?"

Ignoring Rose, Courtright waved his arms at the surrounding onlookers, "Okay, ladies and gentlemen. That's all the excitement for now. Go back inside and raise some more hell. Give us room here."

As the crowd dispersed, Margaret put her hand on Beelzebub's head to comfort him. The dog lifted his snout and moaned in pain. "Mama, he's hurt bad," she said.

"Beebub's hurt," Jody said as he began crying.

Daniel cleared his throat and his Adam's apple bobbed up and down as he said, "I'm a pretty good hand with injured animals. Perhaps I can help you."

Daniel turned to Courtright and asked, "With your permission, Marshal?"

Rose grabbed Marshal Courtright by his elbow and said, "Jim, these folks need help. They wouldn't be in this fix if you had shot those wild dogs."

"Okay," the marshal said as he tugged at his mustache and pulled his arm away from Rose's grasp. "Daniel, you may assist this fine family."

"Let's find a wagon and get him down to McGregor's Stable," Daniel said. "We'll put him in one of the stalls. Margaret, you best not touch any of his wounds. He might have—" Daniel let his voice trail off.

Sarah looked up in alarm. "Do you think those dogs might have rabies?" she asked with fear gripping her heart.

"I don't know," Daniel said. "We can't take any chances."

Chapter 6

Sarah walked ahead of Margaret and Jody as they entered the McGregor Livery Stable. The pale pink orb of the sun was barely above the eastern horizon, and breakfast at the hotel had been a tense, hurried event. The gate to one of the stalls was open, and Daniel Worthington's jacket and vest lay draped over it. Horses, chomping noisily on piles of hay, occupied several other stalls. The two rear doors of the barn were ajar, and a clutch of baby chickens entered and began pecking around on the dirty floor in their eternal search for stray oats and bugs. It was still cool in the building and, although it reeked of horse manure and urine, it hadn't reached the overpowering ripeness Sarah knew from experience that it would attain during the warmth of the afternoon.

When Sarah arrived at the open stall, Daniel, covered by a woolen blanket, was sleeping soundly with his head resting on an old saddle. His Adam's apple was bobbing up and down in concert with his snoring. Beelzebub lay at the end of the enclosure, tied by a short rope. While Sarah was awakening Daniel, she could see the rise and fall of the dog's chest and hear the rasp of his breathing. The wounds in his hide had been sewed up and covered with salve.

"Oh, goodness," Daniel said as he awakened and looked up at Margaret and Sarah. "I fell asleep. I am sorry."

He lurched hurriedly to his feet with straw scattered all over him. As Margaret playfully brushed particles off the long bangs of his hair, he took a step backward.

Jody had discovered the baby chickens and began stalking them with a stick he had picked up on the way to the stable. "Here, chickee ... chickee," he chattered at them as they scattered before him.

"Don't be concerned, Daniel," Sarah said. "Did you stay here all night?"

"Yes, Ma'am, I did. Wanted to make sure your dog was goin' to survive my patchin' up."

After looking at Beelzebub, Margaret said, "Looks like you did a fine doctoring job. We do appreciate it."

"Well, thank you ... Margaret. I had a lot of experience down on the farm." Daniel colored slightly from the compliment, his large hands hanging self-consciously at his sides.

"Where are you from?" Sarah asked.

"My father had a ranch near Lockhart, south of Austin," Daniel responded. "He was killed at Chickamauga. He fought for the South, he did."

"And your mother?" Margaret asked.

"She was killed durin' the '72 Comanche raids—" Daniel's voice tailed off and he squinted his eyes. "Indians ravaged her."

He swallowed, his Adam's apple bouncing up and down, before continuing, "They even killed the cattle. Just took the horses. I was over to the neighbors deliverin' a foal when it happened. Didn't know about it till I got home, by then it was too late."

"I understand, Daniel," Sarah said quietly.

She remembered that bloody spring when dozens of frontier families were slaughtered and their homes burned. While other Indian tribes had accepted the U.S. Government's offer of food and shelter on the Fort Sill, Oklahoma reservation, the Comanche's had spurned the latest in a long line of promises from their white adversaries. They remained in the sanctuary of the Indian Territory and continued their bloody raids against the settlers in areas they considered their own as far back as the collective knowledge of their forefathers reached. Jim had taken Sarah, Margaret, and baby Jody to the fort in Waco for protection. However, while raids took place all around them, for some unknown reason the Parker Ranch had never been harmed.

Sarah stepped close to Daniel and put her hand on his arm. "We don't mean to pry. You are a fine young man, and we do appreciate what you're doing for Beelzebub."

"That's okay," Daniel said. "I don't mind talkin' about it."

"What brought you to Fort Worth?" Margaret asked.

"I come up the trail with a cattle herd early last year."

"You go and get some breakfast, Daniel," Sarah said. "We'll stay here and watch Beelzebub."

"Okay. I am a mite hungry. I'll go on down to Sadie's Café. It's a good place to eat."

Sarah reached into her handbag, withdrew some coins, and handed them to Daniel. "Here," she said. "The least we can do is buy your meal."

"I don't have to pay at Sadie's," Daniel remarked as he refused the money.

"Why not?" Margaret asked with a quizzical look. "Does Sadie have her cap set for you?"

Daniel looked flustered as he responded, "Marshal Courtright assigned me to eat there. It keeps the problems down if one of us peace officers drops in now and then."

After Daniel left, Sarah gave Margaret a long look. "I am surprised at you," she said. "Why would you care if Sadie is looking out for him?"

"No reason," Margaret said as she averted her eyes. "Just asking."

"Just asking? Well he is a nice young man. And he does have a manner about him."

"Mama, doesn't he have the greatest voice?"

"Voice?" Sarah responded. "Yes, I suppose he does. Speaking of voices, I haven't heard anything from Jody. Where did he go?"

At that moment, Sarah heard a sound in the hayloft above them. Looking up, she saw Jody climbing a ladder leading upward in the barn. Ahead of him, whimpering in fear, a snow-white cat scampered up the rungs.

"Jody," Sarah shouted with one raised eyebrow. "What are you doing? Leave that cat alone and get down here."

Jody turned from his lofty perch on the ladder and looked down at his mother. "But, Mama, I want to play with him."

"You climb right back down. Now!"

Jody looked up at the cat pulling away from him and hesitated, but he stayed where he was. Sarah started to the ladder leading to the loft. As she passed a nearby stall, the horse inside, a large black stallion, reared up and flailed his hoofs at her, causing her to step backward. When she reached the loft covered with piles of straw and hay, Jody climbed down toward her. She snatched him off the ladder as soon as she could reach him and plopped him onto a mound of hay. She was about to admonish him when she heard a man's voice from below. She recognized him immediately, and she shushed Jody so she could hear what he was saying.

"Hello, Miss Whitman," the man barked in a gruff and unfriendly manner.

"Sheriff Wilson," Margaret responded. "You look like you've been riding all night. What are you doing here in Fort Worth?"

"I'm looking for you ... and your mother. You both know a hell of a lot more about those robbers than you told us. Where the hell is she?"

Sarah looked over the edge of the loft just as Sheriff Wilson, who was standing with his back to her, spit a stream of tobacco near Margaret's feet. Sarah held Jody against her bosom and waited for the response that she knew was coming from her daughter.

"My mother's not here," Margaret said with an apprehensive glance toward the loft. "But I do recall she had words with you about spitting, Sheriff. It is a nasty habit. I'll thank you to never do it around me again."

"Don't get smart with me, young lady. I'll spit where the shit I want to. I'll ask you one more time, where the hell is your mother?"

"I don't respond to threats, or to the devil's language, sir."

As Sheriff Wilson stepped up to Margaret and seized her arm, Sarah looked around the loft for something she could use as a weapon. Lying near the ladder was a splintered wooden singletree that fit nicely in her grasp. Holding on to a roof support with one hand, she leaned out and swung it through the air with the other. It crashed through the sheriff's hat and impacted his skull just above his ear with a resounding crack. He crumpled to the floor, uttering a soft moan.

"Mama!" Margaret cried. "I was wondering when you'd do something. I didn't know you'd do that."

"Someone needs to teach him some manners," Sarah said as she climbed down from the loft with Jody under one arm. "He's just lucky I'm the one who whacked him."

"What are we going to do now?" Margaret asked as she looked down at Sheriff Wilson sprawled face down. He lay near the stall holding the frisky stallion that had nearly kicked Sarah. His hat had been knocked off, and a large knot protruded over his ear. "He knows we have the money."

"I'm not sure about that," Sarah said. "He may just have his suspicions. I do think Jack Kilpatrick isn't far away."

Looking at Sheriff Wilson, Sarah mused, "He never knew I was in the loft. For all anyone else knows that horse over there kicked him in the head."

Turning to Margaret, she added, "If anyone asks, that's what happened."

Margaret looked at her mother for a long moment before responding, "I understand. Remind me to never get you mad at me."

"And remind me to never curse or spit near you," Sarah said with a smile. "We better get a doctor. He might have a concussion."

"I hope he does," Margaret said as she massaged her arm where the sheriff had grabbed her. "It serves him right."

While Margaret went to find a doctor, Sarah and Jody entered Beelzebub's stall and quietly approached him. He was sleeping uneasily, his breath ragged and shallow. Flies were buzzing about his wounds, forming a small cloud over him. Every now and then, he would shake his ears and raise one paw to scare them away. But his eyes remained close.

"That's close enough, Jody," Sarah said, as they stopped just outside the reach of the rope.

"Want to pet Beebub," Jody whined. "Beebub is hurt."

"Yes, he is hurt. But we can't pet him. He might have sickness in his wounds. We have to be careful."

"Poor Beebub," Jody said, standing by his mother with a thumb in his mouth.

As they watched Beelzebub thrash in the throes of his nightmare, a cluster of flies chose a long slash on his muzzle to dine on. Sarah took off her wide-brimmed hat and waved them away.

"Mama," Margaret shouted from the barn entrance.

Sarah turned as her daughter entered with a tiny, baldheaded man carrying a black bag. A huge Mexican man, wearing a sombrero big enough to cast shade over a city block, was shuffling along behind them.

"He's a doctor," Margaret said. "I saw him on the sidewalk outside."

"Good morning. I'm Dr. Hinton," the man, hardly big enough to reach Sarah's shoulders, said as he knelt by the unconscious body.

He inspected the large, discolored swelling on Wilson's head, and then he rolled him over. Peeling back his eyelids, he peered into his eyes. Opening his bag, he removed a stethoscope and started to place it on the sheriff's chest.

"I'll be darned!" Dr. Hinton exclaimed as he stared down at Wilson's badge. "He's a lawman."

Turning to Sarah, he asked, "What caused this nasty bump on his head?"

"He was standing near that stall," Sarah said as she pointed at the stallion pawing and snorting at the commotion. "That horse must have reared up and hit him."

"That would certainly explain a blow like this," the doctor said as he listened to Wilson's heartbeat.

"Is he going to be alright?" Margaret asked apprehensively.

"Don't know for sure yet. Best get him down to my office. He may have a cracked skull. Probably a concussion. Has he been awake at all since he was hit?"

"No, I don't think so, Doctor," Sarah responded. Fear gripped her tightly as she wondered if she was responsible for another man's death. With uncertainty swirling in her thoughts, she said a silent prayer for Sheriff Wilson's recovery.

"Jose," Dr. Hinton said, motioning to the big Mexican blocking the doorway. "Get my buggy and bring it here."

"Si," Jose responded. He turned and moved ponderously out of the barn, the brim of his sombrero waving up and down like the wings of a giant bird.

Dr. Hinton took a vial of smelling salts from his bag, uncorked it, and held it under Sheriff Wilson's nose. Wilson responded with a snuffle and a gasp, but he did not open his eyes. The doctor shook his head and stood up. Looking around the barn, he found an old blanket and draped it over the sheriff's body.

"I'm afraid he might go into shock," he said in response to Sarah's questioning look.

Jose arrived with the doctor's buggy just as Daniel returned from his breakfast. Apparently, he had found a place to freshen up because he was clean-shaven and wore a new shirt. He carried a guitar over his shoulder, which he hitched self-consciously around to his back to shield it. Margaret looked at him appraisingly and, apparently liking what she saw, smiled in welcome.

"Whatever happened here, Mrs. Whitman?" Daniel asked as he watched Jose pick Sheriff Wilson up and place him in the rear of the buggy.

"A horse must have kicked him," Margaret said after a glance at her mother.

Daniel looked at the circled star on Wilson's chest and exclaimed, "He's a sheriff!"

"He's the sheriff of McLennan County down in Waco," Sarah said as the doctor's buggy clattered out of the stable. "His name is Wilson."

"Goodness sake," Daniel said. "I stopped by the office, and no one told me about a sheriff visitin'."

"Was Marshal Courtright there?" Sarah asked.

"Yes. He never said nothin' about no sheriff."

"He never said anything about a sheriff," Margaret interjected.

"No, he didn't," Daniel agreed. "He never said nothin'."

"Daniel," Margaret bore in. "The proper way to say it is, 'He never said anything about a sheriff.'"

Daniel looked at Margaret wide-eyed for a moment, and then comprehension dawned on him. He responded in an open and forthright manner, "You're right Margaret. I don't always speak proper words. Thank you."

"How far did you go in school?" Sarah asked.

"Learned a little readin' and writin' … and cipherin'," Daniel said. "Had to help Mama on the farm, so couldn't do much schoolin'."

"I see you have a guitar," Sarah said with a twinkle in her eye. "Are you going to sing for us?"

Daniel kicked at the dirt floor before responding, "I just like to play and sing a little. It keeps me company. I learned to sing from my mama. She had the voice of an angel."

"Daniel," Sarah said to change the subject. "Beelzebub is either sleeping or unconscious. He hasn't been awake since we arrived."

"I'm not surprised, Mrs. Whitman," Daniel said as he went to Beelzebub's stall. "Those bites were pretty bad. It's hard tellin' what those dogs been scroungin' in. I expect he has fever from infection. Marshal Courtright gave me the day off, so I can stay here. We got to keep him cool and make sure he drinks lots of water for a while."

"I want to talk with the marshal," Sarah said. "Margaret, you and Jody stay here and help Daniel while I'm gone. Watch that Jody doesn't climb up that ladder again."

"Mrs. Whitman," Daniel said. "May I speak with you outside?"

"Certainly," Sarah said as she followed Daniel out the rear door.

The fenced-in stable stretched out behind the barn for a quarter mile or so before it ran into a small hill covered on the top by a copse of trees. The ragged outline of the post oaks and elms looked like a bad haircut above a giant's elongated forehead. Separate corrals near the barn held horses and mules. Above the top rail of one tall enclosure stretched the heads and humps of four large animals.

"Those are camels, aren't they?" Sarah asked? "I've never seen any except in books."

"Yes," Daniel responded. "The U.S. Calvary tried usin' them to chase Indians, but their feet are made for sand, not the rocks out there in the territory. Mr. Mac traded some mules for them."

Holding his hat in his hand and kicking the ground with one toe, Daniel said quietly, "Mr. Mac don't want the dog in the barn with the horses. Afraid he'll spook them. Even his snorin' is loud. Now that sheriff got hurt, folks'll be blamin' him. Mr. Mac said there's an old tool shed not bein' used out back a piece. It's in those trees just over the top of that hill. If you don't have no objections, I'll move him out there."

"No," Sarah said as she suppressed a smile. Margaret's latent teaching talents would get a workout with Daniel's crude vocabulary, she thought. "Find out how much Mr. Mac wants for rent for the shed, and I'll pay him."

She paused for a moment, and then asked, "Do you think Beelzebub has rabies?"

"It's too early to tell. The fever is from the wounds and loss of blood. I cauterized his cuts and sewed them up good as I could. The rabies gets in the bloodstream and sets awhile before gettin' into the creature's head and givin' it the slobberin' fits. I seen it bust loose as long as four weeks after the bites."

"Four weeks?" Sarah asked. "Are you telling me he'll have to stay penned up for four weeks?"

"Either that or he'll have to be shot. Can't take no chance on him turnin' into a mad dog. Folks can get rabies too. The marshal says I should shoot him right now, just in case. For you … and Margaret, I'll do what I can to keep him alive. Mama believed dogs are God's creatures too. Guess I go along with her."

"Bless you Daniel," Sarah said with a sigh. "Looks like our stay here in Fort Worth will be longer than I expected. But you can't spend all your time with him."

"No, I can't. After I get him settled, I'll look in on him before and after work. See he's fed and watered proper like."

"I am going to pay you for your time," Sarah said. "I will not abide any objections."

"You don't have to do that, Mrs. Whitman. I got all I need now. Marshal Courtright pays me thirty dollars a month and found. I can't even spend all of it."

"Perhaps so, but I will still pay you. And please call me Sarah."

"Gosh," Daniel said. "I'd feel mighty uncomfortable doin' that. You are Margaret's mother."

"Okay," Sarah said with a laugh. Pointing at the camels, she said, "Please show them to Jody, he'll enjoy it."

"I will," Daniel said. "We won't get too close. They bite."

Sarah looked at the hill in the distance that would be Beelzebub's home for the next month. He would be very lonely out there by himself, she thought. They would have to visit him as often as possible while she continued to look for Jim. The event with Sheriff Wilson still bothered her. She surmised that when he came out of his coma, he'd probably tell Marshal Courtright about his suspicions. Lurking in the back of her mind was the presence of Jack Kilpatrick with his searching, penetrating eyes. But, as her father often said when talking about making a commitment, "In for a penny, in for a pound." The old English expression certainly fit her present situation. She was in for a pound, perhaps a lot more.

Suddenly, Sarah realized where she could hide the valise full of the stolen government gold and silver. It was a problem that had been vexing her like an infected tooth since they arrived in Fort Worth. It wouldn't be long before someone searched the hotel room. If they found it there, she had no doubt that she would be arrested. She had thought about stowing it under a pile of straw in the stable, but that didn't set well with her. Who would think about looking for it in a shed, buried under a dog the size of Beelzebub, a dog that might have rabies?

"Daniel," Sarah said. "I think I should be here when you move Beelzebub. Right now, I have an errand to run. Please wait until I return."

Chapter 7

As I pensively put pen to paper, the hour of noon descends on Fort Worth like carrion settling on its prey. A warm fall sun blankets the sprawling cow town with a malicious malaise that lingers over from the long, languid summer. The mid-day lull calls for those who can spare the time to sit in the shade, take a nap, eat a leisurely lunch, or dilly dally with a sporting woman, if that be their inclination and they can afford it. Even the destitute dogs seem to realize that time slows down during this part of the day, and they seek shade and avoid confrontation with their fellow canines and with the general population.

Speaking of naps, I say the siesta is the best thing we ever received from the sovereign nation south of our border known as Mexico, although our illustrious mayor, G. H. Day, insists it is hot chili peppers and tequila.

Speaking of dogs, I say it is time for the city to appoint an animal control officer to extricate the canny carnivores that roam our streets at will. Marshal Courtright has neither the manpower nor, it seems, the will to effectively exterminate the scurrilous scoundrels. Only yesterday, a young boy was bitten on the left leg right on main street. Was the diabolical dog rabid? We can only pray for the youngster's sake that it was not.

Speaking of sporting women brings us to the crux of this erudite editorial. If our fair city desires to take its place among the foremost in this country, it is time for us to rid it of the worst pestilence since Sodom and Gomorrah. Yes, I speak of that thicket of thieves, that purveyor of poisonous licentious libations, and that provider of pernicious prostitution known far and wide as Hell's Half Acre. If Marshal Courtright has not the resolve to decimate that demonic blight on our civic conscious, then I say the time is nigh for a new law officer to step into the breach and battle the iniquities that run rampant in our streets. Let us not delay, dear citizens, lest one day soon we look back at that palace of pusillanimity and turn into pillars of salt; a fate similar to that which befell the family of Lot.

C. W. Heddings, Editor-in-Chief and Proprietor

Sarah smiled to herself as she placed the *Fort Worth Beacon* she had been reading on the table next to a clear vase containing a single yellow rose. She picked up a delicate china teacup, with a blue floral pattern. What a pleasure, she thought, to sip tea and read a newspaper at leisure. She felt guilty about leaving Margaret, Jody, and Daniel with Beelzebub at the shed, but she wanted to see Marshal Courtright when he returned from lunch.

Looking at the newspaper, she thought about the editorial she had just read. While she knew most of the words, one perplexed her. She thought about the advice her father had given her about learning new words. He told her that when she came across something she did not understand, she should put it into a place in her mind called the "New Words Room." She was to keep it there until she learned the meaning of it, and then she could let it out. To keep the room from becoming too crowded, he had given her a dictionary for her twelfth birthday. If she was going to read city newspapers with words like "pusillanimity," she would have to keep such a reference close at hand. For the time being, she would put it in her "New Words Room."

Sarah looked up at the clock on the wall behind the serving counter. It was nearly noon. She noticed that the tea was listed at three cents, as was a newspaper called *The Gazette*.

The waitress, a huge black woman dressed in a blue gingham dress with a white bonnet, approached her with a steaming teapot. Sarah allowed herself the luxury of another cup.

"Thank you," she said with a smile. "My name is Sarah Whitman."

"Why, you's welcome," the woman said with a white-toothed smile that lit up her broad features like sunshine breaking through dark clouds. "Pleased to meet you. I's Sadie."

"You serve excellent tea, Sadie," Sarah said. She thought that Margaret certainly wouldn't have to worry about Sadie being a competitor for Daniel's affections.

"Thank you, Ma'am," Sadie said, glowing with pride.

"I have a question," Sarah said. "Why is this newspaper, the *Beacon*, free when you charge three cents for the *Gazette*?"

"It's cause of the man what writes that," Sadie pointed at the paper on Sarah's table. "Nobody can't read what he writes, so it's free. Only comes out once a week on Fridays."

Sarah picked up the thin paper and glanced at a short article on the front page below the editorial:

William Tate Meets His Maker

> The nefarious and notorious horse thief and escaped murderer William Tate was summarily executed at the dawning of day yesterday. When this astute observer arrived at the place of perdition, Mr. Tate was sporting a hemp cravat and dangling like a modifier. Having nary next of kin to neither cast lots over his worldly possessions nor claim his corpus delicti, his remains will eternally reside in Potter's Field in the local graveyard in an unmarked grave within the reach of the capricious clutches of the ferocious fires of Hades.

Sarah finished her cup of tea and glanced at the clock again. She still had over an hour before Marshal Courtright was due back in his office. Leaving five cents on the table, she returned the newspaper to the stack on the counter.

"Come back and see me, y'hear?" Sadie said, wiping flour from her hands on her apron.

"I will, Sadie," Sarah responded as she walked to the door of the café.

When she reached Main Street, Sarah looked at the displays in the storefronts along the way. She had never seen such an array of goods and services for sale. Passing a laundry, she saw a window sign that offered washing, drying, and pressing for five cents per item. She gave herself a mental reminder to bring the dirty clothes from the hotel room. She also thought that she would have to buy additional garments for herself, Margaret, and Jody since they would be staying longer than intended. If she did not find Jim, they could return home and wait out the quarantine month for Beelzebub, but she was reluctant to put all the responsibility of caring for him on Daniel.

Just past the laundry was a milliner shop with a wooden mannequin in the window dressed in a floor length dress. The blue velvet material looked as soft and inviting as lamb's wool. The hemline, sleeves, and the high neck were trimmed in elegant white lace and embroidery, and a line of embroidery ran down the front of the dress to the thin belted waistline. Petty coats and a rear tassel gave the outfit a full, formal look. The model was holding a parasol in one raised hand, and a wide-brimmed white hat bedecked with blue silk ribbons perched on her wig of brown hair. Highly polished black leather shoes with narrow toes and full-length laces completed the ensemble.

Sarah could see her reflection in the store window beside the mannequin. Comparing herself to the image, she felt like a country bumpkin. She was wearing a long, black wool skirt with a single cotton shift underneath and a long-sleeved, white cotton shirt buttoned up to her neck. Her wide-brimmed, black hat, one that she had worn for many years, was definitely showing signs of wear. And her shoes, wide toed and scuffed, resembled men's brogans.

Looking closer at the woman model, she noticed how thin and graceful her hands were. Her own were roughened from the rigors of farm work; the past months without a man's helpful strength. She glanced at her fingernails, which, although she had recently trimmed them, also showed the effects of that manual labor. The model's waist was so tiny that she could probably put her hands around it. Her own waist, she thought, was still small for a woman of her age. She supposed that if she were a member of the elite in a city like Fort Worth, she would have to wear corsets with their restrictive and painful stays to give her the hourglass figure that seemed to be in vogue. Riding horses and hoeing in a garden, as she did, certainly didn't lend themselves to such foppery.

The model's face looked like a sanded fence post and was devoid of features, so Sarah could not compare with her. However, after looking into the mirrored glass, she thought that she was reasonably attractive. She had always imagined that her nose was too small and turned up on the tip, but Jim had disagreed with her. He thought it enhanced her fiery red hair and emerald green eyes.

The mannequin's chest was made up of two small mounds, which hardly filled out the bodice of her dress. Sarah thought that her breasts were still firm and full. They were certainly larger than the sexless creature behind the window. Of course they were nowhere near the prodigious mountains that Rose Travis sported, not that she would ever want such a burden. She knew most men appraised her chest when they looked at her, but she wouldn't want them to gawk at her the way they did at Rose.

Thinking of her breasts turned Sarah's thoughts to Jim. She missed his strength and calm demeanor in times of stress. And, mostly at night, she missed his hard, lean body and his gentle caresses. A shiver came over her as the realization dawned on her that he was dead. If he wasn't, she felt certain he would have returned to her or found some way to contact her.

Turning away from the window, she continued down the street passing a dentist office, a barber shop, and a store that sold men's and boy's apparel. She didn't think she would have any problem finding a place to buy clothes for herself and her children.

The buildings along the board walkway abutted each other with no room between. Only a few of them were painted, as if that were a frivolous expense. If a fire were to start in any one of them, Sarah thought, they would all be consumed by the conflagration. The owners tried to distinguish their facilities by putting up distinct signs announcing their wares and services. The signs ran the gamut from professionally painted masterpieces replete with colorful birds, animals, and scenes to hand-scribed boards bordering on the illiterate. Sarah found herself smiling as she read one of them:

MILLER BROS. SHOE STOAR

For Aching and Burning Feet

Our Bimbo Shoes Are Best In West

She had never heard of Bimbo Shoes, but she wasn't sure she wanted to shop in an establishment that couldn't spell "store."

A commotion in the street drew Sarah's attention. A freight wagon apparently had hit a rut and bounced off part of its load of buffalo hides. Horse and buggy traffic going both ways had to detour around the obstruction, and the riders and passengers didn't take kindly to the delay. Sarah could hear their protestations and gestures, most of them bordering on the blasphemous. The wagon driver, a huge man wearing dirty coveralls and sporting massive, tobacco stained whiskers climbed down from the seat and began tossing the hides back onto his wagon.

Sarah's gaze was drawn across the street to a one-story wooden building with an alley running down each side. A white sign, with shadowed black lettering on the false front above the door, proclaimed:

FORT WORTH BEACON
C. W. Heddings, Editor and Prop.

Two windows framed in white perched on either side of the dark wooden door of the newspaper office like black eyes alongside the beak of a carrion bird.

The "New Words Room" in her mind opened and the word "pusillanimity" peered out. She thought she might as well find out the meaning from the man who wrote it. Watching the surge of traffic diverting around the pile of buffalo hides, she made her way across the street.

The interior of the building consisted of one large room with a counter across the front. A strange rhythmic sound, like the pounding of a cloth covered hammer on an anvil, issued from the rear where a tall, thin man with a green visor operated a printing press that whooshed and banged as it spewed out paper. The sharp odor of printing fluid cut through the dusty air.

Sarah approached the counter as a tiny man, several inches shorter than she was, sidled toward the door and nearly ran into her. He was dressed in a variety of bright colors: shiny black boots, blue trousers as pale as a robin's egg, a purple silk shirt closed at the neck with a pink bow-tie, and a wide-lapelled, white jacket with two yellow roses peeking from the chest pocket like baby chicks. Flashing black eyes had been flung into his round, florid face beneath hair as white as snow. Sarah immediately thought of the multi-colored, scissor-tail flycatcher she had seen along the Bosque River. And, as soon as the strange little man opened his mouth to talk, he reinforced that comparison as he bounced up and down with the cadence of his speech.

"Oh, bless me, dear heart," he chirped rapidly as he placed one hand over his chest in a grandiose display of contrition. "Please forgive my ostentatious display of ineptitude." The words, high and girlish, gushed forth on a waft of breath carrying with it the distinct odor of alcohol mingled with the cloying aroma of sweet cologne.

"Good morning," she responded with a smile. "I am Sarah Whitman."

Bowing deeply, the little popinjay responded, "C. W. Heddings at your service, dear heart."

Sarah looked down at the tiny row of white teeth showing through his wide and infectious smile. It reminded her of a woodcut drawing of a grinning Cheshire cat in a book of fairy tales. "I just read your editorial and, I must admit, I didn't know one of the words," she said. "Perhaps you would be kind enough to tell me the meaning of pusillanimity."

Heddings' smile grew larger until it seemed to cover half of his face. "Only one, dear Sarah Whitman?" he asked as he bounced delightedly on the toes of his shoes in a futile effort to increase his height. "You warm the cockles of my heart. Most of the uncouth and uneducated riffraff who take my missive in their grubby hands fail to comprehend any of the wonderful writing that flows so fortuitously from my pen. Alas, instead of using it for erudite education, too often, they wield it as a supercilious substitute for delicate paper used after a movement of their bowels. Please excuse the scatological reference, dear heart."

"Pusillanimity, Mr. Heddings?" Sarah asked to stem the torrent of words bombarding her before any more made their way into her "New Word Room."

"Yes, dear heart. Pusillanimity is a 14th century English word most favored by the Bard of Avon, William Shakespeare, himself. It means the quality or state of being pusillanimous. In plain vernacular it means cowardliness. I assume you are referring to my description of our demonic den of iniquity, Hell's Half Acre, as a palace of pusillanimity?"

"Yes," Sarah answered.

"Ah, dear heart. Would that others shared your ability as a wordsmith. Most of them suffer from cranial vegetation. Alas, I tearfully fear that more often than praise, I suffer the slings and arrows of outrageous and unfounded criticism. Tell me, what brings you to our fair burg?"

"A visit, sir." Sarah found it hard to talk to Mr. Heddings without adopting a formal manner. "My home is on the Bosque River south of here."

"Please," Heddings said with a wave of his hand. "Now that we are formally introduced, you may address me by the name my dearly departed mother—God rest her soul—bestowed upon me at birth." With another deep bow, he added, "Clarence, if you please."

"Thank you, Clarence," Sarah said with an unconscious curtsey. "You may call me Sarah."

"May I be so bold as to inquire if you are bound by the holy and sacred bonds of matrimony, dear Sarah?" A sly look stole over Clarence's face like that of a small boy asking what he would get for Christmas.

"Yes, I am married," Sarah responded.

She decided to take Clarence into her confidence and added, "That's why I came to Fort Worth. I'm looking for my husband, Jim … James Whitman. He came here two months ago to sell some horses to the army. I haven't seen him since then."

"Oh!" Clarence placed his hand on his chest again in a theatrical gesture. "Perhaps I can be of some service. My newspaper is at your disposal. Even the rapacious riffraff are enticed by the mystery of lost persons. I must ask you for a description of your dear mate of matrimony."

While Clarence picked up a pencil and a pad of paper from the counter, Sarah gathered her thoughts. Although she had lived with Jim for years, it was difficult to recall details of his physical appearance. More than his looks, she remembered his strength and his calm attitude under stress.

Clarence unconsciously licked the tip of his pencil while he waited for her to begin. Sarah took a deep breath to steady herself and said, "Well, he's about six feet tall, thin, brown hair—it was cut short when he left. His eyes are brown also. Oh, and he has several smallpox scars on his cheeks."

"I see a handsome and virile knight in my mind's eye," Clarence said with his charming smile. "I am reminded of the exalted Shakespeare's delicious description of a man in *As You Like It*, dear heart:

> All the world's a stage,
> And all the men and women merely players.
> They have their exits and their entrances,
> And one man in his time plays many parts,
> His acts being seven ages."

Clarence continued with a trace of moisture in his eyes. "Oh, that we might give your James his seven ages. Does this man of masculinity have any distinguishing traits that make him stand out from the capricious crowd?"

"Yes," Sarah said after a pause. "He walks with a slight limp. One of our old bulls hooked his left leg while he was riding in the pasture. It still bothers him some, especially when it rains."

"Of course. Such a debilitation will certainly help to identify our James. Have you given a thought to the repugnant remuneration commonly offered for news of missing persons?"

"Remuneration? Do you mean a reward?"

"Yes, dear heart."

Sarah thought about the valise of gold and silver buried under Beelzebub. She had added some of her own savings to it before removing enough of the silver coins to pay their expenses for the present. Offering a reward would require her to use some of the gold bars, which might lead the authorities—especially Jack Kilpatrick—to tie her to the government robbery money.

"How much do you recommend?" Sarah asked to gain time to think.

"It should be minimal so as not to call forth the scurrilous scoundrels who feast like carrion of the misfortunes of others. We would end up chasing false leads and dis-interring anonymous bodies. Alas, it should be enough to stimulate those knaves who might have knowledge of value. Enough, dear heart, to provide the common cowboy, roving mule skinner, and citizen John Doe with the holy trinity of tobacco, liquor, and women."

"How much do you suggest?" Sarah asked.

"Can you afford to put up cash collateral with one of our nefarious nabobs of industry, also known as a benevolent banker, of the sum of $100?"

Sarah, who had been thinking of five times that amount, readily assented, "Yes, I can."

Clarence flashed his Cheshire cat smile as he wrote a name and address on one of the pages of his notebook, tore it out and handed it to Sarah. "This gentleman will assist you with establishing the collateral. In the meantime, I will pen an item for tomorrow's issue and print a few hundred handbills to be expeditiously distributed by my young assistant of colored persuasion."

"What do I owe you for this, Clarence? I must pay you for your expenses."

"Dear heart, you offend my sensibilities. I would not consider remuneration from one as learned and beautiful as you. A word of thanks and a kiss on my proffered cheek would be sufficient."

"I do thank you," Sarah said as she leaned down and kissed Clarence's pudgy jowl. The odor of his breath was stifling, and she quickly stood up again.

"I must ask you," she added. "Why do you have two roses in your jacket?"

"You are most observant," Clarence said as he pulled one of the flowers from his pocket and offered it to Sarah with a bow. "I present one yellow rose each turn of the sun's orb to a perceptive person of merit. For as Juliet said to Romeo, 'What's in a name? That which we call a rose by any other word would smell as sweet.' You are the recipient on this fine day."

"Thank you," Sarah said as she placed it in her chest pocket. Backing out the door, she said, "I'll wear it with pride."

She felt breathless from the conversation with Clarence, and she wanted to savor the fresh air outside. The last view she had before the door closed behind her was of him nodding his head down in an exaggerated bow of farewell. Her "New Word Room" had several new occupants, and she would either have to stay away from Clarence or buy a dictionary to prevent over crowding. Taking a deep breath, she started down the street toward Marshal Courtright's office.

Chapter 8

At the far end of Main Street, Sarah could see the buildings on each side terminate in front of a huge structure, still under construction, that blocked the road. She recalled someone at the hotel telling her the courthouse had burned down earlier in the year, and it was being rebuilt. Since she had a little more time to spend, she decided to take a closer look at it.

The monstrous building, perched on a bluff overlooking the Trinity River, was the largest Sarah had ever seen. Wide stairs led from the street up to the first floor, which was nearly completed. The uncovered wooden supports of the upper stories stretched skyward like the skeleton of a prehistoric monster. A tall gantry reached to the top where a pulley system, drawn by a team of sweating horses and lashed on by a huge, bare chested man shouting blasphemous phrases, lifted construction material to workers perched on the narrow supports.

When Sarah shaded her eyes against the blinding mid-day sun to look up, she heard whistles and catcalls from the men staring down at her. Blushing at the tone of their voices and the suggestive nature of their words, she walked quickly away toward the edge of the bluff.

As the sounds of the construction and the voices of the men faded behind her, she could see the river far below. The water, at a low level as the year marched slowly on toward winter, meandered snake-like from west to east. She knew it ran by Dallas on its convoluted way south where it joined with the drainage of other rivers, including the Bosque River of her home county, to feed into the Gulf of Mexico. Across the river, in the distance, she could make out a number of stalls and sheds surrounded by herds of cattle bustling around feed troughs. Beyond the buildings stretched fields cut out of the trees like white squares on a checkerboard. On the northern horizon, the smoke from burning brush rose high into the clear sky before dissipating.

Sarah felt a pang of homesickness come over her as she looked down at the stream again. The north winds would soon strip the leaves from the cottonwoods and elms along the river bottom back at her ranch. She wondered if she would be there to see it. A sense of helplessness gripped her, and a dark blanket of gloom and apprehension fell over her shoulders. She felt like a stranger in a strange land. The hustle and bustle of Fort Worth, while temporarily stimulating, was beginning to wear on her. And she worried about the influence of the town, with its undercurrent of vice and violence, on Margaret and Jody. She missed the quieter sounds of her home: the lively chirping of the birds, the bubbling laughter of the flowing water, and the mournful keening of the wind in the trees.

From far off in the distance came the clear peal of a church bell. The beckoning tones carried above the dissonant sounds of the city behind her like doves carrying news of salvation, and they brought tears of joy to her eyes. As she thought about church, she pictured the little white chapel where her father had ministered and where she had first became aware of the power and the love of the Lord.

Suddenly she recalled something he had told her about being distraught, "Don't worry about tomorrow until it comes. Today has enough worries of its own. Remember Psalm 37 verse 5: 'Commit thy way unto the Lord. Trust also in him, and He shall bring it to pass.'"

Sarah took a deep breath and lifted her slumped shoulders. She mouthed the words, "Thank you, Father." Turning, she walked to the city hall where Marshal Courtright had his office. The rays of the sun warmed her and lifted her spirits, and strength began to flow through her again.

As Sarah walked up on the porch beneath the marshal's sign, she could hear voices coming out of the open door. She started to enter the office when she heard her name being spoken. She knew at once who was talking: Jack Kilpatrick. Stopping, with most of her weight on one foot, she listened carefully.

"We searched her ranch, but didn't find anything," Jack continued.

"You don't think she had anything to do with the robbery, do you?"

Sarah identified the second voice as that of Marshal Courtright.

"No," Jack said. "I do think she met those three renegades. For some reason, she's not saying anything about it."

"The money, do you reckon?" Courtright asked.

"Could be ... could be. You might keep your eye on her. See what she's spending money on. There's no way a stump rancher has much cash to spread around. With your permission, I'll search her hotel room."

"I'll send one of my officers to help you."

"No need to do that, Jim," Kilpatrick said. "I—"

Sarah had to shift to take the strain off the leg that was bearing her weight. When she did, a board creaked loudly, and the voices from inside stopped immediately.

Continuing into the office, she saw Marshal Courtright seated behind a large desk with his feet propped on an open drawer. Across from him, his legs crossed and his boots resting on the desktop, Jack Kilpatrick leaned back in a wooden chair. His hat was pushed back to the top of his head, which exposed a white expanse of forehead and a receding hairline that detracted from the perfect image Sarah carried of him. He was wearing a white silk shirt tied together at his neck with a thin tie. A black suit and vest with a matching, wide-brimmed hat made his face seem thinner than Sarah remembered. She saw an open sore on his upper lip that she hadn't noticed before.

He was doing something rather strange with one hand. A silver coin flowed around the long, slender fingers of his left hand like a shiny fish surfacing and diving in the water. The coin appeared and disappeared as if by magic. It was one of the most unusual things she had ever seen.

"Good afternoon, gentlemen," Sarah said as Jack's chair came upright with a clatter and Marshal Courtright struggled to his feet, one cheek bulging with tobacco. He looked around at the cuspidor behind him and, after a long hesitation, turned and spit into it with a loud splat.

"Why, Mrs. Whitman," Jack said smoothly as he recovered from his obvious surprise. "I was just talking to the marshal about your missing husband."

"Thank you for your concern, Mr. Kilpatrick," Sarah said.

Turning to Courtright, she asked, "What information do you have about him?"

Courtright, still not fully recovered from his astonishment at Sarah's arrival and the near disaster of swallowing his tobacco, stammered before answering, "Well ... well, I ... I really don't have any new leads. Jack and I were just reviewing the missing person file." He picked up several sheets of paper from his desk and peered at them.

"Would you mind sharing what you have with me, Marshal?" Sarah asked.

"Certainly, Mrs. Whitman," Courtright said as he smoothed his drooping mustache with his fingers. "Nothing more than I sent the sheriff down in Waco."

"All Sheriff Wilson told me was that Jim disappeared right after he left the army fort with the money from selling his horses," Sarah said. "No one saw him after that."

"Well, that's about it," Courtright said as he looked down at the papers in his hand. "Captain Anderson, the quartermaster at the fort, paid your husband in government script for forty horses at thirty dollars a head. Twelve hundred dollars in total. It was about four in the afternoon when he left the fort. He told the captain he was going to head south instead of staying the night here. He wanted to get home as soon as he could."

"He hired a hand in Waco to help him with the horses," Sarah said. "Have you talked to the man?"

"Yes," Courtright said. "His name's Cameron. He's from Fort Worth. He was returning from Austin when he heard in Waco your husband needed help to bring a horse herd north."

"Well?" Sarah said as she arched one of her eyebrows at the marshal.

"Well … Uh," Courtright stammered. "He said Mr. Whitman paid him his wages outside the fort and they split up. He swore he never saw your husband again."

"You seem somewhat uncertain about this Mr. Cameron," Sarah said. "Can you tell me why?"

"When I received the missing person report from your sheriff, I called him in. It seems that—" the marshal's voice trailed off as he looked around at the cuspidor again.

"Go ahead and tell her, Jim," Jack Kilpatrick interjected as he took a small leather-bound journal from the desk and, after closing it carefully, put it into his jacket pocket. "She has a right to know."

"Well," Courtright said after he spit again. "Cameron—he's known as Sludge around here. He's always been a big drinker and a loud talker. Thinks he's a card player, but … it seems like after your husband disappeared, he showed up at the saloons with a wad of money. More than your husband paid him in wages. When I questioned him, he told me he'd had a string of good luck at the poker tables in Dallas."

"And?" Sarah arched her eyebrow again at the fidgeting lawman.

"It seems he did, in fact. I questioned him, but I had to turn him loose. There was no way to trace the money he had, and we … well, we couldn't find a body. So we couldn't charge him with anything."

Jack Kilpatrick looked up at Sarah. "Circumstantial evidence might get him arrested," he said. "But no jury would convict him. The marshal has done all he can."

"I see," Sarah said. "If my husband left the fort in mid-afternoon and headed south, someone should have seen him on the road. Have you talked to any witnesses who might have noticed him?"

"Sorry, Mrs. Whitman," Courtright said as he sat down in his chair. "This is a busy town. Lots of people coming and going at all hours. I sent my officers out to ask questions, but by the time I got the missing person report, the trail was cold."

"This Mr. Cameron, what can you tell me about him?" Sarah asked.

Courtright answered hesitantly, "Not much. He lives west of town on the river bottom. His daughter takes in wash and cleans houses to keep the family going. He's a Civil War veteran. Still fights for the south when he gets drunk."

"Have you ever arrested him for anything?" Sarah asked.

"Couple of times for public intoxication and fighting. He's spent a few nights in the town jail."

"Do you think my husband is dead, marshal?" Sarah asked straightforward.

Courtright hesitated. He looked at Kilpatrick for support, but Jack was staring at the ceiling and ignoring him. Finally, he said, "Well, after all this time. Unless he wanted folks to think he was dead." Noticing the piercing look Sarah gave him, he continued, "I must be honest with you, Mrs. Whitman. It does look as if he met with foul play. However, without a body and witnesses, we can't arrest anyone."

"I want to thank for your assistance," Sarah said after taking a deep breath. "If you get any more information on my husband's disappearance, please let me know."

"Are you returning to your ranch, Mrs. Whitman?" Jack Kilpatrick asked with a wide smile as he stood up and pulled his hat down over his forehead. "Fort Worth has a lot to offer. Fine dining and an excellent play house. I would be more than pleased to acquaint you with the town at your convenience."

"Thank you," Sarah replied as she avoided his appraising stare. "I have no need of your services. I will be leaving as soon as practical. Good day, gentlemen." As she left the office, she could feel the stares of both men on her back.

When she reached the sidewalk, she heard a voice reach out to her, "Mrs. Whitman. May I have a word with you please?"

"Of course, Mr. Kilpatrick," Sarah said, turning to face him.

"I'm sorry Marshal Courtright didn't have any more information on your husband," Kilpatrick said, his voice low and deep with concern.

Sarah was aware of the man's overpowering masculine presence. She looked up into his piercing eyes that glimmered with a reflection of the bright rays of the sun. "I can understand how difficult it must be to investigate a disappearance months after it happened," she said. "I notified Sheriff Wilson two days after Jim was due home. Courtright should have started looking into it by the third day."

"Two days!" Jack exclaimed. "Jim told me he didn't receive a telegraph message from Wilson until nearly two weeks after it happened."

Sarah's shoulders sagged in disbelief. Why would Sheriff Wilson wait so long to start the search for Jim, she wondered? She remembered the visit to his office. She had left Margaret and Jody with the Sigmund's and gone into Waco alone the second day after Jim was due to return. She distinctly remembered that Wilson told her he would telegraph the authorities right away.

"I would pursue this with Sheriff Wilson except he is still in a coma," Jack said shaking his head.

"He is?" Sarah asked.

"Yes. It seems a stallion kicked him in one of the livery stables. Strange, Wilson is an excellent horseman. I can't imagine him letting a horse kick him like that."

"Is he going to live?" Sarah asked. She certainly didn't want to cause the man's death. She had just wanted to stop him from accosting Margaret.

"It's touch and go right now. His family wants him returned to Waco, but the doctor says he isn't ready to travel yet."

"Sorry to hear he's not doing well," Sarah said. "I'll pray for him and his family."

Stepping back, she continued, "Thank you for your assistance, Mr. Kilpatrick. My family is awaiting me. Good day, sir."

"One moment, please," Kilpatrick said softly, his dazzling smile lighting up his face. "I think we know each other well enough to be on a first name basis. Sarah, my name is Jack."

Before Sarah could respond Kilpatrick went on, "I don't know how long you plan to stay in Fort Worth, but I meant what I said in the office. I would be honored to escort you."

His smile widened as he continued, "I know how lonely it can be to lose someone you love and be without a companion. Especially at night."

Sarah arched one eyebrow as she retorted, "I am not lonely, Mr. Kilpatrick. I have my family with me, and I'm looking for my husband. For all we know—and I pray—he is still alive. My name is Mrs. Whitman to you. Good day."

Sarah was looking into Kilpatrick's eyes when she finished speaking. A strange transformation seemed to come over him. His smile froze into place, and a veil covered his eyes. Almost at once the shroud lifted, and she was staring into the eyes of a person unlike any one she had ever met. Kilpatrick's pupils appeared to shrink as they fixated on her with a malevolent intensity. Sarah gasped and raised her hand to her mouth. A shudder came over her. She was unable to tear her eyes from his piercing stare.

Then, as suddenly as it began, Kilpatrick returned to normal. He blinked several times, and his eyes softened. He laughed and said, "I certainly respect your wishes. Good day to you also, Mrs. Whitman."

Sarah turned quickly to avoid any further conversation. As she walked down the street, fingers of discouragement probed at her. She was sure that Marshal Courtright was not telling her everything he knew about Jim's disappearance. But what could she do after all this time? This was not her town; she had very little information to go on and no one to turn to. If the marshal couldn't solve the mystery surrounding Jim, what chance did she have of finding him?

What should she make of Jack Kilpatrick? One moment he seemed like a kindly person, determined to help her find her husband, and the next like a stranger consumed by an inner fire she couldn't understand. She shivered as she recalled the strange look that had come into his eyes when she refused his offer to escort her. It seemed beyond strange; it had an undercurrent of raw evil.

Then, squaring her shoulders, she went on down the street. She decided that she would not be dissuaded from the arduous task in front of her. Yes, Jim was undoubtedly dead, but she would find out what happened to him. When she did, those who were responsible would pay for their transgressions. Then, and only then, would she and her family return home. And they would take Jim's body with them for interment in the graveyard on the Bosque River.

Chapter 9

Sarah stood on the sidewalk across from the Red Bull Saloon. She had told Margaret that she would return directly to the hotel after she visited with Marshal Courtright but, as she walked along the street, she thought about Rose. She sensed that Rose had wanted to talk to her about something the night before when they were interrupted by the dog attack on Jody. Perhaps now was the time to hear what she had to say and get some information from her. The thought of entering the saloon again overwhelmed her. She knew the men inside would stare at her, expecting her to be friendly to them; perhaps even drink with them. Why else would she go in a place like that?

A noise behind her caught her attention, and she turned around. A small Mexican boy, his clothes ragged and dirty, was holding out a clump of blue and white wild flowers, dirt still clinging to the stems.

"*Dos centavos, Senora?*" the grubby little boy asked, averting his eyes.

Sarah smiled as she looked down at the lad. He looked like he hadn't had a decent meal or a bath in a long time.

"*Dos centavos?*" the boy asked again.

Sarah took two pennies out of her purse and handed them to the tiny flower peddler with a smile and a pat on his bowed head.

As he stuffed the money in his pockets, a smile snuck onto the youngster's face like a returning long lost friend. "*Muchos gracias, Senora,*" he said as he turned to run away.

"Wait!" Sarah said. She held out a five-cent piece, and the boy stopped immediately, his eyes widening. "Do you speak English?" she asked.

The little boy shook his head slowly while looking hungrily at the coin Sarah held in her hand.

Sarah pointed at the saloon across the street. "Rose," she said. Then she put her hand on her chest, "Sarah." Aiming her finger at the building, she repeated, "Rose." Then turning the finger at herself once more, she said, "Sarah."

The boy seemed to grasp what she was saying immediately. Looking at her, he said, "Sarah?"

"Yes. Tell Rose to come to Sarah."

The boy glanced briefly at the coin once again, and then he scampered across the street in front of a wagon loaded with lumber. The driver sawed on his reins to divert his horses around the darting youngster and shouted at him in anger. Sarah held her breath until he reached the far side and disappeared into the saloon.

Several minutes went by while Sarah stood in the shade of the store overhang and waited. Just when impatience was beginning to well up in her, the door to the saloon opened, and the Mexican boy burst out. As the swinging doors closed, they were thrust open again by Rose as she strode through them. Sarah held her hand up and waved. Rose looked up and spotted her immediately. After looking up and down the street at the traffic, Rose walked regally toward Sarah, her pace slowed by her high-heeled shoes.

When Rose reached the sidewalk where Sarah stood, she paused to brush dust from her bright blue dress, swelled out by petticoats. "Goodness, Sarah," she said in her low, husky voice. "I couldn't understand what that little *muchacho* was saying, but he sure was insistent. I'm glad to see you."

Rose raised a small fan and waved it back and forth in front of her rouged cheeks. A light afternoon wind stirred the wispy ends of her hair, which was piled on top of her head like a massive beehive.

Sarah turned to the boy who was staring at her in anticipation. Handing him the five-cent coin, she said, "Thank you ... *gracias.*"

The youngster grabbed the coin and, without responding, ran quickly down the walkway.

"Rose," Sarah said. "Thank you for coming. I hope I haven't interrupted anything?"

"Just a nickel and dime poker game," Rose said with a laugh that made her ponderous breasts jiggle. "Can't win much at those stakes. Most of the action takes place when the sun goes down. Guess that's when sin becomes acceptable. Well, honey, what brings you here?"

"I just wanted to talk with you," Sarah said.

"I'm glad you came," Rose said. "We didn't have much time last night. How's your family doing? You have a beautiful daughter and a fine looking son."

"Thank you. They're fine. Fort Worth is very exciting to them. Maybe too exciting." Looking down the street, Sarah added, "Let's go to Sadie's Café. I do enjoy the tea there."

"Are you sure you want to be seen in public with me?" Rose asked seriously. "I don't have the best reputation among the folks in town."

"Of course," Sarah smiled. "You've been my friend since our school marm days, even if you have been gallivanting all around. Are you sure you want to be seen with a country bumpkin, with no sense of style, like me?"

Rose's handsome face lit up in a smile, and she placed her long, graceful fingers on Sarah's shoulder. "Gracious, honey. I haven't had tea in the afternoon since I left San Francisco."

Sadie seated them at a table near the window of the small café where they could see the traffic pass by outside. Sarah and Rose were the only customers in the room. After she served them tea and small sugar cakes, Sadie quietly withdrew to her kitchen.

"Well, honey," Rose said as she sipped her tea carefully from the dainty cup. "What brings you out of God's country to this dusty den of iniquity?"

"In due time, Rose. First, tell me what you've been up to? How did you get from that little school house on the Bosque River to Fort Worth?"

Rose took another sip of tea before replying, "After I left my worthless husband, I got restless feet. They took me all over the United States and to Europe."

"Europe?" Sarah exclaimed. "I didn't know you went there. Tell me about it."

"I loved Paris," Rose responded. "So many lights and the people are so stylish. And the men—"

"Yes, what about the men?" Sarah asked as she saw a twinkle in Rose's eyes.

"Such gentlemen," Rose answered. "Not like the uneducated ruffians here."

"Why didn't you stay there?" Sarah asked.

"Another one of a long string of mistakes," Rose said with a sigh. "I met a man who convinced me he was of royalty. But he just wanted to use me as an excuse to come to the United States to escape the authorities who were after his rear. It was fun for a while. New York, Saint Louis, and finally San Francisco. Then our money ran out, or I should say my money. Louis never worked a day in his life, and he and had no intention of ever starting. So I had to do something."

Rose glanced down at her massive chest, which was only partially covered by her dress, and continued, "I was somewhat attractive then."

"You still are," Sarah said.

"Thank you," Rose smiled. "But not like you. Your beauty went all the way to your soul. It seems you still have that beauty, as well as your figure. I often thought of you when I was traveling."

"And I of you," Sarah said. "I looked forward to getting your letters and cards. I would dream of visiting the places you went. As I remember, the last letter I received was from San Francisco."

"That was when I started ... well, this business I'm in now," Rose said quietly. "I hope you don't judge me too harshly."

"Judgment is not mine to make," Sarah said. "One of my father's favorite sayings of Jesus was, 'Judge not lest ye be judged.'"

"Your father was a wonderful man," Rose said. "You must miss him very much."

"Yes," Sarah said as she sipped the tea. "Every day in so many ways. Thank you for your concern."

"You seem a little depressed," Sarah said after she composed herself. "Are you all right?"

"No," Rose said as she ran her hand through her hair to smooth it down. "I lost one of my favorite girls. Little Lu we call her. She's been with me since Denver."

"Lost her?"

"Yes. She just up and disappeared last week. The boarding house where she lived is only six blocks away. She left the Red Bull about one in the morning and never arrived at her room. One of the other girls saw her start home alone."

"Could she have run off with someone?" Sarah asked.

"Not my Little Lu," Rose said with a sad shake of her head. "Not her. She was my little pink flower. She always wore pink, you know, wouldn't put on any other color."

The door opened and a small, thin woman dressed in a black dress with long sleeves entered. A thin, gossamer veil fell from her narrow-brimmed hat like a spider web and concealed her features. She floated past Sarah and Rose with tiny, mincing steps and took a table near the counter.

After seating herself, the woman looked up and stared at Rose. When Sadie walked up to ask her for her order, she stood up and said sharply, "I will not take tea with a harlot."

As she strode toward the door, the woman stared though her veil in disapproval at Rose who gazed back at her with a wide smile. Making a clucking sound, the woman said, "Well, I never—"

"I hope you have, honey," Rose said laughing at the woman as she left the room.

"Rose, I—" Sarah started to speak.

Rose held up her hand, "Don't worry about it. That's Mrs. Dalton. Her husband owns one of the local banks. She's the president of the Fort Worth Women's Club. They're committed to ridding the town of liquor, gambling, and prostitution. Probably to protect their spineless husbands. I think they all swore an oath to make life as miserable as they can for me."

"Why do they single you out?" Sarah asked.

"It seems that I am a paragon of non-virtue," Rose responded, a wide smile softening her face. "They think all the girls in town work for me. I kind of enjoy their pompous meddling. Of course, I don't normally show myself in public in the daytime like this. I hope I haven't cost Sadie any business, but it's given Mrs. Dalton a lot to talk about at the next club meeting."

Rose chuckled and added, "I would like to see the expression on her face if she found out how many of the pillars of the community frequent places like mine when they are off on business trips, including her husband."

After a long moment of silence, Sarah said, "I didn't get a chance to tell you last night, but I'm looking for my husband, Jim Whitman."

"I recall his name from your letters," Rose said. "What happened to him?"

"Two months ago he came to Fort Worth with horses to sell to the army. After they paid him, he left the fort and was never seen again."

"I am so sorry, honey," Rose said. "What a burden this must be on you. Has Marshal Courtright looked into it?"

"Yes," Sarah answered. "But he didn't get word until two weeks after it happened. The sheriff in Waco didn't notify him for some reason."

"You poor dear," Rose said as she reached across the table and patted Sarah's hand. "Is there anything I can do to help?"

"Perhaps there is," Sarah said. "Do you know a man named Sludge Cameron?"

"Cameron?" Rose said. "Yes, I guess everyone in town knows that worthless son-of-a-bitch. I apologize for the language, honey. He is one of the most despicable men I've every met, and I've met more than my share. Is he a suspect in Jim's disappearance?"

"Possibly," Sarah said noncommittally. "What can you tell me about him? I heard he was a good card player."

"Hah!" Rose snorted. "When he's sober, which isn't much of the time, he's not too bad. But when he's drunk, he'd draw to an inside straight. And mean!

He's nasty when he gets drunk. He'd pick a fight with a grizzly bear, if the bear was wearing a Union cap. Sludge can't let go of the Civil War."

"My husband hired Cameron in Waco to help him bring the horses up to Fort Worth," Sarah said. "The officer at the fort said they split up after Jim paid him. Then Jim started home."

Rose put her chin in her hand as she thought for a moment. Then she said, "It seems like I remember. Let's see, about two months ago? Yes, it was about that time. Sludge didn't have much when he showed up at our place, but I heard he'd been to every saloon in town that would let him in. Do you think it was your husband's money?"

"I don't know," Sarah answered. "Marshal Courtright said he made some money gambling in Dallas. He couldn't trace what he had to the army currency. I understand he has a family near here?"

"Yes," Rose said. "His wife was nearly as mean as he is, and bigger. Sludge weighs about as much as a skunk and smells like one. I don't allow my girls near him."

"How does he support his family?" Sarah asked.

"His wife died a year or so ago," Rose answered. "Some say she was beaten to death, but no charges were filed against him."

"Courtright mentioned a daughter," Sarah said.

Rose took a deep breath and shook her head before answering, "Yes. About sixteen. She does laundry and house cleaning. Never seen her, but I hear she's tiny as a bird. Sludge ... Are you sure you want to hear all this, Sarah?"

"Yes," Sarah answered. "Nothing you say can offend me. Please be frank."

"Sludge was arrested for assaulting his daughter ... sexually. When it came time to file charges, she told the sheriff she wouldn't testify against him, and she didn't want to go to a foster home. I can put up with a lot of things from men, but molesting their own children is not one of them."

"How do I find the Cameron place?" Sarah asked.

"Now wait a minute, honey," Rose said. "You're not going out there, are you? Sludge might be small, but he's mighty dangerous. I called him a skunk, but when I lived in Denver, there was a vicious little creature called a wolverine in the woods. It'd stand off a bear. That's what Sludge is, a wolverine."

"You just said the Cameron girl does laundry," Sarah said. "I have some clothes at the hotel that needs washing."

"Can I talk you out of this?" Rose asked.

When Sarah shook her head, Rose said, "Their shack is along the river bottom about three miles southwest of town. You take the right fork in the road from the fort. They live just past the Hudson Plantation. You'll see the sign. If you're going out there, don't go alone."

"One other question," Sarah continued, ignoring Rose's warning. "Do you know a man named Jack Kilpatrick?"

Rose raised her eyebrows and stared down at Sarah. "I do, honey. I sure do. Handsomest man I ever saw. When he first came to town, I told him he could put his spurs under my bed anytime he wanted. But, I wasn't his type. He's very particular. Just likes—"

Rose's voice trailed off into a brief silence. "Sorry, Sarah," she said. "I shouldn't be talking like this to you."

"It's okay," Sarah said. "You can be yourself with me, you know."

"How did you run across Jack?" Rose asked.

"He was with the county sheriff down near Waco. They were looking for some robbers when I met him. This morning, when I went to see Marshal Courtright about Jim, Kilpatrick was in his office. I assume he's a lawman also."

"A lawman!" Rose said. "Well, not really. He's a Pinkerton agent."

"What's that?" Sarah asked.

"Pinkerton is a company from back east that does security work for the government and private companies," Rose answered. "Jack works out of the Saint Louis office."

"Saint Louis?" Sarah asked. "He doesn't live here?"

"No," Rose responded. "He spends a lot of time traveling in Texas: Dallas, San Antonio, Houston, and here."

Sarah decided to avoid telling Rose about Kilpatrick's proposition to her and the strange look that came over him when she refused. To change the subject, she looked at the stack of papers on the counter and said, "I met the most interesting person this morning, Rose. He owns that free newspaper over there, the *Fort Worth Beacon*. His name is Clarence Heddings. Do you know him?"

"Clarence!" Rose exclaimed. "I know him as C. W. Heddings. You must have made quite an impression on him to get his first name. Clarence, huh? Wait until I see that little turd again."

"You know him?" Sarah asked. "I just read an editorial he wrote about getting rid of the saloons."

"Honey," Rose said. "He thinks that will sell his papers."

"Sell?" Sarah said. "I thought he just gives them away?"

"If you read his editorial, you know why he can't sell them. No one, especially the cowboys and buffalo hunters we get here, knows what he's saying. I just love him to death. He reminds me of a little mocking bird. Chatters all the time and uses words only God knows."

"He does," Sarah agreed. "And I've never met anyone who bounces up and down like he does."

"He does that to make himself taller," Rose said with a laugh. "He's about the size of a bean sprout."

"How can he afford to print a newspaper that doesn't sell?"

"Family money, I hear," Rose answered. "He has a sister back east. The two of them inherited their father's fortune. Old money from clothing factories or something like that."

"What's he doing in Fort Worth?"

"He fancied himself as a thespian," Rose answered. "He bought a traveling stage show and set out to make his fame and fortune as a Shakespearean actor."

Sarah recalled the references to Shakespeare that Clarence had used when talking with her earlier. "He certainly seems well versed in the subject," she commented.

"Oh, the memory work was not the problem," Rose said. "But you've heard his voice. He sounds like chalk scratching on a blackboard when he tries to emote. The first night the show went on the road, they threw him off the stage."

"Threw him off the stage?"

"Yes," Rose continued. "Supposedly, a rowdy bunch jumped on stage during *Romeo and Juliet* and tossed him into the audience. His supporting cast quit on him, and he came west to fulfill his second calling as God's gift to the newspaper industry. Only problem is, he can't separate his two loves: Shakespeare and writing."

"The poor man," Sarah said. "I feel sorry for him."

"But don't you just love the little gnome, honey?" Rose asked with a laugh. "I wouldn't be too concerned about him. He can afford to indulge in his newspaper hobby, and he's starting an acting school. I couldn't be one of his students; he'd wear me ragged with his twittering. He also likes the ladies."

"He does?" Sarah asked with an astonished look.

"Sure does. He's like a banty rooster. All the girls love him because he's such a gentleman. Always sending them flowers and gifts with quotes from Shakespeare. Little Lu was one of his favorites because she's more his size."

Oh Lord, Sarah thought. Is there any man in this town who doesn't visit the "girls" as Rose calls them? Suddenly an image of Daniel and Margaret came to her mind. She didn't want to pry, but Margaret was her daughter and only sixteen. "Rose," she asked, "what can you tell me about the young man, Daniel Worthington? He's one of Marshal Courtright's deputies."

"Daniel?" Rose looked at Sarah with a perplexed look.

Then she responded, "Oh yes, honey. Your daughter, Margaret. Well you can rest easy about him. If I had a son—heaven forbid—I'd want him to be like Daniel. We all have adopted him. If you want to know, he doesn't drink or take up with the girls. Somewhere in his upbringing he developed a strong faith in the Lord. Probably from his mother. When I asked him about it, he was embarrassed. Just said he was saving himself until he was married proper like."

When Sarah didn't respond, Rose asked, "Have you heard him sing? He has a voice that warms your heart one moment and brings tears to your eyes the next. If Clarence wanted a stage act, he should hire Daniel. I've never heard a better voice; not in Europe or San Francisco."

"No," Sarah said. "I've never heard him sing. I'm looking forward to it, though."

Looking at the flower in Sarah's pocket, Rose said, "I see Clarence made you a 'Yellow Rose of Texas', honey."

"He did give me this. I couldn't stay long enough to ask him what it meant. As you said, he wears me out too."

"He read somewhere about the big yellow roses in Texas and decided to make them his calling card," Rose said. "He gives one away every day to someone he meets."

Rose turned and waved her hand across the room. "See all the roses on the tables? He thinks Sadie is the best cook in town, so when he can't get anyone else to accept his flowers, he presents them to her. She thinks he's the cat's meow."

Sarah looked at the clock on the wall behind the counter. "Goodness. I must go. I told Margaret I would be right back after I saw Marshal Courtright."

"It's past time for me too," Rose said as she pushed her chair back from the table and stood up. "The tea is my treat, honey. It's so good to see you again after all these years. I'm just sorry it's under these circumstances."

"Everything has a meaning," Sarah said. "I truly believe we were meant to meet at this time and place."

Rose put her arm around Sarah's shoulders and escorted her from the café. "As much as I like tea … and crossing swords with Mrs. Dalton, we need to find another place to meet," she said. "Where are you staying?"

"The Mansion Hotel," Sarah said.

Rose reached into her purse and withdrew a small ivory handled pistol. Handing it to Sarah, she said, "I don't know if you know how to handle a gun. But you best put this in your purse. Can't ever tell when you might need it in a place like this."

When Sarah looked at it hesitantly, Rose said, "It's only a .25 caliber. It holds five shells. It'll scare off the ruffians more than hurt them."

Sarah took the gun and put it in her purse. "Thank you, Rose," she said. "I hope I won't need it."

"Me too, honey," Rose said as she engulfed Sarah in a massive hug. "You take care of yourself and your family, you hear. This is no place for you. Get out of here as soon as you can and go back home. And let me know if you need anything, anything at all."

"I will," Sarah said. Turning, she started down the sidewalk so Rose wouldn't see the tears forming in her eyes.

Chapter 10

▼

When Sarah entered her hotel room, she sensed that something was amiss. The two beds, made up earlier by the maid, were slightly rumpled. She thought Jody might have caused that while playing, but the beds themselves seemed to have been moved slightly away from the walls on either side. Then she noticed that their extra shoes, which she had lined up under her bed, were also out of place. Apprehensively, she opened the chest of drawers where she kept their underwear and stockings. She remembered folding them neatly that morning. While they were not in disarray, they had been moved. Someone had searched the room, someone who didn't care if she knew it or not. She shuddered at the thought of a stranger touching her personal items. She felt like she had been violated in some way.

A folded piece of paper lying beside the water basin caught her eye. It was a note from Margaret. Whoever had ransacked the room—she had her suspicion that it was Jack Kilpatrick—had probably read it, which upset her even more. If he stooped low enough to paw through her clothes, he certainly wouldn't stop at reading a letter. Picking it up, she moved to the light from the window and read Margaret's tiny and precise cursive:

> Mother,
> Jody and I are with Daniel at Beelzebub's shack.
> We waited for you until noon. Please come join us. Margaret

Jody had signed his name with a large scrawl across the bottom of the page. Looking at the note, Sarah began thinking about schooling for both of them. She had been able to give Margaret a good foundation in reading, writing, basic ciphering, history, the classics and, thanks to her father's legacy, the Bible. But, while Margaret could perform farm chores and housekeeping tasks very well, she lacked even rudimentary knowledge of social graces. Her world, up to now, had been centered on the ranch in the country. Fort Worth, although it was not a large city, had exposed all of them to some of the baser aspects of human nature, which appalled Sarah. She longed for the simple life back on the river, but she knew Margaret would be changed forever by her experience here.

As Sarah walked up the narrow, rutted road leading from the main road east from downtown Fort Worth to the shack on the hill, the black oak, dogwood, elm, and beech trees and varied bushes were resplendent with the brilliant colors of fall. The red, gold, yellow, and brown hues brought to her mind the biblical story of Joseph and his coat of many colors. And like Joseph coming back from adversity, she knew the deciduous plants would come alive again in the spring after being dormant through the winter, and their leaves would burst forth in their various shades of green and earth tones, which would be their coat through the long summer days.

Above the chirping and crackling of birds on the hillside, Sarah heard a strange noise. It sounded like someone singing. As she approached the top of the rise, she could see the shack through the brush. The voice she had heard now came clearly to her. She recognized it as Daniel's. Accompanied by the strum of a guitar, his low tenor voice filled the afternoon air with an aching sound that touched her heart. Margaret and Jody were sitting on the ground in a clearing in front of the small building and staring at Daniel in awe.

Not wanting to interrupt them, or cause embarrassment to Daniel, Sarah stepped behind a tree to hide her from their sight and listened as Daniel continued singing.

> Down in the valley, the valley so low,
> Hang your head over, hear the winds blow.
> Hear the winds blow, dear, hear the winds blow,
> Hang your head over, hear the winds blow.

Silence descended on the clearing as the last words of Daniel's song soared above the trees and faded away into the afternoon sky. The only sounds Sarah could hear were the rustle of the wind in the treetops and the far off chirping of birds. She stepped around the tree and quietly approached the shack.

"Oh, Daniel," Margaret said. "That was wonderful. You have such a great voice."

"Bessie Pike," Jody shouted. "Sing Bessie Pike."

"You mean *Sweet Betsy from Pike*," Margaret said as she looked up at her mother approaching them.

"Oh, Mrs. Whitman," Daniel said, scrambling to his feet. His face colored as he stammered, "I ... I am sorry."

"No need to be sorry," Sarah said with a smile. "You are a wonderful singer. I'm the one who is sorry. I'm sorry I missed the rest of it."

Jody ran up to Sarah, and she took him in her arms. "Mama," he chattered gaily. "Daniel sang to us."

"How is Beelzebub doing?" Sarah asked.

"He's better," Daniel answered as he opened the door to the small shack.

Beelzebub, lying on the straw covered dirt floor, looked up at the sudden intrusion of light from outside. When he saw Margaret and Jody, he lurched to his feet and plodded forward to greet them. A chain dangling from his wide leather collar held him back. Snuffling through his nose and rattling in his throat, he seemed mystified by the restriction.

"I had to chain him up," Daniel said. "He about chewed through the rope I had on him."

Jody wanted to run forward and take Beelzebub in his arms, but Margaret grabbed him and held him back. "No, Jody," she said. "We can't pet him yet. He's still hurt."

"I played the chain out the back," Daniel said. "That way, I can cinch him up tight when I feed him and clean out the place."

Sarah wrinkled her nose at the dank odor emanating from the closed room. "Why don't we leave the door open?"

"Can't do it while we're not here," Daniel answered. "No tellin' what may wander in. You know, skunks and whatever."

"This is a lot of work for you," Sarah said.

"It's not bad. Just have to water and feed him mornin' and night. And muck out."

"Well," Sarah said. "We'll do our share. Margaret and I will take care of the feeding. You have enough to worry about with your job."

"Oh, no trouble," Daniel said with a sidelong glance at Margaret, his Adam's apple bobbing as he swallowed. "Don't mind doin' it at all."

"Mama," Margaret said. "Daniel said there is a traveling circus in town today. He asked us to go with him this afternoon. Can we?"

"Can we, Mama?" Jody chimed in. "Please?"

"You're welcome to join us, Mrs. Whitman," Daniel said.

"Thank you for the invitation," Sarah said. "It sounds like fun. I have an errand to take care of. Why don't the three of you go?"

She removed several silver dollars from her handbag and handed them to Margaret. "I'm going to take the laundry out," she said. "Why don't we meet at the hotel for dinner about seven? Please join us, Daniel."

"Oh, please do," Margaret said quickly as she stepped close to Daniel. Then, self-consciously, she glanced at her mother and backed away with color rising in her cheeks.

"Margaret," Sarah said. "Let me speak with you for a moment. Daniel, will you watch Jody? We'll be right back."

"Of course," Daniel said.

Turning to Jody, he asked, "Do you want to learn how to play my guitar?"

"Yes, yes," Jody squealed.

After they walked down the road out of view of the shack, Sarah stopped and faced Margaret.

"I hope you're not upset because we didn't wait for you and came up here with Daniel?" Margaret said.

"No, I'm not upset," Sarah said. "I can't think of anyone you'd be safer with. He's a fine young man. I heard some nice compliments about him this morning."

"Really, who from?"

"I had tea with Rose. She said Daniel was one of the finest young men she had ever met. And …" Sarah decided to share it all with Margaret. "She said he does not drink nor visit any of the … well, soiled doves, as your grandfather would say."

"Thank you," Margaret said smiling sweetly. "But you didn't need to tell me that. I just know he is a gentleman."

"Let's not rush anything. I think it would be best if you two don't spend time alone. Do I have your promise on that?"

"Yes, you needn't worry," Margaret said.

"Okay," Sarah said. "I went to see Marshal Courtright. He doesn't have any information on Jim's disappearance. For some reason, Sheriff Wilson didn't notify him until two weeks after it happened."

"Oh, no!" Margaret said. "Why not?"

"I don't know," Sarah answered. "But the marshal has pretty much given up on finding out anything."

"I'm so sorry, Mama," Margaret said with tears forming in her eyes. "I know how you wanted to find him. I miss him."

"So do I," Sarah said.

"Are we going home now?" Margaret asked as she looked longingly back up the road toward where Daniel and Jody waited.

"Not just yet," Sarah said, noticing the wistful look in Margaret's eyes. "We can't leave Beelzebub with Daniel. It wouldn't be fair to him. And, knowing him, he'd be out here every day. No, not yet."

Sarah looked at Margaret for a moment, and then she said, "There's something else I must tell you. Please don't be frightened, but Jack Kilpatrick is here in Fort Worth."

"Does he know what happened at our ranch?" Margaret asked apprehensively.

"I don't think so, but he certainly suspects something," Sarah said. She decided to not tell Margaret about the search of their hotel room. "I want you to know the money we brought with us is buried under the floor of Beelzebub's shack."

"It is?" Margaret asked wide-eyed.

"Yes," Sarah said. "I just want you to know where it is. In case—"

"In case of what, Mama?" Margaret said with a gasp. "Ain't nothing going to happen to you is there?"

"I don't think *ain't* nothin' goin' to happen to little ole me," Sarah said as she raised one of her eyebrows.

"Oh no," Margaret said. "Did I use that word again?"

"Yes," Sarah smiled. "How do you expect Jody and Daniel to learn proper English, if you don't use it?"

When Margaret didn't respond, Sarah continued, "By the way, why don't you get Daniel to put the 'g' on the end of his words? That would be a good start toward his education. But do it kindly."

"You know I will," Margaret responded.

"There is one other thing," Sarah said. "The man Jim hired to help him with the horse herd lives here. His name is Sludge Cameron."

"Is he a suspect?" Margaret asked.

"Not to Marshal Courtright, but I have my suspicions," Sarah said.

"Maybe Daniel can help," Margaret offered. "He is a police officer."

"Perhaps," Sarah said. "Not yet. I only have suspicions to go on. I don't want him to get crossways with his boss."

Sarah reached out and took Margaret in her arms. "Give me a hug and then go back to Daniel and Jody. Enjoy yourself this afternoon. And please be careful."

"You too," Margaret said quietly, trying not to cry.

Chapter 11

▼

Sarah clucked to the horse pulling the small carriage she had rented at the livery stable and pulled around a slow moving wagon heavily laden with split wood. As she went back to the right side of the wide, dusty road, she could see the fort rising in the distance. A United States flag fluttered in the brisk afternoon breeze from a pole over the entrance gates, which were open to allow a steady stream of traffic to flow in and out. Soldiers and civilians, afoot and mounted, mingled with horse and oxen drawn wagons as they entered and exited the huge structure. Large poles, sharpened on the top and mounted vertically, formed the walls, which enclosed a number of wood frame buildings surrounding a parade ground and a stable.

As Sarah passed the opening, she glanced inside. She had heard that the fort had not been active since before the Civil War, but an army detachment was using it temporarily to train recruits for the campaign further west against the Apaches. She could see a small group of Negro soldiers, clad only in black boots, blue pants, and long red underwear marching bare-headed in the open field at the command of a brassy-voiced sergeant dressed in full uniform, his large white sleeve stripes bright in the sunlight. A white man, stripped to the waist, was riding a bucking horse in one of the stables accompanied by the catcalls of several watchers, in various degrees of dress, seated on the fence.

Sarah's horse shied, and she had to pull on the reins to get him under control again as a cannon boomed from the rear of the fort, which overlooked the Trinity River. She couldn't see the gun, but a trail of smoke rose above the walls to be blown away by the restless wind. The marching soldiers seemed oblivious to the firing, as they continued to move back and forth in mindless obedience to the bellowing of the drill sergeant like a flock of mourning doves flowing to and fro to avoid the bark of a hunter's shotgun.

Turning away from the fort, Sarah took the right hand fork of the road leading south. Looking down the bluff, she could see the river below as it stretched out like a gigantic snake without a head or a tail. Overhead, high cumulous clouds piled on top of each other. Further to the west, the clouds were ominously tinged on their bottoms with dark gray. To the northwest, dark slanting elements of rain enhanced the gray underbelly. As the faint rumble of distant thunder disturbed the air and the first tentacles of cool air tugged at her like a child seeking attention, Sarah pulled her shawl closer about her shoulders and tightened the ribbon holding her wide-brimmed hat.

The height of the bluff decreased as Sarah left the fort behind. Dropping down toward the river, the road narrowed as it cut along the hillside. At the bottom of the decline, widening fields stretched out to the side of the carriage. The indigenous trees and shrubs had been removed to make room for crops of cotton, wheat, and alfalfa. Off to the right, the stark white outline of a three-story plantation house contrasted with the dark green and brown of the dormant fields awaiting the onslaught of winter. Here and there, she could see Negro workers in the fields and outside a large shingle-roofed barn set back from the massive main house. As she passed the gate leading to the house, she read a large sign with black letters on a white background: HUDSON PLANTATION.

A half-mile past the plantation gate a copse of trees encroached onto the land all the way from the river to the road, which took a turn to the right into the forest. For a moment, Sarah lost sight of the stream, although she could hear it murmur in the distance. Looking up, she could see massive oak tree branches reach out to each other like the hands of separated lovers and form a canopy over the roadway. The daylight, diminished by the clouds covering the sun and filtered through the leaves, was dim, gray, and lifeless. Occasional wind gusts, pushed ahead of the approaching weather front, found their way through the overhanging trees and stirred the loose dirt in the wagon ruts, giving life to dust angels that rose in brief merriment to escort the carriage as it made its way along.

The road passed through a small creek, the water barely over the horse's hoofs. A side road, not much wider than a game trail, went off to the left along the side of the stream. After a short distance, it disappeared in the thick underbrush.

Sarah clucked at her horse as he balked at the raucous crackle of a large black bird perched on a nearby tree limb. When she looked at the bird, she noticed something strange in a bush below it: a flash of bright pink, like a small ribbon. The vibrant color seemed out of place among the earth tones of the trees, bushes, and underbrush. She started to halt the carriage so she could get a better look at the object, but a shiver of apprehension ran through her as she thought of confronting Sludge Cameron. Flicking the reins, she increased the carriage's pace and went on down the road.

Suddenly, Sarah burst out into a clearing on the right side of the road that extended all the way to the river. The field, with corn stalks broken and bent over like the defeated soldiers of an ancient battle, fronted a ramshackle shack surrounded by the flotsam and jetsam of years of cast off garbage, building materials, farm implements, and animal excretion. Chickens pecked incessantly throughout the yard, and several pigs lay sleeping next to the steps leading up to a narrow porch at the front of the small shack. A mongrel dog, ignoring Sarah's approach, sniffed around the corner of a decrepit outhouse and headed toward the house. A dilapidated corral held a swayback horse, frozen in place with a tuft of grass in his mouth as if he had died in the standing position, and a huge blue-black mule swatting flies with his tail.

Sarah turned the carriage onto the path leading away from the road. Apprehension gripped her as she stared at the hovel that appeared unfit for human habitation. Overcoming her fears, she pulled up next to the building and stepped to the ground. Taking the bag of dirty clothes from the seat, she walked up on the porch, accompanied by loud creaks from loose boards. The door was ajar, but a screen door, with holes in it large enough for a cat to jump through, blocked her. She started to knock on the doorjamb when she heard a shrill noise come from inside, like a muffled scream.

She listened carefully, but the sound did not recur. After a moment, she called out, "Miss Cameron. I have some laundry for you."

A long period of ominous silence was the only response to her voice. Once again, the feeling that she was intruding where she wasn't wanted came over her. She started to leave, and then turned and said again, "Miss Cameron. I am staying at the Mansion Hotel. They said you would do some laundry for me."

When she did not receive a response, she turned to leave. As she walked around the carriage, the creak of the screen door startled her. Looking up, she saw a tiny waif of a girl, barefooted, and dressed in a simple cotton shift, standing in the darkness of the doorway staring at her with large, limpid eyes damp with moisture.

"Hello," Sarah said as she walked back toward the porch. "Do you do laundry?"

For a moment, the girl didn't respond. Then she said in a voice, quiet and trembling, "I do your washin'."

Sarah opened the screen door and handed the girl the sack of clothes. The scrawny youngster, slender as a willow, averted her face as she took the bundle. Thin, stringy hair fell down to her shoulders and across her face, partially obscuring dark bruises and jagged cuts on her nose and her cheeks. Dirty, broken teeth lined the child's mouth beneath her bruised lips.

"Oh, you poor child," Sarah said as she started to reach out. But the skittish girl jumped backward into the room and stared out at her with fear in her eyes.

"What is your name?" Sarah asked quietly as a crash of thunder echoed against the house.

"Annie," the girl said so softly that Sarah had to strain to hear it.

"Well, Annie, I am pleased to meet you. My name is Sarah. How much will the laundry cost?"

The girl looked up with wide, innocent eyes. Wiping her runny nose on the sleeve of her dress, she answered, "About two bits."

Sarah held out a silver dollar. "Here take this."

"Oh!" Annie said trying to return the coin. "That's too much."

A sound came from the rear of the room, but it was too dark inside for Sarah to see anyone. The small, dirty windows had been covered with waxed paper, so little light penetrated. Annie turned her head toward the noise, reminding Sarah of a mouse reacting to the growl of a cat. Then she gripped the coin in her tiny hand and held it against her side.

A bright flash of lightning lit up the yard, and Sarah could briefly see into the shack. At the rear of the room, a door stood partially open, but she could not see anyone other than Annie. She had a feeling someone else was with the girl, and that was the reason for her bashfulness.

"When can I pick it up?" Sarah asked, hoping to draw Annie into a conversation. She was reluctant to leave her with whoever else was in the house. Someone—she suspected it was Sludge Cameron—had recently beat her, adding to her existing scars.

"Be tomorrow," Annie said as she closed the door and left Sarah standing on the porch.

The first raindrops from the approaching storm began pelting the dirty yard, raising tiny dust motes and scattering the chickens. Flashes of lightning, coming at shorter intervals, were lighting up the gray sky, and booms of thunder began to roll across the clouds like the crescendo of an orchestra of the gods. A sudden gust of wind slammed into Sarah, blowing her hair into disarray and rattling the screen door. She turned back to speak to the girl again, but she was gone. She thought of knocking, and then she realized that whoever was with Annie would not want her to come into the house.

Walking quickly to the carriage, she climbed up under the leather roof. It extended over both seats, but it was open on the sides and in front, which allowed near freezing windblown rain to pelt her like shotgun pellets. Drawing her legs back under the seat, she pulled her hat down over her eyes.

The heavens opened up and flung down a deluge accompanied by wind, thunder, and lightning, as if all the gods in the sky were venting their fury at once. In a few short minutes, the yard was a quagmire of running water, and the rain created hundreds of small rivulets snaking their way toward the river. Sarah shivered as the damp cold reached through her clothes and chilled her. She looked at the shack, nearly obscured in the downpour, but it was dark, silent, and forbidding.

Sarah snapped at the reins to start the carriage in motion and thought about Margaret, Jody, and Daniel being outside in the storm. She hoped they would find some shelter. But as she considered it, she felt confident that Daniel would take care of them. He was a competent young man.

When she turned onto the main road toward Fort Worth, the rain slackened slightly and settled into a steady drizzle. The image of Annie, frightened and abused, wouldn't leave her. With each step of her horse, she was getting further away from the poor girl. Then, with a gut wrenching impact, the thought hit her that the man, who had probably killed Jim, was assaulting his own daughter, a scared and defenseless girl.

When Sarah came to the creek she had crossed earlier, it was running deep and wild, filling the roadway with a torrent. Her horse stopped at the rushing sound of the roaring stream and shook rainwater from his head.

Sarah held him back. But it wasn't the rushing water that stopped her, it was the realization that she had to do something about Annie, and she had to do it right away.

Backing up the carriage, Sarah headed it onto the creek-side pathway, which was still above the water level. Then she reversed direction and turned back toward the Cameron shack. As she did, she saw the outline of a mounted man approach her. When the rider neared, she saw that he was astride a large, unsaddled mule, plodding head down through the rain. Sarah's carriage blocked the roadway, and the man came to a halt facing her.

He was a small wisp of a person with a dark, scruffy beard. Rain, collected by the wide brim of his black hat, streamed down in front of his face and obscured his features. He seemed shocked to see Sarah stopped in the road, and he peered at her through the downpour.

"Good day," Sarah said as she reached into her handbag and put her fingers around the grip of the pistol Rose had given her.

"Get out of the way," the man said in a hoarse whisper, barely noticeable over the sound of the driving rain and the swirling wind.

"Are you Mr. Cameron?" Sarah asked as she pulled the gun out of her purse and, concealing it in her scarf, stepped to the ground. The steady rain began soaking into her clothes as she approached the mule.

"It's none of your damn business who I am," the man barked. He kicked the mule and attempted to go around Sarah and the carriage.

Sarah reached up and grasped one of the reins as she pulled the pistol from her scarf and pointed it at the rider. "Stop right there," she said loudly. "Get down or I'll shoot you where you sit."

"Gawddamn," the man shouted. "What the hell are you doin' with that?"

"I said get down," Sarah said decisively. "Now! On this side, where I can keep an eye on you."

As the man slid to the ground, Sarah stepped back and leveled the barrel of the gun on his chest. He was short and slight, the top of his wet hat only came up to her forehead. Through the rain, she could make out his narrow face and beady black eyes. Rose was right, she thought, he is one of those wolverines.

"I got nothin' you want, lady," he said his eyes never leaving the pistol barrel. "Put that damn thing away before someone gets hurt."

"The only one who is going to get hurt is you," Sarah said.

"What … what do you want of me?"

"We'll start with your name," Sarah said ignoring the rain soaking her to the skin.

"Name? By gawd, what do you want my name for?"

"I'll thank you to not blaspheme the Lord," Sarah said sharply. "Mr. Cameron isn't it? Or Sludge?"

"Okay. So you know who I am. What do you want?"

"You helped my husband, Jim Whitman, bring a herd of horses from Waco two months ago. I want to know what happened to him."

"Husband, by gawd," Cameron said, ignoring Sarah's admonishment. A sly look came over his face as he continued. "I don't know nothin' about him. He paid me off and went south. That's all I know."

"I think you know more," Sarah said. "He never returned home. Tell me what happened to him."

"And if I don't?" Cameron said as he moved a step closer.

Sarah cocked the hammer of the pistol and extended it in front of her, the barrel aimed at Cameron's throat. At the sound, he drew back against the mule, his bravado evaporating.

"I think you will, Mr. Cameron," Sarah said. "I believe you killed my husband, and I know you beat your own daughter and maybe worse. I have no reservations about shooting you."

"I wouldn't do that, Mrs. Whitman," a commanding voice slashed through the rain.

Glancing out of the corner of her eye, Sarah saw a tall rider clad in a dark slicker with his hat pulled down over his eyes. His horse was standing at the rear of her carriage. A lever action rifle rested across his saddle horn with the barrel aimed toward Cameron.

"Jack Kilpatrick!" Sarah said in astonishment. "What are you doing here?"

"Just passing by," Kilpatrick said. "Guess I saved you from doing something you would rue later."

"I didn't ask for your help," Sarah said sharply, looking up through the rain. She kept her pistol on Cameron.

"No," Kilpatrick responded. "You didn't. But as a law officer, I can't stand by and see a man shot down in cold blood."

"I heard you were a Pinkerton detective, not a law man," Sarah said.

Kilpatrick laughed, "Technically, you're correct. However, the sheriff has a standing order appointing me as a deputy whenever I'm in his county."

"Gawddamn," Cameron said. "I'm gettin' tired of standin' out here in the rain."

"I must apologize for the inconvenience, Mr. Cameron," Kilpatrick said.

Turning to Sarah, he continued, "Why don't you get in your carriage, Mrs. Whitman. Be a might drier there."

Sarah looked at Kilpatrick in frustration. Whatever advantage she had over Cameron was gone. If she shot him now, she had no doubt she would end up in prison. Margaret and Jody relied too much on her for that to happen.

"Okay," Sarah said as she lowered her pistol. "But I do believe Mr. Cameron had something to do with my husband's disappearance."

"Perhaps," Kilpatrick said. "Only he can tell us if he's involved."

As Sarah climbed into her carriage, she took her eyes off Cameron for a second. Suddenly, the sound of a gunshot split through the drum of the rain. Startled, she looked up to see Cameron fall to the ground, blood staining his left shoulder. Turning, she saw wisps of smoke coming from the barrel of Kilpatrick's rifle. His hat was still pulled down, and she couldn't see his face.

"Oh Lord!" Sarah said. "Why did you shoot him?"

"He was reaching for a gun," Kilpatrick said as he kneed his horse up and looked down at Cameron's body. "I don't know who he was going to shoot. Could have been either one of us."

"Are you sure he was armed?" she asked.

"Quite certain," Kilpatrick said as he dismounted. Looking up at Sarah, he said, "You best leave now. I'll take care of this."

Sarah looked through the rain toward the Cameron shack. She wondered if Annie had heard the shot that hit her father. Turning to Kilpatrick, she said, "I'm going to get his daughter. I can't leave her out here alone."

"Suit yourself," Kilpatrick said.

Sarah snapped the reins and started down the road. Her mind was in turmoil. Everything had happened so quickly. She didn't know if she would have been able to shoot Cameron. She didn't think revenge was strong enough in her heart to bring her to that point. But now he was dead, and with him had died any chance she had of finding out what happened to Jim. Tears mingled with the rain on her face as she snapped the reins over the horse's rear.

When Sarah reached the turnoff to Cameron's shack, the rain had diminished to a fine mist. The clouds to the west were beginning to lighten with the promise of an end to the brief storm. The chickens, which had disappeared during the worst of the deluge, were pecking animatedly about the muddy yard searching for worms and other bugs enticed out of the dry ground by the standing water.

Sarah pulled the carriage as close to the door as she could and stepped down to the porch. She heard the muted bang of a far off gunshot. It sounded like it came from down the road where she had left Kilpatrick and Cameron. Strange, she thought, did Kilpatrick shoot again? And, if so, why?

Chapter 12

Sarah stood at the foot of the bed and looked down at Annie Cameron while Dr. Hinton examined her. Under the light from the window and a lamp burning on the bedside table, the girl's bruises and contusions stood out against her pale skin like blight on a field of cotton. Her eyes were closed, and she moaned incoherently each time she was touched. Although the doctor had bathed her with a washcloth, a dank odor still permeated the air. Her hair, thin and blond as corn silk, was matted and filthy.

Dr. Hinton, his bald head shining in the light, kept saying, "Tsk ... tsk ... tsk," as he bent to his task. Standing, he wiped his pince-nez glasses on a towel and looked at Sarah. "This child has suffered severe abuse," he said. "I've seen trampled cowboys who looked better. I gave her a dose of laudanum. She'll sleep for awhile."

"How bad is she, doctor?" Sarah asked.

"Some of the injuries are new, the ones on her face and neck, but there's evidence she's been beaten for a long time. I found scar tissue on several ribs that had been broken and healed. Her mouth is in a horrible state. She needs a dentist badly. But, that's not the worst of her troubles. She's—"

"Mother!" Margaret exclaimed as she opened the door and stared into the room. Daniel and Jody were standing behind her in the hallway. "What's happening? Who is that girl?"

Sarah took Margaret's elbow and escorted her out of the room, closing the door behind them.

"Mama," Jody said excitedly. "We went to a circus. They had bears and tigers and clowns." He was grasping the remnants of a large candy cane in his grubby hand.

Sarah looked at Margaret's questioning eyes and said, "Her name is Annie Cameron. She's been hurt. The doctor is tending her. Go down to the restaurant and wait for me. I'll join you in a moment."

"But—" Margaret started to speak.

"Hush, now," Sarah said. "I'll explain it to you when I come down."

Turning to Daniel, she said, "Thank you for attending to my family this afternoon."

Forcing a smile on her face, she added, "I see you are all dry. How did you avoid that rainstorm?"

"We were in a big tent, Mama," Jody answered. "A big tent." He spread his arms wide in description. "It go boom outside."

"Good, Jody," she said. "I'm pleased you had a good time. Daniel, will you select a table? I'll join you very soon."

"Yes, Ma'am," Daniel said as he took Margaret's arm and guided her down the hall. Sarah noticed that Margaret went with him willingly, as if she were used to his attention.

When she reentered the room, the doctor was washing his hands in the small basin. Annie had stopped her thrashing, and she appeared to be in a restful sleep.

"Mrs. Whitman," he said. "I can sew up the child's cuts and salve her bruises, but—"

"But what, doctor?" Sarah asked.

"Alas," Dr. Hinton said as he dried his hands. "She is with child."

"Oh Lord! The poor girl."

"Yes," Dr. Hinton said as he waved at the bed. "The person who did this, do you know who it was? It's my responsibility as a man of the medical profession to report these occurrences to the authorities."

"I believe it was her father, Sludge Cameron," Sarah answered.

"I've heard stories about that man. I understood the sheriff was going to arrest him."

"That's true," Sarah said. "But Annie refused to testify against him. She was probably afraid he would hurt her even worse."

"I see," Dr. Hinton said with a sigh, as he closed his medical satchel. "I will inform the authorities."

"No need to," Sarah said quietly, afraid Annie would hear her. "Her father was killed this afternoon."

"Killed?" the doctor looked up in astonishment. "The scoundrel certainly deserved whatever happened to him. How did it happen?"

"Jack Kilpatrick, a special sheriff's deputy, shot him. Apparently Cameron had a gun, and he was about to use it."

"Hmm ..." Doctor Hinton said looking at his patient. "I need to remove her to my office where I have a patient room. It's also where I reside. I can keep closer watch on her there."

"How soon is the baby due?" Sarah asked.

"Hard to tell. She's such a small girl. And undernourished. I estimate she is in her fifth or sixth month."

"The poor child," Sarah said. "Will she be able to birth?"

"I don't know," Dr. Hinton said as he shook his head. "She is so weak now, and suffering from trauma. I'm afraid she will lose the child. Probably best for both of them. The fetus is not developed enough to survive the rigors of birth. It may be touch and go just to save her life."

"I'll pay you for your services, doctor," Sarah said.

Dr. Hinton smiled for the first time since he arrived. The corners of his eyes wrinkled under his glasses, as he said, "No need to worry, Mrs. Whitman. I know she's not your family. Besides, I have enough wealthy patients who overpay me for prescribing elixirs for their imaginary illnesses."

Looking at Annie, still in a restful sleep, he added, "My assistant will come for her straight away. I'll tell the maid to put fresh linen on the bed and air the room out. Might be a tad difficult to sleep in here otherwise."

"Thank you so much, doctor," Sarah said as she followed him out of the door. "Will you join us for dinner?"

"Not tonight," Dr. Hinton replied. "I've already taken sustenance. At my age, a little is better than a lot. Food that is." He chuckled quietly at his private joke as they went down the stairs.

The dinner was a hectic affair as Sarah explained the reason why Annie Cameron was in their hotel room. She didn't go into the details of Sludge's shooting, the severity of Annie's injuries or her pregnancy. Jody kept interrupting her with vivid descriptions of the circus, complete with shooting imaginary bullets at targets around the dining room.

When she finished her story, Sarah turned to Daniel. During the meal, she noticed that he and Margaret were holding hands under the table. She was unsure how to handle the situation, so she decided to let it pass for now.

"Daniel," she said. "It might be best if you don't pass any of this on to Marshal Courtright. Let's keep it among us. I expect he'll pay me a visit soon."

"Certainly, Mrs. Whitman," Daniel said, self-consciously putting both hands on the table. He glanced at Margaret, who was staring adoringly up at him, before turning to Sarah and adding, "Thank you for the fine meal. I have the early shift tomorrow. I best be getting along."

"You are welcome," Sarah said. "We'll feed Beelzebub tomorrow. I appreciate you taking Margaret and Jody to the circus."

Looking at her son, who was still shooting at imaginary wild animals behind the other tables, she added, "As you can see, he enjoyed it."

"I did also, Mother," Margaret said, extending her hand to Daniel. "Thank you."

Uncertain of what to do, Daniel grasped Margaret's hand and shook it vigorously. "Uh, goodnight, Margaret," he stammered.

After Daniel left, Sarah asked Margaret, "Did I hear him say *getting* and you say *mother* not *mama*?"

Margaret took on a serious demeanor as she responded, "Yes. Daniel is an apt student. He just hasn't had the opportunity to learn properly."

"And, *mother*?"

"I think it is the appropriate way for an adult woman to address her mother," Margaret said. "Mama is for children."

At the breakfast table the next morning, Sarah was sipping a cup of tea watching Margaret and Jody finished their apple pie, when the door to the dining room opened and Marshal Courtright entered. He was wearing a brown, three-piece suit, a hat of matching color, and a black cravat. His long brown hair, full and luxuriant, glowed in the early morning sunshine pouring through the door. He had recently shaved, and Sarah noticed that his ruggedly handsome face was fixed in a scowl as he searched the room with his dark piercing eyes. Locating her among the diners, he strode toward her table.

"Good morning, Marshal," Sarah said, looking up.

"Top of the morning to you, Mrs. Whitman," he said. After touching the brim of his hat to Margaret, he turned back to Sarah, "May I speak with you?"

"Certainly," Sarah said, standing up. "Margaret, after you finish, please take Jody upstairs and start his lessons."

"Okay, Mother," Margaret responded. "When are we going to feed—?"

Margaret stopped when she saw Sarah raise one eyebrow. Looking at Jody she said, "Don't play with your food. We have school lessons to attend to."

Sarah followed Marshal Courtright to an alcove past the registration area. She sat on a small settee while Marshal Courtright occupied a high-back chair facing her. The clerk, who had been sitting in a chair reading a newspaper, stood up and began wiping the counter top with a rag. After a look of disapproval from the marshal, he returned to his chair, out of sight.

"What can I do for you, Marshal?" Sarah asked.

"Jack Kilpatrick said you and he were involved in an altercation out on the river bottom yesterday," Courtright said, twirling one end of his mustache. "Can you tell me what happened?"

"I'm sure Mr. Kilpatrick informed you about Mr. Cameron, didn't he?" Sarah asked to gain time to think about what she would say.

"He did," Courtright responded. "Jack said Cameron accosted you on the road for some reason. He happened to come along just as Cameron was drawing a gun. He had to shoot him."

"Yes," Sarah said thinking rapidly. The marshal hadn't mentioned that she held a gun on Cameron. Perhaps Kilpatrick didn't tell him.

"That's the way it happened," she said.

"Why were you on that road, Mrs. Whitman?" Courtright asked as he stared into Sarah's eyes.

"Someone told me the Cameron girl did laundry," Sarah answered, returning the marshal's gaze.

"Long way to go for laundry," Courtright said. "We have several places here in town. In fact, there's one right next to this hotel."

When Sarah didn't react, Courtright continued, "You were going out to see Sludge, weren't you?"

Sarah took a deep breath before responding, "Yes, I was going to see him. I wanted to ask him about my husband."

"I see," Courtright said as he pushed his hat up on his forehead and leaned back in his chair. "Did you learn anything?"

"No," Sarah said truthfully. "We met on the road. It was raining quite hard. We were just starting a conversation when Mr. Kilpatrick came along. Then he shot Cameron. It all happened so fast."

"I'm sure it did," Courtright said. "So Jack rode up as you two were talking. When he did, Cameron pulled a gun and Jack shot him. Is that the way you see it?"

Sarah noticed that Courtright leaned forward to scrutinize her, and she answered carefully, "Yes. That's about it."

"And the Cameron girl?" Courtright asked. "I understand you brought her to the hotel with you?"

"Yes, she's now at Dr. Hinton's office," Sarah said. "She was badly hurt. Her father abused her terribly. And you peace officers let it happen."

Courtright held up his hand with his palm turned to Sarah as he responded, "We certainly should have arrested that scoundrel a long time ago. It was the sheriff's jurisdiction."

"Are you avoiding your responsibility, Marshal?" Sarah said, continuing her attack.

"No," Courtright said while he nervously twisted his mustache. He seemed to have lost his confidence in the face of Sarah's accusations.

Reaching into his vest pocket, Courtright pulled out a silver coin and showed it to Sarah. "Jack found this on Cameron," he said. "He'd been broke for a week or so. Don't know where he got this. Could it belong to you?"

"Yes," Sarah said. Then, realizing she might have made a mistake in claiming the coin, she went on, "I gave it to Annie Cameron to do my laundry."

"I see," Courtright said. "If you gave this to the girl, then you must have gone to the house before the altercation with Cameron?"

"Yes," Sarah said. "I did go to the house, but I didn't see Mr. Cameron there. Just the girl. I gave her that dollar to do my laundry. Then I left. That's when I met Cameron on the road."

"Expensive laundry," Courtright commented. Holding the coin up, he said, "This is an 1838 Gobrecht silver dollar."

"Why are you telling me this?" Sarah asked.

"Kilpatrick is investigating the robbery of a large amount of government gold and silver."

"Are you accusing me of stealing that money, Marshal?" Sarah asked sharply.

"No," Courtright said with a thin-lipped smile. "Just thought you might like to know all the silver coins in that shipment were '71 and '72 Liberty Seated dollars."

"Thank you for the information," Sarah said. "Is that all you wish to discuss with me?"

Ignoring the question, Courtright said, "I can understand you wanting to find out about your husband, but it costs quite a sum to come up here from Waco and stay in a hotel. Stage, room, meals, and whatever for three people. Most ranchers don't have two coins to rub together. How did you come by enough money for this trip?"

"Jim and I have run that ranch for nearly twelve years now," Sarah said confidently. "We have several hundred head of horses. Over time, we've sold a lot of stock in Waco and to local ranchers and farmers. We are frugal people. Our wants are few, and we've set aside some cash. I have the sales receipts at my ranch if you care to look at them."

"I don't," Courtright said. "But Jack may want to. You must know by now he has suspicions about you."

"And you Marshal?"

Again, Courtright ignored Sarah's question. Looking into her eyes, he said, "Now that Cameron is dead, there's no reason for you to stay here is there?"

"Are you telling me to get out of town?"

"No," Courtright said, standing and tugging at the brim of his hat. "Take all the time you need."

As Sarah stood, a woman wearing a long, flowing pink dress walked by. She was carrying a white parasol with a pink ribbon tied to the top. Sarah followed her progress to one of the dining table. Suddenly, she remembered the object she had seen on the bush off the road to Cameron's shack.

"Are you all right, Mrs. Whitman?" Courtright said. "You look like someone just walked over your grave."

"Yes," Sarah said, touching her hair. "I'm fine. Just fine. Too much tea so early in the day, perhaps. Good day, Marshal."

Without waiting for a response, Sarah walked past Courtright. She could sense him staring at her as she went up the stairs. Her thoughts swirled around in her head. Could she really have seen a pink object out in the woods? She knew she would have to talk to Rose very soon.

Chapter 13

▼

The residual rain from the previous day's storm shimmered on the fields in the late morning sun as Sarah and Rose started down the incline from the top of the bluff to the river bottom. They were riding in Rose's carriage, which was pulled by a pair of white horses and driven by an elderly black man attired in a dark blue uniform with a stovepipe hat covering his white, closely cropped hair. Sarah was dressed in a dark full-length woolen skirt and a long-sleeve blouse buttoned at her throat. Recalling the sudden shower of the day before, she had donned a wide-brimmed hat and carried with her a long coat and a shawl. Rose, dressed more sedately than usual, wore a long, gray, high-necked dress without the normal opening over her breasts. Her shoulders were covered with a white shawl, and her only jewelry consisted of several rings on her fingers and a large mother-of-pearl brooch pinned to her bodice.

"It could have been something else," Sarah said as she looked at Rose with concern.

"You said it was pink?" Rose asked quietly.

"Yes, it certainly appeared to be," Sarah said. "Of course, it was raining pretty hard. I could have been mistaken."

Several field hands at the Hudson Plantation shouted and waved at their carriage as they passed. Rose ignored their greetings and stared straight ahead past the driver. "Oh, Sarah," she said. "I'm so afraid we'll find her out here, lying in the woods. Poor Little Lu."

"Perhaps we better turn around and go back to town," Sarah said. "I don't think you're up to this. I'll tell the sheriff what I saw and let him take a look."

"No," Rose said. "If she's out here, I want to be the one to find her. I'll be all right. Just stay beside me."

"I will," Sarah said, placing her hand on Rose's shoulder.

They rode on in silence for several minutes. The only sounds came from the far off murmur of the river, the dim shouts of the field hands behind them, and the clip clop of the horses' hoofs on the dirt road.

Sarah pointed to the left of the road and said, "It's just past that small creek ahead."

"Thomas," Rose said loudly. "Stop on the other side."

"Yes'm," Thomas said without turning his head.

When they stopped, Sarah stepped to the ground while Thomas assisted Rose. Looking up the small trail she had seen before, she took a moment to gain her bearings, and then she walked to a large bush near the edge of the stream. "I'm pretty sure this was where I saw it," she said when Rose joined her.

"What did it look like?" Rose asked. "Was it a dress or a hat? Little Lu even wore pink hats."

"No," Sarah said as she knelt by the bush. "It was smaller than that. More like a ribbon."

One of the branches had been broken off and lay on the ground. The storm could have caused that, Sarah thought. The gusts were very strong at times. The ground showed no evidence that anyone had been there recently.

Standing, she said, "It's gone now. The wind may have blown it away."

Looking up the trail to where it disappeared into the overgrown underbrush, she felt a strange foreboding. Turning to Rose, she asked, "Are you sure you're up to this? Should we search up there?"

"Yes, honey," Rose said as she started toward the end of the pathway. "We haven't come this far to turn back now."

Sarah caught up with Rose as she was pushing the brush aside to go further up the trail. The creek, back to a gentle, burbling flow after the heavy rain, widened out as it flowed over rocks, pebbles, and brush roots. A small turtle, frightened by their approach, scrambled into the water and submerged. Overhead the trees blocked the direct sun, only allowing thin shafts of dancing beams to penetrate the shadowy glen. Wind rustled through the branches and dislodged dying leaves, which fluttered through the air like red, brown, and orange butterflies. When they struck the ground, already covered with foliage, they made tinkling sounds like tiny hailstones falling on a newly mown field.

Suddenly, the clear, fall air became contaminated with an oppressive odor. A few steps ahead, Rose stood looking down at the ground. As she approached,

Sarah could see Rose's large shoulders shake and hear her sobbing. Stepping up to her side, she looked down at the partially buried body of a young woman: a dark haired woman dressed in a low-cut pink dress.

The recent storm had washed the topsoil and leaves from her head and torso leaving her lower limbs still covered. Her young, almost childlike, face was white and bloodless and appeared unmarked. But a gaping wound across her throat gave evidence to the violence that had taken her life. Whoever had put her in the shallow grave had placed her hands on top of each other on her chest, as if the act of tenderness would somehow atone for causing her death.

Sarah held Rose while she cried uncontrollably. "I am so sorry," she said. "Come now, let's go back to town and let the sheriff know what we found."

Rose stared down at the body for a long time, tears streaking her rouged cheeks. Finally, she said, "Poor Little Lu. She was like a tiny flower. So pretty and fragile. She wouldn't hurt a thing."

"We'll pray for her," Sarah said quietly.

"Pray?" Rose rasped. "Why would God let this happen to an innocent child like her?"

"I know it's difficult to accept at a time like this," Sarah said. "But there is a purpose for everything. Perhaps God wanted to call her home to be with Him now."

Rose started crying again. After she composed herself, she looked down at the body once more. When she did, she gasped.

"What is it?" Sarah asked.

"Look!" Rose exclaimed as she pointed at the dead woman's chest.

There, stuck in the cleft of her small breasts, partially covered by dirt and leaves, were the faded remnants of a flower, a yellow rose.

The law office of W. A. Thompson was on the corner of First and Main Streets. As Sarah walked up to the door, she could hear the sounds of construction at the courthouse nearby. It was a rare fall afternoon, with sunny skies and balmy temperatures. The promise of winter, with its driving snow and bone chilling temperatures, seemed remote. A false sense of the perfection of nature exhilarated her and strengthened her for the task ahead.

When she opened the door, the tinkle of a bell mounted on the jamb announced her arrival. The entry room was small, consisting of a settee and a straight-backed chair to the right and a row of file cabinets fronted by a desk to the left. Across the back of the narrow room was a closed door leading to another area. The stale, dank odor of cigar and pipe tobacco permeated the area. A young man, dressed in a black suit and wearing a thin tie, glanced up at Sarah with soft, welcoming eyes set back above his pink, chubby cheeks. His hair was cropped closely over his ears, and he had the eager, fresh-faced look of a new bank employee wishing to please the customers.

Rising to his feet, he nodded his head and said, "Good day, Ma'am. How may I be of service?" His voice was high pitched and subservient.

"Mr. Thompson?" Sarah asked.

"No," the man laughed, wind snorting out of his nose like a horse blowing on a cold day. "Mr. Thompson is in his office. I'm his law clerk and assistant. My name is Ben Clanton."

"I am Mrs. Whitman," Sarah said. "I would like to speak with Mr. Thompson, please."

"Oh," Clanton said as he wrung his hands in embarrassment. "I'm afraid Mr. Thompson is quite busy at the moment. Perhaps you would like to make an appointment to see him at a later date."

The sound of someone hitting the wall in the back room caused Clanton to gasp. Turning toward the noise, he exclaimed, "Oh, dear me!"

When the sound repeated itself, louder this time, Sarah said, "Don't you think you should see what is happening?"

"Oh, dear me!" Clanton said again. "Do you think I should?"

"Is someone with Mr. Thompson?" Sarah asked.

"Well, no, but—"

"You should see what that noise is. He may be suffering from a seizure or something."

Clanton sprang into action. Rushing to the door, he flung it open. Gasping in surprise, he stepped back, which opened the view into the room to Sarah.

A huge mound of a man was sitting on the floor in front of a large desk. His legs were splayed out in front of him, and he was drinking from a bottle held aloft in his massive hand, large as a slab of beef. Wearing a black, pinstripe suit with a starched-collar white shirt, his tie was pulled loose and to one side in defiance of any decorum. His large rubbery lips were wrapped around the neck of the bottle sucking noisily at its amber colored contents.

After he drained the last drops from the glass container, he threw it against the wall where it clattered without breaking and bounced back onto the floor at his feet. Belching noisily, he looked up at Sarah and Clanton with a bleary look.

"What the hell do you want?" the man roared in a rumbling bass voice that sounded like it came from the bottom of an empty barrel. "Haven't you seen anyone take a drink before?"

"Oh dear, Uncle William," Clanton squealed as he tried to help the huge man to his feet.

After a struggle, he finally succeeded. Thompson teetered unsteadily on his feet, and he would have fallen if Sarah hadn't taken hold of his arm. With Clanton's aid, she steered him around his desk and helped him plop down in his wooden office chair.

"Goddamn, who the hell are you?" Thompson asked Sarah in a slurring voice, as he peered at her under massive, snow-white eyebrows, which matched his long unkempt hair.

"I'll thank you to not take the Lord's name in vain," Sarah said sharply.

"What … what the hell," Thompson moaned through bubbles forming on his lips.

"You, sir, are drunk," Sarah admonished.

"What the hell time is it?" Thompson demanded as he looked at Clanton.

"Why … it's about half past two."

"There," Thompson said with a triumphant smile as he eyed Sarah. "I can not be drunk. I never get drunk until after dark, except in the middle of summer, of course. Since it is not dark, and it is not summer, I cannot be drunk, Madam."

Turning to Clanton, he added, "How do you like that logic, Ben? Don't you think the jury would return a verdict of not guilty … or not drunk, to you, Madam whoever the hell you are?"

"My name is Sarah Whitman," Sarah said with a raised voice. "I came here to talk to Mr. Hedding's attorney. Instead I find a foul mouthed drunk hiding behind a bottle."

"Oh dear!" Clanton exclaimed as he backed out of the office to get away from the confrontation.

"I'll have you know—" Thompson ran out of words temporarily.

After staring balefully at Sarah under his heavy eyelids for a moment, he continued, "Heddings, you say. Little shit's got himself into quite a pickle, I'd say. Or his pickle's got him into quite a shit."

"I will say he made a very poor choice in an attorney to represent him," Sarah retorted.

"Now hold on," Thompson said after a gut-wrenching belch that spewed alcohol and tobacco fumes all over Sarah. "Get that burr out from under your saddle."

Waving at several certificates mounted on the wall, he continued, "I'll have you know I was awarded a doctor of jurisprudence from none other than the great state of Missouri."

"It surprises me you were able to stay sober long enough to graduate," Sarah said. "Are you sure the certificate isn't for a doctor of inebriation?"

"You are spirited," Thompson replied. "I like that in a horse or a woman."

"I am not a horse," Sarah said. "And I don't like you or your sinful habits."

"I concede the first round to you," Thompson said as he wiped his lips with the back of his hand.

At that moment, Clanton entered with a steaming cup of coffee. Placing it on the desk, he quickly vacated the room.

Thompson picked up the cup and, with one long draught, nearly drained it. Belching again, he focused his eyes at Sarah and said, "Heddings you say? Don't think the little shit had much choice in a counselor. Nobody likes a whore killer. I only took him on because we shared a bottle now and then. After dark, mind you. Or was it because the county attorney told me I had to represent him? No matter. What did you say your name is?"

"Mrs. Sarah Whitman," Sarah said. "And I will thank you to refer to your client as Mr. Heddings. You are showing your lack of class by using descriptions of bodily functions that are best kept private."

Thompson sat up in his chair and shook his massive head. Glowering at Sarah, he said, "You have a mouth like my grandmother, Mrs. Whitman. No one has taken me to task like this since she died, God rest her soul."

"It has been entirely too long a time. If you are going to represent Mr. Heddings, I expect you to clean up your language." Sarah leaned over Thompson's desk and continued firmly, "Because I will not tolerate it."

"Sit down," Thompson said waving at a chair in front of his desk. "You don't need to shout," he whined.

Sarah sat down and asked, "What evidence is there that Mr. Heddings committed this crime?"

Thompson shook his head as if to solidify his thoughts. Then picking up a stack of papers on his desk, he scanned them before answering. "He was seen at the Red Bull Saloon the night Little Lu, Lucille Martell, disappeared. Quite drunk he was."

Thompson glanced up and added quickly, "Not drinking with me. I was in Dallas at the time."

"That's not very solid evidence," Sarah said. "He shouldn't be arrested for just being there that night."

"Now hold on," Thompson said. "There's more. Someone saw him with the whore after she left the saloon."

"Mr. Thompson," Sarah said. "I'll thank you to not refer to the poor girl by that name."

"What ... what name? Lucille Martell?"

"That is her name, but please do not call her a whore. That is a low-class choice of a word."

"But that's what she was," Thompson said raising his eyebrows. "She was a whore."

"You will be representing Mr. Heddings in a court of law," Sarah said. "It will be to his benefit for you to rise above the street level. I'm sure he will expect you to conduct yourself accordingly."

Thompson's chest rumbled with laughter as he said, "Old C. W. said about the same thing. He calls them 'ladies of the night.' Little rooster'd get upset if anyone called them whores."

Sarah stood up and, leaning forward, placed her hands on Thompson's desk. "I can see you are no better than the gutter where you find your liquor. I fear for Mr. Heddings' fate if it must rest in your hands. I assume that at one time in your life, you read the Bible. You may recall the story about a woman who had committed adultery. When she was brought before Jesus for judgment, he said, 'He that is without sin among you, let him first cast a stone at her.'"

"Now calm down," Thompson said, as he fell back in his chair defensively. "I don't want to cast no stones. I assure you I'm concerned about C. W. too. Only problem is the evidence the sheriff has is going to get him strung up."

"You're his attorney, you shouldn't judge his guilt or innocence," Sarah said. "That's for the court to decide. You haven't given me any evidence that would convince me of his guilt."

"The sheriff has the murder weapon," Thompson said.

"He does? Where did he find it?"

"In C. W.'s newspaper office," Thompson replied. "He found a knife in a desk with blood on it."

Sarah slumped back in the chair. When she was first told that Clarence had been arrested for Little Lu's murder, she couldn't believe it. Although she had only met the man one time, it was hard to accept that a gentle soul like him could commit an act of such unspeakable violence. Rose had agreed with her, and it was at Rose's urging that she had visited Thompson to see if they could help Clarence.

"Can I speak with Mr. Heddings?" Sarah asked.

"If the sheriff will let you," Thompson said. "You have to go to the county jail. It's a temporary one over on Second Street. He might be a little skittish about visitors."

"Why?" Sarah asked.

"We have a lot of riff raff in town. Some even permanent folks. They don't take kindly to killing a member of the gentler sex. There's been talk of a lynching."

"Lynching! Surely the sheriff and the marshal won't allow that?"

"This town isn't far removed from frontier justice," Thompson said. "The notion of courts and attorneys and judges don't set well with many. They'd rather have a quick necktie party and get it over with, fit and proper."

"Fit and proper!" Sarah snapped. "What if the man is innocent? That's what a trial is for."

"As a member of the legal profession, I agree with you," Thompson said. "I'm afraid little C. W. has already been found guilty by the folks out there. He's not very popular with the men. Most think he's too much of a dandy. And he comes on to their wives; giving them flowers and such."

After another noisy belch, he went on, "If you get to see him, tell him I'll be over to chat with him this later this morning."

"It's past morning, Mr. Thompson," Sarah said as she rose abruptly from the chair. "It's the middle of the afternoon."

"I'll be damned," Thompson said as he attempted to rise. But the effort proved too difficult for him, and he plopped back into his seat.

"You just might be if you don't mend your ways," Sarah said. "Good day."

As she left the office, she heard the sound of a drawer opening and the clink of a bottle behind her. When she passed Clanton's desk, he stood up looked at her respectfully.

"Good day, Mrs. Whitman," he said. "If there's anything I can do to be of service, please ask."

"You can wean your uncle from that bottle, young man," Sarah said as she walked to the door. "Before it kills him."

Chapter 14

▼

Before the deputy sheriff would let Sarah in the back room where the cells were, he searched her handbag. Then, looking bashfully at her clothes, he asked, "You're not carrying a weapon on you, are you, Ma'am?"

Another deputy, leaning back in a chair with his feet on his desk, looked bemusedly at his companion and said, "Ain't you goin' to search her, Randy? You know what the sheriff says about visitors."

"Why don't you search her, Willis, dag nab it," Randy, a swarthy young man with a large wad of tobacco in his jaw, responded in consternation.

"Not my job," responded Willis, an elderly round, mound of a man without a hair on his head. "You're the one lettin' her back there."

"Gentlemen," Sarah said. "I give you my word. I am not carrying a weapon of any kind. I'm a friend of Mr. Heddings. I came to talk to him."

"Hell, Randy," Willis said. "Let her see him. Just stay with her."

"Do I have to?" Randy whined. "I can't stand being around that man. I don't understand anything he says. And he never shuts up."

"If'n you don't want Sheriff Roberts to get his tail on fire, you'd best go along," Willis said. "Besides, he'll be talkin' to the lady, not you. Give her ten minutes."

After Randy opened the door, he stood aside so Sarah could enter the back room. The stench of human waste overpowered her. There were four cells, two on each side of the aisle. They consisted of two metal bunk beds, small barred windows set high in the brick wall, and front bars from floor to ceiling enclosing narrow doors, also barred. The dim light, coupled with a terrible odor, immediately depressed Sarah.

"Do you ever clean up this place?" Sarah asked Randy. Wrinkling her nose, she looked around for sign of life.

"Well, Ma'am," Randy answered proudly. "We empty the buckets twice a day."

Movement in the far cell on the left caught Sarah's attention. A splotch of white in the near darkness moved toward her.

"Dear heart," Clarence said as he reached one hand through the bars and waved a limp wrist at Sarah. His other hand clutched a handkerchief to his nose. A yellow rose, which appeared as wilted as his spirit, protruded from a buttonhole in his lapel.

Sarah stepped forward and stood in front of him. "Clarence," she said. "I can't believe you are in here."

"A mistake of tragic proportion, I assure you," Clarence said, his squeaky voice more subdued than normal.

He was dressed in a white suit with black trim around the lapels and cuffs. A pale blue shirt with a ruffled front, a black cummerbund, and highly polished black shoes completed his attire. Sarah thought that his clothing seemed more suited for a formal ball than a filthy, ill-lit jail cell.

"Rose and I are concerned," Sarah said. "Is there anything we can do for you?"

"Ah, dear heart," Clarence replied with a grin on his face. "Just to know such fine women are thinking of my travails girds my loins and puts strength in my sword arm. The enemy shall shrink before our combined might. Tis not—"

Sarah interrupted him, "We only have ten minutes, Clarence. Is there anything you need?"

"Twice the orb has turned, since I was taken bodily from my abode. A warm bath with lavender water, freshly pressed accouterments, a bottle of my Cologne de Paree, and an elixir of the gods would send me into ecstasy. Lord, what fools these mortals be. The worthless wastrels running this reprehensible establishment do not understand that a gentleman of the first order requires daily bathing and a change of clothing to be presentable."

In spite of herself, Sarah smiled. "I'll speak to the sheriff about getting you a bath and a change of clothes," she said.

"Oh, my heart will be grateful," Clarence said as he bounced up and down on his toes in joy.

Sarah glanced at the deputy leaning against the door trying to look disinterested before she turned back to Clarence and said, "I just spoke with your attorney, Mr. Thompson."

"I asked not for a solicitor," Clarence said. "I have the faculties to determine my own fate. But, alas, yon gendarme foisted the sot upon me."

"I must be honest," Sarah interjected. "There is a lot of evidence against you."

"Done to death by a slanderous tongue," Clarence emoted in a raised voice. "My heart is pure. The sight of me with the young damsel is not proof of guilt. How—"

"Didn't Thompson tell you they found a knife in your office?" Sarah interrupted again.

"Nay, forsooth," Clarence said quietly. His body shed some of its vibrancy, and he slumped against the bars.

Sarah wondered why Clarence hadn't been notified of the incriminating evidence against him. "Sheriff Roberts found a knife in your desk," she said. "A knife with blood on it."

"Something is rotten in the state of Denmark," Clarence said with a smile, regaining some of his energy. Holding up the middle finger of his left hand, he thrust it toward Sarah. "Look, dear heart. I have suffered a dagger's thrust."

Sarah looked closer and, even in the subdued light, she could see evidence of a cut, still scabbed over, on Clarence's finger. "How did you do that?" she asked.

"Opening a missive from my dear and precious sister," Clarence answered. "Not a fortnight past."

"You mean you cut your finger while opening a letter?"

"Yes," Clarence responded.

Fluttering his fingers in front of him, he added, "I disdain soiling my digits with the paste. Therefore, I use an instrument better suited for such a mundane task."

"What did you do with the knife after you cut your finger?" Sarah asked.

"I cast it aside with impunity."

"Did you tell the sheriff about cutting yourself?"

"Nay," Clarence answered.

"Have you told Thompson?" Sarah persisted.

Clarence replied blithely, "I have had no congress with him when he was not in his cups."

The deputy, standing at the door, cleared his throat and said, "Your time is up, Mrs. Whitman. I must ask you to leave now."

Clarence handed Sarah a piece of paper through the bars. "Please," he said. "Be so kind as to convey this editorial to Stubby Johnson, my illustrious printer, for tomorrow's edition. We must not disappoint our readers who are thirsty for the nectar of my words."

As Sarah took the sheet, she said, "Be of good cheer, Clarence. I'll speak to the sheriff and Mr. Thompson about what you told me. And I'll bring you a change of clothes."

"Farewell, dear heart," Clarence said as he put his hand over his chest. "Parting is such sweet sorrow. Till we meet again."

After leaving the jail, Sarah returned to Thompson's office. Finding him snoring loudly in his office, she decided not to disturb him. At her request, Ben Clanton gave her a quick primer in state law as it applied to prisoner care. When she left the office, she was carrying a large legal book.

At Sarah's summons, Rose came to her hotel room. She brought Rose up to date on the case against Clarence. She also expressed her concerns about his well-being and his chance of getting adequate representation from William Thompson. Then Sarah made a request of her, which Rose readily and cheerfully accepted.

When Sarah entered Sheriff Roberts' office later, he stood up and greeted her warmly. They had spoken several times during the sheriff's investigation into the murder of Lucille Martell. He was a small, sallow-faced man with a large, drooping mustache. Dressed in a black suit with a white shirt and a black string tie, he reminded Sarah of an undertaker she had met in Waco.

Rose didn't think much of the sheriff, and her sessions with him about Lucille had been adversarial. She told Sarah that she thought he was as crooked as the middle fork of the Trinity River. He owned a large cattle ranch north of town that was growing entirely too fast for a county employee making sixty dollars a month. Rose expressed her concern that he would rush Clarence to trial, so he could get himself in front of the public prior to his upcoming re-election campaign.

"Mrs. Whitman," Roberts said. "What can I do for you? How is our illustrious Mr. Heddings today?"

Sarah placed the large tome she was carrying on her lap and sat in a chair across from him. He eyed the book quizzically but didn't say anything.

"I'll discuss that later, Sheriff," Sarah said. "Are you aware he has a scar on his finger where he cut himself less than two weeks ago?"

"No," Roberts answered. "Don't know about that. Don't know what difference it makes."

"Difference! Why it may mean that he's innocent, and you jailed the wrong person. He said the knife you found was the one he uses to open letters."

"Harrumph," the sheriff snorted. "Likely story."

"Don't you think you should interview him and record his statement?" Sarah asked indignantly.

Roberts leaned back and glanced at the ceiling for a moment, to show his disinterest. Then, sitting up straight, he looked at Sarah through narrowed eyes. "The man was seen with the whore at the time she disappeared, Mrs. Whitman," he said curtly. "The corpse was adorned with one of his yellow roses. And we found a knife in his office with his blood on it. I think we have enough evidence to satisfy the good citizens of this county of his guilt."

Frustrated, Sarah took a deep breath before responding, "If there is any possibility Mr. Heddings is innocent, you must continue the investigation. We may have a murderer loose on the streets."

"Thank you for your concern," Roberts said through his tight lips. "I am well aware of my duty to this county. I don't need you to tell me how to do my job." He turned away from Sarah and started to rise from his chair.

Sarah slammed the legal volume she was holding on the sheriff's desk and turned it so the lettering on the spine faced him. "Do you know what this is?" she asked.

After leaning forward and squinting at the book, the sheriff sat back in his chair and said cautiously, "It looks like a law book."

"It is," Sarah said. "It's the rules and requirements for the conduct of county and state officials in charge of jails and prisons, as approved by the Texas state legislature."

Roberts swallowed quickly and remained silent. His partially closed eyes looked warily at Sarah.

Sarah opened the book to a page marked with a sheet of paper. Sliding it around toward her, she read, "The duly appointed or elected officials supervising places of incarceration are charged with the responsibility of providing for the health and welfare of said inmates."

Looking up, Sarah said, "I believe that identifies you, Sheriff. You are responsible for the health and welfare of the inmates in your jail. Am I not correct?"

"Are you an attorney, Mrs. Whitman?" Roberts asked with a snide smile.

"You know women are not allowed to attend institutions of higher learning to study law in this country," Sarah said.

Roberts leaned back with a smug look on his face, as if he had made his point.

Sarah continued, "I am here as a citizen of this state who is concerned about the poor treatment Mr. Heddings is receiving under your supervision."

"Poor treatment? Hell, he's a damn prisoner accused of murder."

Sarah motioned at the book, "Nowhere in this directive does it make reference to the reason for incarceration. The humane treatment of inmates is not based on the severity of their crime. Or in the case of Mr. Heddings, the charges filed against him."

When Roberts did not respond, Sarah extracted a piece of paper from her purse. She unfolded it and placed it beside the law book.

Roberts stared at it for a moment before asking, "What's that?"

"A letter addressed to the governor of Texas."

"To the governor?" Roberts said as he squirmed in his seat. "What's in it?"

"It is a description of the deplorable conditions you have allowed to exist in your jail," Sarah said. "And a request for your removal from office as unfit to serve. I understand that one of your prisoners died last winter because of your dereliction of duty."

"Hell, he weren't nothing but a damn Mexican."

"A man under your care died of pneumonia because you failed to adequately heat the jail," Sarah said continuing her attack.

Roberts blew bubbles of frustration past his shaggy mustache, as he searched for a response.

"In addition to this letter going to the governor," Sarah went on before the sheriff could form his thoughts into words, "a copy will be published in the *Fort Worth Beacon* and distributed widely throughout the county."

With the election just over a month away, Sarah knew the sheriff didn't want any adverse publicity. She had heard that he was facing stiff competition from the owner of the largest gristmill in the area, who was also the minister of a local Methodist Church.

"You can't do that," Roberts finally spit out.

"I can," Sarah said. "And I will, unless—"

"Unless what?" Roberts said as a glimmer of hope came into his eyes.

Sarah took another sheet of paper from her purse and placed it in front of the sheriff. "Unless you agree to these conditions," she said.

Roberts picked up the paper and peered closely at it. As he read, he blurted aloud, "Statement from defendant for record ... daily cleaning of cells ... outdoors exercise ... three hot meals each day."

Jabbing his finger at the paper, he exclaimed, "What the hell is this? I can't approve such balderdash."

"I think you can," Sarah said, picking up the law book and leaving the letter on the desk.

"Good day," she said as she left the office. Behind her, she could hear the sheriff fussing and fuming as he read her list of requirements.

When Rose's valet, Thomas, and his son, George, clad in matching red and black uniforms with top hats perched on their heads, pulled a wagon into the alley beside the Red Bull Saloon and began loading a large item covered with a sheet, no one observed their activity. But when they stopped at the *Fort Worth Beacon* office a few minutes later, several people gathered on the sidewalk to watch as they disappeared into the building only to reappear moments later carrying a bundle and a valise. Others joined those curious onlookers as the two elegantly dressed men stopped briefly at Sadie's Café to pick up several items in paper sacks.

By the time Thomas and George arrived at the county jail, word of their strange behavior had spread like wildfire throughout downtown Fort Worth, and a throng of bystanders, buzzing like a colony of bees in a flower garden, crowded the sidewalk and spilled out into the street. The sheriff was conspicuously absent as the two men uncovered a large object in the bed of the wagon and lifted it to the ground. Oohs, ahs, and laughter spread through the crowd as they realized what it was: an ornate bathtub painted white and decorated around the edges with red and blue flowers. Steam emanated into the cool afternoon air as Thomas and George carried it into the jailhouse.

George soon returned to the wagon, and he removed the articles from the paper sacks acquired from Sadie. Folding a white towel over one arm, he picked up a glass and a corked bottle in one hand and a round, covered metal tray in the other. Carrying the tray aloft like a waiter in an expensive restaurant, he disappeared quietly into the building.

After several minutes, he returned to the wagon again. This time, he opened a bundle and extracted a suit of clothes draped over a hanger. Grasping the valise in his free hand, he re-entered the jail.

After a period of time, during which the crowd outside the jail increased in size and merriment, Thomas and George appeared carrying the washtub. Shooing back those onlookers standing next to the sidewalk, they poured the soapy water from the tub into the dust of the street, and then placed it in the wagon bed. They made one more trip inside to get the serving tray and several other items before climbing aboard. Sitting up straight and silent, they rode away down the street. The murmur from the group of bystanders faded into the distance behind them like the raucous chatter of a flock of chickens.

Chapter 15

▼

When Sarah entered the hotel room, she stopped abruptly at the sight of Daniel sitting on the floor and strumming his guitar. Margaret, on a chair nearby, stared at him rapturously while Jody clapped his hands in rhythm with the tune.

"Oh, Mrs. Whitman," Daniel said as he rose awkwardly to his feet.

"That's okay, Daniel," Sarah responded, closing the door behind her.

Looking at Margaret, she said, "I'm sorry I'm so late."

"Daniel was entertaining us," Margaret said.

"Mama," Jody said as he jumped up and down on the bed. "Daniel is teaching me to play his guitar."

"That's wonderful," Sarah said.

Turning to Daniel, she added, "You have a fine ear for music."

"Thank you," Daniel said. "My mother was from Virginia. When she came west to marry my father, she brought her piano with her. I would sit on her lap and listen to her play."

"Do you play the piano?" Margaret asked.

"Yes," Daniel answered. "My mother taught me to read sheet music and play."

"She sounds like a wonderful person," Sarah said. "You must be very proud of her?"

"I am," Daniel said with a self-conscious shrug.

"Margaret," Sarah said. "I have something I need to do here. Would you mind going down to dinner without me?"

"Not at all," Margaret said. "Can I help you?"

"No," Sarah answered. "I'm going to edit an article for a newspaper."

"Wow!" Margaret said. "I'm impressed."

"Oh, it's not much," Sarah responded. "I told you about Mr. Heddings being in jail. He gave me an editorial for his paper. But I think it needs some work. Now, you all go down and eat."

Margaret paused at the door and looked back at her mother. "I need to talk to you later," she said with a concerned look on her face. Then she smiled and added, "Can I bring you something from the dining room?"

"Thank you," Sarah said. "I've been eating entirely too much since we came here. Perhaps a piece of pie would be nice."

When the door closed, Sarah wondered what Margaret might have to say to her. Hopefully, she wasn't getting too serious about Daniel.

After reading the editorial Clarence had given her several times, she decided it would only cause him greater harm if it was published now. Since he was in jail, his newspaper would be more widely read than before. And, she mused with a smile on her face, after this afternoon's spectacle at the jail, he will be quite a celebrity. His article was filled with his usual outrageous rhetoric, spiced with numerous Shakespeare quotes. But it was the message conveyed by the writing that concerned her most. Instead of protesting his innocence and stating his case in clear terms, he railed against the gods of fate and the local law enforcement officers, who had arrested and jailed him. Sarah could just imagine what the reception would be in the saloons, dance halls, businesses, and bedrooms in the area. Like a pack of wild dogs thirsting for blood, those who were in favor of lynching him would, almost certainly, pick up additional supporters.

As she recalled her conversations with Clarence's attorney, William Thompson, and Sheriff Roberts, she felt certain that they would not look out for his best interests. They would go through the motions of parading him before a court of law but, in the end, she was afraid that he would die for the murder of Little Lu.

Kneeling by the bed and closing her eyes, Sarah prayed for Clarence. She asked God to touch those who held his life in their hands, to give them wisdom and compassion. She recalled the many times her father had prayed with her. "Don't be afraid to ask for the Lord's help," he often said. "We mortals are not strong enough to carry the load we're asked to bear without divine assistance."

Rising, Sarah took Clarence's paper and sat at the small table near the window. An evening wind was blowing the white curtains into the room in a rhythmic motion. The scent of fall was in the air. The thought of Clarence, shining with life and color as he faced the grim harshness of his accusers, was depressing to her. It brought to her mind the onset of winter at her ranch: the trees stripped of their bright foliage leaving only their stark, denuded branches to face the snow and freezing rain. Somehow, she must find a way to help him through his winter of adversity.

She read through Clarence's editorial again. When she finished, she thought about a sermon her father had preached at a local church just before his disappearance. The regular pastor had been caught in a compromising position with one of his congregation, and he was forcibly ejected from the community. About the same time, a black field hand had been accused of molesting a young white girl. Without benefit of a trial, the man, who vehemently protested his innocence, was taken into the woods and hanged by the youngster's father and several other members of the church.

Preacher Parker had stayed up through the night, prior to the Sunday service, writing his sermon. When Sarah brought him coffee the next morning, he was on his knees praying, tears in his eyes.

Sarah remembered the powerful message he delivered, as if it had been yesterday. With pointing fingers and flashing eyes, he told the congregation, in no uncertain terms, that mankind, fraught with weaknesses, sinned against God when they violated any of the *Ten Commandments*, as the pastor had done when he committed adultery. Then, he turned to the pews where the men who had taken part in the lynching sat. He told them that they had violated not only God's commandment against murder, but also the lawful precepts of the Declaration of Independence and the Constitution of the United States. Those documents state that all men are created equal with the right to life, liberty, and the pursuit of happiness, and they provide for every citizen to have the right to a public trial by an impartial jury.

As Sarah reviewed her father's sermon in her mind, an idea for the newspaper article came to her. She knew that she had to walk a fine line between human rights and frontier justice. Many local citizens, and a large percentage of visitors to the city, still chafed under the rule of the Reconstructionists appointed by the Washington lawmakers. Rose had told her that the derogatory terms "Carpetbaggers" and "Copperheads" were still shouted in a whiskey fog around the saloons by the ex-Confederates. To them, the court system was just another form of Yankee imperialism implemented to keep southern sympathizers in line. And many thought that the edicts of the Bible were fine for women, children, and old men facing their final judgment, but they couldn't take the place of the gun and the rope, which dispensed swift, violent, and final justice.

When Sarah finished her article, she started to sign her name to it but stopped. She realized that books, magazines, and newspapers were written by men only. Women did not have the right to vote, hold public office, preach the Gospel, attain medical or legal degrees or, it seemed, write for the public. It wouldn't do Clarence any good to put something in the *Fort Worth Beacon* that no one would read. After some consideration, she wrote "S. Parker, Concerned Citizen" on the bottom of the page.

After Margaret and Jody returned from dinner, Sarah ate the pie they had brought to her and read to Jody before putting him to bed.

Then, with the oil lamp on the table providing light, Margaret read the piece her mother had written.

"Oh," she said quietly, "this is very good. Do you think it will help Clarence?"

"I hope so," Sarah responded with more confidence in her voice than she felt inside. "Please don't tell anyone I wrote this. I think it's best no one knows it was a woman."

"All they could talk about in the dining room was how he had murdered that … woman," Margaret said. "And you need to explain to Jody what the word 'whore' means."

"I will," Sarah said.

Then, dreading the response, Sarah asked, "What did you want to talk to me about?"

A frown descended on Margaret's beautiful face like a thin, gray veil. "While we were feeding Beelzebub this afternoon, I heard the sound of guns in the distance. Lots of shooting. When I asked Daniel about it, he got very serious and wouldn't tell me what was going on. He just said it was something he disagreed with. I could see he was upset, so I didn't push him. What do you think it was?"

"I certainly don't know," Sarah responded with relief. At least she didn't have to face a situation involving Daniel at the moment. "Where were the shots coming from?"

"You know the main road going east of town?" Margaret asked. "I think if you stayed on it instead of turning up the trail to Beelzebub's shack you'd come to the place where they came from."

"Perhaps it's a firing range the military uses for training," Sarah offered. "I saw a lot of soldiers in the fort the other day."

"If it was just a firing range, why did Daniel get so upset?" Margaret queried.

"I don't know. It is strange. Let's not worry about it tonight. That's what your grandfather's worry bag is for."

"Can I watch you put this worry in the bag?" Margaret said with a smile that brightened up her face and displaced the gray veil.

"No," Sarah said, also smiling. "If you watch, it will escape and run around the room all night. You won't get a wink of sleep for worrying about where the worry is."

Margaret yawned and said, "I'm too tired to do that. I trust you to take care of it."

After Margaret went to bed, Sarah took a book out of her purse that she had found in Clarence's room. By the flickering light of the lamp she began reading *Plays and Sonnets of William Shakespeare.*

When Sarah entered the *Fort Worth Beacon* office the next morning, it appeared to be vacant. Going to the counter, she peered into the area containing the printing press and Clarence's desk. Motes of dust floated like tiny, wandering insects in the golden shafts of sunlight streaming through the windows behind her. The odor of tobacco, ink, and cleaning fluids, combined with the floating dirt particles, irritated Sarah's nose.

She squeezed her nostrils to try to stop it, but a loud sneeze forced its way out, "Ah choo!"

The sound of chair legs hitting the floor, followed by a throaty hack and a clanging spit into an unseen spittoon, came from behind the printing press.

"I'm Sarah Whitman," Sarah said to whoever was stirring in the back. "I have an article for today's paper."

Then, feeling self-conscious about the noise she had made, she added, "I'm sorry about that sneeze. Are you Mr. Johnson?"

A thin, bony man wearing low-slung trousers held up by wide suspenders draped over long red underwear shuffled up to the counter. He squinted and shaded his eyes with his ink-stained hands as he stared at Sarah. His back was bowed so far forward that it thrust his head into a position where he stared down at the floor. For him to look Sarah in the eye, he had to crane his neck and peer up under his bushy white eyebrows and snowy hair like a shaggy dog looking up for a handout. He responded to Sarah's question as to his identity with a slight lifting of the left side of his lips and a squint of his eye on that side.

Sarah looked at him for a long moment, not knowing what to make of the strange man. She wondered if she should ask him his name again but thought better of it. Finally she asked, "Has today's paper been printed yet?"

The man responded by turning down the right side of his lips and closing his right eye at Sarah.

Exasperated by the lack of oral response, Sarah handed him the article she had written and said, "Mr. Heddings gave me an editorial at the jail for the paper. But after reading it, I thought it might do him harm. So I wrote something to replace it."

Even as she said it, Sarah felt uncomfortable. Perhaps, she thought, she was taking too much on herself to re-write something from the owner of the newspaper, even if she deemed it in his best interest. She hadn't given much consideration as to how Clarence would respond. After all, she had made the decision on her own to discard his editorial.

Snatching the paper from Sarah's hand, the contorted gnome returned his head to its natural position, with his neck parallel to the floor, and quickly scanned it. When he finished, he gawked tortuously up at her. Once again his left lip and eye rose, this time more prominently than before. Then he spun around and shuffled back to a table in front of the printing press. After one more accurate spit, which brought a resounding clang from the spittoon, he began laying out letters with dexterous fingers that danced over the type box like a classical musician over piano keys.

Sarah started to speak again, but she decided it wasn't worth the effort. She realized that she had been summarily dismissed, and she wasn't sure what to make of it. After standing at the counter for a long moment, she turned her back on the silent old man and went out the door.

Chapter 16

The afternoon sun, dimmed by low, gray clouds that held the promise of rain, was dipping into the western sky when Sarah left the hotel. She stopped at the livery stable and rented a carriage. Margaret's concern of the night before was on her mind. She couldn't understand why people shooting guns outside of the downtown area would upset Daniel. In addition to being a law officer, Sarah thought he was an honest and conscientious young man with fine Christian morals. If he was upset, there had to be a good reason.

Sarah decided to go by the jail and talk to Clarence about the newspaper article she had substituted for his editorial. The paper wouldn't be on the streets until early in the evening, and she didn't want him to read it before she discussed it with him.

When she pulled up in front of the jail, the sheriff was just leaving. As she stepped down from the carriage, he turned to her and said, "I hope you are satisfied, Mrs. Whitman."

"I don't know what you mean," Sarah responded with a smile.

"I have become the laughing stock of the city," Sheriff Roberts said. "Letting a prisoner eat brought-in food and have a change of clothes. And ..." Sheriff Roberts blustered. "And take a bath!"

"Why, Sheriff," Sarah said sweetly. "You are just looking out for the health and welfare of your assigned prisoners."

"Harrumph," Roberts said as he strode down the board sidewalk with his head lowered like a mad bull.

When Sarah entered the cell area, she noticed a distinct difference from her last visit. The odors, which had been overwhelming before, now were almost acceptable. The faint aroma of flowers emanated from Clarence's cell.

"Dear heart," Clarence said as he bounded up from his bed where he had been sitting. He was wearing a white suit with red stripes that made him look like an over-sized stick of candy. A fresh yellow rose peeked out of a buttonhole in his lapel.

"Hello," Sarah said with a smile at his boyish enthusiasm.

Bowing nearly to the floor, Clarence waved one hand across in front of his face and said, "Tis my honor. I thank you and Rose of Sharon for the remarkable repast, lovely lavation, and admirable accouterments."

"Clarence," Sarah said seriously. "I must tell you something."

Handing him the paper she had written, she continued, "I read your editorial, and I was concerned that it would inflame those people out there who believe you are guilty. I know it's not my place to interfere, but I want to help you. I wrote this and took it to the *Beacon*. Please read it and let me know what you think. It's not too late to put your article back in."

Clarence took the sheet to the window in his cell where a dim light poured through. After reading it, he returned to the bars at the front of the cell and extended his hand to Sarah.

"Be not afraid of greatness, dear heart," Clarence said with tears in his eyes. "This states my cause much better than ever I could."

"Thank you," Sarah said with relief. "I am concerned about your trial. I asked Sheriff Roberts to talk to you about the cut on your finger from the letter opener. I told him he should reopen the investigation."

"Dear heart," Clarence said as he bounced up and down. "With you beside me, my right arm is strong as the mighty wind."

"That may not be enough," Sarah said. "You're going to need a good attorney when you go to trial. Mr. Thompson is nothing but a drunk, as you know. I—"

"Fear not, dear heart," Clarence said. "Be of good cheer."

"I'll try," Sarah said as she turned and walked away; the burdens she had carried in with her still weighed heavily in her mind.

She wanted to help Clarence, but she didn't know what she could do. And the thought came to her that she shouldn't be spending so much time and energy on him. She had her own family and her own problems to be concerned about. She was sure that Sludge Cameron had murdered Jim for his money. Now that Cameron was dead, finding Jim's body would be nearly impossible. If he was buried in a shallow grave like Little Lu, someone might find him by chance. But she couldn't justify staying in Fort Worth for that. If he was found, Marshal Courtright or Sheriff Roberts could notify her at the ranch. And, of course, she had to consider Beelzebub. She couldn't leave him alone with Daniel.

Then something Jody said after he returned from the circus came to her, "Mama, does God make bears and lions?"

When she told him He did, Jody pursued his line of questioning, "If He does, why are they in cages? They don't look happy in there."

An image of the cages the animals were kept in came to her. Perhaps Daniel could find a cage to put Beelzebub in so they could take him home. She could pen him up in a corner of the barn until the quarantine period was over.

The thought of returning to her home on the Bosque River excited her. Separating Margaret and Daniel would be difficult; however Margaret was too young for an intense relationship. A separation might be best for both of them.

The air was chilled from a gusty north breeze when Sarah rode along the road leading east from the downtown area. She drew her blanket tightly around her legs and slowed the horse pulling the carriage to a walk to reduce the wind on her face. She could see the bluff of the hill above the river to her left, although she couldn't see the water. To the right, trees and brush obscured the landscape. The rustling of leaves and the ululation of the wind in the tops of the post oaks and elms, combined with the tittering of small birds and the rhythmic stepping of the horse, caught her attention and calmed her jumbled thoughts.

A few minutes after she passed the trail leading to Beelzebub's shack, Sarah heard a strange sound, which she couldn't identify. It started as a low, guttural moan, and then rose in volume and pitch until it screeched like a crosscut saw being sharpened. Suddenly it stopped, only to be repeated moments later. Sarah shivered and pulled her scarf up around her face and ears.

The main road turned to the left to follow the river, and a narrow path led to the right into a dense group of trees. The strange noise appeared to be coming from that direction. Clucking at her horse and sawing the reins, Sarah turned the carriage onto the trail. Within a few feet, huge trees, with branches intertwining overhead to form a canopy, surrounded her. The sound she heard earlier had died out, as if the forest was aware of her encroachment and silenced it to keep its identity secret.

Suddenly, the narrow road opened onto a large clearing. The charred remnants of tree stumps and blackened earth gave evidence that a fire had recently decimated the area. Ash rose under the carriage wheels and Sarah covered her mouth and nose to avoid breathing it. As she did, the stench of decay overwhelmed her. Her horse, frightened by the odor, reared in his harness and refused to go any further.

After Sarah got the carriage under control, she looked at the burned area. Horror gripped her like a vise as she realized what lay before her: an animal killing field. Dozens of dogs, cats, horses, and other animals, in various stages of putrefaction, were strewn haphazardly here and there. Some of them had been trussed with ropes and wires before they were killed. Many were nearly torn to pieces as if their killers had used them for target practice long after they were dead. Carrion birds fluttered over the bodies and competed with swarms of flies and maggots for the sustenance from the decaying flesh and bones.

Sarah leaned over the side of her carriage and vomited onto the ground. An utter sense of disbelief and horror consumed her. So this was Marshal Courtright's solution to the animal problem that plagued Fort Worth, she thought.

Her horse, feeling a relaxation of the tension on his reins, whinnied and reared again, fear showing in the whites of his eyes. Thrusting backward, he nearly turned the carriage over before Sarah could gain control and quiet him. She avoided looking at the carnage in the field as she backed away down the trail.

After she reached a small clearing, she started to turn the carriage when she heard the sound that had startled her before. Forcing herself to look back at the field of death, she saw movement near the roadway. A small, black dog with white splotches was pulling itself along on its front feet toward her. As she looked closer, she could see a dark splash of blood on the animal's rump. Then the keening wail reached out to Sarah again as the dog howled in agony.

Tears flooded Sarah's eyes as she watched the plight of the poor creature as it inched painfully closer. Tying the reins to the front bar of the carriage, she removed the pistol Rose had given her and walked back toward the field. When she approached the animal, it stopped crawling and looked mournfully at her. She couldn't tell if it was male or female. Its mottled coat was covered with soot and dirt, and its face was wet with tears and saliva.

Raising the gun, Sarah stared over the sights at the pathetic animal. She knew she should put it out of its misery. It appeared as if a bullet had broken its back, and it had no control over its hind legs. As her finger tightened on the pistol's trigger, the dog wailed again. Then it did a peculiar thing. Cocking its head, it issued a tiny, sad bark while it looked up with large, limpid eyes.

"Oh Lord," Sarah said as she dropped the barrel of the gun. Impressed by the little dog's fighting spirit, she knew she couldn't kill it.

Daniel would know what to do, she thought, as she went to the carriage for a blanket. When she approached the animal again, it lay quietly and watched her. She wrapped it in the blanket and placed it in the bed of the carriage. As she climbed into the driver's seat and started down the road, she felt the dog's sad eyes on her back.

When Sarah pulled up to Beelzebub's shack, Jody rushed up to greet her. "Mama," he shouted. "Beebub is all better. Can I play with him now?"

"I think it's too soon," Sarah said. "Daniel will let us know when he's well."

"Oh!" Margaret exclaimed as she approached the carriage and saw the dog whimpering in the back. "The poor thing is hurt. Where did you find it?"

"Down the road," Sarah answered. She glanced at Daniel who had joined them and asked, "Will you take a look at it?"

"Is it a he or is it a she?" Jody asked impatiently. "Or is it a he she?"

Laughing at Jody, Daniel unfolded the blanket and inspected the dog. Even though he handled the animal carefully, it howled in pain. When he finished, he said quietly, "It's a female. Young, probably less than a year old. She's been shot. The bullet grazed her spine, but it's not broken."

"Will she survive?" Sarah asked.

"Can't say yet," Daniel answered. "She needs some doctoring and a few good meals."

"Oh," Margaret said. "We must help her. Can we keep her here with Beelzebub?"

"Yes, Mama," Jody chimed. "Beebub is Maggie's dog. I want one too."

Sarah looked at Daniel, who nodded at her before answering, "We'll do what we can."

"Who would shoot a little dog like her?" Margaret asked.

"I don't know," Sarah responded with anger in her voice. "Perhaps Daniel can tell us."

Daniel glanced down at the ground before responding, "It was Sheriff Roberts' idea. I tried to talk Marshal Courtright out of helping him. I told him I would take no part in it. He said I didn't have to. The sheriff's deputies do all the killing. They're paid extra by the businesses in town."

"Doesn't Fort Worth have an animal shelter where strays are sent?" Sarah asked.

"No, Ma'am," Daniel said. "Nobody wants to spend the money to build one and keep it up."

"So they take the animals out in the woods and shoot them?" Sarah shook her head sadly.

"Mama," Jody said, jumping up and down with joy, as he looked at the pathetic little creature. "She's my dog, can I name her?"

"Yes," Sarah replied. "Please don't get too attached to her. She's been hurt badly, and she may not live."

"Oh, she will," Jody said boisterously. "I'll take care of her and feed her."

"Okay," Sarah said. "I guess we can keep one more invalid."

As Sarah watched, Daniel carried the dog into the shack with Jody and Margaret following. She suddenly decided where she would spend the first of the stolen government money. The sight of the slaughtered animals in the forest glen was still vivid in her mind, and she knew it would stay with her the rest of her life. Something had to be done to stop such senseless cruelty.

Chapter 17

When Sarah entered the *Fort Worth Beacon* building, a week had passed since her article had been printed and distributed. For the first time in the paper's existence, Stubby had to print extra copies of an edition. And, for the first time, customers actually paid for the paper. She wasn't sure if the success was due to her input or simply the fact that the *Beacon's* owner and editor was facing a trial for murder. She thought it was the latter. Many readers throughout the county had discussed the impassioned plea for civilized justice, and then wondered who S. Parker really was. She hoped that only Clarence, Margaret, Rose, and Stubby knew she used that *nom de plume*.

Sarah handed Stubby the article she had written for the next edition. Clarence had approved it, with one exception: he asked her to sign it as "City Editor." After discussion—because she thought that title was too generous—they agreed on "Contributing Editor."

Stubby snatched the paper from Sarah's hand and, bending over in the light from the windows, perused it rapidly. After he finished, he curled the left side of his lips up and squinted his left eye, signifying his approval. Then peering intensely at Sarah, he actually smiled at her with a twinkle in his eyes.

Sarah smiled back at him while nodding her head. Unconsciously, she was adopting his manner of communicating with gestures instead of words.

Reaching up to the counter top from his bent position, Stubby removed a piece of folded paper and handed it to Sarah. As he shuffled back to his printing press, she read a hand-scribed note:

> Fort Worth Beacon,
> The letter from a concerned citizen in your last edition was most erudite

and pertinent. I have read many treatises supporting the legal system of our august nation, but never one more clearly stating the need for the rule of justice in a time of inflamed passions. I desire to meet the esteemed writer of said epistle, Mr. S. Parker, at the earliest convenience in my office.

B. B. Paddock, Editor in Chief, Fort Worth Gazette

Sarah was thrilled that someone as famous and influential as B. B. Paddock would compliment her article. She knew he was one of the driving forces behind the railroad coming into Fort Worth. When the construction halted east of town due to lack of funds, he had inspired a citizen's group to work night and day to complete the last fifteen miles of track. They saved the town from becoming a ghost town after many businessmen had fled to the Dallas railhead.

Sarah realized that Mr. Paddock was under the impression that a man had written the commentary in defense of Clarence. She was reluctant to tell him that she was responsible. Then she thought about Clarence. He was like the little wounded dog she had found in the field in the forest: helpless and on the verge of death. To survive, he would need a lot of support as well. He might lose his life because of the lynch mob mentality flaring up like wildfire in Fort Worth. Or, if that didn't occur, he might be found guilty due to the sheriff's shoddy investigation and the poor defense representation at his trial. She had to do everything she could to help him, even if it meant admitting that she authored the article.

The *Fort Worth Gazette* on Second Street would have contained three or four offices the size of the *Beacon*. A multi-story building, it stood alone among its neighboring businesses like an immense oak tree in a group of small elms and mesquites. As Sarah approached it, she was still having misgivings about seeing Mr. Paddock.

Standing on the sidewalk in front of the wide stairs leading to the entrance was a young boy holding an arm full of papers and screaming in a falsetto voice, "Read all about it! Only in the *Gazette*! Democrat Samuel Tilden favored to defeat Ohio Republican Governor Rutherford B. Hayes for President! Read all about it! National election only three weeks away! Get your paper! Only three cents! Read all about it!"

Sarah stopped and bought a paper. The boy quit shouting long enough to thank her, and then he began bellowing again as he waved another copy in the air. Glancing at the front page, she noticed that there was no mention of Clarence's upcoming trial; in fact there was no local news at all. The headlines topped stories from all over the United States—especially from Washington D.C. and

Austin—but none from Fort Worth. She thought that was strange, and she made a mental note to ask Clarence about it.

When she entered the newspaper office, the first thing she noticed was the noise and the hectic pace of the workers. Three large presses were hammering out page after page of newsprint and spewing them onto piles on the floor where several boys waited to snatch them up, fold them, and stack them in piles. A tall, thin man, wearing a green eyeshade, stood near a counter piled high with some of the stacks. He was shouting at two young boys, frantically tying them into bundles, to hurry or they would miss the stage to Weatherford. In the far corner of the office a smaller press clanged out advertising handbills, which were quickly seized and thrust into carrying bags slung over the shoulders of a group of black youngsters. Sitting at a table in front of one of the presses, a shriveled up old man was reviewing written material before handing it to the printer. And in a far corner of the open space, Sarah could see another man bent over a desk pounding out Morse code on a telegraph machine, which seemed to be attached to his hand as it vibrated furiously.

Sarah was unsure of what to do. Then she noticed a glass enclosed room to the left side behind the counter. A mustached man in shirtsleeves was writing on a pad of paper on a large desk. A sign over the closed door identified the office: Editor in Chief.

The green-visored man at the counter noticed Sarah, and he murmured something that she couldn't hear over the noise in the room. Handing him the paper Stubby had given her, she said loudly, "Mr. Paddock?"

Nodding, the man shouted at the boys bundling papers on the counter once more, and then walked to the editor's office. He knocked and waited until the man at the desk looked up before entering. Sarah couldn't hear what they were saying to each other over the murmur of voices and the clanging of the presses. Accepting the sheet Sarah had sent to him, the mustached man scanned it quickly before staring at her, and then beyond her to the door, as if he was expecting someone else to be with her. When he seemed satisfied that she was alone, he raised his hand and beckoned for her to come to him.

As Sarah approached the office, the man inside went to a peg on the wall and took down a jacket, which he donned as she entered the door. When she closed it behind her, the racket outside diminished to a dull roar.

"Good day, Ma'am," the man said in a low voice tinged with a slight hoarseness, as if he had been shouting over the cacophony hammering at the window panes for hours. "B. B. Paddock at your service."

He motioned Sarah to a chair in front of his desk, and then he sat down across from her. The wall behind him was adorned with framed copies of newspapers and a large print of a map, which was titled *Railroad Map of Fort Worth* in large block letters. To Sarah, it looked like a large spider with long, spindly legs had squatted down on top of the map.

After all she had heard about Mr. Paddock, Sarah expected a larger man. However he was about her height. His black suit and dark cravat surrounding a starched high-neck white shirt, a stiff bulldog posture, a square-jawed face with piercing gray eyes, and dark hair parted neatly down the middle made him seem much larger than life. Unlike Jack Kilpatrick, who was extremely handsome, but also cold and calculating with a mysterious undercurrent of violence, Mr. Paddock was physically attractive in a straightforward and honest manner.

"Thank you, sir," Sarah said as she sat down. She pointed to the paper he held in his hand and continued, "I am Sarah Parker Whitman. I wrote that article for Mr. Hedding's newspaper."

Paddock's thin eyebrows rose slightly, and he stared at Sarah with a look of disbelief.

"I know women don't write for newspapers," Sarah went on. "So, with Mr. Heddings permission, I signed it with my maiden name, S. Parker."

"I see," Paddock said as he recovered from his surprise. "I must say I have followed Mr. Heddings' plight with journalistic interest. Unfortunately, we have never become friends. Perhaps, that was due to the conflict of our business interests. However, I know excellent writing when I see it. I meant what I said in this note." Paddock looked at Sarah appraisingly.

Conscious of Paddock's interest in evaluating her, Sarah raised her hand and touched a wayward tress of hair peeking out from the front of her hat and returned his forthright look.

A loud bang caused Paddock to shift his eyes from Sarah out into the room behind them. "Damn," he said, and then looked contritely at her. "I beg your pardon. The rollers on that press keep breaking down. We can't seem to repair it properly. Each time it shuts down, we lose half an hour of printing. And, in this business, time is money."

"If this is not a good time, Mr. Paddock, I can return later," Sarah said.

"No," he responded. "The foreman knows more about it than I do. As I was saying, your treatise certainly helped calm some of the hot tempers in town. I am surprised that you ... a woman wrote it. You appear to be well versed in grammar and syntax. But most impressive was the logical way you incorporated the Constitution and the Bible into your argument for Mr. Heddings rights. Do you have a formal education, Mrs. Whitman?"

"No," Sarah answered. "My father was a Baptist preacher. He educated me at home. I did teach school for several years."

"That makes this even more remarkable," Paddock said as he glanced at the note he had sent to the *Beacon*.

"Why did you request me ... S. Parker to come see you?" Sarah asked.

Paddock smiled for the first time as he responded, "In addition to being a journalist, I have a deep interest in seeing Fort Worth become a major city of the West. With the Indian problems behind us, the number of settlers moving into this part of Texas is increasing rapidly. Free land is available for the taking. Of course, the buffalo will soon be exterminated, so that trade will die. But now that we have the railhead here, there is every reason to believe we will become a major shipping point for cattle to the East and Northeast."

"I understand you were responsible for bringing the railroad into town," Sarah said.

Paddock smiled again. "No," he said. "A lot of concerned citizens made it happen. I just help provide the vision for them."

Turning to the wall map Sarah had noticed earlier, he pointed at it and said, "My dream is for Fort Worth to be the central hub of tracks leading in all directions from here."

"It looks like a giant spider," Sarah said with a smile.

"Yes ... yes it does," Paddock responded with his own smile. "It's been called the *Tarantula Map*. Each leg of the spider is a rail line. So far, we only have the one in from Dallas, but in time—" Paddock stopped and looked back at Sarah. "I'm getting a little carried away," he added with a shrug of his shoulders.

"My father told me dreams can't become reality without hard work," Sarah said. "I'm sure you've put a lot of effort into it. But tell me, how does the fate of Mr. Heddings fit into this?"

"That's an excellent question," Paddock responded. "In addition to businesses and people, a town needs a number of things before it can take on the role of a city: fire protection, potable water, garbage disposal, police, newspapers, hospitals, schools, and so on. But the most important feature, which is less tangible, but may be more important, is that a local government must rule by the precepts of law and order and not by lynch mob mentality. If that doesn't happen, we are left with anarchy."

Paddock shook his head and continued, "Your friend, Mr. Heddings, must be afforded a trial conducted by the proper authorities or all our other efforts to bring this community into prominence is doomed to failure."

Smiling again, Paddock said, "That's why I am so interested in your article, Mrs. Whitman. Your words did more to quell the civil unrest brewing among our populace than any measures we town leaders, including the marshal and the sheriff, have taken. I want to reprint it in the *Gazette*. With all due respect to the *Beacon*, my paper has far wider distribution. I can also send it on the telegraph wire to news outlets in the major cities throughout the United States. We need to let the rest of our country know we are not a tribe of wild frontiersmen, but a city of respectable and law abiding citizens."

Sarah took a deep breath before responding, "I'm not sure what to say. I do appreciate your kind words. My intention in writing that article was to help Mr. Heddings get a fair trial. I believe he is innocent of the charges against him."

"I must admit," Paddock said with a wide smile that lit up his face and crinkled the corners of his eyes, "I was expecting a man not a beautiful and well spoken woman such as you."

"Does that mean you won't reprint the article?" Sarah asked, color rising in her cheeks.

"I will," Paddock said quickly. "However, it may be prudent to keep our readers unaware that it was written by you. I believe quoting it verbatim with S. Parker as the author would be appropriate."

"If you think that's best," Sarah said. "I don't want to call attention to myself, and I don't want to harm Mr. Heddings' cause."

Sarah stood up and faced Paddock, who had also risen from his chair. "When will a woman be able to write for your publication, Mr. Paddock?" she asked.

"I don't know," Paddock replied as he stepped around the desk and took Sarah's hand in his. "Perhaps the time will come."

"Perhaps sooner rather than later," Sarah said as she withdrew her hand. "It is far overdue. Good day, sir."

As Sarah left the glass-enclosed office, the broken printing press that had been silent now banged into life. Lifting high above its metal table, it slammed down on the white newsprint sliding under it like the giant hammer of an angry Greek god. Spewing out printed papers at a rapid rate, it settled into its normal rhythm as it whooshed and banged, adding to the deafening noise in the room. When she reached the door, she turned briefly to see Paddock staring at her with a smile and a lifted hand.

Chapter 18

▼

When Sarah reached the sidewalk across the street from the Red Bull Saloon, she looked around for the Mexican boy she had used for a messenger before. But he was not in sight. After lingering for several minutes, she decided to go up to Rose's room. It was the middle of the afternoon, and she thought she might find her there.

Crossing the street between a stagecoach and a mule-drawn wagon laden with hay, she started up the stairs at the side of the saloon. Just as she reached the landing at the top, the door opened and a young black woman, scantily clad in a short, blue nightgown with a lace collar above her breasts, backed out screaming. Her hands were out in front of her as if she were defending herself against an attacker.

Shocked, Sarah stopped. Reaching into her purse, she pulled out Rose's pistol and stepped up beside the hysterical woman.

"It's okay now, Ellen," a voice came from inside, which Sarah recognized as Rose's. "He's dead. Won't bother anyone else."

Sarah put the pistol back into her bag and stared through the open door. She expected to see a body lying on the floor.

"Why, hello," Rose said to Sarah as she emerged from the hallway waving a folded newspaper.

Turning to the distraught woman, who was holding her face in her hands and sobbing, she said, "Ellen, get in here. How many times have I told you not to go out of your room without being properly dressed?"

Ellen, still sniffling and wide-eyed, skirted well away from Rose as she stepped through the door. When she disappeared, Rose laughed heartily and said to Sarah, "Who were you going to shoot with that gun, honey?"

"Oh, Rose!" Sarah said. "You gave me such a fright. That poor girl. What scared her so?"

Still laughing, Rose extended the newspaper so Sarah could see what had caused so much consternation. The body of a black roach stuck to the paper, its legs still quivering in the throes of death. "Ellen's afraid of her shadow," she said. "I never met a body so frightened of God's creatures."

Tossing the paper and its dying passenger over the railing into the alley, Rose put her arm around Sarah, "I'm glad to see you, honey. What brings you here?"

"I need to talk to you. Is this a good time?"

"Certainly," Rose responded, glancing toward the street below. "Why don't we go into my boudoir? That is, if you don't mind entering a den of iniquity; being a preacher's daughter and all." Rose's large breasts, barely contained by the purple sateen dress she was wearing, shook with her laughter.

"You're not trying to corrupt me, are you?" Sarah said, also laughing.

Turning serious, Rose said, "I don't think that's possible, honey. I know you too well."

Sarah followed Rose as she entered a door inside the hallway that opened to the left. It was a large area, formed by taking out the wall of an adjoining room. The scent of perfume and makeup permeated the air, and Sarah had to hold her nose to avoid sneezing. The windows were lavishly decorated with red velvet curtains, which, in combination with the red brocaded bedspread on the enormous, high-post canopy bed, and the red patterns accenting the pink wallpaper, gave the room a vibrant, shimmering quality. An ornate dressing table, white with gold trim, sat against one wall below a large mirror. Vases of flowers, containers of makeup, dainty glass vials, and spray bottles of perfume overflowed the tabletop. Between the two windows sat a delicate, white settee and matching chairs that looked like they had been taken from the parlor of the king of France. A free-standing clothes closet, large enough to walk into, abutted the wall beside the bed. Against the far wall, a white bathtub with colorful floral designs perched on clawed feet beneath a large, exquisitely framed portrait of a woman dressed in a dark blue Victorian style dress. The model's hair was piled on top of her head and crowned with a diamond tiara. Sarah had to look at the painting several times before she realized that Rose—although younger and slimmer at the time—was the subject.

"My goodness," Sarah said in wonder as she stared around the room. "You wouldn't take my ranch in trade for this, would you?"

Rose said quietly, "This isn't you, honey."

"I know it's not," Sarah responded, equally serious. "I just couldn't imagine a room like this in my wildest dreams."

Rose steered Sarah to the settee and plopped down beside her. Easing off her red, patent leather high-heeled shoes, she let out a loud sigh, "Oh! What a relief to get rid of those."

Sarah picked up the glittery shoes and compared them with her own sturdy, flat-soled boots. "If I had to wear these," she said, "I'd be afraid to go down stairs."

"It's not easy," Rose said. "It takes lots of practice and a fall or two. But you didn't come to discuss shoes, did you?"

"No," Sarah said. "I want to talk about Clarence. I have a few ideas about how we can help him. Also, I saw something outside of town that turned my stomach, and it's heavy on my mind."

Rose propped her long legs up on a low table in front of the settee and asked, "What's bothering you?"

"Sheriff Roberts is killing stray animals in a field east of here," Sarah said. "Apparently Marshal Courtright is going along with it."

"I heard that," Rose said. "What a terrible thing to do. But what does that have to do with Clarence?"

"I want to buy about ten acres, not too far from town?" Sarah said, ignoring Rose's question.

"What are you up to?" Rose queried.

Sarah smiled and responded, "Do you know if there is any land available?"

"Yes," Rose answered. "There's lots of it around Fort Worth for sale. The government gave out land grants to Civil War veterans. Many of them claimed the property but can't work it, so they sell off parcels. Are you going to tell me what you're up to?"

"Patience was never one of your virtues," Sarah said with a twinkle in her eye. "Do you know a Methodist Minister named Lovett?"

"Everybody knows old fire and brimstone Lovett," Rose said as she furrowed her brow. "He's running against Sheriff Roberts in next month's election. Doesn't have a Chinaman's chance in hell. Why are you asking?"

"I understand he's short of money to run his campaign," Sarah replied. "I also heard he was one of those veterans you were talking about. He may have some land he'd like to sell."

"So?" Rose asked bemusedly.

"Okay," Sarah said. "I'm going to tell you straight out. I want to buy some land to build an animal shelter on. And I want to buy it from Lovett, if possible, so he'll have money to run against Roberts. I believe Clarence is innocent, but Roberts only cares about convicting him so he'll look good going into the election. The fact that Clarence cut himself on his knife while he was opening letters means nothing to him. I don't know Lovett, but he can't be as self-serving as Roberts. If we can get a postponement, and he's elected before the trial, maybe he'll reopen the investigation."

Rose looked at Sarah with sudden fright in her eyes as she said, "You know, if Clarence is innocent, there's a murderer still out there. My girls may not be safe. I hadn't thought too much about that."

"It certainly is possible," Sarah said. "I need your help."

"Of course," Rose responded. "What can I do?"

"I have some gold and silver," Sarah said quietly, as if she expected someone to be eavesdropping on them. "I can't spend it. It can be tracked to me, which I don't want to happen."

"Sarah," Rose interrupted wide-eyed. "Whatever have you been up to? And you a fine Christian woman."

"It's best if you don't know where it came from," Sarah answered. "Someone might start asking questions, and you can tell them you don't know anything. I want to exchange what I have for currency I can use."

"No problem, honey," Rose said. "I know a banker in Dallas who owes me a few favors. He'll keep his mouth shut, because he couldn't stand for me to say anything in public about him. I'll send Thomas over to see him. Where are you keeping this mysterious plunder?"

"Nearby," Sarah said. "I'll need your help to get it. I think I'm being watched."

"This is getting better all the time," Rose said. "Just who would be watching you?"

"Can you tie Jack Kilpatrick up for awhile, say an hour or so?" Sarah asked.

"Jack!" Rose exclaimed. "Honey, you are into something big, aren't you? Well, I wish I could get Mr. Kilpatrick to come up here for a dalliance but, as I said, I'm not his type."

Appraising Sarah, Rose added, "You are, though. I'm surprised he hasn't hit on you."

When Sarah just looked at her without replying, Rose stopped with a nod of understanding, and then continued, "I see. So he's tried to get you under the sheets?"

Ignoring Rose's question, Sarah said, "I need some time to recover the gold and silver."

"Jack's a sucker for a big stakes poker game," Rose said. "There are a couple of high rollers in town looking for some action. Businessmen from Kansas City. I could set something up. I need to let you know somehow. I can't use Thomas all the time or folks might get suspicious. You don't want them talking about you the way they talk about me."

Rose thought for a minute and, then after looking at several ribbons draped over a peg on the wall, she said, "I'll tie a red ribbon on the door knob outside if Jack's busy downstairs. Will that work?"

"Yes," Sarah said. "The money will be in a large valise. How can I get it to you without being noticed?"

"Thomas lives south of downtown with his son and their families. It's about three blocks from the train station on Third Avenue. A brown house with a white picket fence. I'll tell him to watch for you. He can take the bag to Dallas. He has a brother over there he can spend the night with if it gets too late."

"It's a lot of money, Rose," Sarah said.

Laughing, Rose responded, "Don't you worry, honey. I'd trust Thomas with my life. In fact, I have several times. That gold will be safer with him than if it was in a bank."

Satisfied, Sarah said, "I won't worry about it then."

Pausing for a moment, she added, "I can't buy the property in my name. Do you have any ideas?"

"This has all the makings of a conspiracy," Rose said gleefully. "We certainly can't put it in my name. That would be a lark. The city fathers would accept it, but they'd have to go home to leftover chicken and a cold bed."

"I want to buy it anonymously and donate it to the city after the kennels are built," Sarah said. "You know, I wrote that newspaper piece for Clarence using a pen name. Why can't we use a fictitious name to buy the property?"

"Well, the title has to be registered at the Land Office to become legal. Then papers have to be drawn up to transfer it to the city. You should have a bank account; that's a lot of money for a cash transaction. Let me give it some thought. I just happen to know—in the Biblical sense—some local gentlemen who might help us. Have you thought of a name to use for this?"

"No," Sarah said. "Any ideas?"

"Should be a name no one around here knows," Rose said. "Let's see ... Smith? No, that's too common."

With a twinkle in her eye, Sarah asked, "Remember that little girl in your class at school who told us the story about the bear with bad eyes?"

Rose thought for a moment, and then laughed. "Yes, I do," she said. "She thought the hymn, *Gladly, The Cross I'd Bear*, was about a bear with bad eyes named Gladly."

"How about Mr. Gladly for a name?" Sarah suggested.

"Sure, honey," Rose said as she continued the play on words. "You are Gladly." Putting her arm across Sarah's shoulders, she said, "Hello, Mr. U. R. Gladly."

"One more question before I leave you," Sarah said. "What can you tell me about Clarence's attorney, Thompson?"

"Wet Willie?" Rose said with a frown that raised several furrows on her high forehead. "He was known as 'Slick Willie' before he took up drinking. William Quincy Thompson. I heard he was tall, handsome, and very smart in his younger days. Guess he's still tall. He was one of the original attorneys here in Fort Worth. He came from Chicago, I believe. The old timers say he could talk the fleas off a dog before a court of law. He wasn't here long till he married Clara Dalton."

"Dalton?" Sarah asked. "Haven't I heard that name before?"

"Yes," Rose answered, "Clara's brother, Todd Dalton, is the esteemed husband of my favorite admirer, Tilly Dalton, the president of the swarm of hornets known as the Fort Worth Women's Club."

"Doesn't Clara have some influence on Thompson's drinking?" Sarah asked.

"That's the sad part of the story, honey," Rose said. "About four years after the marriage, Willie made a name for himself handling some high dollar cases in Dallas. He had to stay over some nights, and he left his wife alone. At least, he thought she was alone. Seems like she got religion about the same time they got married. Willie wasn't much for listening to anyone's words but his own, so he stayed home on Sundays. The church Clara went to had a young preacher who was born with a silver spoon in his mouth and pants that wouldn't stay buttoned. He picked out some members of the fair sex from his congregation to consort with. Clara was one of them. Willie being gone and all gave the preacher the opportunity to exorcise his demons, so to speak."

Rose stopped and looked at Sarah, "I hope this talk about wayward preachers isn't upsetting you honey?"

"Yes it is," Sarah responded. "But it would be upsetting no matter what the man's profession was. My father said the only real saints were those who walked with Jesus in person. Everyone after that has had to deal with the sins of the flesh in their own way. Some don't handle it well."

"This one sure didn't," Rose said. "I guess he got into too many drawers, and the husbands caught him. By the time word got around, he'd spoiled several of his flock. Clara's name came up as one of them. The preacher was tarred and feathered and run out of town on a rail."

"Oh, no!" Sarah exclaimed. "What did Thompson do?"

"Willie wouldn't believe it at first, of course," Rose said. "Couldn't accept the fact Clara would look at anyone except him. But she withdrew from him and started wasting away. Wouldn't let him touch her. He was a teetotaler up till then, but it became too much for him, and he started drinking. You've seen him, honey. He's a big man. He can put away booze like you've never seen. He used to come into the Red Bull when he still had money. After he'd inhaled all the hard liquor behind the bar, he'd start in on the beer. Fortunately, he was a gentle drunk. He'd just put away a few gallons, mumble to himself and pass out."

Sarah recalled Thompson falling on the floor in his office when she visited him the first time. "What happened to Clara?" she asked.

"She stayed in her house all the time with the curtains drawn. The doctor who attended her said she lost all her color and didn't weigh more than a child. She wouldn't eat and just kept quoting Bible passages that didn't mean anything to anyone but her. One day, Willie found his way home after a week long drunk. She'd died sometime before. In a crazy rage, he burned down the house with her in it. The marshal, at the time, investigated but didn't press charges. The doctor told him Clara could have died anytime. She had no will to live, just wanted to go meet Jesus. Willie hasn't been sober since. He lost most of his business, of course. He hangs on to his shingle, thanks to Ben Clanton. The boy worships him. He's about the only thing Willie has going for him now."

"Oh, the poor man," Sarah said. "I was impressed with his nephew. He seems to be very knowledgeable about the law."

"He's actually Tilly's brother's son, so they don't have any blood connection," Rose explained. "She tried to get Ben into her husband's banking business and away from Willie. But when it came to figures, he didn't have sense enough to pour piss out of a boot if the directions were written on the heel. I have heard he's doing fine as Willie's scrivener."

"Scrivener?" Sarah asked.

"Law clerk, honey," Rose answered. "He does all the writing, transcribing, filing, and such. Willie just signs the papers put in front of him, when he's not passed out drunk."

"How do they handle a trial?" Sarah asked. "Thompson has been appointed Clarence's defense attorney. He'll have to go into the court room."

"They mostly do property and stock transactions," Rose responded. "It's scary to think Clarence's life may depend on Wet Willie."

"Yes," Sarah said as she stood up. "It is scary. Thank you for your time and your help."

"No problem," Rose said, rising ponderously on her bare feet and taking a deep breath.

As they walked to the door, Rose put her arm around Sarah's shoulder and asked, "When are you going back home, honey?"

"I don't know," Sarah answered wistfully. "Soon, I hope."

Chapter 19

"Next week!" Sarah said with disbelief in her voice. "The trial is next week?"

Ben Clanton cowered back in his chair to distance himself from Sarah. The door to Thompson's office was closed and an ominous silence dwelled within.

"Yes, Mrs. Whitman," Ben answered. "I filed for a continuance like you asked, but the circuit court disapproved it. Judge Nathaniel Blackwell from Austin has been assigned the case. He'll be here Monday morning."

"Are you and Mr. Thompson ready to put on a defense?"

Squirming in his seat, Ben glanced hopefully toward Thompson's office, as if he expected him to come to his assistance. Finally he responded, "I don't know."

"You don't know!" Sarah said sharply. "A man's life is at stake, and you don't know if you're ready for trial."

Seeing that Ben was close to breaking down, Sarah continued in a soft voice, "I know it's not your fault. I'm just concerned about Mr. Heddings. Did you also request the court replace Mr. Thompson as the defense attorney?"

"I did," Ben said eagerly. "Since he was dully assigned to the case as a bona fide member of the legal profession, the only reason they will accept for replacement is unavailability due to severe illness, death, or being occupied with another trial at the time this one comes up."

"Well none of those apply, unfortunately," Sarah said. "Did you get a doctor to certify that Mr. Thompson is not competent to try the case?"

"Doctor Hinton came to see him," Ben said. "But Uncle William threw him out. I mean he really did throw him out. Right out on the street. It was horrible."

"I see," Sarah said. "It looks like we have a trial to conduct, young Ben. Can you keep Mr. Thompson sober long enough to get through it?"

"I wouldn't know how to do that," Ben said apprehensively. "He's a large man, and he drinks a lot. He had me bring in a cot, and he took to sleeping in his office."

As Sarah thought of Thompson holed up in his office like an animal, she envisioned Beelzebub quarantined in his shack. What if Thompson was locked up until he was sober so he wouldn't hurt himself or outsiders?

A loud noise issued from Thompson's office. A moment later, the door opened and Thompson's massive head emerged like an ancient lion coming through the African bush country. He stared at Sarah and Ben through bleary, unfocused eyes. His hair was tousled, and he sported a week-old, scruffy beard.

"Benny Boy," he wheezed. "It is getting dark. Go get me a bottle of whiskey. Now, damnit." The door slammed shut and, after a few scurrying sounds, quiet descended again.

Ben fidgeted in his seat and looked at Sarah in despair.

"Do you know someone who can do a quick construction job for us?" she asked.

"Yes I do," Ben responded. "What do you have in mind?"

"I want you to get your uncle a bottle of whiskey, a big bottle," she said.

"Really, Mrs. Whitman?" Ben responded in disbelief. "Don't you want to sober him up?"

"I do," Sarah said. "But as you said, he's a large man. If the doctor couldn't even get in to see him, it would be quite a chore for you to dry him out. We'll get him drunk one last time. Then, while he's passed out, have the windows and the door boarded up so he can't get out. We'll make sure he has enough water and food to last a few days and some openings for air to circulate. And a large night bucket. It might be a good idea for you were to pass the word around to your neighbors to ignore any noise coming from here the next few days."

Fear showed in Ben's eyes as he stared at Sarah. "My gosh, Mrs. Whitman. He'll kill me if he finds out I had anything to do with something like that."

"Just tell him it was my idea," Sarah said. "In fact, I'll tell him myself when he's sober enough to talk to. Let's not worry about what he'll do right now. We have four days to get ready for Mr. Hedding's trial. It looks like we will have to prepare the case. If we can get Mr. Thompson alert enough, maybe he can use what we give him. If not, you'll have to conduct the trial."

"Me?" Ben said aghast. "I'm not an attorney."

"I know you're not," Sarah said. "But you are intelligent and knowledgeable in the law. If we have to, we'll tie Mr. Thompson in a chair while you do the talking."

"Tie him," Ben moaned. "Oh, dear me. Can we get away with that?"

"Hopefully, we won't have to resort to that," Sarah said. "He was a brilliant attorney at one time. With our help, perhaps he can be one again."

Sarah waited until early on the morning of the first day of the trial to remove the boards imprisoning William Thompson in his office. Ben Clanton wanted to absent himself, but Sarah insisted that he attend. She assured him that his life was not at stake.

"Oh, it was so terrible," Ben told her. "I thought he was going to tear down the walls. Mr. Purcell, the owner of the general store next door, wanted to call the marshal. He thought someone was being murdered. It was all I could do to talk him out of it."

"You did very well, Ben," Sarah said. "When this is all over, your uncle will thank you."

After the carpenter removed the last board securing the office, Sarah and Dr. Hinton entered cautiously, leaving the door open behind them. The desk and all the chairs were overturned. Most of the wallpaper had been torn off, and bloody fingerprints stained the walls. The stench of urine, feces, vomit, and other unrecognizable odors was overpowering. Rose had prepared Sarah for the occasion by giving her a lace handkerchief daubed liberally in perfume. Holding the cloth over her nose, she approached the inert mass lying on a cot beneath the boarded up window. At first, she thought Thompson was dead because he was so still. Then she saw the movement of his massive chest as it contracted and expanded in breathing.

Dr. Hinton stepped past Sara and bent over Thompson's body. After checking his heart beat with a stethoscope, he pried open his eyelids, which were stuck together with mucus. As he did, Thompson reared up and struck out with his forearm, which was as huge as the leg of a mule. Jumping backward, Dr. Hinton avoided the lethal blow.

"What ... what the hell is going on?" Thompson uttered in a weak, hoarse voice. Looking up at Sarah and the doctor, he blubbered, "Who the hell are you?"

"Doctor," Sarah said. "I think he's going to live. Please go out and close the door behind you. I want to talk to Mr. Thompson alone."

"Do you think it's safe?" Dr. Hinton asked wide-eyed.

"I can take care of myself," Sarah said with a disarming smile. "Please do as I ask."

After Dr. Hinton left, Sarah looked down at Thompson lying on the cot. He was trying unsuccessfully to sit up. Taking hold of his feet, she placed them on the floor, and then she put her arm behind his large frame and helped him into a sitting position.

"Thirsty," Thompson croaked. "I'm thirsty."

Sarah reached into the pocket of her coat and took out a bottle of water. Uncapping it, she held it up to Thompson's mouth and poured it between his lips.

After taking several draughts, he sputtered and spit. "Water. Gawddamn. What are you trying to do to me, woman? Where's the liquor?"

"My name is Mrs. Whitman, not woman!" Sarah said. "And you're through with liquor for a while, Mr. Thompson," Sarah said. "Maybe a long while."

"Jesus Christ. What the hell are you talking about?" Thompson shook his head and tried to focus his eyes.

"I'm talking about you, and I'm talking about your responsibilities to yourself and to those who love you," Sarah said forcefully. "And I will thank you to never use the Lord's name like that again. Never!"

"Damn, you're touchy," Thompson said as he looked around at the destruction in the room as if he was seeing it for the first time.

"Not half as touchy as I can be," Sarah said.

Thompson stared at Sarah for a long moment before saying "Gawddamn Ben—"

Sarah slapped Thompson soundly across his beefy cheek. The blow landed with a sharp crack and raised a red welt on his skin. Tears of pain came to his eyes, and he stared at her in disbelief.

"I have told you for the last time, Mr. Thompson, I will not tolerate that kind of language," Sarah said standing stiffly over him. "Ben has taken up for you long after he should have run away and left you alone."

With a flash of anger in his eyes, Thompson raised his hand, which was nearly the size of a dinner plate, and prepared to strike back. Sarah stood her ground and looked in his eyes without a trace of fear.

"Are you going to hit me, Mr. Thompson?" Sarah asked quietly. "If you feel you must, please go ahead."

Thompson looked at her and took several deep breaths through his flaring nostrils. Dropping his hand, he said, "I can't hit you. It wouldn't be proper."

"Who taught you it's not proper to strike a woman?" Sarah asked softly. "Your mother?"

Thompson's eyes softened as he replied, "No, I never knew my mother. My grandmother raised me."

"What would your grandmother think if she could see you in this condition?" Sarah asked. "Drunk every day. Turning your back on the profession you were born for and rejecting those who care for you. I know you lost your wife. It was a terrible thing to go through. But that is over and done with. It's time for you to be the man your grandmother would be proud of."

Thompson closed his eyes and began crying. Sobs wracked his heavy body as tears streamed down his face. Sarah, unmindful of his stench and filth, put her arms around him and held him.

After a long moment, Sarah stood up. Taking Thompson's face in one hand, she raised his chin and dried his eyes with her handkerchief. "Okay," she said. "It's time to move on. I have several gentlemen with me—their names are Thomas and George. They're going to help you bathe and clean up. They have a new suit of clothes for you to wear and something to eat. When you are presentable, there is a young man outside you owe an apology to. Then we are going to court, and you are going to defend a fine man who just may be innocent of a terrible crime."

"I am?" Thompson said in a strangled voice, his body still shaking with emotion.

"Yes, you are," Sarah said. "Unless you want to crawl back into that sewer you've been living in? It's your choice."

Thompson reached out and enveloped Sarah's small hand in his. Looking at her through his bleary eyes, he said, "Thank you. I'm not sure I can, but I'll try."

"No, Mr. Thompson!" Sarah said. "You won't try, you will do it."

Chapter 20

▼

Due to the fire damage at the courthouse, a temporary court was set up in the Opera Hall, a massive wooden structure built by local citizens interested in the arts. Traveling road shows and local theatrical groups used it for performances. Modeled after eastern opera houses, the hall had excellent acoustics, drapery covered walls, and triple-tier seating with private loges. The main floor slanted downward from the entry doors to the band pit area in front of the stage. For the trial, carpenters had installed a temporary floor reaching from the front spectator seats to just below the stage level where the judge and the defense and prosecuting attorneys would conduct their business.

The sound of bells from a far-off church pealed the hour of noon as Sarah approached the hall. Low, scudding clouds covered the sky. An occasional rumble of thunder announced the coming of a storm, but the threat of bad weather didn't dampen the enthusiasm of the throngs of people gathered around the hall waiting for the doors to the court to be unlocked. The crowd included black-suited gentlemen escorting colorfully attired ladies with parasols, cowboys with manure on their boots, soldiers regaled in full uniform, townspeople wearing their daily business clothes, country folks in overalls and shapeless dresses with bonnets, visiting reporters looking like they had slept in their clothes, and Rose's entourage of ladies from the Red Bull Saloon dressed in subdued hues with prim collars.

Standing beside Rose, Sarah read a hand scribed note pinned to the wall beside the entrance door to the hall:

> District Court Rules
> 1. No firearms allowed inside the courtroom. All guns should be

checked at the Marshal's Office. No acceptions.
2. No coloured persons allowed, unless needed for cleaning.
3. Chewing is discouraged. If you have to, bring a cuspidor and try to spit quietly.
4. Smoking is permitted, but be careful of starting fires. Water buckets are available.
5. No alcoholic beverages allowed within 48 feet of the courtroom.
Theo. Roberts, County Sheriff

Sarah turned to a young deputy sheriff standing on the porch and asked, "Did you write this notice?"

"Yes, Ma'am," he said proudly.

"Why does it say no alcoholic beverages are allowed within forty-eight feet?" Sarah asked.

Pointing down the sidewalk, the deputy said, "It's exactly forty-nine feet to the front door of the Texas Trail saloon. I measured it myself."

"Good work," Sarah said with a smile. Then, pointing at the first rule, she added, "That should be spelled 'exceptions' not 'acceptions.' To accept something means you agree to it."

"Oh, gosh," the man said, as a blush spread over his clean-shaven face. "Do you think other folks will notice?"

"Probably not," Sarah said. "The sheriff signed it, so I wouldn't worry about it."

"Honey," Rose said with a smile and a tilt of her head, "Don't you think that lad is a little old for your schooling?"

"We're never too old to learn, are we?" Sarah replied, also smiling.

"Mrs. Whitman!" a voice drifted across the street above the din of the traffic and the murmur of the crowd outside the hall.

Sarah turned to see Ben Clanton walking toward her, his arms laden with books. Waving, she stared at the tall man lurching unsteadily beside Ben. She hardly recognized William Thompson. Clean-shaven and with neatly trimmed hair beneath a gray, narrow-brimmed hat, he appeared to be getting some color back into his face. He was wearing a black three-piece suit with a white shirt and a thin black tie, which made him look like a successful businessman out for a mid-day stroll. A shiny black cane, which he wielded like he'd used one all his life, assisted his ungainly stride.

As he stepped up onto the sidewalk, Thompson doffed his hat and said, "Mrs. Whitman. Top of the day to you."

"Thank you," Sarah responded. "And good day to you."

She could see from the dark spidery veins covering his florid face and his blood-shot eyes that he was suffering terribly from the years of drowning himself in alcohol and from the trauma of his recent withdrawal from the drug. But as she looked at him, she saw an underlying strength in him that she hadn't noticed before.

Sarah extended her hand to Thompson. When he took it in his warm fist, she looked into his eyes and said, "We've never been formally introduced, William. Please call me Sarah."

"It shall be my pleasure, Sarah," William responded. "My pleasure indeed."

Then turning to Rose, who was equal to his height with her high-heeled shoes, he nodded his head and said, "Good day, Rose."

Rose curtsied with a broad smile and responded, "I'm pleased to see you looking so fine, William. All the ladies in town will be swooning after you."

"Mrs. Whitman," Ben said breathlessly. "I went over the case with Uncle William. He has some ideas that will be helpful."

William looked at Sarah and said, "We voir dired the jury this morning. Not much to choose from. All ruffians and neer-do-wells, I'm afraid. We'll just have to make do. It seems that you and Ben have prepared my case extremely well," he said graciously. "There is one omission, however."

"Really?" Sarah asked. "What's that?"

"I read your newspaper article," William said. "It is most erudite and appropriate. I desire to call you to the stand as a witness for the defense and have you read it to the court."

"Gracious," Sarah said. "I'm not sure I would feel comfortable doing that. And as a woman, it may not have much of an impact. Why don't you read it yourself?"

"I'm surprised at you," William said with a twinkle in his eyes. "Can this be the same tigress who imprisoned me in my own office and struck me a mighty blow to bring me to my senses? I do not believe there is any task beyond you."

William pulled a gold watch from his vest pocket and, after unsnapping the cover and glancing at it, said, "I understand the trial is to begin promptly at one o'clock. I wish to consult with the worthy defendant prior to the proceedings. I desire to have you in attendance at the counselor's table, Sarah. But—"

"I understand," Sarah said. "It's not a place for a woman. Neither is the jury box nor the voting booth," she added with a smile. "I leave him in your capable hands."

Walking up to the deputy sheriff guarding the door, William looked down from his great height and announced loudly in his bulldog voice, "I am the defense attorney, Mr. William Thompson. I understand my client is inside. Please be so kind as to escort me and my able assistant to him. At once, dear fellow."

The deputy swallowed and backed up against the wall. He reached into his pocket and extracted a key. Opening the door, he stood aside while William and Ben, still struggling with his load of books, entered. The deputy then closed the door and locked it behind them.

When the door was opened to Sarah and the rest of the public, the noisy, milling crowd made a mad rush toward the entrance like a herd of thirsty cattle rumbling to water. Sarah was swept up in the mass movement and pushed into the hall. Most of the loges and upper seats were already occupied since the sheriff had allowed selected parties in through the side doors. When she was able to separate herself from the throng searching for empty seats, Sarah found herself in the aisle near the front. She looked around for Rose but couldn't locate her in the confusion.

Ben Clanton stepped down from the counselor's floor and came up to Sarah. "We have reserved a place for you, Mrs. Whitman," he said. Leading her to the front row of chairs, he seated her at a level almost even with William and Clarence, who sat at a table facing the center of the stage.

Clarence was wearing a white suit with red piping on the cuffs and lapels. His long, thinning hair was slicked back and fell down over the collar of his purple silk shirt. A bright yellow rose adorned his lapel. Bouncing excitedly on the chair next to William, he looked like a multi-colored bird hopping on a perch next to a gigantic black bear. Sarah couldn't hear what he was saying, but he was chattering non-stop.

When Ben joined them at their table, both William and Clarence turned and looked at Sarah. William nodded his massive head while Clarence, still bobbing up and down, waved at her with a white silk handkerchief. Sarah acknowledged their greetings with a lift of her hand.

At the prosecutor's table on the right side of the floor sat a thin, elderly man dressed in dark gray pinstripes, which contrasted with the snow-white of his unruly hair. His cadaverous face, and his habit of remaining very still, gave the impression that he had died in an upright position, and he was just waiting for the undertaker to come and carry him off.

The jury, all white men between the ages of thirty and sixty, occupied two benches on the left side of the stage. A surrounding low, wooden wall isolated them from the attorneys and the spectators.

"All right!" a deep bass voice thundered over the tumultuous sound of the onlookers, many of them still scrambling for seats. "All right. Get quiet or get out!"

The man calling for order was standing in front of the tall structure that held the judge's lofty seat. His huge, barrel chest threatened to burst through the vest of his tan suit as he sucked in vast amounts of air and expelled them in astounding roars of sound.

The noise in the hall diminished to a dull roar, while the last of the seats were filled, and the overflow lined up against the walls at the sides and the rear. Sarah turned and located Rose and her group of ladies near the middle of the auditorium. Glancing up at the loges, she saw B. B. Paddock seated next to a tall, striking woman dressed in a frilly white dress waving a fan in front of her face. She rested one hand, possessively, on Paddock's shoulder. Just below Paddock and closer to the stage sat Jack Kilpatrick. Before Sarah could look away, he caught her eye and waved at her with a wide smile.

Sarah turned without acknowledging Kilpatrick, her thoughts thrown into turmoil. She had used some of the gold and silver taken from the visitors to her ranch to purchase property east of town from Reverend Lovett under the name U. R. Gladly. She prayed that Rose's money transfer in Dallas would not be traced to her. The barns and kennels for an animal shelter were under construction, and the transfer to the city was scheduled for the following week. Unfortunately, it would be too late to help Clarence. The trial, at the insistence of Sheriff Roberts, had been accelerated so it would take place before his re-election vote. Clarence's fate rested on William's defense and the subsequent decision by the jury.

The voice of the court bailiff burst throughout the hall like a clap of thunder, "Hear ye! Hear ye! Silence in the courtroom. The Third District Court of the State of Texas is hereby in session in the case of the State versus Mr. C. W. Heddings. Please stand for the honorable Judge Nathaniel Blackwell."

Sarah stood as a small, round man, dressed in a black robe, entered the stage through the curtains to the left. His baldhead gleamed from the radiated light from lamps on an overhead chandelier. He walked to his raised platform with short, mincing steps like he was suffering from a bowel disorder as a murmur of conversation rippled through the standing-room-only crowd.

Judge Blackwell banged his gavel several times. "Silence in the court," he shouted in a high-pitched voice. "I will not stand for interruptions. This is a court of law, not a circus."

Turning to the prosecution table, he said, "Counselor, introduce yourself for the record and read the charges against the defendant, please."

The elderly man at the prosecutor's table rose slowly to his feet, as if it was the last act he would ever accomplish on earth. In a surprisingly clear and forceful voice, he said, "Thank you, your honor. I am Robert Stallings, counselor for the prosecution. The state alleges that on or about one o'clock in the morning of September 30, 1876, the defendant, Mr. C. W. Heddings, did forcibly remove Miss Lucille Martell from the streets of Fort Worth and subsequently end her life by violent means. The specific charges are kidnapping and murder in the first degree, your honor."

Judge Blackwell pointed at the defense table and said, "Counselor for the defense, your name for the record. How does the defendant plea?"

As William rose from his table, several catcalls echoed through the hall. "Wet Willie," was heard several times along with derisive laughter.

The gavel slammed down again as Judge Blackwell shouted, "Order! Order in the court! Another outburst like that and I'll have the room cleared."

Looking down at William, he said, "Please continue."

"Thank you, your honor," William said. His voice was strong and deep, as if he had found a special reserve of energy. "Attorney for the defense, William Thompson at your service. My defendant, Mr. C. W. Heddings, pleads not guilty."

Another ripple of noise arose from the audience, but a sharp smack of the gavel silenced it. Looking at Stallings, Judge Blackwell ordered, "Proceed with your opening argument."

Stallings unfolded from his chair and sidled slowly up to the jury box. After looking each of the jurors in the eye, he said, "The state will prove without a shadow of a doubt that during the early morning hours of September 30, the year of our Lord 1876, the defendant—" Stallings turned and pointed at Clarence who was watching him excitedly while he squirmed in his chair. "The defendant, Clarence—"

A rush of laughter swept over the courtroom like a gust of wind. But it was cut short when the judge reached for his gavel. Sarah cringed as she realized that she was one of the few who knew Heddings by the name of Clarence.

"Objection, your honor," William said, standing laboriously. "The defendant's name is listed in the court records as Mr. C. W. Heddings. I implore my esteemed colleague to address him as the same."

"Objection sustained," Judge Blackwell said. Turning to Stallings, he said sternly, "Address the defendant properly, counselor."

Stallings nodded at the judge and continued, "The state will prove that on said date, the defendant, Mr. C. W. Heddings, did snatch Miss Lucille Martell bodily from the street while she was going from her place of employment to her place of residence. Mr. Heddings then removed Miss Martell to parts unknown and proceeded to inflict grievous injuries by slashing her throat with a knife and allowing her to bleed to death. Then Mr. Heddings took the victim's body to a location on Mary's Creek outside the city limits where he interred the young woman in a shallow grave. Those actions by themselves, members of the jury, were most heinous. However, Mr. Heddings was not through with his despicable ways. As if in contempt of every shred of human decency, he left his calling card above the heart that no longer beat."

Turning and pointing at Clarence with a long, skeletal finger, Stallings continued in a voice that sounded like a preacher condemning a blatant sinner. "He placed a flower between her cold breasts ... a yellow rose like the one he flaunts in this very courtroom."

William's objection was drowned in a sea of derisive shouts and boos from the crowded auditorium. Pieces of paper and other sundry items were flung through the air toward the floor where Clarence sat white-faced in fear, cowering beside William.

A man's voice, which sounded like it had been well oiled with alcohol, erupted from one of the rows just behind Sarah, "Lynch the dandy son-of-a-bitch. Whore murderer."

Judge Blackwell stood and banged his gavel furiously, while the bailiff added his thunderous voice in a call to end the pandemonium. When some semblance of order was restored, the judge pointed to the man who had screamed for Clarence's demise and said loudly, "Bailiff, I want that man removed from this courtroom at once. He is not to return for the duration of the trial."

Then glaring at Stallings, he said, "I will speak to both counselors immediately."

While Judge Blackwell was conferring with the attorneys, the bailiff with the assistance of two sheriff's deputies forcibly ejected the agitator from the auditorium. When the restive crowd settled down to a low murmur, the judge dismissed William and Stallings with a wave of his hand.

Then he looked out at the sea of faces in the hall. The heat from the lamps near his head was causing him to perspire heavily, which increased the shine on his bald head. "Apparently you ladies and gentlemen here in Fort Worth take the performance of a duly appointed court of law lightly," he said loudly and firmly. "The right of an accused to a fair trial in this state is guaranteed by our constitution. The right of the public to disrupt such a trial is not. I have the authority to conduct these proceedings behind closed doors. I can assure you that I will do so if we have another incident such as just occurred."

Looking down at Stallings, he said, "For the record, the objection by the defense is sustained. Continue counselor. Without the theatrics."

Stallings, looking somewhat subdued, stood in front of the jury box and said, "The prosecution will prove beyond any doubt that Mr. C. W. Heddings did commit this odious crime. You members of the jury will have no recourse but to find him guilty on both charges. Thank you." Returning to his table, he folded back into his chair.

William rose slowly, as if a great weight was draped across his shoulders. His face was pale, and he appeared to lack the strength to stand. When he skirted the end of the table, his hand struck a glass of water, sending it to the floor with a loud crash. Ben Clanton sprang to his feet and began picking up the broken shards. William stood quietly until Ben finished, and then he walked ponderously to the jury box, tapping his cane with each step.

Instead of looking at the jurors, as Stallings had done, William raised his eyes and stared at the ceiling for a long moment, as if he were requesting divine guidance. Finally, he dropped his head and addressed the box, "The prosecution would have you believe that the defendant committed a violent act of murder against a helpless young woman; a woman who he was quite fond of, actually. Yes, murder is a heinous crime. Taking another person's life is a violation of the religious and moral foundations of our united country. But it happens. Yes, it happens all too often. Why does one commit such a crime? The legal term answering that question is called motive."

William stopped and glanced at Clarence before continuing in a strong voice that rumbled off the stage and filled the auditorium, "The prosecution conveniently neglected to address the motive Mr. Heddings had for perpetrating this crime. Why? Because they know he had no motive. What is a motive, I ask you? It comes from the Latin word *motivus*. It's an emotion or desire that influences the will and incites one to action. Motive can be negative as well as positive. Greed, avarice, jealousy, and hatred are examples of negative motives. They can lead a person to commit a crime such as Mr. Heddings is charged with. But did he exhibit any of those negative motives toward Miss Martell? Quite to the contrary, he was filled with positive motives toward the young woman: concern, friendship, and, yes, even love."

The jurors leaned forward in their seats and listened intently to William as he dropped his voice and went on, "Lacking a motive, the prosecution will have you believe that circumstantial evidence will prove their case against the defendant. Was Mr. Heddings the only one seen with Miss Martell that night? No, he was not. Did anyone actually see Mr. Heddings abduct her? No, they did not. Did anyone see him murder Miss Martell? No, they did not. The prosecution will also have you believe that, because a yellow rose was found on the victim, he is undoubtedly guilty. However, anyone could have placed that flower as a ruse to throw suspicion on Mr. Heddings."

William leaned on his cane and took a deep, audible breath before continuing, "The prosecution has the responsibility to prove Mr. Hedding's guilt beyond any reasonable doubt. However, the defense will prove during the conduct of this trial that Mr. Heddings had no motive for this murder and only the barest of circumstantial evidence connected him in any way. It will be up to you, members of the jury, to consider that lack of motive and absence of solid evidence and return the only proper verdict in this trial for Mr. Heddings. Not guilty!"

As William lumbered to his table, Clarence daubed at his eyes with his handkerchief. Silence descended on the courtroom, and the sounds of William's feet shuffling and his cane tapping the wooden floor could be heard by everyone.

After a long moment, Judge Blackwell announced, "The court will recess for one half hour. If you spectators are not in your seats on time, you will be locked out."

Sarah thought she might go back and talk with Rose during the break, but the aisle was clogged with people, some standing in place and chattering and others rushing madly for the rear doors. Then a voice caught her attention, and she turned around to see William standing near her.

"Sarah," he said quietly. "Clarence insists that he take the witness stand in his behalf. I think it's in his best interest not to. He walks like a lovesick girl strolling through a garden, and you know how he talks. If Shakespeare hadn't of been born, I think he'd be mute. Most of what he says will go right over the head of the judge, let alone the jury. If he takes the stand, dressed in his gaudy clothes with that yellow rose stuck in his lapel, it might not matter what he says. The lynch-mob movement in that crowd out there could go berserk. Judge Blackwell and Sheriff Roberts might not be able to hold them back. Perhaps you can reason with him."

"I can try," Sarah responded in agreement. "Do we have time now?"

"No," William said. "It's a short recess. I expect it will be tomorrow before I get to call any witnesses. Perhaps you can see him in the jail tonight."

"I will," Sarah said. "Have you asked him to not wear a flower during the trial?'

William sighed and turned his palms upward, "It's like talking to a child. He's enjoying the spectacle. He thinks they're having the trial in this theatre to give him a stage to stand on and moralize to the world."

Chapter 21

▼

By the time the court re-convened, Sarah knew that the forty-nine feet to the Texas Trail Saloon had been traversed by a number of court watchers, and many of them were on the downward spiral to inebriation. Several tried to accelerate it by carrying mugs of beer and bottles of hard liquor to the hall, but they were intercepted by sheriff's deputies and turned away.

After waiting a few extra minutes for the noise to subside, the judge banged his gavel and told the bailiff to lock the entrance doors. Then looking down at Stallings, he said, "You may call your first witness, counselor."

Stallings stood up and turned around to face the jury. "The prosecution calls Sheriff Theodore Roberts to the witness stand," he said.

Roberts, in a gray suit and carrying a white, wide-brimmed hat, mounted the stairs to the stage floor and marched stiffly up to the bailiff in front of the witness stand. His thinning hair, recently trimmed, was slicked back over his forehead with oil that glimmered in the lamplights.

The bailiff extended a bible and, when Roberts placed his hand over it, exploded in an elephantine roar, as if he wanted everyone in town to hear him, "Do you swear to tell the truth, the whole truth, and nothing but the truth, so help you God?"

Taken back by the blast of sound from the bailiff, the sheriff hesitated before answering, "I do."

"Please be seated," the bailiff said.

Stallings approached Sheriff Roberts. "Please state your name and occupation, sir," he said.

"Theodore Roberts, duly elected by the majority of the voters, sheriff of Tarrant County."

A titter of laughter, ignored by the judge, swept through the hall at the sheriff's obvious reference to the upcoming election.

"Please tell the court how you were notified of the death of the deceased, Miss Lucille Martell," Stallings asked.

"I was in my office at four o'clock on the afternoon of October 6 this year when two women, Mrs. Sarah Whitman and Miss Rose Travis approached me. They informed me they had found a body near Mary's Creek southwest of town."

"I see," Stallings said. "And did these two women say who the corpse might be?"

"Yes," Roberts replied. "Rose ... Miss Travis said she identified it as Lucille Martell."

"And what did you do then, Sheriff?" Stallings queried.

"I accompanied them to the place where they said they found the body," Roberts said. "I found Miss Martell lying in a shallow grave. Most of her was covered with dirt and leaves."

"Did you notice anything unusual about the body, sheriff?"

"Yes," Roberts answered. "Several things, actually. Her throat was slashed open, and her hands were clasped on her chest like she was praying. And there was a flower between her—" Roberts stopped and looked up at the judge before continuing quietly, "On her chest."

"Can you describe the flower?" Stallings asked.

"Yes," Roberts replied. "It was a rose ... a yellow rose."

"Do you see such a flower in this courtroom?" Stallings asked in a quiet voice.

Sheriff Roberts was pointing at the flower in Clarence's jacket when William lurched to his feet. "Objection, your honor," he said. "The prosecution is attempting to alienate the jury against the defendant again. The fact that he is wearing a flower should not be held against him. It's a well-known fact he is partial to roses, and he wears them every day."

Judge Blackwell hesitated for a long moment before replying, "Objection sustained. It has not been proved that the defendant placed the flower on the body of the deceased. Continue counselor."

Stallings turned back to the witness stand and said, "What did you do then, sheriff?"

"I asked the county coroner to examine the body and remove it to the mortuary," Roberts responded. "Then I started my investigation."

"And where did that lead you, sir?" Stallings asked.

"I went to the *Fort Worth Beacon*, where Mr. Heddings works, to speak to him," the sheriff said. "But he was not there."

"And what did you do then?" Stallings queried.

"I searched his office and found a knife with blood on it," Roberts said.

"Is this the knife you found," Stallings asked, holding up a silver-coated dagger with a tag tied to the handle. A dark discoloration smeared the edge of the blade.

"Objection, your honor!" William shouted as he stood up and leaned on the table. "A warrant duly approved by a representative of a court of the state is required before a person's personal property can be searched. Sheriff Roberts had no such warrant. Anything he found at that location cannot legally be admissible as evidence in this case."

"Your honor," Stallings interjected. "The said location searched by the sheriff was not personal property; it was a public place of business. Authorities, if required in the conduct of a criminal investigation, can search such a location without a warrant. The state supreme court in the case of 'The State versus Henry Milton' in 1874 upheld a ruling in a similar situation."

"Your honor," William said. "The knife was found in Mr. Heddings' desk. That certainly fits the definition of personal property."

Judge Blackwell peered down at the two attorneys for a long moment. Finally he said, "Objection overruled. The newspaper office is considered a public place of business. The evidence the sheriff found is admissible to the court."

Turning to Stallings, he said, "Please continue, counselor."

"Sheriff," Stallings said. "After you found the knife with the blood on it, what did you do?"

"I proceeded to the Red Bull Saloon, where I found Mr. Heddings and arrested him," Roberts said.

"I see," Stallings said. "Did the defendant make any statement to you?"

"Statement?" Roberts asked.

"Yes," Stallings pursued. "Did he make any statement as to his guilt or innocence?"

"Said he was innocent ... or at least that's what I think he said," Sheriff Roberts replied with a quizzical look. "Something about slings and arrows of fortune, or some such."

At the defense table, Clarence leaned over and spoke excitedly to William, which elicited a glare from Judge Blackwell.

"Did he expect to be arrested?" Stallings pursued.

"Objection," William shouted again. "Any statement the sheriff could make about the defendant's state of mind at the time of arrest is pure conjecture and is not admissible."

Judge Blackwell leaned forward and said, "You are correct, counselor. Objection sustained."

"No further questions, your honor," Stallings said abruptly as he shuffled slowly to his table.

William stood up ponderously and looked at the sheriff for a long moment before he approached him, walking slowly and carefully with his cane. A sudden hush fell over the room as the spectators leaned forward in anticipation.

"Good afternoon, Sheriff," William rumbled. "I have a few questions to ask you. The young lady disappeared on the thirtieth day of September. When did you begin your investigation?"

"Miss Travis told Marshal Courtright she was missing the afternoon of the following day. His deputies interviewed the, er ... clientele and staff at the saloon. Then they searched the city for her. When they didn't find anything, my office was notified, let's see, the next day. I sent my men out to look around the county."

"And did the initial investigation by the marshal and your office turn up a suspect?" William asked.

"No," the sheriff answered. "Nobody's name come up. Everyone seemed to like Little Lu. She was a good whore, not like most of them."

A tittering of laughter swept through the auditorium. Judge Blackwell brought it to a halt with a bang of his gavel.

"Sheriff Roberts," William growled after he glanced down at Sarah. "Miss Martell's profession is not on trial here. I ask you to not use a derogatory name to describe the deceased."

Roberts looked confused as William continued, "The break in the case came when Mrs. Whitman and Miss Travis notified you they had found a body at Mary's Creek nearly a week later."

"Yes," Roberts responded.

William paused as if he was collecting his thoughts, and then he continued, "As you told my esteemed colleague, there was a yellow rose on the deceased. Could someone have put that flower there to throw suspicion on the defendant?"

"Objection, your honor," Stallings squealed as he rose from his chair. "The defense is leading the witness to state a conclusion based on inadequate facts."

"Your honor," William said, turning to the judge. "That is exactly what this witness did when he searched Mr. Heddings' office without a warrant and pointed him out in this courtroom. He arrived at the conclusion that the defendant, and only the defendant, could possibly have placed the flower on the body. In the absence of credible witnesses, such a conclusion cannot be valid. It is only conjecture, sir. Conjecture is a conclusion deduced from incomplete, defective, or presumptive evidence and is arrived at by surmise or guesswork. The esteemed prosecutor is well aware that conjecture has no place in a court of law. I ask that the Sheriff's conclusion as to the defendant's action in this matter be stricken from the record."

Judge Blackwell looked up at the ceiling as he considered William's comments. Finally he said, "The counselor for the defense is right. There is no evidence that the defendant, or anyone else for that matter, placed the rose on the body. Any references will be purged from the trial record."

Turning to the jury box, the judge added, "You jurors are instructed to disregard any comments that suggested the defendant placed evidence on the deceased."

Several of the jurors looked at the judge in consternation, while others nodded in agreement. The foreman, a thin, well-dressed elderly man with half-glasses setting low on his nose, stroked his neatly trimmed beard as he considered what had transpired.

William returned his attention to the witness chair, "Sheriff, I have one more question ... actually a two part question. I understand you entered the defendant's place of business and removed a knife, the one entered in evidence. How did you surmise the blood on it came from the deceased? In fact, could it not have come from the defendant himself?"

William turned toward the prosecutor's table, expecting an objection to his question. But Stallings sat quietly with his chin on his hand staring at the sheriff.

"Well ... I assumed it was her blood," Roberts said hesitantly. "The coroner said it looked like human blood."

Stallings stiffened in his chair as William bored in on the sheriff, "Assumed? You assumed it was the deceased because it looked like human blood? Did you examine the defendant to see if he had cut himself ... on his own knife, in his own office?"

Sheriff Roberts squirmed in his chair as he stammered, "No ... No, I didn't."

"Yet, the defendant showed a cut on his finger to several persons after he was arrested," William said forcefully. "Those persons will be called as witnesses. They will attest that the blood on the knife, which you assumed was the deceased, could have been from the defendant. They will also attest that, even after you were informed of the defendant's injury by the defense counsel, you refused to inspect it or take his statement about the incident."

"Objection, your honor," Stallings said with an edge of disgust in his voice. "The counselor is badgering the witness. And he is conjecturing—if I may use his own word—that he knows beforehand what witnesses will attest to."

"Objection sustained," Judge Blackwell said. "Do you have any further questions for this witness, counselor?"

William sighed and looked at Clarence before continuing, "No, your honor. Just a clarification if you will."

Turning to Sheriff Roberts, he said, "What the defendant said when you arrested him was, 'Alas, I tearfully fear that more often than praise, I suffer the slings and arrows of outrageous and unfounded criticism.'"

After the closing arguments on the third day of the trial, the jury was sent to a secure room in the rear of the hall for deliberations. During the waiting period, Sarah and Rose walked up to the defense table. William appeared tired and listless, and he slumped heavily in his chair. Ben Clanton, a look of pride on his face, stood beside him with one hand on his shoulder.

Clarence managed a weak smile, but he also seemed drained by the ordeal of the trial. When Sarah had told him it was in his best interest not to take the witness stand in his own defense, he had reluctantly agreed, and then he lapsed into a period of quiet depression.

"Dear hearts," he said with a limp wave as Sarah and Rose approached him. "Sir William is a master at elocution and argument. He is truly the noblest Roman of all."

"I agree," Sarah said. "You have my most sincere congratulations, William."

"And mine," Rose added. "If I ever have need of legal representation, I hope you will be available for me."

"Thank you both," William responded. "Now it's up to the capriciousness of the jury."

Clarence looked up with a sudden spark in his eyes and said, "Fair ladies, would you do me the service of providing me with a fresh rose. The one above my beating heart is wilted. I wish to be properly attired when the august body determining my fate returns."

"Certainly, honey," Rose said with a smile as she leaned forward and smothered Clarence in a bosomy embrace. When she straightened up, tears pooled in her eyes and ran down her cheeks.

As Sarah looked at the flower on Clarence's jacket, an idea came to her. When a swarm of newspaper reporters crowded them away from the table, she took Rose's arm and drew her aside. Lowering her voice so no one else could hear her, she passed her thought on to Rose.

Rose wiped the tears from her face and smiled at Sarah's suggestion. "Wonderful, honey," she said. "I'll send a couple of my girls out straight away."

When the jury returned to their box, word spread immediately to those waiting outside and in the surrounding saloons. The deliberations had taken nearly three hours, which was time enough for those whose imbibing rate was several whiskeys an hour to get slightly drunk and mildly boisterous, and for those who swigged liquor non-stop to reduce themselves to staggering, mumbling characterizations of sub-humans.

During the wait, a number of fights had broken out between those convinced of Clarence's guilt and those swayed by the logical defense put forth by his attorney, William Thompson. Judge Blackwell, anticipating such an outcome, ordered Sheriff Roberts and Marshal Courtright to station additional deputies at the entrance to cull out those likely to cause a disruption inside the courtroom.

The selection process took nearly half an hour, and several arrests and whacked heads occurred before the doors could be closed and locked. The bailiff had to bellow for order for several minutes before the spectators settled into their seats and stopped murmuring.

Sarah adjusted the yellow rose on the bodice of her dress and looked around the room with a satisfied smile. She could see Rose and her entourage seated near the center of the hall. Each of them wore a similar flower. When she turned to the attorney's area, she could see that Clarence was adorned with one, as was William and Ben. Then, mysteriously, yellow roses began to appear throughout the auditorium. She could see them scattered from the floor seats at the rear to the box seats on each side. Even Jack Kilpatrick sported the flower. When she looked up at Jack, he caught her eye and waved jovially at her.

The judge seemed perplexed by the proliferation of yellow roses among the spectators when he entered the stage. He stared around the room for a long moment before banging his gavel and turning toward the jury.

"Gentlemen of the jury," he said in a loud voice. "Have you reached a verdict?"

"We have, your honor," the foreman said as he rose to his feet.

"Will the defendant please rise?" Judge Blackwell asked.

Clarence bounced to his feet like a child being excused from a dinner table, while William rose slowly and carefully, leaning on his cane for support. Ben stood beside him with his hand on his arm.

Sarah realized that she was holding her breath. Exhaling slowly, she bowed her head and said a silent prayer for Clarence.

"And how do you find on the charges of kidnapping and first degree murder?" Judge Blackwell asked the jury.

The foreman turned to Clarence with an anguished look on his face. He coughed into his fist before proclaiming, "We find the defendant, Mr. C. W. Heddings, guilty on both charges."

Pandemonium suddenly broke loose in the courtroom. Fights started all over as those who wore yellow roses fell upon those who had disdained them. Flying objects, which included hats, half-smoked cigars, and filthy spittoons, bombarded the main floor and the stage area. Shouts of lynching rose above the raucous sounds of the out-of-control horde threatening to tear the hall apart.

Ben ran down from the attorney's floor and, taking Sarah's arm, led her up to the stage. The judge, too stunned by the outbreak of violence to move, sat immobile on his raised podium. Deputies of Sheriff Roberts and Marshal Courtright rushed forward and formed a protective line at the front of the stage with swinging batons and drawn pistols.

When the battle raging in the auditorium threatened to break through the cordon of officers, a white-faced Sheriff Roberts took command. He shepherded those on the stage, which included the judge, the bailiff, the defense and prosecuting attorneys, the jury members, Clarence, and Sarah, through the back curtains to the room where the jury had been sequestered. As he closed the door behind them, the sound of several gunshots came from the auditorium.

Sarah huddled in one corner of the room with William, Clarence, and Ben. William leaned against the wall and gasped for breath until Ben grabbed a chair from the long table and sat him down. Clarence appeared unruffled by the flurry of activity, and he smiled broadly at Sarah as he re-arranged his rose until it met his satisfaction.

Sarah looked at him in astonishment. He didn't seem to realize that he had just been found guilty of murder and a vicious mob was clamoring for his lynching.

"Sheriff," Judge Blackwell said in a quavering voice, fear showing in his eyes. "I have never in all my days as an attorney or judge seen a more deplorable demonstration of lack of control. I find you personally responsible for this ... this—"

A chastened Sheriff Roberts responded weakly, "I am sorry judge. The jury was out so long it gave those ruffians too much time to drink."

"Dang burn it," Judge Blackwell said. "Don't blame it on the jury. I find you in contempt of court. You can be assured the fine will be the maximum I can levy. Now, I want you and your men to get me out of here to the train station. I'll not stay in this place of savages any longer."

"Judge," Stallings spoke up as the judge began removing his robe. "The jury has found the defendant guilty, but you have to pass the sentence before the trial is complete. I'm sure you don't want a mistrial and have to go through this again."

Clearly flustered, his face red and shiny with sweat, Judge Blackwell pulled his robe back on and responded curtly, "No. I certainly don't. Fort Worth is off my travel list from now on."

Turning to the bailiff, he said, "We'll adjourn the court right here in this room. I declare the rest of these proceedings closed to the public. Please carry on."

"Yes, your honor," the bailiff said. Raising his voice, he barked, "The court will come to order. The honorable Judge Nathaniel Blackwell presiding."

He positioned the prosecution on one side of the table and the defense on the other. The jury was herded into a standing position at the rear of the room, and a chair was placed at the head of the table for the judge.

Sarah sat next to Clarence with William and Ben on his other side. She was surprised that no one raised an objection at her being there. As silence descended on the room, she reached out and took Clarence's hand and squeezed it tightly. He turned to her, his face pale and his shoulders sagging.

"Mr. Heddings," Judge Blackwell said with his hands spread palms down on the top of the table. "You have been found guilty of kidnapping and murder by a jury of your peers. Do you have anything to say before I pass sentence?"

Sarah felt the warmth go out of Clarence's hand. Tears came to her eyes as she waited for him to speak.

A long moment passed before Clarence raised his chin and looked around the room. He seemed disappointed that his audience was so small. Finally he looked at the judge and began in a strong voice, "I thank my esteemed counselor, Sir William, and my many friends—"

Looking at Sarah, he smiled bravely before turning back to Judge Blackwell. "My many friends who believed in this soul. What's gone and what's past help should be past grief."

His voice faltered as he continued, "Although I am innocent, I go, and it is done; the bell invites me."

Then he seemed to find a reserve of strength. Standing, he placed his hand over his heart as he continued, "I leave you with the words of Hamlet.

> To-morrow, and to-morrow, and to-morrow,
> Creeps in this petty pace from day to day,
> To the last syllable of recorded time;
> And all our yesterdays have lighted fools
> The way to dusty death.
> Out, out, brief candle!
> Life's but a walking shadow."

Clarence's head dropped forward, and he fell into his chair. Only William's strong arm kept him from sliding to the floor. Sarah slid her chair closer, and she put her arm around Clarence and held him tightly.

"Ah hem," Judge Blackwell cleared his throat. "Yes. Admirably spoken, Mr. Heddings. I, too, often seek solace in the words of Mr. Shakespeare. Now it is my sworn duty to pronounce sentence upon you."

Looking directly at Clarence, he said, "It is the judgment of this court that on the morning of November 2, 1876, between the hours of eight and ten, you will be taken from the place of your incarceration to a place of execution and hanged by the neck until you are dead. May God have mercy on your soul."

Forgetting that he did not have a gavel in his hand, Judge Blackwell smacked his fist sharply on the table. Wincing from the pain, he gasped, "Court is adjourned."

All of the strength went out of Clarence, and he slumped onto the table. Sarah moved close to him and put a comforting arm around his shoulders. For a long moment, the only sound in the room was his quiet sobbing.

"Judge, our appeal," William said quietly, as Ben stood up and carried a stack of papers to Judge Blackwell.

"I expected no less," Blackwell responded while he removed the robe covering his dark suit. "I will carry it to the Court of Appeals in Austin. Their ruling will be returned by courier forthwith."

Chapter 22

▼

The unusually temperate weather continued into November. During most years, winter would have arrived by now, but its polar winds had yet to reach south of the Red River. As Sarah walked up the slight rise from the buggy, the bright morning sun warmed her through her coat and scarf. Walking under a wrought iron sign with the words *Fort Worth Memorial Park* on it, she turned right and went to the corner of the burial ground. Just beyond the perimeter fence, large oak trees, denuded of leaves, stood watch like ancient sentinels guarding a sacred ground. A whisper of wind stirred their bare limbs into slight movements, as if to show they were still alive and vigilant.

Sarah knelt by a large headstone fronting a newly dug grave. After placing a single yellow rose at its base, she stood and read the inscription carved on the face:

> Clarence L. Heddings
> Born April 10, 1832
> Deceased November 2, 1876
> *Give me my robe, put on my crown;*
> *I have Immortal longings in me.*
> W. Shakespeare

Clarence had chosen the quotation to accompany him on his journey to the hereafter. Beside his name, the craftsman had etched a single flower, a rose, at Sarah's request.

Sarah knew that convicted murderers put to death by the state's legal system normally would be interred in an unmarked plot in the Potter's Field portion of the graveyard. The custom of the time was to bury such criminals without a marker, facing south so they would not be able to see the Lord Jesus when He returned to earth. But, with the assistance of Rose and others, she had raised the funds to purchase a space in the public area. The money left over had been used for a stone monument.

During the scant few weeks between Clarence's trial and his execution, Sarah had come to know him quite well. The daily visits with him in the jail were times of emotional stress, and yet they were also times of spiritual growth for both of them. Clarence had turned away from religion when he was a teenager. Rebelling against his strict parents, he had substituted Shakespeare as a father and God figure. Now he came back to the Lord on bended knees, with tears in his eyes. Sarah, watching his conversion, felt a strengthened sense of her own spirituality and purpose of life.

The magnetic pull of her ranch weighed heavily on her. Winter was at the doorstep, and Lars Sigmund was spending much of his time preparing it for the onslaught of the strong, freezing winds and sleet about to sweep across it. Beelzebub was still in quarantine, but she couldn't use that as an excuse for staying in Fort Worth. She had remained because she could not leave Clarence alone during his last days. When the trial appeal was rejected, as William predicted, she knew Clarence needed her. She became his soul mate, his confident, and his friend. As the days passed, she became even more convinced that he was incapable of taking another person's life. On the day of his execution, he had smiled and chatted with her effusively. Then he had gone to his death bravely, marching like a tiny soldier on parade, with a yellow rose in his lapel and a prayer on his lips.

U. R. Gladly had made a generous donation to the fund to build a public school in Fort Worth. Sarah had wanted to designate it in memory of Clarence, but Rose talked her out of it. Rose told her that he was a convicted murderer interred by the state, and his name might taint the benevolent aspect of the donation.

"I'm sorry, Mama," a quiet voice said to Sarah.

Looking down at Jody through the tears in her eyes, Sarah responded, "Thank you. He was a good man. When you grow up, I want people to say that about you."

"They will," Margaret said as she joined them, putting her arm around her mother's shoulder. "Jody is a special person."

"Ahem," a voice came from behind Sarah. Turning, she saw Daniel standing behind her with his hat in his hands.

"Is there anything I can do for you, Mrs. Whitman?" Daniel added.

Sarah smiled. She had become quite fond of him over the past month. He was the most sincere and forthright person she had ever met, and he had strength of character coupled with gentleness that reminded her of Jim. When he asked her for Margaret's hand in marriage, she wasn't surprised. She knew Margaret was in love with him. When she suggested that they wait until her seventeenth birthday in the spring and have the wedding at the ranch, they both agreed.

"Is everything ready for us to leave in the morning?" Sarah asked as she turned and walked toward the cemetery gate.

"Yes," Daniel said, hurrying to keep up with her. "I have a cage to put Beelzebub in. Best we wait another week or so before we let him loose, just to be sure he's okay."

"How is Patches doing?"

When she had asked Jody why he chose that name for the injured dog she had found in the animal killing field, he related that Daniel had told him he would have to cover her with patches to make her well.

"Much better," Daniel said. "She wants to bedevil Beelzebub all the time. She'll be as good as new in a few weeks."

Sarah was turning the carriage on the road toward town with Daniel riding along side, when she noticed a rider coming out of the trees. It took a moment before she recognized Jack Kilpatrick.

"Afternoon, Sarah," Kilpatrick said with a smile, as he pinched out a cigarette and flipped it on the ground. He reined his horse up to the carriage, blocking its progress. "Mighty nice of you to pay your respects to the dearly departed."

"Mrs. Whitman!" Sarah said sharply. "Are you following me?"

She was surprised at his appearance. His face, normally tanned and relaxed, was pale and lined as if he had been ill. Even his voice lacked its usual timbre.

"Why, Sarah," Kilpatrick said, ignoring her admonishment. "Why would I do that?"

Tipping his hat to Margaret, who was sitting beside Sarah, he said, "Good day, Miss Whitman."

"Good day, sir," Margaret responded coolly. She reached out and took Daniel's hand as he sat on his horse near her.

"And to you, Daniel," Kilpatrick added. "I hear you're giving up the law. Is that true?"

Daniel quieted his horse and moved closer to Margaret as he responded, "Yes sir. I've signed on to work for Mrs. Whitman."

"I understand you are returning to your ranch," Kilpatrick said to Sarah.

"Yes," Sarah answered. "Now if you don't mind, we have things to do."

Kilpatrick started to back his horse up to let the carriage pass, and then he stopped. Reaching into his vest pocket, he withdrew something and tossed it to Sarah. The sunlight glittered off the object as it arced through the air and fell through her fingers onto her lap.

Sarah picked it up and glanced at it. Then she looked up at Kilpatrick with a questioning look.

"It's a '72 Liberty Seated silver dollar," Kilpatrick said.

"I see," Sarah said as she held her breath. "Am I supposed to guess where you got it?"

She tossed the coin back to Kilpatrick who caught it with a sweep of his left hand and made it disappear from sight. The motion reminded her of the time she had seen him do a coin trick in Marshal Courtright's office. Something about the sideways movement of his hand when he caught it bothered her, but she couldn't fathom what it was.

Kilpatrick started to laugh, but it turned into a cough that racked his body. A long moment passed before he was able to compose himself and respond, "No. I just wanted you to know something before you left Fort Worth. We'll be searching your ranch. Who knows, we may turn up more silver like this … and maybe even some gold."

"You better have a search warrant," Sarah snapped. "My ranch is not a newspaper office."

"Don't worry. It's a bona fide warrant signed by the proper authorities."

Sarah turned away as her face reddened with anger. She snapped the reins and started the carriage past Kilpatrick, who had to back his horse up to avoid being hit.

After they left Kilpatrick behind, Sarah shivered as she wondered why he would warn her about searching her ranch. The way he talked, the warrant had already been issued. The thought of strangers violating her property disturbed her. Her desire to return home as soon as possible grew even stronger.

When they reached William Thompson's law office, Sarah asked Margaret to leave her there and continue on to the hotel. Entering the building, she noticed that Ben Clanton was not at his desk. The door to William's office was ajar, and she stopped to knock on it.

William looked up from his desk with a smile on his freshly shaven face. "Why, Sarah," he said, standing to greet her. "Come in. Please sit down."

He was wearing a black three-piece suit with a pressed white shirt and a short black tie. The office was clean and orderly, and an open window afforded an entrance for fresh air from outside to circulate through the room.

"I want to say goodbye," Sarah said. "And to thank you and Ben for helping Stubby Thompson at the *Beacon*. I'm still surprised Clarence left it to me."

"Our pleasure," William said. "Ben said there are enough merchants who want Stubby to do their marketing printing to keep him and his wife in provisions."

"I offered the paper to him, but he refused to take it."

William turned down the right side of his lips and winked his right eye at Sarah. "Is this how he responded?" he asked.

Sarah laughed. "Yes. That's his way of saying no."

"Clarence knew what he was doing when he gave the paper to you," William continued. "Stubby is a fine printer, but he can't communicate with the public, as you know. I do wish you would consider staying here and running it. You have a God-given ability to write and a passion to give it meaning. Besides, B. B. Paddock needs some competition to keep his prices down."

"Thank you for the kind words," Sarah responded. "My ranch is waiting for me and my children. Looks like we'll have an addition to the family in the spring when Daniel marries Margaret. I came to Fort Worth to search for my husband, Jim, as you know. Now that Sludge Cameron is dead, I don't think there's any chance of finding his body. It's time for me to go home."

"I am sorry about your loss," William said. "As you told me, you have to put that behind you and go on with your life."

"I know," Sarah responded. "I will. The ranch is the place to do that. A trip back up here before Margaret's wedding may be in order. I'll never forget what you did for Clarence when he needed help. And Ben. He's a very talented young man. He worships you, you know. I hope you're going to make an attorney out of him."

"I certainly intend to," William said. "He reaches twenty one—next month—and Judge Barlow will give him his examination. When you return, that shingle outside will read Thompson and Clanton, Attorneys at Law."

William smiled as he added, "I'm going to miss you, Sarah. I want to thank you for slapping some sense into me. I've decided it's time for me to take a woman in my life again."

"That's great!" Sarah exclaimed. "Who is the lucky person?"

William waved his huge arm around in front of him as he said, "Fort Worth. I'm going to help her become a city to be proud of. A law-abiding city. I plan to start by getting rid of Sheriff Roberts. His re-election was a travesty, and I aim to see he doesn't serve it to term."

"Do you know something I don't?" Sarah asked.

"Could be," William said with a twinkle in his eye. "Could be."

"Speaking of the sheriff reminds me of a question I want to ask you," Sarah said. "Did the coroner take photographs of Lucille Martell's body?"

"No," William said as he narrowed his eyes. "I asked him, and he said the body was too deteriorated when he got it. There is a new photographer in town who uses what he calls a dry plate process. Apparently it gives a better quality image than the daguerreotype cameras, but the coroner didn't know about him at the time."

William sat forward and looked closely at Sarah as he asked, "What do you have in mind?"

"I'm not sure. Just something bothering me. Was she attacked from the front or back?"

"According to the coroner's report, someone came up behind her, pulled her head back, and cut her throat with one deep slash," William responded. "I have a copy if you'd like to read it. Kind of gruesome."

"No," Sarah said. "That won't be necessary. I was wondering if the person who did it was right or left handed."

"Strange you would ask that," William said. "I posed that very question to the coroner. He said he couldn't tell. Probably didn't look that close. And, of course, by the time I came out of my funk and took the case, the body had been in the ground too long."

"Thank you," Sarah said. "I have to be going. Will you join us for dinner at the hotel?"

"I'm sorry," William responded as he stood and offered his hand to Sarah. "I'll say goodbye here. I have a client coming in on the seven o'clock train from Dallas. He wants to catch the return at nine."

Sarah ignored William's outstretched hand. She walked around his desk and embraced him. For a long moment, they held each other in silence. When she backed away from him, both of them had tears in their eyes.

Chapter 23

Sometime during the night, the strong northerly winds, which had been held in check by a high-pressure area, stormed across the Indian Territory and moved to the southeast against its weakened opposition. The massive cold front hurtled the Red River and slammed into the Cross Timbers area of north central Texas with a pent up fury, as if to make up for its late arrival. The balmy temperatures of the day before plummeted to below freezing.

Sarah awoke to the sound of the wind buffeting the windows in the hotel room. She felt the chill in the air through her nightclothes when she rose and awakened Margaret and Jody.

"Mother, it's so cold," Margaret said, shivering as she held her blanket around her shoulders.

"Yes, it is," Sarah responded. She roused Jody and dressed him.

"We should have left yesterday," Sarah said. "This cold weather will probably last for a while. We'll just have to bundle up and do the best we can. We must get back to the ranch."

When Daniel, wearing a long overcoat with a scarf tied about his neck and his hat set low over his forehead, pulled the carriage up in front of the hotel with his horse, Buttermilk, tied on behind, a low, gray line of clouds obscured the morning sunlight. The wind, still gusting strongly, swirled along the street, hurling dust and other loose objects in joyous abandon. Beelzebub was snoring contentedly in a large cage stowed in the wagon's rear storage area, as if it was a mild autumn day. Beside his pen, Patches lay shivering under a blanket, whimpering softly.

A canvas top with rear and side panels enclosed the passenger area of the carriage. It rattled and banged in the wind as Sarah and Daniel loaded their personal items. Margaret and Jody climbed into the back seat, swaddled in blankets and surrounded by their baggage. At Jody's insistence, Patches was moved up with him and lay snuffling at his feet.

When Sarah took the reins in her gloved hands and, following Daniel, pulled away from the hotel, the tails of the two horses pulling the carriage flailed in the strong breeze and steam spurted from their nostrils with each breath.

After they reached the outskirts of Fort Worth and started south, Sarah hailed Daniel. He stopped his horse and waited for her to come up along side. "Why don't you tie Buttermilk on behind and ride with us?" she asked. "It will be warmer out of the wind."

Daniel held the brim of his hat and peered out from under it with eyes tear-streaked from the blustery weather and replied, "Thank you, Mrs. Whitman. I'll do that. Let me do the driving."

"Oh, goody," Jody chimed in, clapping his red woolen mittens. "We can sing songs."

Daniel transferred to the front seat and took the reins from Sarah. After glancing back at Margaret, who unwrapped the scarf from her face to smile at him, he started the carriage rolling. Tiny particles of frozen precipitation crackled against the canvas top and ricocheted off the horses.

"Sing Bessie Pike, Daniel," Jody said.

"I will," Daniel responded. "But you have to sing along with me. I'll do a verse, and then you join me, okay?"

"Okay," Margaret interjected gaily. "Mother, will you sing with us?"

Sarah, lost in her thoughts, almost missed Margaret's request. The time they had spent in Fort Worth would always remain in her memory: meeting Daniel, being reacquainted with Rose, becoming a confident and soul mate to Clarence only to lose him to a travesty of justice, making friends with William Thompson and Ben Clanton, nursing Beelzebub through his quarantine, and finding Patches in the animal slaughter field. And, above all, coming to the realization that Jim was indeed dead, and she would never see him again, never know his strength or feel his love. She was going home, but it would never be the same again.

Wiping tears from her eyes, Sarah said, "Of course, I'll join you. I don't know that song, Daniel. You'll have to teach it to me."

"I know it," Jody squealed. "It's about Bessie Pike who had a hog, a rooster, and an old yaller dog."

Daniel laughed and began to sing.

> Did you ever hear tell of sweet Betsy from Pike,
> Who crossed the wide prairies with her lover Ike,
> With two yoke of cattle and one spotted hog,
> A tall Shanghai rooster and an old yaller dog?
> Sing-too-ral-li-oo-ral-li-oo-ral-li-ay,
> Sing-too-ral-li-oo-ral-li-oo-ral-li-ay.

Daniel's rich, vibrant voice filled the carriage with warmth, life, and joy. When he started the chorus again, Sarah, Margaret, and Jody chimed in with him. As they sang, the cold wind and the miles of travel ahead became insignificant, pushed aside by the love and camaraderie they shared. Even the horses seemed to settle down and, instead of fighting the traces, trotted smoothly onward.

The miles and the songs fell behind them and the wind slackened. Although the gray clouds still formed a low ceiling overhead, the temperature increased slightly as the dim sun climbed higher. Sarah unwrapped her scarf and let it fall across her chest. She removed her gloves but, after feeling the chill still in the air, put them back on.

"Look!" Jody said with wonder in his voice, pointing his mittened hand toward the front of the carriage.

Snowflakes were falling, turning, and swirling in wondrous flight. At first they were widely scattered, then they increased in size and number until they filled the air, large and pristine white floating objects. Within a few minutes the roadway and the grass and bushes alongside were completely covered with a soft winter coat. Only the internal warmth of the horses as they jogged briskly along kept the snow from accumulating on their backs.

"We must sing a Christmas song," Margaret exclaimed, sharing Jody's amazement at nature's spectacular display.

"I have one," Sarah said. As she began to sing the others joined in:

> The first day of Christmas my true love sent to me
> A partridge in a pear tree.
> The second day of Christmas my true love sent to me
> Two swans a swimming
> And a partridge in a pear tree.

As they sang, the snow continued to accumulate. Soon, the ruts in the road were barely visible ahead of them, and the horses were beginning to slow down to cope with the drag against their hoofs and the carriage wheels.

After finishing the song against Jody's protests, Sarah turned to Daniel. "Can we keep going if this snow continues?" she asked. The joyous mood brought on by the snowfall and the singing faded into one of concern.

Squinting to see through the flurry, Daniel responded, "As long as we can see the road, we'll be okay. Should be able to make it through a foot or so. I may have to walk ahead and lead the horses if it doesn't slack off. There's a ranch and stage way-station about two miles ahead. I know the family who runs it; the Williams. We can stop there if we have to."

"Mama," Jody shouted. "I have to go peepee."

"Jody!" Margaret admonished. "That's not a nice way to say it."

"But I have to go peepee," Jody retorted.

"I'll take him, Mrs. Whitman," Daniel said as he stopped the carriage.

Lifting Jody down from his seat, he carried him out to the side of the road where he helped him unbutton his coat and pants. Sarah could barely see the two of them through the world of swirling whiteness.

Then, suddenly, out of the fringes of that white world a moving object appeared. Like a dark ghost, it grew larger as it swiftly approached Daniel and Jody. Sarah shouted in fear, her voice cracked and strained, as the wraith formed into a rider on horseback, "Daniel, watch out!"

But the warning came too late. As Daniel turned, the strange apparition swung a club and struck him to the ground. Continuing on, the rider disappeared into the snowstorm like a puff of black smoke dissipating into a cloud. Then another rider appeared out of nowhere. Swerving to miss Daniel's body, he leaned off the side of his horse and snatched Jody from the ground with a sweep of his arm. Like the first attacker, he continued on until the whiteness swallowed him up.

Unable to breathe, Sarah stared in the direction of Jody's disappearance. Faintly, she heard his terrified voice call to her, "Mama! Help me! Mama!"

Then there was silence, a silence that clutched at Sarah's heart and stopped her breath.

"Daniel!" Margaret screamed as she jumped down from the carriage and ran to where he lay face down with his arms spread wide.

Before Sarah could shake off her paralysis, she saw another figure. He wasn't moving like the first two, it was as if he had suddenly been spirited from some far away place to the peripheral of the falling snow. Black and featureless against the backdrop of white, he sat quietly, facing her. Through the snowy mist, she could see that he was wearing a buffalo robe, and a cap with two small, curved horns covered his head. In one hand, he held a long lance with feathers blowing in the wind from the tip. For a long moment, they stared at each other. Then the ghostly being began walking his horse toward her.

Sarah reached for the pistol in her purse but, hampered by her gloves, she dropped it on the floorboards. Looking up in panic, she could see the face of the intruder as he closed in on her. Beneath his buffalo horn cap, his thin, brown face was covered with streaks of red, yellow, and black. A wide, vivid scar slashed across his left cheek. It started just beneath his eye, ran down across his lips and ended at the right side of his jaw.

The man's penetrating dark eyes stared fixedly at Sarah, primal hatred narrowing his pupils, as he raised his lance to his shoulder. Sensing the futility of further resistance, she said a silent prayer and stared back at him without fear.

Suddenly a shattering roar arose from the back of the carriage. Beelzebub, startled by the commotion and, perhaps aware of the danger to Sarah, was attacking the bars of his cage in a furious rage. The approaching rider stopped suddenly, his eyes widening at the tremendous noise, which cut through the falling snow like the thunder of an avalanche. Backing up rapidly, he wheeled and galloped furiously off in the direction of his two companions.

Sarah tore off her gloves and picked up the pistol, the metal cold against her hands. She started to shoot in the direction of the riders who had disappeared into the storm. Then, realizing that Jody was with them, she lowered the gun. Anguish wracked her body as the memory of his cries for help echoed in her ears.

"Mother, please come!" Margaret screamed. "Daniel is hurt."

Sarah shook the stupor of fear and surprise from her mind and climbed to the ground. Margaret, who was sitting on the snow, had turned Daniel over and was cradling his head in her lap. A large contusion covered the right side of his face and his eye was swollen shut. His breath came in shallow, weak gasps.

Sarah ran to the carriage and returned with several blankets. Covering both Daniel and Margaret, she said, "We have to get him up off this cold ground. He'll go into shock."

"Oh!" Margaret said, tears streaming from her eyes. "Is he going to die?"

Sarah put a finger on Daniel's neck and felt for his pulse. It was fluttering rapidly and weakly. "No," she said with a conviction she was unsure of. "Let's get him into the carriage."

With Margaret's assistance, Sarah drug Daniel to the wagon and lifted him into the back seat where they covered him with blankets. He was still unconscious and did not respond to their voices. Margaret, who was nearing a state of panic, wanted to sit with him, but Sarah grasped her arm and pulled her into the front seat on the driver's side. The heavy snow was diminishing, and the visibility was improving.

"Margaret," she said firmly. "You have to be strong. Daniel needs your help. He said there's a ranch about two miles ahead. It looks like the snow is ending. You can still see the road. Take him there as fast as you can."

"Me!" Margaret said in surprise. "You want me to drive. What about you?"

"I'm going after Jody," Sarah said as she walked to the rear of the carriage and untied Daniel's horse.

"Jody!" Margaret cried. "Where is Jody?"

"They've taken him," Sarah said. "Three Indians. One hit Daniel and another took Jody."

"You said three?" Margaret said as she looked wildly about her.

"Yes," Sarah responded. "Beelzebub frightened the third one off."

After removing some money and her bible from her purse and placing them in her coat pocket, Sarah put it back under the front seat. Pulling on her gloves, she checked to make sure that she still had the pistol. Then she shortened the reach on the stirrups, mounted, and pulled Buttermilk up next to the carriage.

"Be brave," she said as she reached out and touched Margaret's arm. "Daniel needs your strength."

"You can't go running after those Indians," Margaret said in anguish. "They'll kill you."

"I'm going to track them," Sarah said. "Tell the men at the Williams ranch to follow after me. Daniel will need a doctor. Wait for me at the hotel in Fort Worth. Now, go. Hurry!"

Sarah wheeled Buttermilk around and galloped in the direction where the three riders had disappeared. About four inches of snow covered the ground, and she could make out the tracks of the Indian's horses where they left the road. Daniel's saddle was too large for her and the stirrups still set too low, and she started bouncing up and down with Buttermilk's gait.

Although the wind still blew snow flurries in her face, she hadn't started feeling the cold except on her exposed face. She was wearing pantaloons, which came down to her long boots, and a heavy woolen dress with wrist-length sleeves. Rose had given her a lined full-length coat with a fur collar as a going away gift, and it was keeping her warm. She also had a woolen scarf, which was wound tightly around her neck and stuffed down inside the front of the coat.

The lurching ride was causing difficulties with her head covering. Instead of the bonnet she normally wore, she had donned a stylish, wide-brimmed hat for the trip home. Lacking a tie string, it bounced loosely on her head, even though she pulled it down as far as she could. Then, as Buttermilk jumped over a fallen tree, the hat flew off her head. Looking back, she could see it sailing through the air. She thought about turning back for it, but the pain in her heart over Jody changed her mind, and she continued on as fast as she could stay in the saddle.

A stand of timber loomed ahead. The wind, which had nearly stopped a few minutes before with the ending of the snowstorm, now blew with increased fury. The soft, white ground cover was lifted aloft and floated through the air like mist rising over water in a tropical swampland. The gray overcast thinned and the dim sun cast an eerie pall, as Sarah leaned forward to search for the tracks left by the horses she was pursuing. When she left the slight protection of the trees and entered a vast expanse of prairie, the drifting snow obliterated any sign of them.

Realizing the futility of continuing without seeing evidence that the three Indians had gone in the direction she was headed, she stopped Buttermilk and dismounted. Holding the reins in her hand, she walked in front of him peering at the ground. But the shifting snow revealed nothing. She felt the wind on her right cheek and stopped perplexed. Somehow, she thought, she had turned away from the direct wind, which meant she was headed toward the northwest or even west. Turning and looking back over her trail, she could no longer see the copse of trees she had come through. Twisting, turning tentacles of wind-blown snow covered the flat prairie around her.

The sense of pain and loss she had felt since Jody disappeared was suddenly replaced by anger. The fury that came over her caused her to tremble. One of her father's favorite Bible passages was from *Ephesians*: "Let all bitterness, wrath, anger, clamor, and evil speaking be put away from you, with all malice." But, at this moment, she wanted to catch those who had injured Daniel and stolen Jody and visit her wrath on them. Lifting one hand into the air, she formed it into a fist and shook it in rage.

After a long moment, she forced herself to turn away from her murderous heart. Until now, she had not felt the cold because she was so intent on finding Jody. Now it descended on her with a bone chilling impact. Shivering, she returned to Buttermilk and began adjusting the stirrup length. A feeling of helplessness seized her. Even an experienced tracker would be helpless in this snowy terrain. She knew she would have to return to the road and go to the Williams Ranch.

As she was about to mount, Sarah saw a movement behind her, a flash of dark against the white vapors obscuring the ground. Caught in a grip of fear, she tore off her right glove and reached into her pocket for her pistol. The Indians must have realized she was tracking them, and one of them circled back, she thought. Aiming the gun at the growing dark mass, she began to pull the trigger.

At the last moment, something stilled her finger. The form was almost upon her when she dropped the pistol back into her pocket and sank to her knees. "Beelzebub!" she cried.

The huge dog, hair matted and wet from the snow, lumbered up to her with a low rumble in his throat. Sarah put her arms around his neck and hugged him while tears streamed down her cheeks. "You gave me such a fright," she said. "What are you doing here? Did Margaret send you after me?"

Ruffling his ears, she looked into his eyes and said, "Well, we're in this together. We can go back, or we can look for Jody."

At the mention of Jody's name, Beelzebub gave a throaty bark and stared ahead in the direction Sarah had been going. "Okay, old dog," she said as she stood up. "I guess you made the decision for us. I hope you're up to it. Let's go find Jody."

Beelzebub, released from Sarah's embrace, bounded forward past Buttermilk and trotted into the swirling mist. Sarah mounted as fast as she could and followed him.

In time, the wind abated and the blowing snow settled back onto the earth, piling up against trees, rocks, and bushes. Sarah could see no sign of the passage of horses, but Beelzebub continued on with a shambling gait, just faster than a walk. Looking up at the weak afternoon sun, she was almost certain they were headed west. Recalling the recent stories about the Indian situation, she thought that most of them had surrendered to the U.S. Army and were on the Fort Sill Reservation in Oklahoma. But that was almost due north.

Then Beelzebub stopped in front of her. At first Sarah thought he had lost his way but, as she watched, he went to a drift up against a large rock and began eating the snow, wolfing it down in gulps. It took a moment for her to realize that he was thirsty. Coming to her senses, she looked down at Daniel's saddle. Tied to the horn by a leather cord was a canteen. She raised it and shook it, listening to the sloshing inside. Unscrewing the cap, she took a long drink of the cool water.

Turning, she noticed that a bedroll, wrapped inside a thin rain slicker, was tied at the rear of the saddle. Behind her, bulging saddlebags draped over Buttermilk's flanks. When she started out after Jody, she hadn't thought about food or water. The water, at least, had been provided for her. Saying a silent thank you to Daniel, she nudged the horse into a fast walk to catch up with Beelzebub.

The wind, never entirely still, swirled and buffeted Sarah as she headed across the desolate wasteland. Beelzebub rested briefly now and then, but he kept moving onward, never deviating from the half lope, half walk he had started with. As the hours passed and the sun dropped lower in the afternoon sky, Sarah worried that he would die from exhaustion. Several times, she dismounted and gave him water from the canteen and some beef jerky she found in one of the saddlebags. Each time, he drank and ate quickly, and then broke loose from Sarah's embrace with a whine and continued on.

As the dim orb of the sun neared the western horizon, they came to a river. Sarah, almost asleep from Buttermilk's rocking gait, heard the sound of the water and roused herself. Looking down the slope, she saw Beelzebub standing on the bank staring across at the far side. Ice was beginning to form along the edges of the river where backwater eddies formed areas of quiet water. Several scrub mesquite trees and a few scrawny bushes kept lonesome watch over the turbulent waterway.

"Wait, Beelzebub," Sarah shouted as she rode up to him.

The river was about thirty feet wide, and the water on the dark surface roiled and swirled rapidly. It was impossible for her to tell how deep it was. Dismounting, she searched the bank for signs of the Indians they were following. When she could not find any, she knelt on the bank beside Beelzebub.

"Old boy," she said. "That river looks pretty deep. I might be able to keep above it, but you'll get soaked."

Ruffling the hair on his neck, she added, "You'll freeze if you get wet, and I can't get you up on Buttermilk. You're just too heavy."

Beelzebub looked up at Sarah with a plaintive whine. Then he turned back to the river, his eyes fixed on the far side.

"Besides, Beebub," Sarah said as she stood up. "We don't even know if they came to this river. We must go back for help."

Her shoulders sagged in defeat and tears came to her eyes as she realized that she had used Jody's term of endearment for Beelzebub. Memories of Jody's painful cries for help returned to her, stopping her breath and threatening to suffocate her in a shroud of black depression. She forced the thoughts into a new room in her mind, "Jody's Room." She told herself she wouldn't open it just yet. She wouldn't think about him now, perhaps in time.

A sharp bark from Beelzebub brought Sarah back to reality. He bolted down the bank about twenty feet and splashed into the river. A dead limb jutting out into the stream held a flash of red color that caught Sarah's eye just before Beelzebub obscured it. Snatching it in his jaws, he wheeled back on the bank and ran swiftly to Sarah, water flying from his hair.

"Oh Lord!" Sarah cried as she fell to her knees and took the object from his mouth. "Jody's mitten." Encircling Beelzebub's neck with her arms, she kissed his snout with joy. "Forgive me for doubting you."

Looking at the river, Sarah said, "I can't ask you to cross. We don't know how deep it is."

Beelzebub pulled away from Sarah's embrace and, without a backward look, leaped into the water. After several long jumps, he settled into a frantic swimming stroke. The strong current carried him downstream, but he began to make headway toward the far bank. As Sarah watched fretfully, he finally emerged on the far bank. Shaking water from his coat, he stared back at her with an air of impatience.

Sarah was able to make it across the river without getting wet by raising her feet up and placing them on Buttermilk's neck when they reached the deepest part of the ford. When she reached the other side, Beelzebub was waiting for her, his massive body shivering from the cold water. Dismounting, she removed the blanket wrapped in Daniel's rain slicker and dried him as well as she could. Tiny particles of ice were forming on his mane, and his breath spewed forth in clouds of steam.

"I'm sorry," she said as she finished. "I'd like to start a fire and warm us up, but we better keep moving if we want to catch Jody."

At the mention of the boy's name, Beelzebub pulled away from Sarah and started running up the low embankment. When Sarah reached the top of the rise, she could see him loping away across the snow covered plain toward the north. The outline of the sun behind the gray overcast to her left was settling on the horizon and flattening out in preparation for its nightly disappearance. Already, the absence of direct light was blurring the edges of rocks, bushes, and other ground objects. To the north, the cloud cover appeared to be ending as a dry area behind the cold front pushed southward.

Beelzebub looked like a black ghost against the darkening landscape, and Sarah had to speed up Buttermilk to keep him in sight. The thought of traveling on the prairie at night concerned her, but she was driven onward by a primeval motherly urge to save her offspring. It took all her concentration to keep "Jody's Room" in her mind from bursting open and overwhelming her.

Finally the time came when Sarah could no longer see the ground in front of her, and Beelzebub was lost in the dark distance. Afraid Buttermilk would step into a hole or run into some unseen object, she pulled back on the reins to stop him. But the horse kept walking forward, slowly but steadily. Ahead, under the diminishing cloud cover, she could see the first stars of the evening peer down at her.

Then, surprisingly, since the sun had set, she could make out details on the snowy trail: here a tuft of sagebrush reaching upward through the whiteness, and there a rise in the ground casting a dim shadow. As her eyes adjusted to the darkness, she discovered that she could even see Beelzebub far ahead. Buttermilk had adjusted his gait to match his, and the dog remained at the peripheral of her sight. The cloud cover drew back from the sky, as if pulled by some unseen heavenly giant, and provided enough light to continue. The twinkling lights from a myriad of stars overhead accompanied them on their nighttime trek.

Then Sarah became aware of a decrease in the temperature. With the clear skies came a brisk, bone-chilling wind; not strong, but incessant. Tugging at the edges of the scarf she had wound around her face below her nose, the breeze sought out bare skin on her cheeks, ears, nose, and forehead. At first, she felt a tingling from the frigid air, but that quickly turned into a deep painful ache. Holding the reins with one hand, she pulled the scarf up until it covered the lower part of her face to just below her eyes, teary from the stinging wind.

She looked up into the northern sky. The starry outline of Ursa Major, the Big Dipper, formed brightly in her vision. She couldn't remember ever seeing it so clearly. Following the two pointing stars at the end of the dipper, as her father had taught her, she located the North Star in Ursa Minor. It was directly ahead, in the direction Beelzebub was heading. The Indians had started out to the west after they took Jody, she thought. Then, after many miles, they turned back to the north, perhaps toward the reservation in Oklahoma.

Why, she wondered, would they take a white child there? Surely the Indian Agent would take him from them and keep him in safety. If she could find the reservation, Jody might be waiting for her. With that thought in mind, she lifted her slumping shoulders and took a deep breath of the cold air through her scarf.

After what seemed like an eternity, she felt Buttermilk come to a stop. She had been dozing in the saddle, the rhythmic jostling and the long stressful day stealing her energy and dulling her senses. Opening her eyes, she saw Beelzebub lying on the snow in front of her.

"Oh Lord!" she exclaimed as she dismounted slowly and painfully.

The wind, blustery and swirling before, now blew steadily from the north, carrying with it even colder temperatures. Her muscles didn't seem to want to work. She had no feeling in her lower extremities, and she had to force her legs to move.

When she dropped to the ground, the numbness in her feet gave way to sharp pain. Even her hands were stiff and sore. When she touched her exposed forehead, there was no sensation, which frightened her. She knew it was cold enough for frostbite to ravage exposed skin. She remembered a friend of her father who had lost several fingers and the tip of his nose after being caught out in a blizzard.

Beating her hands together and stomping her feet to gain circulation, Sarah knelt on the frozen ground beside Beelzebub. Ice encrusted the hair on his body and jowls, and only the warmth of his breath kept it from forming on his nose. His eyes were closed, and he panted slowly in exhaustion. Buttermilk stood beside them, his head drooped as clouds of steam poured from his nostrils.

Sarah held Beelzebub's head in her gloved hands. Looking upward to the points of light sprinkling the dark night sky, she prayed silently for help. Then, once again, her attention was drawn to the North Star. The face of her father appeared in her thoughts, and the words from Shakespeare he had spoken to her so many years before, when he showed her how to find her way at night using the stars for guidance, came back to her, "I am constant as the northern star."

Although she wanted to collapse on the ground with Beelzebub, she knew she had to listen to her father's voice. The star, barely above the northern horizon, beckoned to her. Jody was out there, in that direction. She could not rest here and give in to the cold and the demands of the long journey. She must go on. They must go on.

She felt a sudden urge to urinate. The thought horrified her. How could she remove her clothes and expose herself to the brutally cold wind? What if she fell in the snow? How would she ever dry herself? On the other hand, if she lost control and went inside her pantaloons, it would freeze and be even worse. She decided that, somehow, she would wait, even if it took all of her will power and energy.

Rising to her feet, she removed the blanket from behind Buttermilk's saddle. After several minutes of tousling and rubbing Beelzebub with it, he regained his senses. Raising his snout, he nuzzled Sarah's hands and licked her face. She inspected his paws and recoiled in horror. The pads, surrounded by dirt and ice, were cut and bleeding. As carefully as she could, she cleaned and dried them. With each touch, Beelzebub whined in pain.

"Okay, old boy," she said soothingly. "I wish we had Daniel to help us. But we haven't come this far to quit now."

Returning to the horse, she removed some more of the beef jerky. Even in the deep cold, the appetizing aroma of the meat brought saliva to her mouth. Tearing off a piece with her teeth, she chewed and swallowed it. Pain in her throat caused her to gag, and she almost vomited into the snow. Removing the canteen, she discovered that it wouldn't open; the screw cap was frozen shut, and her hands lacked the strength to break it loose.

Then, thinking of Beelzebub, she offered some of the meat to him. But he ignored it as he struggled to breathe, his eyes closed in exhaustion. Sitting on the ground next to him, Sarah bit off a piece of the meat and chewed it to soften and moisten it. Then she opened Beelzebub's teeth and placed it in his mouth. Stroking his snout and his throat, she encouraged him to eat. After several seconds, he gulped and swallowed the chunk whole. When she put the next portion close to his mouth, he opened his eyes and snatched it from her hand. After wolfing down several more pieces, he struggled to his feet and started plodding slowly and ponderously through the snow and the darkness.

Sarah watched Beelzebub stagger onward toward that guiding star on high. "What are we to do?" she cried into the night.

Then in the distance, beyond Beelzebub, she saw the vague outline of an object that looked out of place in the dim surreal landscape. The edges weren't wavy or jagged like the trees, rocks, and shrubs she could discern; they were straight and sharp as if constructed by man, not nature.

Sarah grabbed Buttermilk's reins and shuffled toward the object. "Wait, Beelzebub," she shouted hoarsely. Leaning forward to keep from falling, she realized that she had no sensation in her feet. From her thighs downward, she felt nothing. It was as if she were walking on some other person's legs, forcing them to move forward through sheer will power.

Suddenly, her disembodied feet struck something in front of her and she fell sprawling, Buttermilk's reins flying from her stiff hands. Scrambling painfully to her hands and knees, she realized that she had tripped over Beelzebub who was lying on his side near her. Small wisps of steamy air rose from his nostrils only to be snatched away by the brutally cold wind as he struggled to breathe. Crawling to him, she sat on the ground and placed his head in her lap where she cradled it with her arms.

Blowing into Beelzebub's face, Sarah wept as she tried to force a will to live into him. She tried to talk to him, but no sound came through her parched and frozen lips. For a long moment, he lay still, not breathing. Just when she thought she had lost him, he snuffled and coughed weakly. Opening his teary eyes, encrusted with frozen excretion, he looked past her at something behind her.

She followed Beelzebub's stare, and her eyes widened in disbelief. Almost upon them, blocking out the stars, loomed a building. Although it was stark and austere, it filled her with hope.

Laying Beelzebub's head on the ground, Sarah stood up. She ignored the numbness in her feet and hands as she walked slowly to Buttermilk, who hadn't moved since she dropped his reins. He opened his ice-rimmed eyes and raised his head when she put her hand under his jaw. Nuzzling her face against him, she felt the warmth of his skin against her cheek.

"We made it, Buttermilk," she croaked weakly. "Let's see if Daniel left us some matches."

Searching clumsily through the saddlebags, she found a tin can containing something that rattled when she shook it. After several attempts, she was able to put enough pressure on the lid with her gloved hands to turn it. Although it was too dark to see clearly, her spirits lifted when she shook out a bundle of tiny wood sticks tied together with string. Now she could build a fire for warmth and to thaw out the canteen water. Her mouth salivated at the thought of a drink.

Placing the matches carefully in her coat pocket, Sarah led Buttermilk to the building and tied his reins around a hitching post. It was a small shack with a door, slightly ajar, facing to the south. As she pulled at it, it creaked and sagged on its leather hinges, clearing a semicircle in the snow. It was too dark to see into the interior.

Then Sarah heard a sound from within; a sound of scurrying feet. Jumping back, she almost fell. Regaining her senses, she held her breath and listened. Again the noise came, but this time she recognized it. It's just mice, she thought. She needn't be afraid of them. Even so, she removed one of the matches and struck it on the doorframe to give her light. The flickering illumination penetrated only a few feet into the room, but she could see the reflection of several pairs of tiny eyes staring at it. Then they disappeared with a scratching sound.

Stepping inside, Sarah held the match out in front of her as she scanned the interior. A small window set in the rear wall was open to the outside. Broken glass gave evidence that it once contained a windowpane. The room, covered with dust and mice dropping, was bare of furniture. The only item she could see was a dirty blanket lying in a heap in one corner. As she looked at it, small humps moved beneath it. That's where the mice disappeared, she thought. Before the match burned down to her glove, she could make out a rock fireplace in the wall to her left.

Returning to Beelzebub, she knelt and picked up his head. "We'll be okay, old boy," she said. "We just have to get to the cabin. Come on."

Beelzebub opened his rheumy eyes and looked up at Sarah. When she stood, he made an attempt to rise but fell back to the ground. Taking his wide leather collar in her hand, she pulled at it until she was able to get him to his feet. Before he could collapse again, she pulled him toward the shack. He stumbled several times, but she was finally able to get him through the door and into the room near the fireplace. Then the last reserves of her strength gave out, and she sprawled beside him, forcing herself to breathe deeply of the cold air.

Just as she felt herself plunging into unconsciousness, a cough forced its way past her sore throat, and the resulting spasm brought her to her senses. She couldn't go to sleep, she thought. She had to start a fire. Then she could rest.

Sitting, she put her hand on Beelzebub's chest. It rose and fell slowly as he struggled for breath. She could smell the dank odor of his wet hide. Reaching into her pocket for the matches, she was surprised at her inability to grasp them with her stiff fingers. She had experienced sub-freezing weather before. The blue northerners that swept down from the Arctic Circle often visited Central Texas, but she couldn't recall being so cold that it affected her ability to use her hands.

Beating her fists against her chest and massaging her fingers, she was finally able to extract a single match from the bundle. When she tried to strike it against the floor, the head broke off before it could fire. Using all the feeling she could muster in the cold, oppressive darkness, she pulled out another match. This time, she brushed her glove across the floor to clear it of dust before attempting to scratch it. But, again, the head broke off from her clumsy movements.

Despair overwhelmed her. She knew she would have to remove her gloves if she wanted to get the matches to light. But when she tried to pull off one of them, she was unable to grasp it tightly enough. Then, using her teeth, she removed it. Dropping it on the floor, she blew on her bare hand to warm it as she flexed her fingers.

Reaching into her pocket, Sarah removed the matches again. This time, she was able to pull a single one loose. But when she did, the bundle fell into the darkness beneath her. She didn't hear it hit the floor, which she thought was strange. As quickly as she could, she struck the match she held on the floor. Her heart leapt with joy as it flared. Then the flame subsided into a dull glow before finally extinguishing. But she didn't dismay. There were plenty of matches, she thought. She would soon have one of them going.

Thrusting around in the darkness, she couldn't locate the remaining bundle. A sudden panic overcame her, and she had to force herself to calm down. After taking several deep breaths, she felt around with her bare hand. When she didn't feel anything, she widened the search area until she encountered Beelzebub. As she touched him, he snuffled and rolled over onto his stomach.

Running her hand over his hair, which was wet with ice and melted snow, Sarah explored him to see if the matches had fallen onto him. When she couldn't find anything, she crawled around to his other side and felt about on the floor. But, as before, the search was fruitless. The bundle was missing.

Then, realizing that Beelzebub had rolled onto his stomach, she reached under him. When she did, she felt the matches under his haunches. Saying a silent prayer of thanks, she pulled them out and placed them in her gloved hand. But when she felt the tips with her bare fingers to pull one loose, she gasped. They were sodden with the melted snow from Beelzebub's hair, and they crumbled under her touch.

"Oh Lord!" Sarah said frantically.

Removing one of the matches, she attempted to light it. But her efforts were in vain. The tip scraped off and wouldn't fire. She tried another and another. Finally, when she couldn't feel her fingers, she put on her glove and placed her hand inside her coat to warm it.

Overcome with weariness, she thought she would rest for a moment, and then try the matches again. Her last conscious thought was falling onto the floor and striking it with the side of her head. Instead of trying to rise, she placed her hand under her cheek and surrendered to the exhaustion weighing her down.

Sometime later, she was aware of urinating. For a brief moment, she was conscious of warmth flooding her hips and legs, and then she drifted into a dreamless sleep.

Chapter 24

A sound penetrated Sarah's senses. As awareness came to her, the sound repeated, this time louder. She thought that someone was shouting. Unable to raise her head, she lay quietly and explored her bodily sensations. The tip of her nose and her ears were tingling with pain. As her eyes focused, she could see her breath form tiny clouds on the floor beneath her cheek, which rested on her gloved hand. Her lower body seemed detached from the rest of her. It felt like it was encased in ice and frozen. Try as she might, she couldn't move her legs.

Then she felt a touch on her shoulder. All she could do was open her eyes and stare at the floor. Again she was aware of someone touching her, shaking her.

"She alive, boss?" she heard a gravely voice ask.

"Just barely," another voice, higher pitched and more pleasant, responded. "Pert near froze. Looks like the dog's dead, though."

Sarah shuddered. Beelzebub couldn't have died, she thought wildly. Not after all he did to get us this far.

Again the pleasant voice spoke, "Get some wood from the wagon, Hugh. Start a fire, while I bundle her up in some blankets. Bring the coffee pot and another one to boil water in. Hurry!"

Sarah closed her eyes and tried to sleep again, but the cold penetrating her body and the pain in her exposed skin kept her awake. Then she felt someone turn and lift her while wrapping her in a soft blanket. As the internal heat from her body warmed the cocoon around her, she surrendered her consciousness once again.

When she awoke the next time, she was aware of several sensations: the smell and sound of coffee perking, heat on her face, the bright flame of a fire just in front of her, and excruciating pain in her fingertips, her nose, and the tips of her ears. The numbness she had felt below her waist had given way to a damp, clammy feeling. Coughing, she reawakened the soreness in her throat.

"Are you okay, Ma'am?" a man asked as he raised her to a sitting position and held a cup of steaming coffee to her lips.

Looking up, Sarah saw a burly, round-faced man with a handle bar mustache and kindly blue eyes smiling at her. Unable to pull her gloves off, she wrapped them around his hands and took a sip of the coffee. The hot liquid burned her lips and tongue, and she spit it out as she coughed again.

"Sorry ... sorry," she managed to murmur. "Throat hurts."

"Of course," the man said. "Cowboy coffee is a bit harsh."

Removing the cup from her lips, he disappeared for a moment, and then returned. This time, the mug contents were cooler and the coffee had a tart aroma to it. He gave her a sip, which she was able to swallow without coughing.

"What ... what is it?" Sarah asked as the after-taste warmed her mouth and brought tears to her eyes.

"My father's cure for a cold and sore throat," the man said with a twinkle in his eye. "Coffee, honey, and a dollop of Kentucky Bourbon. Guaranteed to cure what ails you, he always said."

Sarah pushed the cup away. "I don't drink alcohol," she said in a weak voice.

"I understand," the man said. "Don't you think you might make an exception just this once?"

"No," Sarah said. "Just coffee and honey, if you please." Although her throat was still very sore, she found that she could talk without too much effort.

When the man knelt beside her and handed her another cup, he said, "I admire a woman of conviction. Burk Burnett at your service. That ugly old squirt over there is Hugh Grossman, my foreman." His voice, though quiet and even, conveyed a sense of authority.

Sarah coughed weakly again and lifted her head as she said, "Thank you. I'm Sarah Whitman."

Then thinking of Beelzebub, she turned to his inert body. Steam was rising from his wet fur as the fireplace heated the small room. "Are you sure he's dead, Mr. Burnett?" she asked fearfully.

"Think so," Burnett answered as he looked at the massive heap in the middle of the floor. "Haven't seen him breathing."

Then looking back at Sarah, he said, "Pleased to meet you, Mrs. Whitman. I saw you at Mr. Heddings' trial."

Ignoring Burnett, Sarah scooted over to Beelzebub. Suddenly, she became aware of the dampness of the clothes covering the lower part of her body. As the room heated, she was also aware of the odor of urine. Horrified, she realized that it was coming from her. Sometime during the night, she had wet herself.

Turning to Burnett, she asked, "Would you mind heating some water so I can wash myself and my clothes, please?" She was unable to meet his eyes.

"Already done, Mrs. Whitman. There's a pot on the fire. And I brought some soap and towels for you. Hugh and I have to tend to the horses. Take your time and let us know when you want us to come back in."

Sarah fought back tears as she said, "Thank you. I will never be able to repay your kindness."

"Our pleasure," Burnett said. "We'll talk when you're ready. Finding you way out here alone in a snowstorm is perplexing. Perhaps you'll tell us about it."

"I will," Sarah said as the two men left the shack, closing the door behind them.

Sarah leaned over Beelzebub and felt his nose. It was cold, but she could feel the warmth of his breath on her hand and her heart lifted. Ruffling his hair, she tried to stir him, but her efforts were in vain, he didn't respond. Looking around, she saw the cup of coffee Burnett had given her. The contents had cooled a bit, but the sharp aroma of the alcohol still lingered.

"I can't drink this, Beebub," she said. "But I see no reason you can't, as long as you don't make a habit of it."

Lifting Beelzebub's snout, she poured some of the liquid into his mouth. He snorted weakly and swallowed. When she gave him another drink, he opened his eyes and licked his lips. After the cup was empty, he whined for more as he rolled over onto his paws.

"That's enough for now, old boy," Sarah said as she rubbed his face with a towel. "Be patient while I clean up."

Sarah removed her clothes under the blanket. Using a washcloth, she scrubbed herself in the soapy water. Wrapping the blanket around her, she washed her coat, dress, and under garments. After wringing most of the water out, she spread them in front of the fire. She realized that the heavy woolen dress would take a long time to dry. Taking the pot of wash water to the window, she threw it out. The wind had subsided, and a bright morning sun gleamed off the snow-covered ground. Thinking about the two men standing outside in the cold dismayed her.

A knock on the door caused her to start. She turned at the sound of Burnett's voice from outside. "Mrs. Whitman," he said. "I have some clothes you might be able to wear."

Holding the blanket closely about her naked body, she opened the door a crack and looked out.

Burnett, averting his face, handed her a paper sack. "Just a skirt the wife ordered," he said. "Don't have a blouse, but you might be able to wear this shirt."

"Thank you," Sarah said as she took the clothes and closed the door. The black wool skirt looked like it would fit well enough, but the red flannel shirt was very large.

Sarah picked up her shift and pantaloons. They were still damp but warm. After holding them up in front of the fire for several minutes, she put them on. Then she donned the skirt and her stockings. When she tucked the shirt in her waistband, it bagged out around her chest and emphasized her breasts, but she didn't see any way to avoid it. Drying her hair with a towel, she combed the snarls out of it with her fingers.

The tip of her nose and her ear lobes still smarted after nearly losing their bout to frostbite. She wondered if the pain would ever go away. Looking at Beelzebub, she realized that he had taken a worse beating. The floor under him was bloody from his mangled paws. He had crawled closer to the fire and was sleeping soundly again, steam rising from his hair.

Going to the door, Sarah opened it and looked out. The cold wind still keened in from the north, and a high, gray overcast obscured the sky. Burnett and Grossman were standing by a wagon pulled by two large draft horses. Two other horses, a white mare and a big brown stallion, were tied to the tailgate, munching on hay strewn on the ground. With a shock, she saw Buttermilk, still secured to the hitching post in front of the cabin. She had forgotten about him. His saddle had been removed and a blanket placed over his back. He was also eating hay from the ground.

"Mr. Burnett," she called. "Please come in and get warm."

"Right away," Burnett said as he spat a wad of tobacco with the wind.

When the two men entered, Beelzebub opened his eyes and growled a deep rumble that seemed to shake the whole room. Sarah went to him and, leaning over him, said soothingly, "That's okay, Beelzebub. They're friends."

Grossman threw some more wood on the fire and set up a skillet with a slab of bacon in it and a pot full of beans. When Sarah asked him if he needed help, he just shook his head and smiled. The smell of the food cooking made her realize how hungry she was.

Burnett stood close to the flames warming his hands. Looking down at the huge dog snoring beside him, he said, "Why, I'll be. Thought he was dead. Where'd he get a name like that? And what is he? Never saw a dog that big."

"My father was a preacher," Sarah answered. "He named him after the fallen angel who was Satan's cohort. He's part German shepherd and part Gray Wolf. If it wasn't for him, I'd still be out there." Sarah pointed to the door.

"Good thing you're not," Burnett said as he poured Grossman and himself a cup of coffee. "It must have been below zero last night."

Grossman, a small, wiry man, with a long gray handlebar mustache standing out from his leathery face, glanced beneath his bushy eyebrows briefly at the dog, and then at Sarah. He filled a plate with beans, bacon, and a thick slice of bread. After handing it to her, he backed away from her thanks with a nod of his head. Going to Beelzebub, he placed a large slice of uncooked bacon in front of him. He sat down next to him, crossing his legs like an Indian, and ate from the plate on his lap as the dog wolfed down the meat.

After Sarah finished eating and wiped her hands on a towel, she turned to Burnett and said, "I know you're wondering what I'm doing out here."

"Thought you'd get around to telling us in due time," Burnett said with a smile that lit up his face and crinkled the corners of his eyes.

Picking up a burning stick from the fire, he lit his pipe. He took a deep draught and blew the pungent smoke out before continuing, "Didn't think you'd pick this spot for a vacation, but before you start," he said, looking directly at her. "I want to tell you I read that article you wrote in the paper. I have a copy of it in my saddlebag, as a matter of fact. I didn't know Heddings, but I felt he was being ramrodded. My wife read his newspaper to see what new words she could pick up. What you wrote, and spoke about at the trial, helped put some sense in a lot of folks. Sorry the way it came out. Don't know why the law is always in such a hurry to hang a man."

"Thank you for your kind words," Sarah said. "Were you there … for the trial?"

"Yes, I was," Burnett said. "The wife too. Her name is Ruth. She admired your letter. Read it to our daughter and son."

Sarah wrested her thoughts back to the present. She couldn't think of Clarence's last days without crying inside. Although William Thompson had tried to talk her out of it, she had attended Clarence's hanging. The sickening sound as he plunged downward and was caught up by the rope was indelibly etched in her memory. But it was a memory that she had to put away for now. Jody's plight had to be foremost in her mind.

"My family and I were on our way back to our ranch west of Waco yesterday," she said. "My daughter Margaret and little Jody—he just turned five. Daniel

Worthington was with us. He hired on to help me. He and Margaret will be married in the spring."

Sarah found that it was easy to talk to Burnett. He followed her words with interest and concern in his eyes. She was also aware that Grossman was listening as he sat quietly, staring into the writhing flames of the fire.

"We were south of Fort Worth. I don't know how far; perhaps thirty miles or so when the snow started. Jody ... Jody had to go to the bathroom. Daniel took him to the side of the road. Then ... an Indian came out of nowhere, and he hit Daniel with a club. It knocked him unconscious. Another one—" Sarah stopped as the vivid memory brought tears to her eyes.

Silently, with compassion in his eyes, Burnett reached into his vest pocket and withdrew a white handkerchief. Without speaking, he handed it to Sarah and waited for her to go on.

Sarah daubed the moisture from her eyes and took a deep breath before continuing, "Another Indian came out of the snow behind the first one. He grabbed Jody and ... and took him away."

"Just two of them?" Burnett asked quietly.

"No," Sarah said. "I looked up and saw another one sitting on his horse staring at me. He started toward me, but Beelzebub let out a roar, and he rode after the first two."

"I see," Burnett said looking down at the sleeping dog. "I bet he can roar some fierce. The first Indian was counting coup."

"Counting coup?" Sarah asked.

Burnett took a sip of his coffee and replied, "An Indian gains stature with his fellow warriors if he can get close enough to touch his enemy with a stick and get away unharmed. This one got a little carried away. Can you describe them?"

"Not the first two," Sarah said. "They came out of the snow storm and were gone before I got a good look at them. I did see the third one, though. He wore a buffalo horn cap, and he had a scar down across his face." Sarah traced a line down her cheek and across her lips.

"It's that damn Buffalo Scar. Beggin' your pardon, Ma'am," Grossman said in a low, hoarse voice that sounded like it was being drug over a gravel creek bed.

"You know him?" Sarah gasped.

"Unfortunately, we do," Burnett said. "Guess we better let you know who we are. I own a cattle ranch north of Fort Worth. Hugh there runs it for me. When he's not tending his fruit orchard, that is."

Grossman snorted and returned his stare to the fire as Burnett continued, "We've been up at Fort Sill in Oklahoma Territory talking to Quanah Parker about running a herd on the reservation and another one near Palo Dura Canyon."

"I thought all the Indians were on the reservation," Sarah commented. "They don't own the land outside do they?"

"Not legally," Burnett said. "At least they don't have written deeds to it. But much of the land in the panhandle is still considered Indian Territory. And, no, not all of them are on reservations. They're still a few renegade families living out in the brush. I'm surprised they're still making raids this time of the year. Guess they had enough meat to make them feel like warriors again, and they probably thought the warm days would last. They can't forecast the weather any better than we can."

"Does Buffalo Scar live on the reservation?" Sarah asked hopefully. Surely, if he took Jody there she could find him.

"Only when he wants government beef," Grossman growled.

"That's true," Burnett said. "Some of the warriors haven't given up their wild ways yet. They'll spend the winter on the reservation, then come spring they start feeling their oats and go on raids. Pretty hard for the Indian agents to control them."

"Isn't Quanah Parker their chief?" Sarah asked. "Can't he make them stay?"

"The Comanche braves only listen to their chiefs if they agree with them," Burnett said. "If they don't, they're free to do as they please. The government folks in Washington never did figure that out. Just kept trying to get peace treaties signed. Didn't understand they meant nothing to any Indian who didn't make his mark."

"And not much to those who did," Grossman snorted.

"And Jody?" Sarah asked apprehensively.

"Buffalo Scar won't take him to the reservation," Burnett answered. "He'd be arrested if he did."

"How can we find him?" Sarah asked.

For a long moment, Burnett pondered the question. Then after exchanging a look with Grossman, he responded, "We'll have to go to Quanah and ask for his assistance. He and Buffalo Scar aren't the best of friends, but we may be able to offer him enough to get the boy."

"Offer him what?" Sarah asked. "Money?"

"No," Burnett said. "Most of the Indians are wary of white man's money. They want solid goods: beeves, guns, horses, blankets, and other stuff they can trade in turn."

Sarah wasn't sure how much money she had with her. "I'll get what we need," she said. Jody is out there, alone and waiting for her, she thought. "How much do you think it will cost?" she asked.

"Shouldn't be too much," Burnett responded. "I'll throw in a couple of beeves."

"I can't ask you to do that. He's my son."

"My pleasure," Burnett said. "I have a youngster just a tad older than Jody."

"He's got so many cows now, he can't count 'em anyway," Grossman grunted as he spit into a large can he had brought in from the wagon.

"True," Burnett smiled. "Can we throw in a few of your peach trees, Hugh?"

Grossman didn't answer; he just ruffled the hair behind Beelzebub's ears as he stared into the flames.

"I'm ready to go," Sarah said. "When can we start?"

Burnett paused before answering, as if he were considering different alternatives. Finally, he said, "I can understand your impatience. Be the same way if it was my son. We need to notify the army about Buffalo Scar and—"

"Mr. Burnett," Sarah interrupted, "I am going after my son. Now! I don't want him to be with those horrible men any longer. My maiden name was Parker. Cynthia Ann Parker was my aunt. Maybe Quanah will help me since I'm related to him."

Burnett looked at Sarah with a shocked expression. "Well, I'll be," he said. "The letter in the newspaper was signed by a Parker. Didn't know the connection until the trial."

Waving his hand at Grossman, Burnett said, "Hugh. Let's you and me go outside and palaver."

Looking at Sarah, he continued, "We'll be right back, Ma'am."

After the two men left, Sarah sat on the floor beside Beelzebub. Putting her arms around his neck, she stared into the fire. In the security and warmth of the cabin, she couldn't stop the door to "Jody's Room" from opening. He was so vulnerable, so trusting. She remembered his birthday party at the hotel in Fort Worth only two weeks before. She would never forget the excitement in his eyes as he blew out the candles on the cake in front of her, Margaret and Daniel. "I'm a big boy, now," he had shouted. "I'm five years old."

Sarah wished that Daniel was with her. She could use his strength and morale support. But he would need time to recover from his head wound. She remembered that Sheriff Wilson had gone into a coma from the whack on his head she had given him. Not a day went by without her praying for his return to health. Now she added Daniel to that list.

The door opened and Burnett entered. Sarah stood up as he handed her a gray felt hat with a wide brim encompassed by a rattlesnake band.

"This might fit you, Mrs. Whitman," he said, a smile reacquainting itself with the wrinkles on his mouth and eyes like an old friend. "Need something on your head if you're going out in this weather."

"Going where?" Sarah asked.

"I know you're set on going after your son without delay," Burnett said quietly. "I would do the same. I have to get back to Fort Worth. I got a telegram at Fort Sill that my wife is ill. That's the reason Hugh and I were traveling in the storm."

"Oh," Sarah said raising her hand to her mouth. "I'm so sorry. How is she?"

"Don't know for sure," Burnett answered with a shake of his head. "Just that she's down with fever."

"Then you must go to her. I shouldn't have kept you here."

"I'm glad we could be of service to you," Burnett said. "We couldn't leave you here alone. Hugh will take you to see Quanah at the reservation. You'll take the wagon and his horse. Won't need yours. I'll take him with me and see he gets taken care of."

Looking down at the sleeping Beelzebub, he continued, "You'll have to take him in the wagon with you. Looks like he's plumb tuckered out. A word of warning, though. Don't let him get near the reservation dogs. They're mean as sin and will tear him apart if it takes all of them to do it."

"Mr. Burnett," Sarah said with moisture in her eyes. "I don't know what to say. I hate to put you out like this, with your wife sick and all. I'm even taking clothes meant for your family. The horse belongs to Daniel Worthington. He and my daughter, Margaret, should be at the Mansion Hotel in Fort Worth. Would you mind delivering it to him?"

The child-like smile snuck back onto Burnett's face as he replied, "My pleasure. Let's get this sorted out, then we'll say our appreciations. I know you'd make Ruth's day if you would come have supper with us one night. You and your family."

"You can count on it," Sarah said as she extended her hand. "Please call me Sarah."

"My pleasure, Sarah," Burnett said as he took her hand. "The name's Samuel, but folks call me Burk."

Chapter 25

▼

The wind let up a little as Sarah and Grossman started north. It had taken all three of them to lift Beelzebub into the wagon, where he promptly fell asleep under a blanket. Sarah felt soreness in her throat and the onset of coughing that was beginning to concern her. She knew that she couldn't allow herself to get sick when Jody depended on her.

For the first few miles, neither she nor Grossman spoke. Then, when Sarah mentioned Burnett's comment about Grossman's pears, he opened up and became very communicative. The son of a Kentucky farmer who prided himself in his orchard, he had inherited his father's love for growing apples, peaches, and other fruit trees. By the time they made their first stop at a stage way station in Decatur, they were chatting amicably.

"Hugh," Sarah said as they headed toward the Red River on the Texas and Oklahoma border. "Why is Mr. Burnett interested in a cattle range so far north? The railroad doesn't go up there, does it?"

"No," Hugh answered. "The nearest train spur is over a hundred fifty miles to the east of Fort Sill. Gettin' government supplies to the Indians is tougher than nails. The reservation has some of the best grazin' land in this part of the country. Thousands of acres. Now the buffalo is about gone, there's nothin' to eat the prairie grass. Best thing about it, it's there where we can sell the beef to the government. What we can't sell to them, we can trail up to the railhead in Kansas. If we can get a lease from the Indians, we'll just have to set aside a few head each year to pay for it. Your kin, Quanah, has become the spokesman for many of the Comanches. He can't speak for the Kiowas or Wichitas, but they'll go along when they see what they'll get out of it."

"I don't know much about Quanah," Sarah said as she coughed and wiped her nose with a piece of tissue paper. "My father never met him. After Cynthia Ann was taken back to her family, he visited her in East Texas. He said she didn't even recognize him. She was mourning the death of her baby, Prairie Flower, and she died soon after that."

Hugh stopped the wagon and removed a heavy woolen blanket from the rear, which he wrapped around Sarah's shoulders.

"Quanah's grown up into quite a man," Hugh said as they started up again. "Crafty as a Quaker. Nothin' much gets by him. He'll be rich one day if he can get the rest of the tribes to go along with him on the cattle leases."

"Does he speak English?" Sarah asked.

"A few words," Hugh said with a chuckle. "More than he lets on, I expect. He has a friend named White Cloud who talks good English. He spent some time with a white family when he was a pup. He does the talkin' while Quanah just stares at you. He has gray eyes, did you know that? Unusual for an Indian. Must have come from you Parkers."

"Really!" Sarah exclaimed. "I didn't know that. My father and grandfather had gray eyes." She turned away from Hugh and coughed into her glove.

"Well, watch out for those eyes," Hugh said. "When he fixes them on you, best not tell a lie. I swear he knows what's goin' on in your head."

The grassy landscape, waving in the gusty wind, stretched out in front of the wagon without a hill or a tree to break its monotony, and the sky, cloudless and pale blue, seemed to reach up to eternity. The sun, a bright orb in the afternoon sky, provided light to the day, but little warmth. A thin layer of snow covered the roadway and the ground alongside.

Sarah shivered and drew her blanket closer about her chin. The vast surrounding space made her feel small and alone. Not alone, she thought, just insignificant on the endless plain. Only an occasional rabbit or prairie dog was visible. The soft soughing of the wind, the clopping of the horses' hoofs, and the creaking of their traces were the only sounds interrupting the forlorn stillness. A terrible vision of Jody coming through this emptiness as a captive of the three Indians haunted her. Cold and frightened, he must have felt so forsaken. She shuddered again.

"Big, ain't it?" Hugh said, sensing Sarah's feelings. "Kind of lonesome without the buffalo."

"Did you see them before they were killed off?" Sarah asked, grateful for the conversation to get her mind off Jody.

"Yes," Hugh answered with a smile that drew up the ends of his mustache with the curl of his lips. "Amazin' sight. This was once home to the great southern buffalo herds. They numbered in the millions. You could stand on this wagon in the middle of one of the herds and see nothin' but buffalo. When Mr. Burnett and I first come up here, about fifteen years ago, we rode through one bunch for eight hours before gettin' clear of it."

"Why'd they have to kill them all?" Sarah asked.

Hugh spit off the side of the wagon and answered, "Money. Some shot them for sport, but mostly they were done in for the money the hides brought. The Indians culled out a few for food and other necessities, but not enough to make a difference. Of course, when the buffalo was gone, they had to come to the reservation or starve. That and losin' their horses."

"Horses?" Sarah asked.

"As long as they had mounts, they could find enough stragglers left over from the big buffalo herds to avoid starvation and keep ahead of the soldiers. But the army realized that. Only smart thing they ever did in their war against the Indians. Smart, but a terrible waste of horseflesh, if you ask me. When Colonel Mackenzie found the Comanches in Palo Dura Canyon, he killed their horses. Over a thousand, I heard. After that, Quanah Parker and White Cloud brought their people onto the reservation."

"How much farther is it to Fort Sill?" Sarah asked, watching a hawk swoop down in front of them, and then climb rapidly and disappear into the glare of the sun.

"A fair piece yet," Hugh answered as he checked the time with his pocket watch. "We'll stay this side of the Red River tonight. There's a stage house in Wichita Falls where we can bed down. Best we leave your dog there. We should reach the reservation about noon tomorrow, and don't want him to tangle with the Indian dogs."

Sarah turned and looked back at Beelzebub. He had awakened long enough to eat some meat, before returning to sleep. Since the trek through the snow to the cabin the night before, he had not been able to get to his feet. She was concerned that the ordeal had sapped so much of his energy that he wouldn't recover.

When they left Wichita Falls early the next morning, Sarah was dressed in her own clothes, and she felt better about her appearance. She was relieved that Beelzebub had agreed to stay at the stage house without putting up a fuss. He had lain near the fireplace and looked at her with a plaintive whine when she walked out the door. Assured by the stationmaster that he would look after him, she was able to channel her thoughts and energy to the task of finding Jody. This was the third day of his abduction, and the thought of it lasting much longer was hard for her to imagine.

The hat Burnett had given her was too large but, by rolling her hair and laying it on top of her head, she was able to wear it. The day started out cold and dreary. A thin blanket of snow covered the ground, and low, gray clouds, accompanied by a brisk northwest wind, promised continued winter weather. She could see steam filter through the wool scarf she had wrapped around her face.

After a ferry ride across the Red River, they entered a stretch of country much like the one they had traveled the day before. The plains appeared flat, cold, and uninviting as far as the eye could see.

"How much longer, Hugh?" Sarah asked after they had traveled nearly an hour from the passage across the Red River.

"Been on the reservation since the river," Hugh said. He too had a scarf wrapped around his face to ward off the biting wind.

"We have?" Sarah responded as she looked around for signs of habitation. "Where are the Indians?"

Hugh waved his mittened hand to the left side of the wagon. "The Comanches … Quanah's bunch … are out to the west a couple of hours ride. The Kiowas and Apaches are up north. The army fort and the Indian agency are just ahead of us about eight miles."

"I didn't realize it was so big," Sarah said.

"It was set up by the government after the Treaty of Medicine Lodge back in '67," Hugh responded. "But the first Indians didn't start comin' in until the early '70s. Stretches from the Red River north about halfway to Kansas and west almost to the Texas Panhandle."

"Why aren't we heading toward Quanah's camp?" Sarah asked. In the distance, she could see a corral holding a large number of cattle.

"Got to report to the agent first," Hugh said. "And notify the army commander, Colonel Davidson of what happened. He'll try to talk us out of tradin' for the boy. Give him a chance to rattle his sabre and go after Buffalo Scar."

"Why don't we let the army get Jody?" Sarah asked.

"Would serve Scar right for what he'd done, but your son might get hurt in the battle. Most of the soldiers are new recruits. Heard all kind of stories about wild Indians, but never tasted blood. They might shoot anybody that moves if they come on to Scar's camp. No, I think tradin's the best way. Mr. Burnett has an account at the agency store. We'll pick up some goods there. And we have a small herd of cattle here that ain't been sold yet. I'll cut out a couple to take with us."

"I have money," Sarah said quickly. "I can't let Mr. Burnett pay for the ransom."

Hugh flashed one of his rare smiles, "I ain't one to argue with the man. He told me to do what needed doin' to get the boy back. You and him can settle up when we get back to Fort Worth."

As they approached the cattle herd, Sarah could see tendrils of smoke rising from several small shacks and half a dozen tipis clustered together near a main gate to the corral. A small group of men on horseback were in the main enclosure cutting out some of the cows and guiding them through a side gate leading to a smaller pen. Even at a distance, Sarah could see that most of them were Indians, their heads bare and their long black hair falling in plaits over their shoulders.

One of the riders, a young white man wearing a wide-brimmed hat, looked up and, seeing them approach, waved in greeting.

Hugh pulled the wagon to a stop near the corral. Handing Sarah the reins, he said, "Be back in a few minutes. That young feller over there works for me. Name's Bucky."

Sarah took her hat off and shook out her hair until it fell below her shoulders. The soreness in her throat seemed to be getting worse. It was becoming painful to swallow. She didn't want to cough, because she felt she wouldn't be able to stop.

Feeling the slight warmth of the sun on her face, she watched as Hugh and Bucky conversed near the gate while the Indians filled the small pen with cattle. They rode their horses like they were a part of them. Noticing that she was watching, they whooped and hollered, each trying to outdo the other. Their horsemanship and boyish exuberance was infectious, and Sarah found herself smiling as they performed outlandish feats of riding. One stood up on his mount while dashing among the darting horns of the milling cattle. Another rode past the wagon grinning at her from beneath his horse's neck.

Sarah suddenly became aware that someone else was staring at her. Looking at one of the tipis nearby with smoke swirling around the poles at the top, she saw an ancient Indian woman watching her. Waving at her, Sarah waited for a response. But the old woman, her back bowed from age, just peered at her with black, unwavering eyes, standing motionless. After a long moment, Sarah became uncomfortable and turned back to the corral, breaking the unspoken communication.

Hugh and Bucky walked up to the wagon, both spitting tobacco with the wind and away from Sarah. Bucky, tall, thin and sunburned, seemed embarrassed to look at her, although he did manage a grin that made him seem even younger than Sarah had first thought. He wore black, mud splattered boots, dark cotton pants, a blue flannel shirt, and a sheepskin coat under a black hat that had seen better days. Standing a step behind Hugh in deference to his position, he threw glances toward Sarah's fiery red hair when she wasn't looking directly at him.

"Mrs. Whitman," Hugh said as he pulled Bucky forward and put his arm around him. "This here pup is Bucky Halloran."

"I am pleased to meet you," Sarah said with a smile.

Bucky met Sarah's gaze for the first time as he removed his hat and said, "My pleasure. I heard what happened to your son. Anything I can do to help, I'll do. I told Mr. Grossman he can count on me." The youngster's blue eyes showed his concern.

"Thank you, Bucky," Sarah said.

"Bucky's goin' to separate half a dozen beeves from our herd and take them on to Quanah's camp," Hugh said as he released the boy's shoulders. "We'll meet him there soon as we see the agent and Colonel Davidson."

"I want to take Charles with me," Bucky said, turning and looking at a young Indian perched on the corral fence. "Okay, Mr. Grossman?"

"Might be a good idea, son," Hugh said. "Make sure it's square with his father."

Turning to Sarah, he said, "Charles is from Quanah's Antelope Tribe. Nephew or somethin' to him. Guess they're all kin of some sort."

Sarah recognized Charles as the one who had ridden through the cattle herd while standing on his horse. The stocky young man looked boldly at her and returned her smile, his white teeth gleaming in his dark brown face. He was wearing buckskins and a wide multi-colored headband above two large pigtails that hung far down over his shoulders.

Hugh climbed on the wagon and took the reins from Sarah. He clucked at the horses to start up. "Only a few miles to the fort," he said. "With any luck, we'll be on our way in an hour or so. Should put us at Quanah's by late afternoon."

Several minutes after leaving the corral behind, Bucky, astride a gangly white mare, galloped up alongside. "Mr. Grossman, I need to talk to you," he said breathlessly as Hugh brought the wagon to a stop. "Charles said Quanah ain't at the camp. He went to New Mexico yesterday."

"New Mexico!" Hugh exclaimed. "I'll be damned." Turning to Sarah, he added, "Sorry. Was hopin' he'd be here."

Sarah felt her hopes plummet. They had come all this way to see Quanah, and now he was gone. The image she held in her mind of Jody as he disappeared into the snowstorm returned to her.

"What are we to do now?" she asked quietly.

"White Cloud is there," Bucky said. "He'll probably help you. He and Buffalo Scar ain't good friends. Charles said they been fighting since they was little boys."

"Just might work," Hugh said. "White Cloud was a high muckety-muck medicine man before the Comanches came onto the reservation. Even Quanah listens to him. He stands to gain almost as much from the cattle leases. Don't think he'd be put out if we asked him to help us find Scar."

After telling Bucky to start on with the herd, Hugh snapped the reins and started the wagon rolling. He glanced several times at Sarah, as if he wanted to say something but was unsure of himself. Traffic on the road had increased in both directions: peddler wagons, Indians of both sexes on foot, and white male civilians and soldiers on horseback. Several times, they passed entire Indian families walking with their dogs in the direction of the agency.

Ahead of them, a large stone structure without a roof loomed up out of the prairie. Pointing at it, Hugh said, "That's the Ice House. The Army uses it for a prison for Indians they think are troublemakers. They just throw their food over the walls to them."

"Oh, Hugh," Sarah said with a cough. "That's barbaric."

"Sure is," Hugh agreed. "The new army commander doesn't use it except for hard cases. It doesn't set well with any of the tribes."

Hugh turned and looked at Sarah as if he'd made up his mind about something. "Uh, Mrs. Whitman," he said. "Mr. Burnett and I think it would be best ... well—"

"Hugh," Sarah said with a smile. "You know me well enough now to say whatever is on your mind. Don't you?"

"Well, yes," Hugh said hesitantly. "It'll be a hard road from now on. The Comanche camp ain't any place for a decent woman. And the country west of here is harsh. Sleepin' on the ground and such. Never know when the weather's goin' to get nasty again."

Sarah placed her hand on Hugh's arm and said quietly, "So what do you and Mr. Burnett propose I do while you are out hunting for my son?"

"There's a hotel of sorts at the agency for visitors," Hugh responded. "Has a kitchen that ain't too bad."

"Hugh," Sarah said firmly. "Let's do our business here and be on our way to see White Cloud. I promise you I won't be a burden. Besides, you'll need someone to make coffee. I've tasted yours, and it's nothing to be proud of. Wouldn't want young Bucky to drink much of it. Might stunt his growth."

"I done told Mr. Burnett I'd have to hog tie you to get you to stay here," Hugh said with a relieved smile.

"I don't think you want to try that," Sarah said with a laugh.

"No, I don't," Hugh said, also laughing. "That hotel's not much better than the tent I have in back anyway."

Chapter 26

▼

Sarah heard and smelled the Comanche encampment before she could see it; the raucous sounds and acrid odors were carried to her by the northwest wind. Snow covered the ground, broken only by the muddy tracks from wagon wheels and livestock hoofs. The temperature was still too low to allow thawing, and dark clouds obscured the sun. As they crested a small hill, Sarah could see the camp below. Tipis, spewing smoke into the late afternoon sky, seemed to stretch on for miles along a creek cascading south toward the Red River. Horses and cattle were corralled on the near side away from the village where they had access to water from the stream just after it flowed through the camp. Men, women, and children milled around the area in a flurry of activity as preparations for the evening meal progressed. And darting here and there were hundreds of yapping dogs, singly and in packs.

Wrinkling her nose, Sarah covered it with her gloved hand to shut out the reek of the Indian habitation. She hadn't coughed for several hours, and she had to force herself not to give in to the smells assailing her.

Noticing her reaction, Hugh said, "Kinda rank ain't it? Glad it ain't summer."

"How can they stand it?" Sarah asked.

"Don't seem to bother them," Hugh said as he spit off the side of the wagon. "The agent's been tryin' to tell them to keep the animals further down stream and dig their latrines a ways off. But they can't seem to understand the need. Maybe they don't want to take advice from white men. Before they come on the reservation, they upped and moved when a camp got too ripe. Now, they don't have much room. They have to share the reservation with other tribes, and they don't mix well. They keep the cows and horses close because of thieves, not all of them Indian."

"White men come on the reservation and steal from the Indians?" Sarah asked in surprise.

"Kind of a turnabout, ain't it?" Hugh said with a chuckle. "The territory west of here is crawlin' with white, half breed, and red renegades. The whites and breeds are called *Comancheros*. Many of them are meaner'n any Indian."

"How many Comanches live here?" Sarah asked.

"Over a thousand, I'm told," Hugh responded.

At the bottom of the slope, Sarah could see Bucky and Charles holding a small herd of cattle. As they started down toward them, she turned to Hugh and said, "Bucky is a nice young man. Where's his family?"

"Don't have any," Hugh responded as he smiled and waved at Bucky. "His folks abandoned him when they headed west. Mr. Burnett found him in the streets in Saint Louis about ten years ago and raised him. Smart boy, picked up on school right quick. Expect he'll replace me one of these days. He understands the Indians better'n any of us; learnin' their customs and language like he was born to it."

"You seem to be very proud of him," Sarah said. "Do you have a family?"

Hugh shook his head, "Nope. Never found anyone who could abide me."

"That's hard to believe, Hugh," Sarah said. "You'd be a fine catch for any woman."

"Harrumph," Hugh's face reddened, and he snorted as they pulled up to Bucky and Charles.

"White Cloud's tipi is just across the creek, Mr. Grossman," Bucky said, doffing his hat at Sarah.

"How do you tell one from another?" Sarah asked as she stared at the multitude of dwellings. They all looked alike to her.

"Each one is different," Hugh said. "And the lodge poles are marked with each Indian's special markin': feathers, medicine bags, and what not. Takes a while to notice. The chiefs' tipis are close to the water so their wives don't have to tote it so far."

"Wives?" Sarah asked.

"They measure their wealth in horses and wives," Hugh said.

"Now it's cattle too," Bucky added.

"How many wives does Quanah Parker have?" Sarah queried.

Hugh nodded at Bucky who responded, "Four right now, Mrs. Whitman. One of them's a Mescalero Apache. That's probably why Quannah went to New Mexico. To see her family."

Before Sarah could respond, Bucky continued, "Charles talked to White Cloud. He said we can't see him till morning. They're having a Button Ceremony and White Cloud's the Road Man when Quanah's gone."

"Better tell Mrs. Whitman what's going on," Hugh said before he bit a chew off his stick of tobacco.

"Well," Bucky said. He glanced at Charles who was sitting on his horse nearby, listening. "It's *peyote*, Ma'am. From a cactus that only grows down on the Rio Grande and into Mexico. The top of it looks like a bunch of buttons put together. Gives them a feeling they used to get from starving themselves so they could see a vision. Only the braves can take part. They sit in a circle in a tipi and the Road Man starts the ceremony by singing a song and shaking a rattle. After passing a pipe, they eat the *peyote* and sing some more. Lasts all night. Come morning, the Road Man's wife—they call her the *Peyote Woman*—brings in water and breakfast. That ends the ceremony."

"Gracious," Sarah said. "It sounds like a drug ritual. What does the *peyote* do to them?"

Charles rode up to the wagon next to Bucky and looked at Sarah. "I answer, Mr. Grossman?" he asked.

"Please do," Hugh said, nodding his head.

"*Peyote* give back our freedom," Charles said in a low, husky voice. Waving his hand around the camp, he continued, "One time owned all land. Free go everywhere. Now small land. *Peyote* free mind. Talk to great spirit, great father."

"Do you know about our Jesus Christ, Charles?" Sarah asked gently as she sensed the intensity of the young man's answer.

"I know," Charles said. "Jesus Christ *tahbay-boh* great spirit."

"*Tahbay-boh* is the Comanche word for white man, Mrs. Whitman," Bucky said. Reaching out, he punched Charles on his shoulder. "White man!" he said with a wide grin.

Charles smiled back at Bucky and returned the blow. When their horses settled down, he looked at Sarah and said, "White man go to church talk about Jesus Christ spirit." Holding his hand over his heart, he added proudly, "People go tipi, eat *peyote*, talk to Great Spirit."

"Do you eat the *peyote*, Charles?" Sarah asked.

"Not warrior," Charles said with a shrug.

"Just a kid, right, Charles?" Bucky laughed.

Charles swung the loop on his rope at Bucky, missing him by inches. Before Bucky could retaliate, Hugh glared at him and shook his head.

"Looks like we're stuck here for the night," Hugh said. "Once they start with the *peyote* they'll be at it till mornin'. Let's go up the creek a ways and set up camp. Bucky, you and Charles bring the beeves. Don't want them disappearin' on us."

It snowed a little during the night, but Sarah slept through it and the accompanying wind. She hadn't realized how tired she was until she crawled into the small tent Hugh erected for her. She felt bad about the men having to sleep outside by the fire, but Hugh and Bucky insisted that they were used to it.

When she awoke early in the morning, the grayness of dawn filled the tent with a subdued, diffused light. Sitting up, she started coughing. After it subsided, she felt dizzy, and the tent swirled around in her vision. In spite of the cold, she felt perspiration covering her face and neck. She knew she should rise, but the thought tired her, and she lay back down.

Sometime later, Sarah awoke again to the sound of voices outside the tent. She recognized Hugh's, but there was a stranger talking with him; a stranger with a loud, rasping voice difficult to understand. Shafts of sunlight pierced through tiny openings in the canvas door and shined into her eyes. Able to stand with only a slight weakness in her legs, she dressed quickly. Brushing back her long hair, she thought about putting on her hat, but decided against it. After donning her coat, she noticed the extra weight of her bible in one of the pockets.

When she pushed aside the tent flaps, the bright sunlight caused her to sneeze, and then cough. Shielding her eyes with her hand, she peered at Hugh and Bucky standing by the fire and, beyond them, a man on horseback. She had to move to the side to see him clearly against the sun. He was an Indian, dressed in fringed and beaded buckskin leggings and shirt and a buffalo robe, astride a large black stallion. Wide-faced and swarthy, the man wore his hair parted in the middle with two braids hanging forward over his chest. A single eagle feather dangled over his left ear, and a necklace of bear teeth adorned his dark vest. The mane and tail on his horse was festively decorated with colorful beads, bits of glass and feathers, and a large blue ribbon hung down over his neck just behind his ears.

Hugh turned as Sarah walked up beside him. "Good mornin' Mrs. Whitman," he said. "This here is White Cloud."

Sarah looked up at the stranger staring down at her and said, "I am pleased to meet you, White Cloud."

With a start, White Cloud sat back on his horse, his eyes widening with surprise as he stared at Sarah's hair. Sensing its rider's response, the stallion took a step to the rear.

Sarah, astonished at the man's reaction to her, also stepped backward.

For a long moment, the Indian gazed at her, and then he spoke in a loud and commanding voice, "You Parker family?"

"Yes," Sarah answered. "My father was Robert Parker. Cynthia Ann was my aunt."

"*Naduah*," White Cloud said nodding his head with each syllable, the feather in his hair fluttering in the wind. "Mother Quanah. Husband *Peta Nacona*."

Sarah looked at Bucky, who was listening carefully.

"*Naduah* was Cynthia Ann Parker's Comanche name," he said. "She was the wife of *Peta Nacona*, Quanah's father."

"Thank you, Bucky," Sarah said.

Then looking up at the man on horseback, she said, "You seemed surprised to see me, White Cloud. Have we met before?"

White Cloud's eyes were drawn to the blue ribbon woven into his horse's mane. He looked down at Sarah's hair. "You have child, hair of fire same you?" he asked. "And buffalo dog?"

Sarah inhaled sharply. How would this Comanche know about Margaret and Beelzebub, she wondered. She was certain she had never seen him before.

"Do you know White Cloud?" Hugh asked with a surprised look on his face.

Before Sarah could respond, White Cloud reached forward and removed the blue ribbon from his horse. Dismounting, he handed it to Sarah with a bow of his head.

Sarah was surprised at how short White Cloud was; their eyes were at the same level. Taking the piece of cloth, she stared at it for a long moment. Suddenly memories of a day long in the past rushed over her in a torrent.

"I was named Wolf Slayer," he said quietly.

Sarah removed the Bible from her pocket. Opening the pages, she took out a faded ribbon; the one she had placed in it when she was a teenager. When she held it next to the one White Cloud gave her, she could see they were identical.

"You were on the hill above our ranch house that day?" she asked, her voice trembling with the remembrance of her childhood experience. She had fantasized that the young Indian who had looked down at her from across the Bosque River was tall and handsome. This short, squat man with a wide, round face shocked her.

"Yes," White Cloud said quietly, his emotions hidden behind his dark eyes.

"How do you know I have a daughter with red hair and a big dog?" Sarah asked. "I was only sixteen years old when you saw me."

"Wolf Slayer *pahu*—" White Cloud stopped and turned to Bucky.

"He was a medicine man back then," Bucky offered in explanation.

"Yes," White Cloud said pounding his chest. "Medicine man of people. I come see child with buffalo dog. Tell people no go there. Tell them dog spirit of buffalo and wolf. *Tahbay-boh* child, hair of fire. When they see, run away."

Now, after all these years, Sarah understood why the Comanches had never attacked the Parker ranch. White Cloud—Wolf Slayer—had told his warriors to avoid it if they saw a large dog and a red-haired, white child.

"Buffalo Scar take boy?" White Cloud asked.

"Yes," Sarah answered. "His name is Jody. He's five years old."

White Cloud shook his head in annoyance, "Buffalo Scar one foot in reservation, one foot in old hunting ground."

"Can you help me get Jody back?" Sarah asked.

White Cloud looked at the cattle Charles rode herd on nearby and at the wagon laden with goods. Shaking his head, he said, "No trade. Buffalo Scar only know fight. We go, we must fight."

Hugh, responding to Sarah's imploring look, interjected, "We don't want to fight if we don't have to, White Cloud. The boy might get hurt. Try tradin' first."

"Trade!" White Cloud answered, his nostrils flared wide with distain. "Must fight."

Looking at Sarah, he added, "We find boy."

Vaulting onto the back of his horse, White Cloud galloped away toward the Comanche village.

"He may be right, Mrs. Whitman," Hugh said. "Scar don't agree with Quanah and White Cloud that they're better off on the reservation. He's always had a mean streak. He might not give your son up without a fight."

"Will we have a better chance with the army?" Sarah asked, her heart heavy in her chest.

"Don't know," Hugh responded. "What do you think, Bucky?"

Bucky hesitated before replying, "Well, sir. If I had to go to war against Buffalo Scar, I'd rather be with White Cloud than the army. He knows the land better than they do. We might be able to sneak in and get Jody out before the fighting starts."

"Why would Buffalo Scar want Jody?" Sarah asked. "I don't understand why he took him." She felt a coughing fit coming upon her, and she forced herself to stifle it.

Hugh looked at her kindly, "Like White Cloud said, Scar has a mean streak. Might have done it out of pure meanness."

Bucky cleared his throat and interjected quietly, "Might be more than that, Mr. Grossman. Charles says there's talk Buffalo Scar wants to start a new band. Take those away from Quanah and White Cloud who don't agree with them about leasing part of the reservation land to the cattlemen. He thinks he can stay ahead of the army. His women want children to replace those killed in the army raids. He may have taken Jody to satisfy them."

"You're probably right," Hugh said. "But Scar's a darn fool if he thinks he can stay out there. If the army don't get him, some *Comanchero* or settler will."

"Well," Sarah said with a sigh. "It looks like we're going to have to go along with White Cloud, even if it leads to violence. But I can't ask you two to put yourself in danger. I'll go on alone."

Hugh and Bucky exchanged looks. Smiling, Hugh said, "What are you goin' to do, Mrs. Whitman, hog tie me and Bucky to keep us here?"

Chapter 27

"I'm goin' to have Bucky drive the wagon for awhile," Hugh said as Sarah climbed up to the seat. "I want to talk to White Cloud."

"I didn't expect him to bring so many men with him," Sarah commented.

She looked at the braves clustered around White Cloud. She counted twenty. All were armed with lances and either bows or rifles. Black paint streaked their faces and contributed to their warlike appearance. Sitting on smaller ponies, back from the main group, were two youths even younger than Charles. Their faces were not painted, and they carried no weapons.

"Me neither," Hugh responded as he untied his horse from the rear of the wagon. He was carrying a revolver in a holster belted around his waist and tied to his thigh. His scabbard held a long-barreled rifle. "It worries me. He's ready to go to war. You know he was dead set against you goin' with us?"

"I'm sure he was," Sarah replied. "What did you say to him?"

Hugh spit out to one side before answering, "I told him red-headed white women have a temper terrible to behold. And if he wanted a fight with you, go ahead. He thought about it for a while, and then grunted. I took that for agreement."

"Do I have a terrible temper, Hugh?" Sarah asked, laughing.

"Don't think I'd want you riled at me," Hugh replied with a smile as he mounted and rode away.

After the two youngsters from White Cloud's group joined Charles with the cattle, Bucky came over to the wagon. Tying his horse on the tailgate, he scrambled up to the seat and took the reins from Sarah. He also wore a pistol strapped to his leg.

"All set, Ma'am?" he asked Sarah.

"I'm ready," Sarah responded. Feeling flushed again, she was certain that she had a fever. But there was nothing she could do now; Jody was out there waiting for her. The vision of him disappearing into the snowstorm, while crying out for help, hovered at the edge of her consciousness.

When the wagon pulled away from the campsite, the new snow from the night before was beginning to melt under the warmth of the bright morning sun. White Cloud and Hugh led the party toward the north around the Comanche village. Charles and his fellow drovers brought the cattle in trail at the rear.

"How far are we going?" Sarah asked.

"Not sure, Ma'am," Bucky responded. "Charles said Buffalo Scar has a camp in Palo Dura Canyon. Several days from here. That's where Colonel Mackenzie found Quanah and his tribe a few years ago. Didn't kill many of them, but he did slaughter their horses."

"I heard about that," Sarah said. "Do you think he was right to kill the horses, Bucky?"

"No," Bucky replied, his brown eyes tinged with sadness. "He shouldn't have killed them. He had enough men with him; they could have brought them back to Fort Sill. Unlike cows, horses can be moved pretty fast. I guess the colonel didn't want the Comanches to have them."

"Have you met Quanah?" Sarah asked.

"Yes," Bucky responded. "Mr. Burnett let me in on the meetings with him about the cattle leases. Said he wanted me to learn as much as I could. Quanah's a fine man. He don't speak much English, but he seemed to follow what was said. White Cloud did the interpreting."

"What do you think about him having more than one wife?" Sarah asked.

"Well, Ma'am," Bucky responded after giving the matter some thought. "I know it's not right with the Bible, but the Comanches never had the Bible all the years they hunted buffalo on the plains. Charles says it made sense for them to have a couple of wives. It helps spread out the work. It's not easy for the women to keep up with the skinning, cutting up meat, cooking, carrying water, making tipis and clothes, and taking care of the little ones."

Despite her best efforts to quell it, Sarah felt a coughing fit come over her. She covered her mouth with a handkerchief until it passed. The morning fever had definitely returned, and she felt warm and uncomfortable.

"Beg pardon," Bucky interjected with concern in his voice. "I have a bottle of elixir in my saddlebag. Mrs. Burnett sent it up with Mr. Burnett. He said it was good for the croup."

Pulling the reins to stop the wagon, Bucky handed them to Sarah while he walked back to his horse. Returning with a dark brown bottle, he handed it to her.

"Don't know how it tastes," Bucky said as he mounted the wagon and took the reins from Sarah. "Haven't had to use it. You can keep that one. She sent me two."

"Why, thank you," Sarah said.

Unscrewing the cap, she wrinkled her nose against the strong odor that burst forth. Holding the bottle tentatively against her lips, she took a sip. The sharp aroma nearly caused her to sneeze as the thick, dark liquid went down her throat. For a long moment, she held her breath, and then the edge of the soreness in her throat slowly dissipated. She started to ask Bucky if there was alcohol in it. But she decided not to. She didn't want to know. If it would keep her well enough to get to Jody, she would drink it.

As the miles passed, Sarah learned a lot about Bucky. Although he was only twenty years old, he possessed a maturity that she hadn't seen in many men in their thirties or forties. He shared with her his dream to possess his own cattle ranch one day. He even described the house he would put on the property. It would have a covered porch and a second story bedroom with a large window facing to the east, away from the brutal summer afternoon sun. When Sarah asked him if he had a woman picked out to share it with, he reddened and mumbled incoherently.

Late in the afternoon, Sarah asked Bucky if he knew the time. Reaching into his coat, he pulled out a gold-encased pocket watch hanging from a chain attached to his vest. Flipping open the cover, he said, "Few minutes till five."

"What a beautiful watch, Bucky," Sarah said.

"Mr. and Mrs. Burnett gave it to me on my eighteenth birthday," Bucky said self-consciously as he handed it to Sarah.

It was a large, heavy watch, the kind that she had seen bankers and lawyers wear. She was about to hand it back to Bucky when she saw a photograph inside the cover. "May I look at it?" she asked.

"Yes, if you'd like," Bucky said.

Sarah opened the cover to reveal a photograph of a beautiful young woman staring at her with a whimsical smile on her face. Her black hair was swept up to the top of her head, and the high collar on her white dress was adorned with a mother-of-pearl brooch.

"She is lovely," Sarah said as she returned the watch. "Is she the one you're building the ranch for?"

"Guess so," Bucky said quietly, staring straight ahead.

"What's her name?" Sarah asked.

"Sally Henderson. She lives outside of Fort Worth near the Burnett's house. Our wedding's set for next June."

"I wish you both the best," Sarah said smiling. "I would like to be invited to the wedding. I have a daughter named Margaret. She's also going to be married in the spring."

"It will be our pleasure, Mrs. Whitman," Bucky said as he urged the horses to pick up their pace. "I want you and Margaret to be there ... and Jody."

They stopped the first night near the western edge of the reservation. The afternoon sun had melted most of the snow on the ground, and the wagon trail was churned into mud. While Hugh was setting up Sarah's tent, White Cloud and his warriors disappeared.

"They'll camp up ahead a piece," Hugh said. "He'll set out guards for the night."

After a dinner of thin beefsteaks, fried bread, and coffee, Sarah excused herself and went into the tent. Weariness overwhelmed her as she sank down onto the blankets. She took a long drink from the bottle Bucky had given her and lay down. She could hear the murmur of voices from outside as Hugh, Bucky, and Charles talked around the fire. After saying her prayers, her worries and aches and pains floated away, and she fell into a deep sleep.

When Sarah left the tent the next morning, Hugh was frying bacon by the fire. Bucky, Charles and the cattle were nowhere in sight. The sun was already bright in the sky, and the night chill was beginning to disappear. She felt drained of energy, as if a blanket of lethargy had been thrown over her.

"Good morning, Hugh," Sarah said, joining him at the fire and accepting a cup of coffee. "You should have awakened me earlier."

"Mornin'," Hugh replied. "No need to roust you out, unless you can't drink my coffee. I sent the youngsters on ahead with the cattle. We'll catch them before noon."

"Where's White Cloud?" Sarah asked as she warmed her bare hands on the tin cup. She took the plate of beans, bacon, and bread Hugh handed her.

Hugh hesitated before answering, "Haven't seen him. Gone on ahead, I expect."

He had a concerned look on his face, a look Sarah had learned to recognize during the time they had been together. "That worries you, doesn't it?" she asked.

"Yes, it does. Those warriors are out for blood. White Cloud will increase his standin' with the army and the agent if he can get Buffalo Scar and his people to return to the reservation. With the bad blood between them, someone is apt to get hurt."

"Do you think he'll wait for us before confronting Buffalo Scar?" Sarah asked, fear again rising within her.

"No," Hugh said as he shook his head.

"How long will it take for us to get to the canyon?" Sarah asked.

"At the rate we're travelin', two ... maybe three more days," Hugh answered.

He stood up and poured the last of the coffee into Sarah's cup. Throwing the grounds on the fire, he began putting the cooking utensils away.

"I'm slowing us down," Sarah said. "I know that. We can travel later in the day, and you can wake me earlier if that would help. In fact, as warm as it is now, I can sleep in the wagon, and you won't have to put up the tent."

"We'd have to leave the beeves behind," Hugh said. "They ain't swift creatures."

"I want to be there when White Cloud talks to Buffalo Scar," Sarah said. "We have the goods in the wagon. We can tell him the cattle are on the way."

"Let's go then," Hugh said with a relieved sigh. "We got lots of miles to go. We'll take Bucky with us. With the two Indian boys, Charles can handle the herd."

By mid-morning on the third day of their travel, the topography of the plains began to change. Although it was still a vast expanse of wind-blown grass lacking rock formations or trees to give it character and a sense of distance, Sarah could sense that they were on a slight rise. The two horses pulling the wagon were affected by it, and Hugh began stopping at hourly intervals to let them blow and rest. Off in the distance, she could see numerous prairie dogs mounds that gave evidence of a large village of the small creatures that lived underground in their tunnels.

Hugh and Bucky took turns on the wagon. When one was driving, the other scouted ahead of their path of travel. They had brought an extra horse with them so two could rest behind the wagon while the third one was being ridden. Although it was cold at night and a brisk wind blew steadily, the sun provided enough warmth for it to be comfortable during the day.

As noon neared, a narrow stream of flowing water appeared ahead of them, shining brightly in the sun like a golden snake writhing through the plains.

"That's the Prairie Dog Town Fork of the Red River," Hugh said. He had been driving the wagon for the past two hours while Bucky rode on ahead. "We'll stop there for awhile. Need to rest the horses and fill our water cans. That stream flows out of the southeast corner of Palo Dura Canyon."

"Are we close?" Sarah asked.

"If we push it, we should be there about this time tomorrow."

"Let's push it then," Sarah said. The long hours on the trail had given her too much time to think about Jody. So many days had passed since Buffalo Scar and his men had separated them that she was concerned about his welfare. She wondered if he had been injured or beaten by the Indians. She knew he was a strong boy, but was he strong enough to last this long if his captors were brutal to him?

The stop at the river was short, and they pushed on at a fast pace. A full moon rose just after sunset and, with Sarah's urging, they continued on until nearly midnight. She awoke before dawn and, for the first time on the trip, was up before Hugh and had breakfast cooking when he and Bucky rolled out of their bedding.

Several hours after they started that morning, one of the horses in the traces began to falter, limping badly. Hugh filed down the mare's hoof and replaced her shoe. Within minutes they were on the move again.

Sarah rode in silence. She mustered her reserves of strength in anticipation of what lay ahead. Her cold still bothered her, but an occasional sip from the medicine bottle kept her cough under control.

When the sun was reaching its zenith and the land, now devoid of its snow cover, seemed to stretch on to eternity, the plains ahead took on a new hue. Instead of the drab brown tone of the grass and the dark tinge of the muddy ground, the gleam of something white began to appear. Sarah thought she was seeing a mirage but, as they continued on, the white expanded until it dominated the landscape.

Bucky, who had been roaming ahead, came back to the wagon with a downcast look on his normally cheerful face. Holding his hat brim against the wind with one hand, he said, "This is where they killed the horses, Mr. Grossman."

Looking around, Sarah could make out skeletons and individual bones strewn on both sides of the roadway. As far as she could see lay the remnants of hundreds of horses. She and Hugh remained silent as they entered the vast animal bone yard. Bucky rode close beside the wagon, as if he needed the security of their company. Here and there, coyotes and carrion birds picked at the sun-bleached bones of the once mighty horse herd.

An overwhelming sense of loss came over Sarah. What a terrible waste, she thought. Nothing in the descriptions she had heard prepared her for actually seeing the massive slaughter field. The sounds of the helpless, dying animals seemed to hang in the wind keening across the bones. How terrible it must have been for them when they were shot. And how terrible it must have been for the men who were ordered to shoot them, men who depended on horses for their safety, livelihood, and companionship. She wondered how many of them regretted their actions that day and had nightmares even now?

Then, out of the corner of her eye, Sarah saw movement among the scattered bones. Turning, she saw an elderly Indian woman with a shawl covering her head. As Sarah watched, the woman picked up one of the bones and walked slowly to a wide circular area that had been cleared among the carcasses. When she reached the opening, she knelt and placed the bone she was carrying on the ground. Then, rising, she returned to search for another.

"That poor woman," Sarah said. "What is she doing?"

"I don't know," Hugh said in hushed tones. Looking at Bucky, he said, "See what's goin' on. Maybe she needs help."

Bucky started to ride his horse across the field of white, and then he stopped and dismounted. Placing his feet carefully to avoid stepping on the bones, he approached the woman. They were too far away to hear the conversation, but Sarah could see that she was talking animatedly with Bucky as she gestured at the bones strewn around her.

After several minutes, Bucky returned to his horse for his canteen. When he handed it to the woman, she nodded her head several times at him. Then, laying the water on the ground, she turned away and resumed searching among the ghastly remains.

Bucky walked slowly back to the wagon with the brim of his hat pulled down to cover his face. For a long moment, he stood several steps away from Sarah's side of the wagon. When he finally raised his head, she could see tears sparkling in his eyes and running down his cheeks.

"Sorry, Ma'am," he said in a choked voice.

"That's all right, Bucky," Sarah said. "I feel the sadness too."

Finally collecting himself, Bucky said, "Her husband and son were killed when the army raided the canyon. They couldn't get away because their horses were shot. She is collecting the bones out there to make them horses so they ... so they can ride with the Great Spirit."

"Make them horses?" Hugh asked quietly.

"Yes," Bucky answered. "The coyotes and the wind keep moving the bones around. She collects them and makes complete horse skeletons. She takes bones from different places and puts them together."

"How long has she been doing that?" Sarah asked.

"I'm not sure," Bucky said. "She told me she's made many horses. Every full moon, she sits by them and waits for her husband and son to come ride them into the sky where the Great Spirit lives. When they don't come to get the horses, she throws away those bones and makes two more. She's sure they'll return if she can make good horses for them."

"Oh, the poor dear," Sarah said. "What can we do for her?"

"Nothing, I'm afraid," Bucky answered. "She said her people came and took her to the reservation, but she just walked back here. She—" Overcome by emotion, Bucky couldn't go on. He pulled his hat down over his eyes to hide the tears in his eyes.

Thinking of how difficult it had been just to ride from Fort Sill, Sarah shuddered at the thought of the old woman, alone and filled with the memory of her dead family, walking so far to fulfill her obligation to provide them with horses to ride in the hereafter. Although she knew the woman was not a Christian, Sarah said a silent prayer for her.

Hugh cleared his throat and, turning to Bucky, said. "Take her one of the large cans of water and some bread and meat. Least we can do for her."

After leaving the slaughter field, Bucky ranged ahead leaving Sarah and Hugh alone with their somber thoughts. Then he suddenly appeared on the horizon, riding swiftly toward them waving his hat. He stormed up to the wagon and drew his horse to a stop as Hugh halted along side him.

"White Cloud—" Bucky stammered breathlessly.

"Now, just slow down," Hugh said quietly. "What's White Cloud up to?"

"Just ahead," Bucky said. "Coming this way. Looks like he has Buffalo Cloud's people with him."

"Jody?" Sarah said, rising from the seat. "Did you see Jody?"

"They were a long ways off," Bucky said, avoiding Sarah's eyes.

Handing Sarah the reins, Hugh climbed down from the wagon. Going to the rear, he put his saddle on his horse and led it forward. "I'll go see what's happenin'," he said to Bucky. "Bring Mrs. Whitman on."

Bucky tied his horse on the tailgate and, still winded from his ride, climbed up to the seat as Hugh galloped ahead.

"Did you see Jody?" Sarah asked again hopefully.

"No," Bucky said. "They were a long ways off. Looks like they were just coming out of the canyon. All I could see was White Cloud on horseback leading some warriors. A bunch of women and children were following on foot."

"Could Jody have been one of the children?" Sarah asked anxiously.

"I don't know," Bucky said with a shake of his head. "Sorry." He slapped the reins on the rumps of the horses and urged them into a trot.

As they crested a slight rise, Sarah could see the flat plains drop off into a massive canyon in the distance. A large number of people on horseback and walking were streaming toward her. Several of the horses pulled a travois with bodies strapped on them. She could make out Hugh as he stopped beside White Cloud at the head of the procession. As she watched fearfully, Hugh went on down the line almost to the edge of the precipice before turning and galloping toward the wagon.

Sarah couldn't see Hugh's face until he stopped beside her and, removing his hat, looked at her with teary eyes.

"Oh Lord!" Sarah said before Hugh could say anything. She felt the cold, clammy hand of panic seize her and strangle her breath.

White Cloud pulled to a stop in front of the wagon and raised his arm to halt those following him. He stared at Sarah without expression while he waited for Hugh to make his report.

"I'm sorry, Mrs. Whitman," Hugh said in a choked voice. "White Cloud said your son died yesterday. Before they got to Scar's camp."

"Died!" Sarah gasped. "How?" Although she tried to maintain control, sobs wracked her body. Bucky put one arm around her and held her as she cried.

"Scar's son was the one who grabbed Jody," Hugh said quietly, his hat still held in his hands. "He took him to replace a boy of his the army killed in the raid. One of Scar's wives said your son took sick durin' the ride to the camp. They tried to help him, but his fever was too high. She said he died yesterday mornin'. They buried him near the camp."

Sarah looked up through her tears at White Cloud. He nodded his head to her and said slowly, "We hurry. Too late. People no want child to die. Much sadness."

Hugh reached into his coat pocket, removed an object and handed it to Sarah. She had to blink several times to clear her vision before she could see what it was: Jody's other red mitten. Suddenly the realization that he was dead overwhelmed her. As she gasped for breath, she dropped the mitten on the ground. Then she fainted, and she would have fallen out of the wagon if Bucky had not held on to her.

Chapter 28

The jostling motion of the wagon bed brought Sarah up from a state of unconsciousness. Although she was covered with blankets, she felt cold. A shiver ran through her body and her teeth began to chatter. Her first thought was that it was snowing, and she had lost something in the snow and couldn't find it. Before she could grasp the meaning of the thought, she fell asleep again.

In time, she began dreaming. At first, the dream images were soft and vague, like dim shadows on a cloudy day. They swirled around the peripheral of her mind, silent and nebulous. Then the images began to intensify in structure and color until they formed into a familiar scene. She was kneeling on the ground in the family cemetery at her ranch on the Bosque River. She could hear the gurgling sound of the water accompanying the whisper of the wind in the trees. Her mother's gravestone was to her left and, in front of her, the unfinished marker for her father. Beside that, she could make out a slight mound from another grave topped by a white tombstone with no lettering. Then, as she looked at it, a single name appeared upon it: "James."

She sensed that something was missing. There should be another headstone; Jody should be buried here with his family. She looked around, but couldn't find it. Desperation seized her and stopped her breath. She felt weary, as if she had been on a long and arduous journey. But she knew that her ordeal was not over, not until Jody was at rest. She began to cry, tears of anguish and exhaustion.

Then she saw something form in the air over her father's marker. When she looked up, she saw him gazing down at her with his perceptive gray eyes and his kindly smile. She tried to stand, but her legs lacked the strength, and she remained on the ground staring up at him.

In a quiet voice, filled with love and concern, he spoke to her, "Sarah, my child, the grave is empty." Then he smiled at her and his figure dissipated, becoming formless until it faded into the emptiness of space.

A severe bump on her head jolted Sarah into consciousness. Pulling back the blanket that covered her eyes; she looked up into a dull, leaden sky. The continued jostling from the wooden floor of the wagon kept her from returning to sleep. She lay quietly, trying not to think, not to feel. The dream she awakened from came into her memory with vivid awareness.

Her father had told her the grave was empty, but she knew that. His body had never been found and, probably, never would be after all these years. Also the chance of finding Jim was becoming more remote with the passage of time. But what disturbed her most was that she did not remember seeing Jody's grave in the cemetery. She wondered why her father had said "grave" instead of "graves" to her. Was it his way of reaching out to her and telling her to bring Jody's body home with her?

Then she heard the sound of voices, those of Hugh and Bucky. Forcing herself to concentrate, she could just make out their words.

"How long do you think she'll sleep, Mr. Grossman?" Bucky asked as he rode next to the wagon.

"Hard to say," Hugh answered. "Losin' her child after a trip like she made would lay anyone low for a piece."

Sarah was drifting off to sleep again, when Bucky said something that jarred her awake.

"Do you think we should have brought Jody's body with us?" he asked. "Maybe, Mrs. Whitman wants to bury him at home."

"Darn, I never gave that a thought," Hugh said. "Guess we should've. I was too concerned about gettin' her back to Fort Worth. Least we could have done was put up a cross for him. Course findin' where he's buried might be a tad difficult. White Cloud burned the village. Probably wouldn't have if Scar hadn't put up a fight."

"Jody—" Sarah said weakly as she tried to sit up. It took all the effort she could muster to rise to a sitting position.

"Mrs. Whitman!" Bucky said with surprise. "I didn't know you were awake."

Hugh turned around and looked back at Sarah. He had been driving the wagon slowly to minimize jarring while she slept. "How are you doin'?" he asked.

"I'm ... fine," Sarah said weakly. "We have to go back."

"Go back?" Hugh asked incredulously.

"Yes," Sarah said. With great effort, she climbed over the seat and sat next to him. She wrapped a blanket around her to ward off the cold wind that blew strongly from the north. A low, dark gray overcast obscured the winter sun and stole its warmth.

"I want to take Jody home with me," she said. "How far from Buffalo Scar's camp are we?"

"Couple of hours away," Hugh answered.

"Where is White Cloud?" Sarah asked as she looked around for sight of him. All she could see across the flat prairie surrounding them was the undulating buffalo grass as the wind pressed against it in chaotic patterns, swirling and dipping as if orchestrated by some unseen conductor gone berserk.

"He's headed for Fort Sill," Hugh said as he stopped the wagon. "We're goin' southeast to Fort Worth on another route. It'll take us through Wichita Falls so we can pick up your dog. White Cloud's probably not too far that way." He pointed back over his left shoulder. "He can't travel fast with most of the women and children walkin'. There wasn't enough horses to carry everybody."

"I want to find Jody and take him home for burial in our family plot," Sarah said. She didn't mention the appearance of her father in her dream or his words to her.

Hugh tilted his hat back on his head exposing the white skin of his forehead. Spitting carefully with the breeze, he said, "We can try, Mrs. Whitman."

He looked to the north. The clouds near the horizon were tinged with an ominous black underbelly, and the temperature had dropped to near freezing. His breath came in bursts of steam snatched away by the fierce wind. "Looks like we're in for another blue norther," he said. "Are you sure you're up to it?"

"I can't ask you and Bucky to do any more than you already have," Sarah said. "But this is something I must do. If you'll let me use the wagon, I'll find White Cloud and ask him to help me locate Jody. If it snows, we'll never find where he's buried. I ... I can't leave him lying alone out there. We never recovered my father's body or my husband's. I can't let that happen to my son."

Hugh and Bucky turned away as Sarah cried softly. Hugh hawked and spit off the side of the wagon.

Then regaining her composure, Sarah pulled the blanket away from her face and said forcefully, "He's my son. I will not put you in danger. Please let me go on alone."

Hugh and Bucky exchanged a long look. Then it was Bucky who broke the silence, "Mrs. Whitman, I don't remember much about my mother. She left me because she didn't want me. Sometimes at night, I wake up thinking about her. I picture her smiling and reaching out to me. Then, in the light of day, I realize she had no love for me. If she'd been like you, had the love for me you have for your son, I'd still have a mother. I wouldn't have been alone all these years."

Bucky stopped and pulled the brim of his hat down to cover his face. Then he went on, "Whatever you have to do to take Jody home, you can count on me." Turning, he rode away from the wagon.

Hugh bowed his head and said, "I ain't as eloquent as Bucky, but what he said goes for me too. You can count on both of us. Now, that's settled. No more talk of goin' on alone."

Sarah put her hand on Hugh's arm. "Thank you," she said.

"No need for thanks," Hugh said gruffly. "Let's cut White Cloud off and get back to the camp."

Turning the horses into the teeth of the wind, he snapped the reins and urged them into a brisk trot.

They stopped at the edge of the canyon as snow began to fall. In a short time, it covered the ground and swirled around the wagon wheels and the legs of the horses. The low sun struggled to give light to the late afternoon. White Cloud pulled his buffalo robe tightly about his throat and spoke to the two mounted warriors beside him. Then he stared down the narrow trail winding to the bottom nearly a hundred feet below.

Sitting next to them, Buffalo Scar's wife, Summer Water, disdained the cold and wind. Bareheaded, her cheeks were crusted with dried blood where she had cut herself. Most of one ear was missing and two fingers on her right hand had been severed.

When Sarah had asked Hugh about her, he told her it was the Comanche women's way of mourning their dead husbands. When White Cloud killed Buffalo Scar after the confrontation between them broke into hostility, the woman—Buffalo Scar's first wife—slashed herself with a knife while she grieved.

White Cloud spoke harshly to Summer Water, and then he turned to Hugh and Sarah in the wagon. "She say grave hard to find. Can't remember."

Turning back to the woman, he berated her again in Comanche. She bowed her head under the verbal assault, but she did not respond.

White Cloud rode his horse over to the wagon and looked down at Sarah. "We look," he said brusquely. "Maybe no find son."

Sarah was about to respond when Bucky, who had ridden to the edge of the canyon, spurred his horse up to the wagon and said quietly, "There's smoke coming from a fire down there. I saw a tipi from the cliff."

White Cloud rode up to Buffalo Scar's wife and, taking the reins from her, led her horse away from the wagon and back along the trail several hundred feet. Sarah could hear his thunderous voice as he shouted at the woman. She didn't see White Cloud strike the woman, but she heard the blow and turned to see her huddled on the ground next to her horse.

"Hugh, he's hurting that poor woman," Sarah said with concern in her voice. "Can't you make him stop?"

"Best stay out of it," Hugh said, looking down at his hands. "He's the chief of the band. Now that Scar's dead, she's his responsibility until another family adopts her. If we interfere, he'll lose face with his men."

Ignoring the woman, who was still lying on the snow, White Cloud rode back to the wagon. His face betrayed his anger as he spoke to Sarah. "Maybe lie. Say no see bury *tahbay-boh* child."

Sarah caught her breath, "Do you mean Jody could still be alive?"

White Cloud leaned forward and answered, his voice now soft and low, "Her son and wife not in fight. Run from camp."

Turning to Hugh, White Cloud added, "No take horses. Maybe fall."

"Okay," Hugh said as he climbed down from the wagon and grabbed his rifle. White Cloud and his warriors quickly dismounted and, carrying their weapons, headed for the precipice in a crouching run.

"Best wait for us here," Hugh said.

Sarah leaped down from the wagon and almost fell on the snow covered ground. Before Hugh could react, she ran toward the trail leading downward. He followed her in a lumbering gait. Bucky tied his horse to the wagon and fell in behind them.

As the path pitched toward the valley floor, Sarah's feet slipped out from under her, and she fell backward. Sliding on her seat, she almost went over the edge, but was able to grab an outcropping of rock and stop herself. Hugh scrambled to her side and helped her up.

"Careful, it's quite a drop," he said.

As they continued down the trail, he held her arm to slow her down.

When they reached the canyon floor, Sarah could see the ruins of Buffalo Scar's camp ahead of them near a stream that flowed through a small stand of mesquite and cottonwood trees. A number of tipis had been toppled to the ground and lay smoldering in the falling snow. Several dogs were snuffling about the area, snarling at each other as they contested for the food from overturned cook pots. She paused to look around the small village, not knowing which way White Cloud and his warriors had gone.

Bucky came up beside her and said, "The campfire I saw was down that way." He pointed down the canyon where a single strand of smoke snaked upward over a rise in the ground, and then disappeared into the snowflakes and the diminishing light of the dying day. Without waiting for acknowledgement, he ran toward it, followed by Hugh.

Sarah turned to follow them when she heard the flat crack of a rifle disturb the quiet. "Oh Lord!" she said aloud.

Her heart was beating rapidly in her chest, and she had difficulty breathing as she ran, slipping and sliding toward the sound of the shot. Topping the rise, she could see a single tipi up against the canyon wall where it was protected from the incessant wind. White Cloud was facing the hovel with his rifle pointed at an Indian man and woman who were huddled together near the entrance to the tipi. His warriors and Hugh were standing behind him, as if frozen in place. She couldn't see Bucky.

Then the flaps to the tipi opened, and Bucky emerged carrying a child in his arms. At first glance, Sarah could see that it was a young boy with short, cropped black hair and a dark face. He was wearing buckskin clothes and moccasins.

Sarah stared for a moment at the strange boy, so dark and unlike Jody. Then he looked at her, his blue eyes flashing in recognition, and she broke into a run. Tears streamed down her face as she swept down on Bucky and grabbed the boy from his arms.

"Jody," she screamed as she smothered the child. "It's you!"

She fell to her knees in the snow, holding him tightly against her chest. His blond hair had been cut short and dyed black and the pale skin of his face colored with brown stains.

"Mama!" Jody cried, wrapping his arms around his mother's neck. "I knew you would come."

After a long moment, Hugh came up and kneeled beside Sarah. He said quietly, "Mrs. Whitman, dark's comin' on and the snow's gettin' worse. We need to get out of this canyon while we can. We'll have to pitch camp up on top. White Cloud is goin' to take them back to the reservation with him." He waved at the Indian couple who had kept Jody captive.

Tears stained Sarah's cheeks as she looked up. Still holding Jody closely, she said, "Yes. It's time to go home."

Chapter 29

Fort Worth was adorned with a thick cover of snow when Sarah, Jody, and Beelzebub arrived downtown late in the afternoon. A bright sun illuminated the buildings, making them stand out against the white blanket covering their roofs. After a brief visit with the Burnett's, Hugh and Bucky had stayed behind to help feed the livestock. Burk Burnett had insisted that Sarah had no obligation to him for his assistance with Jody's rescue. His wife, Ruth, recovered from her fever, had prepared lunch. Burk's son, William, who was seven years old, and his daughter, Rebecca, a year younger, were enthralled by Jody's experiences. They agreed to let him continue on only after he promised to return and tell his story in detail.

After they pulled up in front of the Mansion Hotel, Sarah was reaching up to help Jody down from the wagon when the hotel door burst open and Margaret ran down the stairs, her arms wide and tears brightening her eyes.

"Oh!" Margaret screamed as she enveloped Sarah and Jody in a tight hug. "I was so worried about you. Mr. Burnett said you were going after Jody. But that was the last word we had."

"I'm sorry," Sarah said. "We had no way to let you know he was safe. We came on a direct route to Fort Worth south of the reservation."

"Hello, Maggie," Jody said as he squirmed away from her embrace. "Where's Daniel? I want to tell him about the Indians."

"How is Daniel?" Sarah asked.

"He's doing very well," Margaret said. "The doctor had to shave his head and give him several stitches. He has a slight concussion, but he should have a full recovery. He went to the telegraph office to see if you'd sent a wire."

Looking down at Jody, Margaret said, "My goodness. What happened to your hair?"

Jody ran his hand over his dark stubby hair. "That's my Indian haircut," he said proudly. "I'm going to keep it like this forever."

"No, you're not, young man," Sarah said with a smile. "Your days of being a wild Indian are over with."

Noticing Beelzebub asleep in the back of the wagon, Margaret went to him and shook him awake. "How are you, old fellow?" she asked.

Beelzebub, still exhausted from his ordeal, raised his head and licked Margaret's hand.

"How did he get out of his cage in the wagon?" Sarah asked.

"I let him out," Margaret answered. "He was having such a fit when you left."

"I'm glad you did?" Sarah said. "I never would have made it without him."

"Mother," Margaret said, suddenly serious. "That horrible man, Mr. Kilpatrick, has been by almost every day to see you. Remember how handsome I thought he was when we met him down by Waco? Well he looks terrible now. I think he's very ill."

"Did he say what he wanted to see me for?" Sarah asked.

"No. When I asked him, he just smiled at me." Margaret shivered from the memory. "Now even his teeth look bad."

"Has he been here today?" Sarah asked as she handed Margaret a bundle of clothes from the wagon.

"No," Margaret answered. "I haven't seen him for several days, now that I think about it. He usually comes when Daniel and I are eating dinner. After he asks about you, he just sits at another table and smokes a cigar and drinks coffee. It really disturbs me, the way he keeps staring at me."

"Well, we'll worry about that later," Sarah said as they walked up the hotel steps. "Jody and I need a bath and a change of clothes. And we must find someone to return Mr. Burnett's wagon to him."

"Daniel should be back soon," Margaret said. "I'm sure he won't mind doing it."

After she bathed and dressed, Sarah pulled Margaret aside while Jody was splashing in the tub. "I'm going out for a few minutes," she said. "I want to see Rose. I'll be back for dinner. Watch Jody while I'm gone. Don't let him out of your sight."

The snow was beginning to settle and melt under the warm rays of the sun as Sarah climbed the stairs on the side of the Red Bull Saloon. When she entered the door, an elderly black woman was mopping the hallway. Looking up, she responded with a nod of her head when Sarah asked for Rose. Leaning the mop against the wall, the woman disappeared down the stairs behind her.

A loud tromping on the steps served notice that Rose was coming up. When she turned toward her, Sarah could see tears streaking down her cheeks. Rose rushed up and enveloped Sarah in a bear hug, nearly smothering her with her ample breasts, which were barely confined by a dark red, low-cut velvet dress. "I was so worried about you, honey," Rose said.

"I'm fine," Sarah said, extricating herself from the embrace. "And Jody's back with me."

Rose took Sarah's arm and ushered her toward her room. "You must tell me all about it. The whole town's been talking about you."

After Sarah filled Rose in on the details of her trip to find Jody, she sipped a cup of tea and said, "Jack Kilpatrick has been bothering Margaret. Do you know what he's up to?"

Rose's smile left her face as she responded, "Something is very wrong with that man. He's like a walking skeleton. Don't know what he's got, but it's not good. And now that he's sick, he's turned nasty. We had to run him out of here last week. He paid for some time with one of my girls, but instead of bedding her, he beat her up. Not bad enough to press charges against him, but—" Rose's voice trailed off as she shook her head.

"Just before we left to go home, he followed me to the cemetery and told me they were going to search my ranch," Sarah said. "Have you heard anything about that?"

"No," Rose answered. "I heard a rumor that Pinkerton fired him, so I don't know why he'd keep investigating that government robbery. Oh, and someone also told me his wife in Saint Louis died. Supposedly Jack was in San Antonio at the time."

"I still have a lot of the money down at the ranch," Sarah said. "Maybe they found it. That could be the reason he wants to see me so badly."

"I hope not, honey," Rose said. "You be very careful. That man's a snake in the grass. Do you still have that gun I gave you?"

"Yes," Sarah said as she reached into her purse and removed the small pistol. "I couldn't shoot it when the Indians took Jody because the trigger guard is too small, and I had my gloves on."

Rose took the gun and laid it on her dressing table. Opening a drawer, she extracted another pistol, which was slightly larger. Turning it over, she said, "Take this one. The trigger guard is removed, so you can shoot it with mittens if you have to. Just be careful. Don't keep a bullet in the chamber; it might go off by accident."

After Rose gave Sarah the gun, she said, "William and Ben have asked about you. They'll be mighty upset if you don't go by and see them."

"I will," Sarah said.

"You know, honey," Rose said. "You have a lot of friends here in Fort Worth. Folks who think the world of you. And I'm one of them. Have you thought about staying here? You still own Clarence's newspaper, don't you?"

"Yes, I do own the paper," Sarah said. "I don't know what I'm going to do with it. But, Rose, my heart isn't here. It's down on the ranch."

After Sarah left the saloon, she thought about going to Marshal Courtright's office to see if she could find Jack Kilpatrick and confront him. She knew she wouldn't quit worrying until she found out why he was looking for her. Her father had told her many times that the only way to get a burr out from under a saddle was to remove the saddle, find the burr, pull it out, and throw it away, and then move on to other more important things. But, she contemplated, there was no reason for Kilpatrick to be at the marshal's office if he didn't work for Pinkerton, so she walked through the slush to see William Thompson and Ben Clanton.

Ben was not in when Sarah entered the office, but William leaped up from his desk and met her in an embrace. For a long moment, they held each other, tears threatening to burst forth from both of them.

After bringing each other up to date on what had transpired since they were last together, Sarah told William about Jack Kilpatrick hounding Margaret and his deteriorating physical condition.

"Yes," William said. "I haven't seen the man for some time, but the rumor is he's quite ill. No one seems to know what's bothering him."

"I understand his wife died recently," Sarah said.

"I don't think that would hurt his conscience much," William snorted. "From what I've heard, he's not one to let the bonds of matrimony keep him from unbuckling his pants every chance he gets."

"Can you find out what happened to her?" Sarah asked. "She lived in Saint Louis. And I also heard Jack no longer works for Pinkerton. I'm curious to know why."

"Curious, huh," William said, cocking his head and looking down at Sarah. "Curiosity killed the cat, they say. Is there something between you and Jack you haven't told me?"

"Yes," Sarah said. "Yes, there is. It's best I don't share it with you now. I promise one day I'll tell you the whole story."

"I'm satisfied with that," William smiled. "The editor of one of the Saint Louis newspapers is a friend of mine. We went to law school together, but he dropped out to become a reporter. I'll see what I can find out."

All through dinner, Sarah kept glancing at the door to see if Kilpatrick was coming in. Meanwhile, Jody kept up a steady stream of boasting to Margaret and Daniel about his experiences with Buffalo Scar's son and his wife. When he embellished his tale beyond reason, Sarah lifted her eyebrow and admonished him to be truthful. The side of Daniel's forehead was swathed in a bandage but, otherwise, he seemed to be well.

The next day, Fort Worth was buried under the deepest snowfall any of the old-timers could remember. The blizzard, accompanied by howling winds, lasted for three days. When it was over, drifts covered some of the buildings up to their second floors. The roads in and out of the town were impassable, isolating the community from the outside world. After the snow stopped falling, the temperature plummeted, freezing the Trinity River so hard that horses and wagons could cross on the ice. Sarah wanted to leave for the ranch as soon as possible, and the delay caused by the weather was disconcerting.

Finally, after nearly two weeks, the cold, high-pressure area that had stretched down the mid-section of the continent all the way from the Arctic Circle retreated back north under the relentless onslaught of a warm-front originating in the Gulf of Mexico. It took several more days for North Central Texas to defrost, but it finally did, transforming its white winter covering into swollen streams and muddy roads and walkways. The steady drip of melting snow accompanied the shouts of pedestrians, horsemen, and wagon drivers sloshing through the deep muck in the streets as the town came out of its hibernation and returned to life.

William was the first visitor Sarah had at the hotel after the weather improved. Sitting in the alcove near the front desk, he removed a telegram from his coat pocket and handed it to her. Unfolding the paper, she read:

> To: William Thompson, Attorney at Law
> Fort Worth, Texas
> Greetings Sir William. Query into Mrs. Norah Kilpatrick. Died at hands of unknown assailant on or about 10 pm July 2nd this year. Investigation still open. Husband apparently in San Antonio at time based on testimony of local hotel owner (female?) As to how she expired? Deep slash across neck severed carotid artery. However, 40 other cuts on body. Some might have been fatal. Homicidal maniac (?) What's up? Send any information you have to me. Need a scoop.

Regards.
Davis Teagarden, Saint Louis, Missouri

"Oh Lord!" Sarah said as she stared at William. "You don't think—" Sarah gasped and let the telegram fall onto her lap.

"I don't know," William said quietly. "Guess I've become a little jaded in my old age, but I look a little harder at circumstantial evidence than I used to. With your permission, I'd like to turn this over to Marshal Courtright and send a copy to a state senator I know in Austin. I'd give a copy to Sheriff Roberts, but he and I aren't on speaking terms right now. I've set the hounds of hell on his backside, and he won't give me the time of day. Besides, he'd just dismiss it as nonsense."

After a long moment, Sarah broke the silence between them, "I wonder why Kilpatrick spent the past months here in Fort Worth instead of going home to Saint Louis. Maybe he's afraid to go back and face an investigation."

"Could be," William said. "In answer to your other question, Pinkerton fired him for poor performance about a month ago. He was assigned to investigate a train office robbery in Arkansas where a large amount of government money was taken. He was supposed to send weekly progress reports to their Saint Louis office. For some reason he stopped sending them in. Never gave—"

William stopped talking as Sarah began to shake as if a chill had come over her.

"Are you all right, Sarah?"

Sarah took a deep breath to steady herself before answering, "Yes, thank you. Still trying to get over a cold. I'll be fine."

Kilpatrick was no longer working for Pinkerton, she thought. If so, why was he still pursuing her and harassing Margaret? The only reason she could come up with was that he was looking for the money for himself. That meant that she and her family were in grave danger, especially if he could commit an act as violent as murdering his own wife. And, though she was afraid to think about it, if he murdered Lucille Martell and placed the blame for it on Clarence.

"You have my permission to do whatever you think is best with that telegram," she said. "I would like to have a copy, if you don't mind."

"Certainly," William said, standing up and putting on his coat.

After dinner, as Sarah was going to her room with Margaret and Jody, the desk clerk stopped her and handed her an envelope. "A telegram for you, Mrs. Whitman," he said.

Sarah thanked the man and, without looking at it, put the message in her dress pocket. William was certainly prompt in getting her a copy of the telegram from Saint Louis, she thought as she climbed the stairs. She would have to go by his office and thank him before they left the next day.

Later, after Margaret and Jody had fallen asleep, Sarah was undressing when the envelope fell onto the floor. She picked it up and started to put it in her valise. Then she looked at her name written on the front. Strange, she thought, it wasn't William's flamboyant cursive. The letters were small and stilted as if the writer had to struggle to complete them.

Opening the envelope gave her a start. The telegram was not the one William had given her. Going to the window, she leaned down so she could make out the letters. Although it was difficult to see in the dim light, her breath caught in her chest as she read:

> To: Mrs. Sarah Whitman
> Care of Mansion Hotel, Fort Worth, Texas
> Dear Mrs. Whitman. We have a patient named Jack Kilpatrick. He has asked for you to visit him. He is in a terminal state and could be called to the arms of the Lord any moment. Time is of the essence. In prayer and obedience.
> Sister Mary Theresa,
> Holy Cross Sanitarium, 811 C. Street, Dallas, Texas

Sarah sat down at the desk by the window. Kilpatrick was dying, she thought. She couldn't remember how many times she had wished he was out of her life since they first met down on the Bosque River. And she had to admit that she had even entertained thoughts of doing him harm when Margaret told her how much he upset her. Now the realization that he was near death caused her to search her soul. He would be gone soon, and she wouldn't have to worry about him. She didn't want to face him, even in his last moments. She would take her family and leave the next day, the telegram put aside until it became just a vague memory.

Tears came to her eyes as she looked out the window into the clear night sky. She knew that her father would have a pertinent Bible passage for her to take strength and guidance from, but she couldn't think of any at the moment. An umbrella of lights sprinkled the heavens as the stars twinkled brightly. She was looking toward the north, and she could see the familiar outline of the Big Dipper. Without thinking about it, her attention slid down to the Little Dipper and the North Star, her father's guiding light, and the light that led her to Jody.

She looked at the star for a long moment as it drew her attention from afar. Suddenly, calmness came over her, and she cast aside her concerns and apprehensions. It was as if a strong hand touched her shoulder, and a wise voice told her what she needed to do.

Folding the telegram, she placed it in the pocket of her coat underneath her gloves. Then she removed the gun Rose had given her from her purse and put it in a bag containing some items she had purchased to give to Rose as a going away gift. It was time, she thought, to trust in the Lord and put away thoughts of hatred and violence.

She stood by the bed and looked down at the sleeping forms of Margaret and Jody. Even in sleep, Margaret looked happy, and so young. It was hard for Sarah to believe that she would marry soon. Jody, one arm flung over Margaret, looked like the little boy she had known before his capture, his hair a vibrant blond again. He seemed to have recovered from his ordeal without any lasting scars or bad memories. She was very thankful for that.

They should leave on the morrow, she mused. But once again, their return home would have to be delayed. She had no choice. One more obligation awaited her before Fort Worth could be put behind them.

Chapter 30

Margaret and Jody did not accompany Sarah to the railroad station. She knew that he would be upset if he saw the train and was not allowed to go with her. After getting used to the roar of the engine, the acrid smoke that drifted in the windows, the clicking of the rails, and the swaying of the passenger car, she rather enjoyed the ride to Dallas. Although she had never been to the city thirty miles to the east, she wasn't looking forward to the ordeal of meeting Jack Kilpatrick.

Her feelings about him were perplexing. She would never forget that day on the street in Fort Worth when he looked at her with pure evil in his eyes. As a Christian she knew she must not judge his soul; only the Lord could do that. If her father was sitting beside her, he would remind her that Jesus said, "Judge not lest ye be judged." Closing her eyes, she said a silent prayer for Kilpatrick.

Holy Cross Sanitarium was too far from the station for Sarah to walk, so she accepted a ride from a young black man driving a taxi wagon. As they traveled down the streets, Sarah was struck by the dissimilarity between Dallas and Fort Worth. She knew that the railroad had come to Dallas several years before it continued on west. That short time seemed to have had a positive impact on it. The streets were wider and better maintained, but it wasn't until they had traveled nearly a mile through the warm afternoon that she noticed a major improvement over Fort Worth: the downtown area was clean, and it didn't reek with the odor of discarded garbage, stale water, and dead animals.

Even the sanitarium looked acceptable from a distance. Sitting at the end of a narrow, dirt culdesac among a copse of mesquite and oak trees, it occupied a large single-story structure that had formerly housed a cattle auction. The surrounding stables had been removed and turned into a vegetable garden, which was tended by some of the patients and staff members. The building, although renovated and painted white, was plain and nondescript. All the windows, except for two in the front, were boarded over, and a large single door served as an entrance. The sign over the door was faded and difficult to read, as if those in charge didn't want to call attention to the true significance of the building: a sanctuary for the insane and terminally ill and the final earthly residence for most of them.

The taxi driver's eyes widened in horror as he pulled the carriage to a stop in front of the entrance and waited for Sarah to disembark. He refused to look at the building, and when she asked him to wait for her, he said, "Yes'm. I'll wait down yonder a ways." Snapping the reins, he galloped away in a cloud of dust as if the devil was pursuing him.

The door opened to a reception room that stretched the width of the building. Dim sunlight streaming through two small windows added to the illumination of several gas lamps fastened on the walls. Dilapidated furniture, cast haphazardly to one side, provided an area for visitors. A large wooden cross and a statue of Mary holding the baby Jesus were mounted on the back wall next to a set of double doors that led to the rear. Several desks and file cabinets were placed to the side opposite the visitor area. A thin, young woman dressed in a black nun's habit sat at one of the desks writing in a large journal. Wearing thick glasses, she was so absorbed in her task that she didn't look up when Sarah closed the door behind her. Left handed, she was contorted over the book with her head bent down to her scratching pencil.

The faint sound of high-pitched wailing came from the rear, accompanied by muffled voices. Although sparsely furnished, the reception room was clean and smelled of lye soap. The absence of fresh air struck Sarah, and she felt a sneeze coming on. She tried, but she couldn't stop it from bursting forth in a crescendo, "Ah … choo."

The young nun jumped up from her chair as if she'd been struck. "Goodness," she said, staring at Sarah.

Then, collecting her wits, she stammered, "I … I'm sorry. I didn't see you come in." Her glasses had slipped down over her nose, and she pushed them back up, which magnified her large, brown eyes.

"That's all right," Sarah said with a smile. "I'm Sarah Whitman. I've come to see Jack Kilpatrick. Sister Mary Theresa sent me a telegram."

"She's with the patients," the nun said. "I am Sister Mary Magdalene. I'll tell her you're here."

Sister Magdalene went to the rear door. Sliding aside a covered opening about eight inches wide, she leaned forward and shouted, "Sister Theresa has a visitor."

A muffled voice responded immediately, and she slid the tiny flap shut. Turning to Sarah, she pointed at the visitor area and said, "You may wait over there. It will be a few minutes. This is lunch hour, and things do get quite hectic."

During the brief time the aperture was open, the wailing that Sarah had heard earlier burst forth with painful clarity. It sounded like women, under severe duress, crying out for help. Sister Magdalene, seemingly unaffected by the expressions of grief from the rear, returned to her desk. Taking up the pencil, she ignored Sarah and began scribbling again.

Several minutes went by, and the scratching of Sister Magdalene's pencil and the sounds from the back of the building began to grate on Sarah's nerves. She looked up at the cross suspended over her as the door leading to the rear opened. A tiny nun, her back bent with age and her pale skin lined with years of worldly concern, approached her.

Holding out a slim, bony hand, the woman said in a soft voice that invited attention and respect, "I am Sister Mary Theresa, Mrs. Whitman. It was so kind of you to come on such short notice. Mr. Kilpatrick has had no visitors since we admitted him." Her pale, gray eyes reflected compassion and intelligence, but they were crinkled at the corners as if she looked at life with a large measure of humor. Releasing Sarah's hand, she sat down beside her.

"Doesn't he have any family?" Sarah asked. She found herself liking the little woman immediately.

"No. His wife passed recently, and he had no children. When I asked him about siblings, he said he had none."

"Do you know why he asked to see me?" Sarah said.

"No," Sister Theresa said with a shake of her head. "I certainly have no idea why he asked for you ... insisted, actually. As I said in my message to you, he is close to passing. I sensed he was a tormented soul when he came to us. Those at the end of their earthly life often express a need to share their last moments with friends or loved ones. Others desire to atone for their transgressions with those who they've wronged. Are you a friend of his?"

"No," Sarah answered quietly. "I'm sorry to say we're not friends. I have only known him for a few months."

"I see," Sister Theresa said with a nod. "When he spoke your name, it was not as one would speak about a friend."

"What is Mr. Kilpatrick's ailment?" Sarah asked. "He seemed like such a strong, energetic man not so long ago."

"What do you know about the disease called syphilis?" Sister Theresa responded.

"Syphilis!" Sarah reacted with surprise. "I really don't know much about it. My father told me it was a disease caught by prostitutes and the men who visit them, but that's about the extent of my knowledge."

"You sound like a learned person, Mrs. Whitman," Sister Theresa said with a tight-lipped smile and a twinkle in her eyes. "Perhaps what I tell you is more than you want to know, but I think it will help you understand Mr. Kilpatrick's physical condition and his frame of mind when you see him."

"Please call me Sarah," Sarah said. She reached out and touched Sister Theresa's hands, which were clasped in her lap.

"Thank you, Sarah. I will. Syphilis is a difficult disease to diagnose and even more difficult to treat. The medical doctors call it 'the great imitator' because many of the symptoms are similar to other diseases. In fact, during the Middle Ages, it was often confused with leprosy. We are most certain it is transmitted only by sexual contact. That's an important assumption for those like me who treat the disease. We are in no danger of being infected by patient contact if we are careful.

"There are three stages to syphilis. During the primary stage, after one is infected, sores appear. These heal without treatment, and most do not realize the disease has infected them. During the second stage, skin rashes may occur. Since other diseases exhibit rashes, syphilis is often misdiagnosed at that time. Also, the patient may have fever, swollen glands, hair and weight loss, and fatigue. Again, these symptoms may fool the doctors. The horrible truth of this disease is that during this stage, the symptoms seem to resolve themselves without treatment. So the patient thinks he is cured of whatever ails him … or her."

Sister Theresa paused and glanced up at the icon of Mary and Jesus, as if she needed to take strength from it. "Since it is a sexually transmitted disease, women are also infected," she continued. "Over the years I have tended syphilis patients, most have them have been women."

"Do any survive?" Sarah asked.

"Very few," Sister Theresa said as she closed her eyes. "Some live longer than others. But, unfortunately, we have no medicine that will cure the disease. All we can do is treat the symptoms and make the patient as comfortable as possible."

Sarah took a deep breath and thought back to the day when Jack Kilpatrick had asked to be her escort in Fort Worth. At that time, he must have known that he had syphilis. Although she admitted to herself that she once thought Kilpatrick was an attractive man, she never stopped believing that she was married to Jim. Even though she was certain that he was dead, she steadfastly maintained her matrimonial vows. Now, she said a silent prayer of thanks that she had not given in to Kilpatrick's overtures.

"Are you all right, Sarah?" Sister Theresa asked quietly. "Perhaps this is too much for you."

"No," Sarah said. "I'm fine. Please continue."

"Well, as I said, there are three stages. The final one begins when the symptoms of the second stage disappear. The infection remains in the body, sometimes for years, sometimes only for a few months. However long it takes, the disease eventually attacks the internal organs, including the brain, nerves, heart, bones, and joints. When that happens, loss of muscle strength, paralysis, blindness, and even insanity occurs. It is a most hideous disease, Sarah."

Sister Theresa looked down at her hands before continuing, "At the end, there is little we can do for the patients. Their death is a painful process. We pray with them and for them."

Sarah sat quietly for a moment before asking, "How long does Mr. Kilpatrick have?"

"He's very near the end. I believe he is willing himself to stay alive until he sees you. Some terminal patients can do that; choose the moment of their death. Just last week, an elderly woman refused to pass until her son arrived from New York. Soon after he came to her bedside, she went to be with the Lord."

"How long ... how long do you think Mr. Kilpatrick has known he has syphilis?" Sarah asked quietly.

"He wouldn't tell me directly, but I surmise he's been aware of it for a year or longer. He went to a hospital in Saint Louis for treatment last year. He must have been in the second stage at that time."

"Did he tell you how he got the disease?" Sarah asked. The memory of seeing Lucille Martell lying in her shallow grave came to her.

"No," Sister Theresa said. "But sometimes, when he loses his senses, he raves about women; how he hates them and wants to hurt them. I don't recall any particular names."

"Thank you for sharing this with me," Sarah said.

"Let us see Mr. Kilpatrick now," Sister Theresa said as she stood. "Are you sure you're up to it? If you haven't been in a sanitarium before, it can be quite unsettling."

"Yes," Sarah said as she rose. "I'm ready."

But nothing prepared Sarah for the shock she received when they entered the main part of the hospital. The noises, which had been attenuated by the closed door, burst over her like a spring thunderstorm: talking, moaning, crying, and banging. The sounds were accompanied by a miasma of odors: lye soap, urine, feces, sweat, and an underlying smell that took Sarah a few moments to recognize: the smell of the dying and the dead. Everywhere she looked there were patients: sitting around tables in a large room just inside the door, shuffling up and down a wide hallway, reclining on the floor, and sitting immobile in wheelchairs. The men and boys were all dressed in dark pants and matching long-sleeve shirts. The women and girls wore one-piece cotton dresses of the same color with loose waists. Scattered here and there among the patients were several nuns wearing black habits and medical aides clad in white pants and shirts to differentiate them from the patients.

Sister Theresa took Sarah's elbow and steered her past the staring eyes that followed them down the hall. They had to step around a young man crouched against the wall. When Sarah first looked at him, he was motionless as a statue. Then his hand shot out, and he snatched an imaginary flying insect out of the air. While she watched in astonishment, he put the nonexistent bug in his mouth and began chewing, a smile lighting up his face. After swallowing, he became immobile again, only his eyes moving as he scanned the air for another prey.

An old man, with rheumy eyes and white stubble covering his face, stepped in front of Sister Theresa and Sarah. With a lascivious look on his face, he stared at Sarah, and then he reached down and began unbuttoning his pants. Before he could go any further, Sister Theresa slapped his hands and told him firmly, "That is not acceptable behavior, Mr. Hanratty. You know better."

Hanratty dropped his head and mumbled, "I'm sorry, Sister. I won't do it again."

"See that you don't," Sister Theresa snapped. "Your daughter will be coming to see you tomorrow. We want to give her a good report, don't we?"

As they progressed down the hall, Sarah could see doors opening to rooms on each side. Most of them were closed, but several stood open revealing beds lined up inside like cots in an army barracks. Many were occupied with patients lying immobile or sitting on them. At the end of the corridor, another door blocked their way. A sign across it read, "Intensive Care."

Sister Theresa stopped and turned to Sarah. "The rooms beyond here are for the terminally ill patients. Mr. Kilpatrick is one of four with his disease. He became violent last week, so we put him by himself in a secure room where he can't hurt anyone. I don't believe he is strong enough now to cause a problem."

"Violent?" Sarah asked.

"Yes," Sister Theresa answered. "He tried to strangle one of his room mates. He accused him of stealing his water. After we calmed him down and put him in a separate room, he tried to commit suicide by hanging himself with his bed sheet. We had to remove everything except for his mattress. He's terribly thin. He hasn't eaten in several weeks. The best we've been able to do is force-feed him some water and broth. Most of it, he spits out."

Reaching into the pocket of her habit, Sister Theresa took out a small, white handkerchief. Handing it to Sarah, she said, "This may help you when we get inside his room. It's sprinkled with lilac water."

What a terribly lonely and unpleasant place to be, Sarah thought. She knew it would take all her strength to meet Kilpatrick. She didn't fear for her safety, but she didn't know if she was emotionally strong enough to go through with it.

As if sensing her apprehension, Sister Theresa put her hand on Sarah's arm. "You are a Christian, aren't you, Sarah?" she asked.

"Yes," Sarah responded. "My father was a Baptist preacher. He raised me with the Bible as his guide."

"I thought so," Sister Theresa said. "I've found it helps me to say a prayer before I go into a dying patient's room. Perhaps it will help you, also."

Taking a deep breath and closing her eyes, Sarah could envision her father standing beside her nodding his head. Reaching out, she took Sister Theresa's hand and prayed silently with her. A sense of calm and purpose gradually replaced the anxiety she had felt. Opening her eyes, she smiled, and they entered the room together.

Sarah had become almost accustomed to the stench of the sanitarium, but the odor in Jack Kilpatrick's room shocked her. Very small, it lacked an outside window to admit light or fresh air. One small, barred opening in the door let in a shaft of light from the gas lamps hanging in the hallway, but it did little to recycle the rancid air inside. The odor of death—the signal to the living that a human being was about to surrender to the ravages of a terrible disease—was much stronger here, she thought. Following Sister Theresa's lead, she took out the scented handkerchief and held it to her nose.

Sarah could make out the form of a man, clad only in dark trousers and a matching shirt, lying on a thin mattress. As her eyes adapted to the dim light, she recognized Jack Kilpatrick. Emaciated to the point of becoming skeletal, he lay motionless on his back. The only sound coming from him was the shallow rasping of his breath.

"He was awake earlier," Sister Theresa said. "If you talk to him, he should respond. I'll wait outside the door for you."

A sudden fear overwhelmed her and, unable to move, Sarah stood over Kilpatrick after Sister Theresa left. For a long moment, she stared down at the form on the dirty mattress. Then, gathering her resolve, she knelt near his head. Even in the near darkness, she could see the bones stretching the skin on his face and the pink expanse of his nearly hairless cranium.

"Mr. Kilpatrick," Sarah said in a quiet and tremulous voice. When she received no response, she put her mouth close to his ear and said louder, "Mr. Kilpatrick. I am Sarah Whitman. You asked me to come see you."

Suddenly Sarah was aware that Kilpatrick was staring up at her, his eyes burning brightly as he focused on her face.

"Sarah," Kilpatrick said in a weak, raspy voice as he tried to lift his head. Then he seemed to gain energy, and he continued, "Information ... your husband."

Sarah's breath was trapped in her throat. She had no idea why Kilpatrick wanted to see her. The last thing she would have thought of was that he had any knowledge about Jim. "My husband!" she said. "What do you know about my husband?"

"Cameron told me—" A dry cough racked Kilpatrick's body, and he stopped talking.

Sarah waited for the spasms to subside, and then she said, "Tell me what Cameron told you. Please, tell me now."

Kilpatrick pulled his thin lips back over his bleeding gums and his brown, prominent teeth in a hideous semblance of a smile. "Not yet," he whispered. "First ... tell me. Government ... money. Where?"

Sarah looked down at Kilpatrick as he struggled to breathe and concentrated on her response. She knew he wanted her to tell him that she had the government money stolen by the three men who had come to her ranch—two of them now dead, killed by her own hand. She had lied to him before, she thought, perhaps the Lord would forgive her if she lied again. Then the vision of Sister Theresa praying came to her, and she realized that she could no longer cover up the truth.

"Yes," she said as she stared into the dilated pupils of Kilpatrick's eyes. "Three men came to our house. They had a lot of money with them. They were going to hurt me and my family. I shot two of them."

Kilpatrick rallied for a moment, and he reached one bony hand up and grabbed Sarah's arm. Before she could recoil, he hissed, "The money ... the money, where is it?"

"I gave part of it to the third man and sent him away," Sarah said with a shudder at the cold, dry touch of Kilpatrick's hand. "I used some of it to build an animal shelter in Fort Worth and start a public school."

"The rest—" Kilpatrick said as he let go of Sarah's arm and relaxed back onto the mattress.

"I still have it," Sarah said.

"Ah," Kilpatrick rasped weakly. "I was right all along ... right about you. Should have—" His voice dwindled off and he closed his eyes.

"I told you about the money," Sarah said sharply. "Now tell me what you know about my husband."

For a long moment, Kilpatrick's eyes remained closed and his breathing stopped. Sarah thought he was dead, when he opened his eyes and stared up at her.

"Cameron—" Coughing racked Kilpatrick's body again, and he arched upward off the mattress, his spine contorting at a grotesque angle. A thin scream, like the rasp of a file being drawn across a saw blade, issued from between his clenched teeth accompanied by the excretion of saliva and blood from his mouth. The sound of his bowels evacuating accompanied the rank odor of feces. Then he fell back onto the bed, his lifeless eyes staring at the cracked, painted ceiling.

Sarah stood and looked down at Kilpatrick. The disappointment of coming so close to finding out what happened to Jim filled her with despair. She put the feeling aside and, with her head bowed, prayed for Kilpatrick's soul. She didn't hear the sound of the door opening behind her, and she was not aware that Sister Theresa had entered the room until she felt the touch of her hand.

"His suffering is over, Sarah," Sister Theresa said. She knelt by Kilpatrick and, after crossing herself, prayed silently for several minutes.

Standing, she said to Sarah, "Come with me."

When they reached the reception room, Sarah had regained her composure. Turning to Sister Theresa, she asked, "What will become of him now?"

"We are not allowed a necropolis here. He will be buried in an unmarked grave in the city burial ground."

"Unmarked?" Sarah asked in astonishment. "He's not penniless, is he?"

"Yes," Sister Theresa said. "He was sent here from the hospital because he was destitute."

Sarah took her bankbook from her purse and wrote out a check. Handing it to Sister Theresa, she said, "This is a draft on a Fort Worth bank. Please see that he receives a proper burial. The remainder is for you to use as you decide."

"May the Lord bless you, Sarah," Sister Theresa said as she took the paper and handed it to Sister Magdalene, who was sitting quietly at her desk listening to the conversation.

"Will you be taking his personal items?" Sister Magdalene asked.

"Personal items?" Sarah responded.

Sister Theresa walked to one of the file cabinets and removed a large envelope. Returning to the desk, she poured out the pitiful, worldly remains of Jack Kilpatrick's life: an unopened plug of chewing tobacco, a pearl handled derringer, a small journal, a folding-blade knife, and a single silver dollar.

"What will you do with these?" Sarah asked.

"The administrator will sell what he can to help with the expenses and discard the rest," Sister Theresa said. "We are very understaffed for the number of patients we have. And medication is often not available. Are you sure you don't want to take them with you?"

"No," Sarah said, her mind still in turmoil after sharing Kilpatrick's last moments. The realization that she would never find Jim weighed heavily on her, but now she and her family could return to their ranch. Although watching Kilpatrick die would be difficult for her to forget, her obligation to him was completed. She felt like a heavy weight had been lifted from her shoulders.

When Sarah stepped out of the front door, a flock of starlings fluttered from the oak tree beside the walkway and settled into another tree along the road leading to downtown Dallas. The sounds of the birds startled her, and she looked up into the bright, blue afternoon sky. Taking a deep breath to clear her lungs of the lingering odors inside where dying and death ruled, she reveled in the fresh air and in the sights and sounds of life outside the building.

Her taxi driver, noticing her standing at the head of the road, started his wagon swiftly toward her. He pulled up beside Sarah in a cloud of dust and waited for her to climb aboard.

As Sarah put her foot on the carriage step, the image of Jack Kilpatrick's personal items came to her mind. Pausing, she thought about the silver dollar. It might be the one he showed her at the cemetery in Fort Worth, the one he said was taken during the government robbery. At least it would not haunt her any longer.

The driver clucked at his horses, and then reined them back in their traces. "We needs to be on our way, Ma'am," he said in a tense, squeaky voice. "This be no place to dally. There be crazy folks in there."

"I'm sorry," Sarah said as she mounted the step and took her seat.

As the taxi tore down the street, cool air blew through Sarah's hair, unraveling wayward strands from under her hat. She was about to tell the driver to slow down when another image came to her: Jack Kilpatrick sitting in Marshal Courtright's office writing in a small journal. She wondered if it were the same one that was taken from him when he was admitted to the sanitarium.

Leaning forward, she touched the driver on his shoulder and shouted, "Stop! Stop!"

The young man jumped as if Satan himself had touched him. Instead of bringing the carriage to a halt, his cry of shock and terror caused the horses to break into a run. Sarah was thrown back into her seat, and she had to hold on to keep from being bounced onto the floor.

After several minutes of wild galloping, the driver finally brought the horses back to a lope. Sarah was able to lean forward again and, without touching the man, she said firmly, "Please stop. Now! I want to go back."

Turning around and staring at Sarah wide-eyed, the young man shouted, "Lordy. I's cain't be goin' back. No, Ma'am."

"Stop the taxi and let me out," Sarah said. "I'll walk."

After Sarah paid the driver, he slapped the reins on the rumps of his horses and galloped furiously away. Turning, she could see the sanitarium in the distance. As she walked toward it, she wondered what had prompted her to return. Surely Kilpatrick's journal wouldn't be of any use to her.

Sister Theresa was still in the reception area leaning over Sister Magdalene's desk when Sarah re-entered the sanitarium. She looked up in surprise and said brightly, "Hello again, Sarah. What brings you back to us?"

Kilpatrick's personal items were still lying on the desk. Sarah pointed at them and said, "You asked me if I wanted to take those with me."

"Yes. Since Mr. Kilpatrick has no next of kin, what we can't sell, we'll burn or discard. You are certainly welcome to take them with you?"

Sarah picked up the silver dollar and examined it. She recognized it as the same one that Kilpatrick had shown her at the cemetery. She wondered if he had kept it as a reminder that the trail to the rest of the money led through her ranch.

Placing the coin back on the desk, she glanced at the knife, one of the most beautiful she had ever seen. It was a long switchblade with inlaid pearl covering the handle. A small silver plate attached to each side was inscribed with the initials "JWK." Unconsciously, she opened the blade. It gleamed in the pale light in the room, and the carefully honed edge looked sharp enough to slice through paper. Horror overcame Sarah as she looked at it. The thought that it might have caused someone's death overwhelmed her.

Snapping the knife closed, she replaced it on the desk and gazed at the notebook. Covered in black leather, it was about four inches wide by six inches long and a half-inch thick. She could see that it had been well used by the frayed page edges and the scratches on the cover.

"I'll just take Mr. Kilpatrick's journal," Sarah said to Sister Theresa. "Perhaps there are some family contacts in it. I'm sure they would want to know of his death."

"Certainly, Sarah," Sister Theresa said. "It's very kind of you to go to the bother. Are you sure you don't want anything else?"

Sarah's attention was drawn back to the knife, fascinated by the evil it might represent. Suddenly, impulsively, she picked it up and put it in her purse with the notebook.

When Sarah said goodbye to Sister Theresa, she felt like she was leaving an old friend. The woman's quiet faith, and her love and respect for her patients, left a deep impression on Sarah. Before she left Fort Worth, she would have to talk to Rose, she thought. A donation to Holy Cross from U. R. Gladly might be in order. She smiled as she thought about the money from the government robbery—a theft Kilpatrick had investigated—helping the sanitarium where he passed away.

Sarah had to walk nearly a half-mile before she met an elderly woman turning her carriage from a side road onto the main street. The woman graciously offered to give Sarah a ride to the railroad station. The train to Fort Worth was in the process of boarding when they arrived, and Sarah was able to go directly to her seat.

As the wheezing, coal burning engine pulled away from Dallas, Sarah's thoughts returned to her visit to the sanitarium and to Kilpatrick's journal in her purse. The more she thought about it, the more anxious she was to read it.

Chapter 31

The late afternoon sun streamed in the window where Sarah sat in the passenger car. Looking to the west along the tracks, she could see a line of low, thin white clouds on the horizon. They held the promise of a colorful sunset as the evening came, a sunset bursting with red, gold, and pink hues. One of the wonders of her childhood, that she always cherished, was the brilliant sunsets along the Bosque River. Her father had told her that God used his paintbrush to create them to show the wonder of the end of the day and the beginning of the night. He likened it to life and death, saying that most people had a horror of death; they looked upon it with fear and anxiety. But, he explained, sunsets were God's way of showing that Jesus was awaiting a person's earthly passing with open arms, welcoming them to a heavenly night they need not fear.

Sarah wondered if this sunset was to welcome Jack Kilpatrick to his heavenly night. Whatever he had been during his life—good or bad—he was now being judged by a higher power. As she looked at his journal in her lap, she was unsure if she would be violating his privacy by reading it. Did he really know anything about Jim's fate, or did he just say what he did at the sanitarium to get her to admit that she knew about the theft of the government funds?

A strong northerly wind was buffeting the right side of the train. Several passengers closed the sliding windows to keep it from streaming into the car. Sarah shivered and drew her shawl closer about her. Drawing a deep breath, she let it out slowly and opened the journal.

At the top of the first page, Kilpatrick had written in a small, precise cursive style that seemed to flow across the lines:

> Property of Jack W. Kilpatrick
> 1812 West River Street
> Saint Louis, Missouri

The first entry was dated long before Sarah met Kilpatrick:

> May 3, '75—Pinkerton Agency offered job as investigator out of St. Louis office. Have to resign deputy sheriff job. Norah wanted me to turn it down due to travel. That is what I like about it, getting away from her. Since second miscarriage, she has turned into a whiner.
> May 17, '75—First assignment to look into railroad embezzlement of funds in San Antonio. Norah putting up fuss.
> May 25, '75—Staying at Texan Hotel in San Antonio. Owner Alma H. Quite a woman. Fell for me straight away. Lost a big hand of poker to a full house. Had three of a kind, can't believe I raised. Expenses high, must find way to get more money from company.
> May 30, '75—Reviewed accountant audit of railroad funds. Filed report on A. Murchison, San Antonio First National Bank to Pinkerton. Recalled to St. Louis for next assignment.

The next twenty pages or so of the journal were filled with Kilpatrick's notes about business assignments throughout Texas. Sarah felt uncomfortable reading them; especially the details of his increasing gambling losses, the lewd comments about women he met in the different towns, and his increasingly crude denigrations of his wife, Norah. Several times, he mentioned leaving her, but he always seemed to return after his travels.

Sarah leafed ahead through the notebook, anxious to see if Kilpatrick mentioned her husband. Nearly halfway into it, she read an entry about concerns for his health:

> November 12, '75—Rash on hands and feet, won't go away. Calamine lotion not helping. If gets worse will see doctor.
> November 30, '75—Damn doctor thinks I may have sexual disease. Can't believe him. Actually seems to be getting better. Sores on lips and neck about gone. Rash on rear end and legs make riding a horse painful. Don't know what the hell is going on. Doctor can't be right.

And then, scanning the pages, she stopped abruptly when she saw her name:

> October 3, '76—Joined posse of Sheriff Wilson, Waco, Texas. Three survivors of gang that robbed train office seen headed west along Bosque River. Met Sarah Whitman and family (daughter Margaret and son) on trail. Fine figure of a woman, so is daughter. Something bothers me about her, the woman is not telling the truth. Her husband Jim disappeared in Fort Worth area. (Talk to Marshal Jim Courtright about him.) Widows need comforting. Play my cards right no reason not to sample both of their charms. Stopped at Sigmund Ranch. No knowledge of suspects. Checked Whitman's ranch. Found '72 Liberty Seated silver dollar new condition, same as in stolen shipment. What is Sarah W. hiding? Sheriff Wilson called off posse to return to Waco against my protests. Will notify federal marshals and sheriffs in West Texas and New Mexico robbers headed into their territory. Just as well we didn't go on. This damn disease is wearing me down. Goddamn whores! I'll teach them not to mess with me.

Sarah noticed that Kilpatrick's penmanship was beginning to deteriorate. At times, it became an almost unreadable scrawl, and he no longer kept his letters between the lines on the page, they wandered downward toward the right side. Promising herself she would read the rest of it more closely later, she leafed ahead, searching for any mention of Jim. Finally she found it:

> October 5, '76 Followed Sarah W. again. She went to see Sludge Cameron. Found them together on river bottom road. She had gun on Cameron, threatened to shoot him to get him to tell of her husband's whereabouts. When she wasn't looking, I shot Cameron in shoulder. After Sarah W. left to go to his house he told me where Whitman is buried. I gave him another bullet in the chest. Don't want Sarah W. to find husband's body and return home. Want her here in Ft. Worth so I can keep an eye on her. Sure she has robbery money or knows where it is. She's a beautiful woman and excites me. Getting her to bed might be challenging. But worth it! When I'm finished with her I'll go after her daughter. They're no better than whores and deserve the same fate. Need that train money then I can go to the clinic in Europe for treatment. All I have is gone.

Anger colored Sarah's cheeks as she thought about Kilpatrick killing Cameron to keep her from returning home and the references to wanting to take advantage of her and Margaret. He knew at that time that he had syphilis. How could he have been so heartless as to give it to them? Recalling Rose's comments about Kilpatrick visiting her girls, she wondered how many other women he might have infected in his anger.

Finding no further comments on her husband, she leafed back through the journal until she found an earlier entry that caught her attention, "September 30, '76—L the first, except for N. They won't be the last. Don't know how much longer I have, doctor won't say. Have to keep going on. About out of money."

Sarah stopped reading, her heart pounding rapidly as she thought about what she had read. Did Kilpatrick kill Lucille Martell and his own wife, Norah? If he did, Clarence Heddings was put to death in his place. The thought horrified her. If Sheriff Roberts hadn't been so anxious to bring Clarence to trial before his re-election vote, he might have found out that Kilpatrick was guilty. She recalled William telling her that he had put the hounds of hell on Roberts' backside. This journal would add the devil to the dogs. She would see to it.

Flipping through the rest of the pages with writing on them, Sarah could find no further reference to her husband. If Cameron did tell where he was buried, apparently Kilpatrick didn't bother to write it down. Of course, she thought, the location of Jim's body meant nothing to Kilpatrick. He didn't want Jim to be found so she would stay in Fort Worth.

Toward the end of the journal, Kilpatrick's writing deteriorated to the point of being unreadable. Sarah couldn't make sense of many of the words he wrote. But, by then, she didn't care. Tears came to her eyes as she thought about Jim. Like her father, he would have a tombstone over an empty grave in their family cemetery. There would be no delay now, she would give Kilpatrick's journal to William and return to the Bosque.

The shrill sounds of the train's whistle roused Sarah from her internal musing. Looking out the window, she could see the first buildings of Fort Worth appear against the colorful rays of the setting sun. Margaret, Jody, and Daniel would be waiting for her to join them for dinner. She wasn't sure how much she would tell them. Her thoughts were still confused and disorderly.

When the train came to a jerking, shuddering stop at the station, Sarah reached across her seat for her purse. She had forgotten about Kilpatrick's journal, which had been setting on her lap, and it fell onto the floor. Reaching down, she picked it up by the cover. She was about to put it in her purse, when she glanced down and saw a crude map drawn on the inside of the back cover. She could make out a line from top to bottom with "Fort" scrawled near the top and a wavy line denoted "TR" running parallel to the line before crossing it just above the "Fort" entry. Another smaller wavy line met the "TR" line near the bottom of the page with a large "X" near the intersection.

Sarah's breath stopped. She was certain she was looking at a map of the area around the old Fort Worth and the Trinity River. The wavy line at the bottom could be a creek that flowed into the river. Did Kilpatrick enter the location where Jim's body was buried after all, she thought. Did she dare hope that she would find him?

The station landing was awash with light from gas lamps as Sarah stepped down from the train. The journal was in her purse, but the map was imprinted in her memory. One more day, Lord, she prayed silently. Please, make it just one more day.

Sarah and William sat on the wagon watching the men spread out and walk through the brush and trees alongside the creek. The rumble of the Trinity River could be heard in the distance. William had a blanket spread over his legs to ward off the cold, which increased the pain in his arthritic knees. Silently mouthing curse words, he was reading Kilpatrick's journal for the third time since Sarah gave it to him that morning. The cold winter temperature turned his breath into fountains of steam that quickly dissipated in the dry air.

Sarah glanced up as Daniel approached her carrying a mangled, partly eaten wide-brimmed hat. He handed it up to her, asking, "Is this his, Mrs. Whitman? We found it under some brush."

Sarah inspected the misshapen item. It was dark gray, the color Jim preferred. Turning it upside down, she looked at the leather lining. The initials "JW" leaped out at her.

"Yes," she said softly, her heart beating rapidly in her breast.

"Then we're in the right area," Daniel said. He dipped his hat and returned to the group searching along the creek toward the river.

Sarah felt William's arm around her shoulders, but she couldn't look at him as tears began to flow down her cheeks. "Jim was such a good man," she said. "I never saw him hurt anything; not an animal or a person. I just don't understand why people have to turn to violence and murder to get what they want out of life. I just don't understand."

William tightened his grip around her and said in his deep, rumbling voice, "I don't read the Bible much, Sarah. But I think that's the only place for you to get the answer. I don't believe another human being knows enough. Guess that's why I never held much with preachers or churches. We all struggle with the good and bad inside. Some, like Kilpatrick and Cameron, just give in to the bad and let the devil and his disciples run their lives."

"If my father was here, he'd have an answer," Sarah said. "You're right, though. He would point to a verse in scripture. I know it will take time—"

Sarah stopped as Daniel stepped out onto the road and started toward her. Before he could say anything, the look on his face told her that they had located Jim's body. She became still and quiet, the winter outside making its way into her soul.

"We found him," Daniel said, unable to meet her eyes. "Big man? Sheepskin coat and a wide belt buckle with a star etched on it?"

"Yes," Sarah responded, as she started to climb down from the wagon.

"Best you don't see him, Mrs. Whitman," Daniel said. "It's not a pretty sight. The coroner is putting his body in a canvas bag. We'll carry the casket over and seal it there."

William grabbed Sarah's arm and pulled her back onto the seat. "He's right, Sarah. You know it's him. You need to remember him as he was when he was alive."

Sarah started to protest, and then stopped. A strange feeling came over her. The anxiety that had overwhelmed her for the past months over whether Jim was alive or dead lifted from her like a wild bird freed from captivity to soar into the freedom of the sky.

"Yes," she said quietly. "Thank you, Daniel. After we get him loaded let's return to the hotel and get Margaret and Jody … and Beelzebub and Patches. I want to leave right away."

"It's getting late," William said with concern in his voice. "You might want to stay the night and get a fresh start in the morning."

"No," Sarah said lifting her chin and trying to smile through her tears. "It's time to leave. It's time to go home."

EPILOGUE

▼

Sarah knelt by her husband's grave and listened to the morning. It was alive with sounds: the clicking of crickets and cicadas communicating with each other in the unintelligible language of the insect species, the warbling of wrens and titmouse as they celebrated the annual birthing of their young, the burbling of the Bosque River on the ebb after the spring runoff as it flowed southeast toward the Gulf of Mexico, the soughing of the wind as it plucked at the trees and rustled through the grass on its joyous journey through the valley, and the strident neighing of the male horses as they raced about the meadows in joyous response to the primordial fires of procreation in their loins.

Nearly two and a half years had passed since Sarah brought Jim's body back to the ranch and buried him in the family cemetery. Jody was past seven now. He was a bright youngster who excelled under Sarah's tutelage, along with his classmate Alicia Mallory. The daughter of a neighboring rancher, Alicia was three years older than Jody. She doted on him as the younger brother she didn't have. Margaret was pregnant with her second child, the first one born scarcely a year after she and Daniel married. Sarah smiled as she thought of the baby named Thomas Henry Worthington after his paternal grandfather. He was an energetic boy with an infectious grin reminiscent of Daniel's and his wobbly steps, often self-destructive, required constant attention.

The ranch had flourished under Daniel's competent management. Buyers came from miles away to purchase his blooded colts, swift stallions, and fertile mares. Neighbors called on him when their livestock suffered illness and injuries. With his quiet demeanor and firm hand, he delivered many a foal facing a difficult birth. Never charging for his services, he looked upon the demands on his time and energy as God's way of using him to serve others.

Daniel brought Sarah back to the church. After he returned from delivering a herd of horses to the U.S. Army in San Antonio, he told her about a Baptist minister, Charles Anderson, who was building a new house of worship an hour's ride away.

The next time she went to Waco for supplies, she stopped and talked to Anderson. A few years older, Anderson had lost his wife to diphtheria ten years before. Declining to remarry, he devoted his time and energy to spreading the Lord's Word. Seeing a need for establishing a house of worship in the country northwest of Austin, he chose a location on the Brazos River. A tall, handsome man deeply tanned from working hatless in the sun, his pale blue eyes showed sensitivity to other's needs and a devotion to the Lord that reminded Sarah of her father.

For the past four months, a Sunday trip to Anderson's church service, followed by a congregational potluck lunch, had become common for Sarah and her family. Lately, she found herself remembering Anderson's smile and the way the corners of his eyes crinkled when he looked at her, even more than his sermons.

The flowers she had planted early in the spring were flourishing now; lending splashes of red, blue, violet, and pink colors to the green of the grass and the white of the tombstones. Looking at Jim's marker, she wondered if he would look kindly on her growing desire to share her life and her love with a man like Charles Anderson. Her father would understand, she thought. Even though his earthly body rested somewhere far away, she felt his presence on the ranch and in the graveyard. And, as she looked at the small-carved stone next to Jim's where Beelzebub's remains rested, she knew the dog's spirit was here also. He was watching over her and her family, especially Jody and little Thomas.

Standing, Sarah looked once more at her father's gravestone. Nothing lay beneath the grass surface now. The last of the stolen government money had been sent to Rose Travis in Fort Worth so she could make a donation in the name of U. R. Gladly to the new hospital being built south of the courthouse and to Sister Mary Theresa at the Holy Cross Sanitarium in Dallas. Now that it was all gone, she felt a sense of relief.

Not a day went by when she didn't pray for forgiveness for shooting the two outlaws: Pete and Breed. When Daniel rebuilt the barn, she had him change the locations of the doors. Fencing in a small area where the two bodies lay, she put up a cross for each of them, simply inscribed, "Rest In Peace."

Sarah brushed her hair back with her fingers as the breeze tugged at it. Turning toward the house, she noticed a movement out of the corner of her eyes. Across the river, a lone rider sat on the brow of the hill staring down at her. Her breath caught in her chest as she realized the stranger was an Indian, an Indian carrying a long lance with a blue ribbon fluttering from the shaft.

Sarah's thoughts flashed back to the day when she was a teenager, and she had seen an Indian boy there on the bluff. She remembered the tremor that went through her at that time, a tremor caused by her awakening desires of womanhood. Now, that emotion was replaced with curiosity. She wondered why White Cloud had returned after all these years.

As she did on that day in the past, she raised her arm in salute. White Cloud returned the gesture, thrusting his lance toward the cloudless sky at arm's length, the ribbon streaming in the wind.

Hearing a noise behind her, Sarah turned. Daniel was coming down the porch steps with a rifle in his hands, cocking it to put a shell in the chamber. The metallic clickings sounded loud and discordant among the soft sounds of the morning.

"It's all right, Daniel," Sarah said. "You won't need the gun. I know him."

"You know him?"

"Yes. He's White Cloud. He helped me get Jody back. I don't know why he came here. We're a long way from the Oklahoma reservation. I'll go find out."

"Best let me go with you," Daniel said. "You know the legislature passed a law forbidding Comanches from entering the state."

"I know," Sarah said. "That makes his visit even stranger. He must have a very good reason."

Sarah went to the dock and stepped into the flat-bottomed boat used to cross the river. After rowing to the other side, she stepped out and pulled the craft up on the bank. Behind her, she could see Daniel standing on the house porch. He still carried his rifle.

When Sarah reached the top of the rise, White Cloud dismounted to greet her. Behind him, she could see four other men on horseback. All of them were dressed in traditional Indian garb except for one who wore high, polished boots, gabardine pants, a red-checkered shirt, and a wide-brimmed hat. Sarah recognized him as Charles, the Indian friend of Bucky Halloran, who had found Jody in the Indian tipi in Palo Dura Canyon. She waved to him as he spurred up beside White Cloud.

Still short of breath from her climb, Sarah smiled at White Cloud and reached out to him. Self consciously, he touched her hand, as if he weren't sure how to greet her. His dark eyes betrayed no emotion as he looked at her.

"Hello, Mrs. Whitman," Charles said with a wide grin. Then, realizing his position, he backed his horse up in deference to White Cloud.

"Hello, Charles," Sarah said, invigorated by his infectious manner.

Turning back to White Cloud, she said, "I am happy to see you again."

White Cloud opened one of his saddlebags and removed an object wrapped in deer hide. Handing it to Sarah, he spoke very seriously, enunciating his words carefully, as if he had rehearsed them many times, "Quanah send you."

Sarah started to speak, and then stopped as she took the item in her hands. A sudden insight came over her. Even before she finished unwrapping it, she knew what it was: her father's Bible. The soft, black leather binding seemed to come alive in her hands as she opened it. Inside the front cover, she saw the words she had read so often as a child:

> Presented to: Robert C. Parker, Baptist Minister
> On this 26th day of Our Lord 1848
> The day of his ordination
> I give you, my son, to God's people
> Serve them well and walk with the Lord
> Let Him be your strength,
> Your guide and your protector
> Hiram T. Parker, Father

Sarah held the Bible close to her chest and looked at White Cloud through her tears. "Thank you, and thank Quanah for me," she said.

"Quanah visit Great White Father in Washington," White Cloud said quietly. "He tell me, you visit him."

"I will," Sarah responded. "Please tell him I will come to see him. I feel like we are very close even though we've never met."

Glancing down at the Bible, Sarah asked the question that had burned in her heart since her father had disappeared on that day so long ago, "Where did you find my father's Bible?"

White Cloud turned and pointed at one of the other riders. "Small Bear have in tipi," he said. "Wife tell Quanah."

For the first time, Sarah noticed that all the Indians, including White Cloud, were armed with rifles in their scabbards, except for one. Shorter than the rest, he sat on his horse with his head down, staring at the ground.

"Where did he get the Bible?" Sarah asked, afraid of the answer.

White Cloud looked up at Charles and nodded at him to respond.

"Small Bear on raiding party in 1866," Charles said. "He and two warriors separate main party. Meet white man. He alone, no gun. He speak no Comanche, they speak no English. Small Bear kill white man. Small Bear take Bible. Think letters inside tracks of tiny animals. Powerful *tahbay-boh* medicine."

Sarah looked at Small Bear, still hunched over and looking downward, as if his spirit had departed him, and he didn't have the strength to hold up his shoulders.

"Where are the ones who were with him when they killed my father?" Sarah asked.

"Dead," Charles said with a shake of his head. "Killed by white soldiers."

For a long moment Sarah stood silently, thinking about what she had just heard. The Comanches did kill her father, and one of them was sitting on a horse near her. She tried to summon up feelings of hatred toward Small Bear, but she couldn't. Her father's image came to her. He wouldn't want her to take revenge against those who killed him. He knew it would poison her for the rest of her life.

White Cloud interrupted her private thoughts, "Small Bear know where father killed. You go with us?"

"Oh, yes … yes!" Sarah exclaimed. Finally, after all these years, she could bring his remains home to rest beside his family.

Sarah and Daniel crested a hill covered with prairie grass and scattered brush in their horse-drawn wagon. Below them, Sarah could see a narrow river winding through a broad wooded valley. The late afternoon rays of the sun gleamed off the water, turning it to gold. Further on, to the northwest, loomed the outlines of high mesas stretching off to the horizon. White Cloud and his companions were waiting down the slope, staring across the river.

"Sacred place," Charles said as he rode up to Sarah. "Many years gone, giant animals live here. Bigger than twenty buffalo. Now only tracks and bones."

"Giant animals?" Sarah asked.

"Dinosaurs," Daniel responded. "I heard they've found evidence of them here. That store owner from Glen Rose, who bought the horses from us, said he has a bone nearly eight feet long."

Sarah thought about her father's bones lying among those of ancient animals that had passed from existence so long ago. She wasn't sure that she believed in dinosaurs. The Bible never mentioned them, and her father said they were just the bedeviled imaginings of people who didn't follow the Lord and His teachings.

When they joined White Cloud, he pointed his lance toward a bend in the river. Then looking at Sarah, he said, "Father there."

Turning, he led them down the slope to the water, the wagon turning back and forth on the hillside to avoid the trees.

After they reached the bank of the river, although it was still warm, Sarah felt a chill come over her. Reaching behind her, she picked up her woolen scarf and wrapped it around her shoulders. Something bothered her. Whether it was a foreboding of the unknown or the thought that she would finally see her father's remains, she wasn't sure. But there was an aura about the valley that was unsettling.

Small Bear, after a verbal berating from White Cloud, dismounted at the edge of the water. He stood looking around a scattering of large boulders that rose up to a bank above his head. The river bed, ground out of rock by the tremendous forces of the movement of an ancient glacier, was covered with a layer of sand, which had been formed over the eons by the action of the water running over the shale surface. Where the water had receded from its spring high, a sheet of smooth rock was exposed.

Sarah gasped as she looked down and saw a large impression in the rock, the mark of a gigantic three-toed creature. And, over four feet away, she could see another footprint similar to the first. Was it really true, she wondered, did huge animals once walk on this land? If they did, what happened to them? And why weren't they mentioned in the Bible?

Small Bear left the riverbank and knelt between two massive rocks, cutting him off from Sarah's view. Then he arose and spoke quietly to White Cloud. Sarah climbed down from the wagon and joined White Cloud as he stood beside Small Bear looking at a gap between the boulders. She felt Daniel's hand on her shoulder, as she tried to see what they were focused on.

White Cloud stepped aside and Sarah could see the scattered bones of a human skeleton. Scavengers had stripped them clean and carried away many of them. Only a shattered skull, a backbone with the ribs still attached, and one upper leg bone remained in the narrow opening. Strangely, she didn't feel horrified at the sight. She knew that her father's spirit was no longer with his earthly remains. Clutching his Bible to her chest, she said a silent prayer for him.

Small Bear moved back from the rocks, his head down in shame. White Cloud turned to Sarah and spoke harshly, "Small Bear will be punished for killing your father. I take him to Tribal Council at Fort Sill."

"No!" Sarah said, shaking her head. "Tell Small Bear to look at me."

White Cloud looked at Sarah with a bewildered look. When he didn't respond, Sarah demanded again, "Tell Small Bear to look at me."

White Cloud stared at Sarah again, as if he couldn't believe what he was hearing. Finally, he turned and said something to Small Bear. But he received no response.

Sarah stepped up to Small Bear and put her face up to his. Finally, reluctantly, he raised his eyes until he was looking into hers. "I forgive you," she said quietly. "I will pray for the salvation of your soul."

Looking at Charles, who was standing nearby, she said, "Please tell him what I said, every word."

After Charles finished interpreting, Small Bear turned his head away without responding.

"Quannah say he must be punished," White Cloud said, looking disdainfully at Small Bear. "Three Comanches kill one white man with no gun. Must be punished."

"No!" Sarah said firmly. "When they did this, we were at war; your people and mine."

She went to White Cloud and put her hand on his arm. Looking into his eyes, she continued, "You are my friend. You kept my family from harm when you were a medicine man. You helped me find my son when he was taken from me. And now you found my father. I am your friend. I ask you to take Small Bear home to his family. Tell Quanah Parker it is time to heal the wounds between us and cast aside the hatred. We have no hope for the future if this is not done."

For a long moment, White Cloud stared emotionless at Sarah. Then he placed his right fist over his heart and said, "You Quanah cousin. You White Cloud sister."

Turning abruptly, he strode to his horse and vaulted on to it. After speaking to his companions, including Small Bear, they mounted and joined him. As they started up the valley, Charles left the group and rode back to Sarah.

"I am sorry about your father, Mrs. Whitman," he said. "My people never forget you. Many talk around the fires about you rescuing your son. One day I return to see you and Daniel. I teach Jody to ride."

Then, before Sarah or Daniel could respond, Charles spun around and galloped away to catch up with White Cloud.

Sarah turned to Daniel, "Let's put my father's remains in the wagon and start home. The moon will be up early."

When they reached the top of the rise above the river, Sarah looked back at the valley. Most of it was in shadow, and it was difficult to see any details. Then she could discern a rider in the distance outlined against the pale silver of the water. He raised his arm in salute, his lance thrust into the sky. She waved back at White Cloud through her tears.

Turning to the misshapen mound under the tarpaulin lying in the bed of the wagon, she said quietly, "Let's go home, Father."

Author's Comments

This book is a work of fiction, although some of the characters and events are real. The dialogues attributed to the real characters are products of the author's imagination.

Jim "Longhair" Courtright served as Marshal of Fort Worth, Texas during the period of this novel. He wore two six-guns with the butts turned forward for a cross-draw. He walked a fine line between upholding the law in the burgeoning "Cow Town" and discouraging rowdy visitors, such as cowboys, buffalo hunters, and other vagabonds looking for liquor, women, and gambling. In 1887, Courtright died in a shootout with gambler Luke Short in the street outside a saloon in Fort Worth.

Newspaperman and civic leader B. B. Paddock was a driving force behind the community effort to extend the railroad from Dallas to Fort Worth in 1876. He conceived the so-called *Tarantula Map* that showed Fort Worth as the hub for a number of rail lines that would service a wide area including Texas, Oklahoma, and New Mexico. He served as the Fort Worth mayor from 1892 to 1900. He edited a major historical work: *History of Texas: Fort Worth and the Texas Northwest*, and he was a two-time state legislator. He died on January 9, 1922 at his home in Fort Worth.

Cattleman Burk Burnett, a close friend of Quanah Parker, was one of the first to sign a lease with the Comanches, Kiowas, and Kiowa-Apaches to use over a million acres of the Fort Sill Federal Reservation grassland for raising livestock. The owner of one of the largest cattle empires in the world, the Four Sixes (6666), with locations in four states and Mexico, he later expanded into banking and the fledgling oil business. When he died a wealthy man on June 27, 1922, his widow left part of his estate to Texas Christian University in Fort Worth.

Cynthia Ann Parker, the mother of Quanah Parker, was nine years old when a band of Comanches and Kiowas kidnapped her from her family home on the Navasota River in Limestone County, Texas on May 19, 1836. She later became the wife of the Comanche Chief *Peta Nocona*. In addition to Quanah, Cynthia Ann gave *Nocona* another son and a daughter named Prairie Flower. Captured with her daughter during a raid on an Indian village by the Texas Rangers in 1861, she was returned to the Parker family. Grieving over her husband and sons, she never adapted to her new environment, even trying to escape several times. Award of a pension by the State of Texas did little to console her and, after Prairie Flower died, she joined her child in death in 1870. Reportedly, she starved herself and died of a broken heart. Cynthia Ann and Prairie Flower were buried in East Texas. Quanah located their graves and had their remains moved to the Post Oak Mission Cemetery in Oklahoma in 1910.

Quanah Parker, son of *Peta Nocona* and Cynthia Ann Parker, was born about 1845 in western Oklahoma into the *Quahadi* (Antelope) Comanche tribe. He became a noted war chief during the last days of the Comanche's conflict with the U.S. Army and the Texas Rangers. When his people took up residence on the federal reservation in Oklahoma, he became one of their leaders during the difficult transition period from being lords of the western plains to wards of the U.S. Government. He played a major part in getting all the tribes to agree to lease reservation land to Texas cattlemen, including Burk Burnett, which improved their standard of living and, eventually, helped make Quanah one of the richest Indians in the United States. A friend of President Theodore Roosevelt, U.S. Congressmen, and cattle ranchers, he made many trips to Washington DC. His former adversaries frequently asked for his advice on political and social issues that affected his people. Rejecting Christianity throughout his life, he was a member of the Native American Church. He was instrumental in introducing the hallucinogenic drug *peyote* to his people and getting it approved by U.S. Government authorities. Named an honorary deputy sheriff of Lawton, Oklahoma, he also had a town in Texas named after him. He died of an undetermined illness on February 23, 1911 and was buried in full Comanche regalia. Today, he rests beside his mother, Cynthia Ann, his sister, Prairie Flower, and other members of his family in the Fort Sill Cemetery.

The *peyote* ceremony described in this novel is based on factual evidence. *Peyote* is a cactus root that only grows in the Chihuahua Desert of Mexico and in the United States between Laredo and Rio Grande City. Also called Cactus Pudding, Dry Whiskey, and White Mule, this sacred plant contains alkaloids and related compounds. Mescaline, similar to the human neurohormone epinephrine, is the main active component of *peyote*. Those who take this hallucinogenic substance say that it gives them an altered state of consciousness akin to the results from ingesting psychedelics artificially manufactured for human consumption (legal and illegal). Sociologists and psychiatrists studying the impact of *peyote* on the Indian psyche liken it to the ancient practice of the young post-puberty Indian male going into the wilderness alone and starving himself until he has an out-of-body experience, a vision that portends the future and gives him his societal name in the form of an image, such as White Cloud or Sitting Bull. When the Great Plains Indians were forced to surrender the nomadic way of life they had enjoyed for thousands of years and restrict their environment to the confines of a reservation, *peyote* became a release, an outlet for their pent up frustrations and their longings for the freedoms of the past. The Native American Church uses *peyote* even today in its religious ceremonies. The fourteenth Amendment of the U.S. Constitution and nine states, including Texas and Oklahoma, preserves the right of the American Indian to use *peyote*. Purchasers of the drug must be members of federally recognized Indian tribes; hence it is one of the most highly controlled substances in the United States.

The slaughter of over a thousand horses belonging to the Comanches occurred during a U.S. Army raid on their encampment in Palo Dura Canyon on September 27, 1874. Led by Colonel Ranald Mackenzie, the attackers forced the Indians to flee out of the canyon. Although they didn't kill many of them, they did take into custody nearly fourteen hundred of their horses, which left most of them on foot and vulnerable to starvation and later apprehension. After burning the encampment, Mackenzie separated a few hundred horses from the captured herd and gave them to his Tonkawa scouts as a reward for locating the village. Then he ordered his men to slaughter the rest, over a thousand. He rationalized his action by saying that he did not want them to fall back into enemy hands. Whether his decision was justified or not, the lack of horses contributed to the Comanche's decision to surrender to the U.S. Army at the Fort Sill Reservation early the following year. The bones of the slain horses rested on the plains for many years before an ambitious entrepreneur gathered them up and shipped them to a fertilizer plant in the East.

About the Author

Ken Miller, a former U.S. Air Force officer and aerospace executive, is the author of two internationally acclaimed historical novels: *Evening of Pale Sunshine* and *Weep Without Tears*. *Evening of Pale Sunshine* captured the sights, sounds, culture, and religious beliefs of Southeast Asia during the conflict of the 1960s and 1970s. It is the story of a love between two people who think they have lost everything only to find that they have so much to live for: each other. Brought together during a historical moment of time, a young American military officer and a beautiful French-Vietnamese woman must survive during a disastrous war that threatens to destroy a sovereign nation and embarrass the United States. The sequel, *Weep Without Tears*, is set in the turbulent post-war times of the 1970s. A stirring adventure story of love, faith, and courage in the face of persecution and impending death, it follows a courageous young orphan boy, a man fighting for his life, and the woman who is determined to unite them at the risk of losing the one she loves. It was a winner of a Lu Spurlock Black Gold Award for an outstanding novel at the Fourth Annual Texans Writing to the World Writer's Conference.

Ken was raised in the mountains of North Idaho. A graduate of Washington State University, he now lives in Fort Worth, Texas. He is a member of the Fort Worth Westerners Historical Association and was the host for the Friends of the Fort Worth Public Library monthly Book Forum. He is an active leader in book discussion groups, public library support, and genealogical and historical research.

978-0-595-44687-2
0-595-44687-6

Printed in the United States
83589LV00002B/250-276/A